I0748577

RED RIBBONS

anna m.l. koski

ISBN 979-8-3288764-90

RED RIBBONS

Also available in eBook with Amazon and Hardcover with Ingramspark.

Cover Image by Joanna Kosinska on Unsplash

Cover Design by The Round Table

To Jennifer Lile.
You found my writing in the dark and brought it into the light.
Thank you

FOREWORD

This foreword came almost nine years after the original posting of Red Ribbons on Wattpad but I figured it was necessary amid the new age where trigger warnings are the norm, I figured the very first book of this series needed its own.

The themes in this book are heavy. Abuse, complex PTSD, trauma responses, and healing from said trauma are things that affect everyone differently and what one person can handle and endure, another might not. This book follows a singular character, trapped in the world that the abuse she endured, that it created. She is flawed, she has setbacks and her healing is not linear because healing from these traumas never are.

That is why I wrote this book. The literary world is filled with tropes and cliches and some of these hurt people, *real* people. When we write misinformation into our books, when we consume it, when we see it, it reinforces negative stereotypes and in turn harms those who suffer from it. The werewolf genre especially is horrible for misrepresenting and misinforming people about abuse and trauma and how people heal from it, whether it be from writer ignorance or perhaps laziness, it is not my position to say.

What is my position, however, is to do this the *correct* way. To combat the negative stereotypes and misinformation using the same medium as they are delivered, to write a story that showcases the gruelling, tasking, and horrible realities that come with these themes in all it's brutal reality.

This book is a gritty, realistic, and occasionally unbearable look at abuse and how it moulds people, how it shapes them, and how they can work through it to get better. To *heal.*

If you want a book where the main character has three months away from her abusers and turns into a badass, this is not for you.

If you want a book where the main character has ability to shrug off her abuse and her healing and turn into a cliched strong and independent individual, this is not for you.

If you want a book where the main character doesn't show emotion, doesn't freeze at her abusers, or she back sasses constantly, this is not for you.

If you want a book where you follow a young woman who has been severely abused and conditioned to live and act a certain way and her brutal growing pains as she attempts to heal from that abuse.

If you want a book where *everyone* is flawed, where they act human, as gritty and illogical it can be at times.

If you want a book where the main character still struggles after *years* because healing from abuse is a life long struggle for the survivors.

If you want a book where you get to see an up close and personal look at just how abuse affects a person's psyche and how utterly hard and painful it is to work towards being better.

If you want a book where we tackle the misinformation about anxiety, abuse, CPTSD, trauma, and everything that comes with it.

This might just be the book for you.

But just remember that healing from abuse is a never ending process and everything I have written is based in reality and experience and there is no such thing as a perfect abuse survivor. We are all flawed, we all struggle, we all have moments where we wish we can give up or we get angry and we *are* allowed to be angry, to be sad, to take *time.*

So here are some quotes that I leave you with:

"There is no timestamp on trauma. There isn't a formula that you can insert yourself into to get from horror to healed." - Dawn Serra

"Post traumatic stress injury isn't a disease. It's a wound to the soul that never heals." – Tom Glenn

"You don't have to save me, you just have to hold my hand while I save myself." – Unknown

"Your anger is the part of you that knows your mistreatment and abuse are unacceptable. Your anger knows you deserve to be treated well, and with kindness. Your anger is a part of you that LOVES you." - Lynds Gallant

"Healing from trauma isn't an overnight process. It's a lifelong journey that requires patience, support, and self-compassion." – Jasmin Lee Cori

To those of you who have survived or are surviving. I'm here for you, however you need me.

ONE

I knew better than to look at his face. I knew better than to make a sound even as he was breaking my heart. I was an omega, a servant and not allowed to look upon the face of my superiors. I was an omega and I would always be an omega. A mantra burned into my brain by the pack I served.

I was grateful to Alpha Lawrence for taking me in when I had been orphaned. I did not resent my station in life. I had been born of two rogues and it had been well within Alpha Lawrence's right to leave me for dead when my dying father had left me on his territory but he had taken me in instead. I owed him my life and I was truly grateful for his insistence of bringing me into the pack.

"Are you listening to what I am saying, omega?" The words were said low and I nodded once. I was glad I wasn't allowed to look at his face. I did not wish to see his irritation in his eyes. It was funny. I did not know what he looked like or what colour his eyes were or even his hair. It was funny because he was my mate and I would never have any clue as to what he looked like. We were destined but not for that, no. I was an omega and would always be below everyone in the pack.

"Yes, sir. No one is to know and I am to never approach you." I bowed my head and a strong hand ruffled my hair gently. I hated the gesture, it spoke of familiarity and I wanted to back away. I didn't like people touching me with familiarity. Only Alpha Lawrence touched me with affection and that was when we were alone, where no one could see. Everyone else ignored me or gave me the occasional slap for something I did wrong.

"Good girl." He sounded so happy and it made my heart clench in my chest but I pushed the pain away. I had a duty to do and I would not be able to do it in my avoidance of him. Alpha Lawrence would have to be informed before he noticed my lack of cleaning the beta son's room.

"Sir, may I ask what I am to tell Alpha Lawrence?" I kept my head down and shifted my clasped hands slightly. My palms were rough with callouses and the light grey dress I wore was getting ragged but it was clean. I always made sure I looked respectable. It was something I could control and I *would* control it.

"We just went over this, omega. You cannot tell anyone." There was an edge to his voice that I shrunk under.

"Sir, it is just that your room is in section two, which is in my section to clean and cater to. I do not wish to shirk my duties in my avoidance of you. If I have something to tell Alpha Lawrence, then perhaps I can get the section switched with another omega." I said the words slowly, not wishing to be hit for my audacity to talk back but I would not give Alpha Lawrence a reason to send me away. I wished to stay with him. He was the closest thing I had to family. Faint memories swirled in my head and I shoved them away with a sharp lurch in my chest.

An Omega does not have memories.

"That's super smart, I didn't think of that. Tell him one of the others made you feel uncomfortable and your request to be changed to a different section. We all know he has a soft spot for you." He sounded relieved, as if he thought I would wish to tell Alpha Lawrence of my rejection. I would not because he ordered me not to but my duty to the pack outweighed everything else.

"Alpha Lawrence is a great Alpha. He cares for all of his pack members equally." It was an automatic response when someone remarked on his slight affection for me. I had been told it wasn't proper for anyone to know of his affection for me. I was a child of rogues and an omega. I was lower than low and Alphas were not supposed to care for people like me.

"Okay. Now I can't quite remember... what do I call you?" He waved his hands slightly before he cracked his knuckles. It looked almost nervous and I bowed my head lower.

"I do not know what it was my parents named me, sir." That much was the truth. I had no memories of a name that I had been called by them. I couldn't remember them to even try to think of any such name. My memories were a painful fuzz and I shoved them away once more.

"You don't know? You have to have a name... *Everyone* does." He sounded slightly surprised and I fought down a smile. Alpha Lawrence had named me, it was more of a nickname than anything but it was mine.

"Alpha Lawrence calls me Mary Mary." Despite the pain that was radiating from my chest I wanted to smile. Alpha Lawrence, who tucked me in when I was little, singing me the nursery rhyme as he pulled the blankets up to my chin, making sure I was covered and would not be cold. The memories were hazy and almost didn't fit together properly but I shook it off quickly.

An Omega does not have memories.

"What?" He sounded startled and I bowed my head once more, the gesture as automatic as breathing.

"That is what he calls me, sir. It is the only name I know of." I didn't wish to explain to him the nursery rhyme, the silly little thing that Alpha Lawrence did for me when I was but a scared little girl. It was my memory and he did not need to know of it. No one did. I shuddered under that.

"Mary Mary... That can't be it... I thought it was..." He paused, "It doesn't really matter now, I guess." He sounded confused before he inhaled deeply, straightening his back. "I, Lucas Simmons, reject you, Mary Mary, the omega, as my mate."

As soon as the words exited his mouth a fire spread through my chest, eating away at everything in its path but I stood firm, keeping my face blank.

An Omega must never show emotions.

"Did it work?" If it was possible the painful fire seemed to burn hotter in my chest at his words.

"Yes, sir." I gritted the words out and focused on breathing. I wanted to curl up in a little ball and let the fire consume me till I was nothing but ashes but I knew it didn't work like that. I would burn forever and it would never let up. I had to be strong but my knees shook slightly and my legs trembled. I wanted to hit the floor, my body begged me for it, but I needed to be strong, I couldn't allow myself to be punished for it.

"How do I know you aren't lying?" There was such a thick disbelief in his voice that I took in a sharp gasp as the fire raged down to my stomach, trying to consume all of me. I felt my legs want to crumple underneath me and burning tears gathered in my eyes

"I am in a fair amount of pain, sir. Please forgive me for my lack of propriety." With that I let my legs buckle and I grasped at my chest, heaving in huge gulps of air, trying to quell the violent fire that raged through me. I let out shuddering breaths and crumpled the fabric of my dress in my hand. The hot tears made burning trails down my cheeks as I tried to fight through it but everything hurt.

"You're a special female, Mary Mary, but thank you for being so understanding. I'm sure you'll find another, more appropriate mate." He ruffled my hair and was then gone, leaving me struggling against the pain. As abruptly as it started it stopped, leaving me feeling oddly empty. I let out several shuddering breaths and forced my cramping hand to release my dress. I took in several more shaking breaths before I forced myself to stand on shaking legs. I used my trembling hands to brush down the crumpled fabric of the dress before I forced my body to move.

Each footstep was agonizing, I felt like I had just ran a full marathon but I needed to talk to Alpha Lawrence. I ignored the cramping and tired muscles and slowly made my way to his office. I felt like the stairs were a mountain but I forced myself through it and finally stood at the solid wood door. I bit the inside of my cheek and lifted a shaking hand and knocked softly on the wood. I wanted to lean against it and slide to the floor. I was exhausted, a bone deep tiredness had filled me. I stepped back slightly as the door opened.

"What is it, omega?" It was Beta John's voice and I gave him a slow curtsy. I wobbled slightly, feeling unsteady on my feet.

"I just needed to speak to Alpha Lawrence, sir, about my work section." My voice warbled slightly and I wanted to curse. I didn't mean to sound that weak, that pathetic, but my body was betraying me.

"Beta John, who is it?" The comforting timbre of his voice made me want to crawl onto his lap and bury my face into his chest and sob out the hurt. It was something I hadn't done in many, *many* years but the urge was still there. I knew that his arms would hold just as much comfort now as they did the last time he held me. I couldn't remember when that time was. Everything hurt and was so disjointed and confusing so I shoved it all away once again.

"It's an omega wanting to talk to you about her work section." Beta John sounded irritated and bored as he looked over his shoulder. I focused on his slightly scuffed boots. They were steel toed. I knew that because I had cleaned them many times before. I had replaced their broken laces and kept them clean for him. He did not notice, they never did, but that was my job. To make sure nothing was noticed.

"Well bring her in, I have a few minutes." He sounded gruff but I knew he needed to be. I hated to come to him with something this trivial but Lucas had demanded that I stay away and I could not remain in my section if I were to do as he said. To be fair, I really didn't want to be around him at the moment either. I did not know if the now fragile control I had over my emotions would last another run in.

"Come in then, girl. Don't keep the Alpha waiting." He opened the door wider and I walked in, trying to keep my shaky legs from giving out. I turned to face the desk and gave another unsteady curtsy. I swayed too far and without thinking I reached out and grasped his desk to prevent my body from hitting the floor. I felt the sudden tension in the air at the action and I brought my other hand to my forehead.

I slowly got my footing back and stared at the hard wood floor. "I am sorry, sir." My voice came out meek and wanted to curse at how faint I sounded. "I am sorry to intrude but there was an incident in my section." My voice warbled and sounded on the edge of tears. I hated how I couldn't hide how emotional I was. I hated how I couldn't trust my own body.

"Get out." The Alpha's voice was low and I could feel his angry gaze on me. I hunched under it and clasped my hands in front of me before turning. Defeat filled me. If he would not listen then I would be stuck tending to Lucas's room. "Not you. Beta John, get out." His voice was rough and I stopped mid-turn and kept my gaze glued to the floor, tears burned my eyes but I refused to let them fall.

"But-"

"Don't argue with me. Obviously this incident has shaken her and having her repeat it to two authority figures will be too intimidating. Leave." There was a distinct order in his voice and I winced as the door slammed behind Beta John. A thick silence fell and I could hear Alpha

Lawrence's heavy breathing. He was angry, I could tell. "What happened?" There was a harsh expectancy to his voice and I trembled slightly.

"It was just boys being boys but I feel very uncomfortable tending that section now." The lies hurt coming out but I had to say it. I had to get away from the section. I had to escape from the pain I knew it would cause. I couldn't stay there and do my job and I didn't want to be banished. I wanted to stay with him, where I felt a feeling of comfort and safety.

"What did they do? Did they hurt you?" He was angry, I knew it wasn't at me but I hated hearing him angry, especially when I partially caused it. He was a good Alpha and I hated it when he was angry with the pack because of me. I wanted to tell him no but the memory of the painful fire that had raced through me wouldn't let me lie about that.

"Yes but I do not think it was intention-."

"Not intentional my ass. Who was it?" His voice was harsh as he cut me off and after a few moments I shrugged. I wouldn't say, I wouldn't tell him. "Look at me, Mary Mary." His voice was a touch softer and I slowly looked up, his face went black with anger as he took in the state I was in. He stood up abruptly. I lowered my gaze from his face to his chest, hating how the tears wanted to escape.

I didn't want to lie to him. I wanted to tell him everything. I wanted to tell him about the rejection, about how empty I felt but I bit my tongue. I wasn't supposed to tell.

An Omega must do as an Omega is told.

I watched as he moved around the desk to stand in front of me. A large hand reached up with a handkerchief and wiped at the sticky residue from my tears. His other hand grasped my chin as he bent down to look me in the eyes.

"Who was it, sweetheart?" His brown eyes were soft, despite the harsh lines of his face. He was an intimidating figure and I could understand why many in the pack feared him. I knew I should have, I knew it deep down but I couldn't. Something in the memories that had been nearly washed away kept me from fearing him.

"I can't say." I felt my bottom lip tremble as his gaze held me captive. He wanted answers that I couldn't give him. I wanted so badly to tell him but I couldn't. I had been ordered and an omega needed to do as they were told.

"*Sweety*." There was a warning tone in his voice and I felt the trembling from my lip take hold of my entire body. Tears filled my eyes and I shook my head frantically.

"I don't know names, I don't know who. I just want to change sections." I felt my breathing come in quicker gasps and without warning I was pulled to a wide chest and comforting arms held me gently. Tears streamed from my eyes but I was too surprised to speak.

"Easy now, little one. I'll change you to section four." His voice was soothing as I shook like a leaf. His embrace was comforting but it did nothing to chase away the empty feeling in my chest.

I blinked rapidly trying to make the tears leave but it wasn't working. "But that is *your* section." I had always been kept the furthest from his section. Ingrid always kept me far away from him, she always told me it was because he didn't want me close. It was odd he would give me that section out of all of the other ones.

"I want to be able to keep an eye on you so this type of thing won't happen again. You're a member of this pack, you're special and you deserve to be treated fairly. You're *not* a plaything to the others." He spoke carefully and slowly as he tightened his grip on me, holding me just a fraction closer. I nodded, burying my face into his chest. I didn't like how empty I felt, how *exhausted*. I just wanted to curl up and sleep.

He let me go but grasped my shoulders gently, looking me in the eye before wiping at my new tears with his handkerchief. "You look ready to collapse. Lie down on the couch and get some sleep. I'll let Ingrid know that you're not feeling well. No one has to know about why you're in here. I want you to feel better." Much to my shock he bent down and pressed his lips to my forehead in a fatherly kiss. Something he hadn't done since I was just a young girl. His stubble scratched my skin and for a brief moment I was six years old and he was kissing my forehead after he had bandaged my scraped knee. I shoved the memory away harshly.

An Omega has no memories.

He pulled back and patted my head before gently pushing me towards the sofa sitting in front of the fireplace. I made my way over to it on unsteady legs before sitting down. Without saying a word I shifted on the firm cushion, pulling my legs to my chest I lay curled up. I felt small and insignificant as I pulled my bare feet under my dress. I hadn't expected my mate to accept me. I hadn't expected a happy ending.

I was just happy to be alive and to have a place to stay. I was content with the work I had but I didn't know how to deal with the burden of such a sharp rejection. I did not blame him for rejecting me. I knew he needed a more suitable mate than an omega. He needed a mate that matched his station. I just wished we had never been paired in the first place because the pain and then the empty hole I felt in my chest was almost unbearable. I felt cold and listless, like I would never be happy or warm again.

I closed my eyes and wrapped my arms tighter around myself. I wanted to sleep, everything in me wanted me to fall backwards into unconsciousness but the empty feeling was a heavy burden. The fire had been incredibly painful but the emptiness was a different sort of pain. It was like an unending ache deep within me that wasn't enough to take my breath away but enough to make it hard to think at times.

I took several deep breaths to push away the pain and I succeeded a tiny fraction. I hated feeling out of control. There was little I could control in my life and controlling my body was one of the biggest things I had and now it was gone.

The door opened and Beta John's scent appeared in the room. I could hear him muttering under his breath and I tried to block the sounds out. I didn't wish to eavesdrop on them. It was not my business what Alpha Lawrence discussed with Beta John.

"Well, what was it she wanted?" He sounded irritated and I made note to avoid him in the present future. I knew when pack members were irritated by me it usually ended up in a stinging cheek or a harsh shove to the floor. I did not know what he would do but I did not want to find out. I squeezed my eyes together tightly, trying to block out the conversation but with the harsh silence in the room, it was like I was focused completely on it.

"She was attacked in her section by some pack members she didn't know. Remind me later to let the pack know that omegas are not toys to be abused. They're people and part of this pack and do *not* deserve that sort of treatment." Alpha Lawrence's voice was low with warning. He was a good Alpha, I knew this and many others knew this. He was strict but he treated everyone the same, even the omegas. I knew there were many packs that allowed their omegas to be mistreated and abused harshly and I was glad he did not abide by such a thing.

"They are *omegas*." There was an edge of distaste to Beta John's voice. No one truly liked omegas, I heard in faint whispers that there were some Alphas that did not have omegas and those that did have them, the omegas weren't like us. They were merely timid creatures that the packs loved and cared for, protecting them intensely. I had always wondered if it were a lie to make other omegas feel better about their station in life, to give hope that there was something better out there.

"Did I stutter, beta? Omegas may be in that station in life but they're still members of this pack and I treat all members fairly. You're no better than an omega in my eyes and they are no better than you." His voice had a harsh finality to it. He would speak of the subject no more. He had used that tone on me many times as I asked numerous questions about my life and about the world around me. I respected the tone. I could hear someone inhaling loudly and I felt my heart thump hard against my rib cage.

"She's still here." There was a low growl in Beta John's voice that I shivered at. The growl did not mean good things for me. I tightened my grip around my legs, closing my eyes tighter. I didn't want him to come closer. I didn't want to be caught listening.

"She's sleeping as she's not feeling well after the incident. I'm having Ingrid change her quarters and I will not force her to continue cleaning her section after today." The warning tone was back but his voice had an icy edge to it. He was losing patience with Beta John, it wasn't something I ever got to witness and I felt bad for listening to it.

"Omegas do not get time for-"

"Do not test my limitless patience, Beta." Alpha Lawrence snapped each word out, he did not like being disrespected. He had made it clear it was the end of the conversation and Beta John had ignored it. I tucked my knees closer to my chest and shifted my head on the rough, decorative pillow that rested against the arm of the couch. Alpha Lawrence was a good Alpha. He was a good leader. Memories slowly swept across the edges of my mind. They taunted me, daring me to take a step into the unknowns that would get me punished.

I closed my eyes tighter, trying to drown them out and sleep, murmuring the mantras inside of my head.

An Omega does not have memories.

TWO

A harsh slap to my cheek yanked me out of the darkness of sleep and I immediately got up, looking down at the floor, knowing better than to look up or touch my burning cheek. "Ungrateful child! Shirking your duties and sleeping in the Alpha's office. I should beat you for this." Ingrid's voice was a sharp, hissed whisper and I rolled my shoulders forward, clasping my hands in front of me.

The door to the office opened and the familiar footsteps of Alpha Lawrence sounded out, much to my relief. "Ingrid, back up and leave her alone." There was a heavy warning to his tone that dared her to retaliate or to do anything more to me. "You do not get to punish anyone. You need to do your job of arranging omega duties and mind yourself." His voice was cold and sharp as he spoke to her, clipped tones that spoke of his clear agitation. I never knew where it came from, never knew what caused it. My memories were too fuzzy to focus on and I didn't want to. Ingrid would take me back to the classroom and I couldn't do that again. I shuddered underneath the thoughts it brought.

I could practically feel Ingrid shaking with anger. She believed I needed to be punished for my supposedly impudent behaviour. "Yes, sir." She gritted the words and I looked at the bottom of her dress. It was the same colour as mine but it was in much better shape. I received the hand-me-downs from the other omegas as it was all Ingrid would give me. I cherished each one I received though. They were my possessions and I took great pains in making sure they were respectable looking despite their thin and ragged state.

The sound of a chair creaking had me glancing towards the Alpha's desk. He settled into his chair, his sharp gaze on Ingrid. "Did you move her quarters?" His voice was cold and I lowered my gaze as he turned his head, as if moving it to look at me.

"Yes, sir." Ingrid was grinding her teeth together and I wanted to wince. I would be punished severely for her anger. I always was.

I glanced over at him from the corner of my eyes and he was shuffling papers on his desk, seemingly ignoring us both. "Section two was only partly cleaned, Ingrid. I want you to finish it before you go to bed." It was an order. I could hear it clearly and I slowly glanced at Ingrid to see that her hands were shaking hard.

She clenched them into fists and I could feel her outrage, her blatant *hate* she had for me and the order. "I cannot possibly clean two sections today." She spoke quickly and I lifted my head slightly.

"I was more than three quarters done before the... *incident*. I only had linens to do, ma'am." I quickly lowered my head once more as she turned to me. All that anger was immediately directed at me and I could feel it like a heavy push against me, a hot brand against my skin that threatened to burn me to ash.

"I did not give you permission to speak, omega." She hissed the words on low and heated tones. I lowered my head further. Even with the other omegas I was lower than them. Ingrid made sure to remind me of it again and again.

"What did I *just* say, Ingrid? *Leave. Her. Alone*." Each word was said with a heavy shove of growling dominance that had her bowing underneath each one. "You do not *command* the omegas, you *organize* them. You are no higher than the rest of them. Remember that. Take her nicely to her new quarters." His voice softened slightly, the dominance lessening but the order was no less apparent. Ingrid grabbed my wrist and tugged me towards the door. Her grip was painfully tight but I said nothing about it because I knew if I did the punishment would be worse. She pulled open the door and took a step.

"Ease up your grip, Ingrid. I said *nicely*." That sharp icy edge of warning was back to his voice and Ingrid released my wrist quickly. "I do not believe in punishing omegas but you're testing my patience for that. You do not get to take your anger out on her. If you have an issue with my orders. You take it up with *me*." Each word was said slowly and seemed to be covered with crackling and frigid ice, to the point that I could see a small tremor in Ingrid's form. She feared him like I was supposed to but could not.

"Do you have an issue with my order?" The question was baiting Ingrid, daring her to say yes, daring her to do something, anything against her Alpha.

"No, sir." She gave him a curtsy before leaving the room quickly. It was as if she expected him to call her out on the lie and chase her through the house. Her boots thumped against the wood floor quickly, showing her rapid movements away from the office.

I turned and gave Alpha Lawrence a deep curtsy. As much as I feared being alone with Ingrid and her anger, I appreciated him protecting me and reminding her of her place. "Thank you, sir." I stood up straight, relieved that the trembling from before had disappeared and happy that I could feel a bit safer with him around, could stand a fraction taller.

His brown eyes looked at me, they swirled with numerous emotions and he swallowed. "If she... If she hurts you. I want you to tell me, okay? If she hurts *anyone*, you need to tell me." He stared at me, his eyes almost sad and I wanted to ask him what was wrong. To ask him why he looked at me like that but I couldn't find it in me, I couldn't find the courage to do anything as my eyes lowered. "You deserve more than that, you truly do. I am right *here* for you, you can tell me. *Please* tell me." There was a faint edge of a plea to his voice and I gave a small nod and another deep curtsy, keeping my eyes on the desk he sat behind.

I shoved at the memories that always surged so close to the forefront when he was around. "Yes, sir, and thank you, sir." I gave him one more curtsy before lifting my skirt slightly and rushing after Ingrid, leaving those hazy memories behind.

She hadn't made it far before I fell into step behind her. Her anger rolled off of her in waves and I knew she wanted to say something as her boots thumped ominously against the wooden floorboards. I knew the other omegas would be scurrying around, quickly trying to do their tasks before her wrath would be brought down on them. She wanted to say something horrid and cruel but I knew the icy and threatening words Alpha Lawrence had said probably kept her mouth firmly closed.

We moved to the very back of the section and she pointed to a small door before turning around, slamming her shoulder against mine as she moved past me. I stumbled backwards from the force of it but ignored the pain the action brought and slowly moved forward and pushed open the small door. It was a little bigger than my previous quarters and as I looked around the room I noticed that Ingrid had taken all the furniture out of the room. Even the mattress was bare on the floor.

I let out a small sigh. She had taken the bed frame and I would have to go to her to ask for it back. The thought brought on a chest tightening sense of anxiety and I immediately shook the thought away. The mattress would be fine for now, at least she had left me that.

I moved to a small pile of linens and pulled out a sheet before slowly making the bed. The ache in my chest wasn't easy to ignore but I knew with time I would be able to better ignore it or even grow used to it. I grabbed the thin blanket and spread it over top of the mattress before looking out the small, dingy window. The sun was setting and despite the sleep I had on the couch, I was still tired, a bone-deep, aching exhaustion that clung to my form and attempted to drag me down towards unconsciousness.

My clothes lay in a heap by the door and I slowly made my way over to them. I picked them up and brought them back to the mattress, folding each dress carefully before moving onto my nightgowns. The pure white fabric had started to turn slightly grey with age and the thickness had been worn down to barely anything. I folded two of them but left the third one out before moving to my undergarments. Once they were folded, I tucked them into a pillowcase and laid it at the head of my bed carefully. Ingrid had even removed the luxury of a pillow. I stood up and slowly undid the buttons on the front of my gown before letting the fabric pool on the floor at my feet.

I sat down on the mattress and carefully and gently took the knots out of my brown curls with my fingers before picking up my discarded dress and folding it. I looked at my pale and thin arms, the blue veins were visible underneath my skin and I absently traced them with the tips of my fingers. It was like dark lightning against a white sky, an inverse of nature and reality. I let my hand drop and stood up before picking up the nightgown. The door to my quarters burst open and I looked over my shoulder in slight surprise.

"Omega! I can't find my-" A younger male looked at me with wide, almost brilliantly blue eyes and I blinked before lowering my gaze and carefully pulling on my nightgown.

I let the thin fabric settle before facing him. "What is it, sir? What do you need help finding?" I clasped my hands in front of me and the silence felt intrusive before he let out a small cough. I resisted the urge to look up at him, I could do so with Alpha Lawrence but I did not know this pack member and I did not wish to be punished feeling as I did.

"Where is the other omega? The one who used to stay here." His voice was slightly strangled and I clasped my hands in front of me before glancing up at him briefly. His blue eyes were wide and his face was slightly pink, from the exertion of running or something else, I wasn't sure.

"She was assigned to a different section, sir. I am the omega for this section now. What is it you are looking for? I could help you find it, if it pleases you." I curtsied at him. I was not ashamed or embarrassed that he had seen me naked. We were shifters, nudity meant very little to us. Despite the fact I had not shifted in years, my wolf was still there but omegas were rarely allowed to shift. Our wolves were subservient and rarely came out, too downtrodden and beaten to show even the tips of their noses.

"It would have pleased me for you to leave the nightgown off-" A strangled cough cut him off and when I glanced up again his face was bright red. "*Please* don't tell Alpha Lawrence you heard me say that because he would literally rip my junk off." He winced at the words and his face flushed a bit more, turning a touch darker. "Seriously, please don't tell him I said that." He almost stuttered for a second as he swallowed and looked around at everything but me.

"You don't have much in here." The words were blunt and I blinked, feeling a touch of shame. I never felt conscientious about how my room was before but how he said it made me want to flush red and hunch over with shame. "Do they really make you stay like this?" He was staring at me, I could feel his gaze like a warm touch to my skin that made me want to move away. It made me uncomfortable.

"I just changed sections, sir. My room was just moved." I didn't want him questioning why. I didn't want him looking like that anymore. I was starting to feel more and more uncomfortable, like a piece of me was recoiling from him. it wasn't me but it was something inside of me that was sending half broken signals to my brain for me to stay away from him

"Still. Not even a bed?" He sounded agitated at the thought, as if he couldn't believe I was not given that luxury. I knew it was my punishment but he did not seem to believe it was just or fair. "I'm going to ask Alpha Lawrence, that doesn't seem right." An immediate alarm sounded in my head and my heart lurched in my chest at the words. Something inside of me screamed at me that Alpha Lawrence wasn't to know.

"It's okay! I'm fine. I am alright, sir." I swallowed thickly, realizing I had allowed my voice to rise at a pack member. I flinched, expecting a hit that didn't come. After a tense moment of silence I slowly forced myself to move out of the flinched and tense position. "What can I get you sir?" He was staring at me again and that uncomfortable feeling was once again there. I didn't want him to remain there and make it continue.

He shifted on his feet, shoving his hands into the pockets of his jeans. "I feel like a real jackass but I don't know where that other omega put my blankets. I came here to ask her where they were." He was wincing, I could hear it in his voice. "I really don't want to bother you with it and looking at your room... I mean I feel like a complete and total ass for bitching about blankets when you don't even have a proper bed." I was taught not to ignore a pack member but him focusing on my room made me anxious that he would go to Alpha Lawrence.

"I shall go check in the laundry room, sir." I wanted him to focus on anything but the state of my room. The less he thought about it the less he would think about going to Alpha Lawrence. He couldn't go to Alpha Lawrence. That voice inside of my head was screaming the warning at me over and over and over again.

"You really don't have to. I can go find another set and maybe like a spare bed for you?" He gestured to my mattress and I couldn't help how I stiffened at that.

"Please, sir. It is my job to take care of this section. Do not worry about me, let me worry about you." I needed him to stop questioning things, it hurt my head and made me feel panicky. The mantras were running rapidly through my head over and over again, a litany of rules that were blurring together. "What room is it you are staying in? I need to know to bring you back your blankets once I have found them." I gave him a low curtsy and he fell silent and I allowed myself to glance up at him.

He looked puzzled. "Why did they change your section?" Despite his curiosity, I gritted my teeth as my eyes wanted to burn at the reminder of the rejection that still had its mark deep inside of my hollow chest. "What's your name?" He asked it softly and I hoped that if I appeased his curiosity that he would leave me to do my job.

"I am called Mary Mary at times, sir, omega at others. Please, I need to know where your room is so I can better serve you." I bowed my head and waited patiently, hoping he would tell me the information I needed to do my job.

I wanted this strange encounter to be over. "Mary Mary... that's cute. *Really* cute." He scuffed his foot against the floor. The gesture was strange for me because it spoke of bashfulness or nervousness. "If you're really intent on the blankets, I'm on the first floor, room fourteen. If you can't find them, don't worry. I'll make do for the night." He cracked his knuckles slightly, once again scuffing his foot against the floor.

I gave him a small nod. "It is no issue for me, sir. I will try my best to find them." I gave him another curtsy before I slowly moved past him and into the hall, unable to help how I hunched my shoulders forward as his gaze followed me.

"*Wow*... she's *really* beautiful." The words were nearly whispered, as if he hadn't wanted me to hear them and I felt a shudder run through me at them. I knew I would never be touched because of my station but the fact someone thought of me as beautiful made my chest feel warm with contentment, even though his glances made me uncomfortable. I tried not to let him see the blush as I moved away. I rarely received compliments, in fact outside of Alpha Lawrence I could count on one hand the times that I had received a compliment.

I slowly made my way to the servant's stairs and took the creaky wood down to the laundry room. I went to section four's machines and opened the dryer. Thankfully some blankets were in there. I pulled them out and folded them precisely. Each room needed a comforter, a sheet, and a spare blanket. I put each blanket in an appropriate stack before going to the spare linen cupboard and pulling out the rest of the linens I needed. I filled out the rest of the stacks before putting them all away except one, I picked it up and went back to the servant's stairs.

I walked up the stairs, ignoring how cold the wood was on my bare feet as I pushed open the door to the first floor. I looked at the numbers on the door before reaching room fourteen. I balanced the blankets on one arm before gently knocking. The door opened slowly and I held out the blankets for the young male.

"Your blankets, sir." I looked down at the floor, before glancing up to see a slightly surprised look on his face.

"Shit, that was fast. You did that in no time at all." He sounded impressed and I resisted the urge to shrug. It was an impolite gesture that usually ended in a slap for my impropriety. I didn't want him to hit me so I kept everything held tightly inside, unwilling to let myself be improper for even a moment.

"It is an inconvenience for you to not have your linens, sir. I do not wish to fail in my duties as an omega." I didn't wish to be banished. I liked the pack and I didn't want to be away from Alpha Lawrence. I held the blankets out further and he took them quickly and with a small cough of what sounded like embarrassment.

"I don't mind being inconvenienced. It's just I expected you to take longer than five minutes. The other omega who worked here, the cranky one, she always took forever to get shit done. This is nice, so don't think I'm complaining." He was rambling and I wasn't sure how to deal with it. I had more than enough long conversations for the day.

I also had more than enough interaction with him. That feeling was still there, swirling around in my chest as if it had no true place to go. It felt so strange. "I apologize, sir, for any inconvenience brought upon you by us omegas. Is there anything else, sir?" I stared at his bare legs, he had changed out of his jeans. Sparse black hair covered them and I could see him shifting his weight from one leg to the next. Another action that confused me.

Why was it that people who spoke to me had such nervous gestures? Other than Ingrid and Alpha Lawrence that is. Ingrid was always one to slap and Alpha Lawrence would offer a kind smile, there was nothing nervous about their actions. It didn't make sense.

"No. You can go. Thank you. For the blankets I mean and for listening to me ramble like an idiot. I'm sorry. I'm really tired." He sounded apologetic and I wanted to tell him it was alright but all I could do was curtsy once more before moving towards the servant's stairs. "Thank you again, Mary Mary. If I find a spare bed I'll bring it right to you" His voice echoed through the empty hall and I lowered my head, slowly picking up my pace.

He seemed like a nice male, he was kind and I hoped he found a mate just as kind as he was. Perhaps if he had a mate he would no longer make me feel as uncomfortable as he did.

I entered the servant's stairs as I slowly made my way up to the second floor, stepping out of the servant's door I then took my time moving towards my bedroom. "Mary Mary, what are you still doing up?" Alpha Lawrence's voice sounded behind me and I turned around quickly, clasping my hands in front of me. "And what are you doing wearing *that* around the house?" I looked up at him and he looked almost horrified at my attire. Another rolling wave of shame coated me as I faintly picked at the worn fabric of the nightgown.

"A pack member did not receive his blankets back from the laundry. He requested I get them for him. I had already changed into my nightgown and it was just a short walk. I did not see the harm in retrieving them for him, regardless of my attire." I looked at my bare feet. I didn't have shoes, none of the omegas did, except Ingrid. She wore boots that thumped against the floors as she walked. Everyone knew where she was when she cleaned. It made it easier to avoid her.

"Ingrid forgot to give him his blankets. Sounds about right." He gave a faint hiss of irritation before he looked at me once more. "Okay, you go to your quarters and next time, change back into your dress. That... *scrap* of fabric you are wearing is damn near see-through. Why don't you have a better one?" He sounded agitated at the thought I didn't have what he believed to be proper attire and I hunched my shoulders forward. I didn't like it when he was irritated or agitated. I was supposed to make sure he was happy because if he was happy then he wouldn't banish me.

"I must take the hand-me-downs, sir. It is all they have for me." I knew the rules, omegas wore hand-me-downs. I was given the oldest ones because I was born to filthy rogues. It was what Ingrid told me again and again.

"That's *bullshit*. I give Ingrid enough money to keep you in good clothing. Not hand-me-downs. *Especially* when they look like that." The words were a heated hiss that had me wanting to almost flinch but I refrained. I knew Alpha Lawrence would never hurt me. "That looks like it would fall apart if you tried to wash it and if it got wet it would pretty much show everything you are trying to cover. Come with me, sweetheart." He didn't give me any warning as he took my hand and pulled me down the hall.

I felt my heart thump against my chest as he squeezed my hand reassuringly. Hearing that he gave Ingrid enough money to clothe all of the omegas surprised me. She always made it seem like we drained the pack dry, that we were an unnecessary, unneeded, and unwanted expense so the more we cleaned and did our jobs without fail, the easier it was for the pack to keep us around. The more we relieved the financial burden we posed, the better it was for the pack.

"I think Ingrid might be spending too much money on herself. I'll have to delegate the omegas' clothing purchases to someone else. Someone more reliable." He muttered the words under his breath as he pushed open the door to his bedroom. I wanted to freeze in the doorway but he tugged me inside before letting my hand go and moving to his dresser.

His room was like he was, everything was in order but there was a hidden warmth to it. I tried not to look around but I couldn't help myself. A multitude of little picture frames sat on a desk he kept by the window and they tugged at something in my mind. I wanted to move closer to see what they were but he was back in front of me and the memories were threatening with a familiar pain.

"Okay, I'm giving you these. They aren't nightgowns but they will cover you better than that thing." He handed me a small stack of shirts and I looked up at him in surprise. He patted my cheek affectionately with a small smile on his face. "I don't wish to have anyone do anything else to you. You're *safe* here. I want you to remember that, okay? I am always *right here* for you. You can tell me anything and everything." It was once again that look that spoke of a faint pleading, as if he were looking for something in me that I couldn't remember.

I said nothing but nodded before taking the white shirts from his hands. "There you are." He cupped my cheek and pressed another kiss to my forehead as if he had sensed my hurt, my broken heart that needed comfort. It was as if he had sensed all of my turbulent emotions and had known that the fatherly gesture would help soothe those stings away.

"Thank you, Alpha Lawrence." I felt a faint smile on my face as he let his hand drop and he pulled away.

"Now go to bed and burn all your old nightgowns tomorrow. I don't want you running around in them." There was an order to his voice but also a clear note of affection. I nodded and curtsied before leaving his room and closing the door behind me. I clutched the shirts to my chest. They were a gift of kindness, I did not get them often. The fact they were from Alpha Lawrence made a warm feeling envelope the emptiness in my chest for a brief moment before it retreated, making the hollow feeling seem almost worse.

I did my best to ignore it as I made my way to the small door that signalled my quarters. I opened it and slipped inside before looking at the shirts. There were three of them, white button up shirts that were made from a nice thick fabric. I quickly placed them on the mattress before kneeling down and pulling the other two nightgowns out of the pillowcase. Alpha Lawrence had told me to burn them so I would.

I pulled the other nightgown off and set it with the rest beside the mattress before grasping one of the button up shirts and sliding it over my head. It was large on me, the sleeves went over my hands and it settled just a bit shorter than my nightgown did. I pulled back the blanket on the mattress and lay down, ignoring the faint hunger pains in my stomach. It was too late to go and get something to eat and if I tried to sneak down to get something I knew I would be punished.

I rolled over and pulled the thin blanket around my form. It wasn't very comfortable with the mattress on the floor and not a bed frame but I knew I would get used to it. It was something I was very good at. I was adaptable. I could adapt to the rejection, I could adapt to my new section, I could adapt to the mattress on the floor. Everything was minor. I had a place to sleep, I was safe, I was wanted. I let the words run around in my head.

I could adapt.

THREE

A month later

My limbs shook and ached as I scrubbed the floor. I did my best to focus on the motion, trying to get lost in it, to jump my mind into auto-pilot. When I could let my mind drift away, let it go blank with the monotony, I could escape the hollowness of my chest, the yawning abyss it had become. I did my best to adapt, to push through it, but it was like a slow descent into a place I knew I couldn't come out from.

I had started to throw up my meals, as sparse as they were. I needed the food but it was getting harder and harder to keep anything down. The lack of it made me feel weak and dizzy. It was why I was trying so hard to lose myself in the work, to lose myself in the motions.

Back and forth, back and forth, again and again, Back and forth, back and forth. I was trying so hard but the dizziness and the trembling in my limbs wouldn't let me drift away.

"You are missing spots, *omega*." Ingrid's voice was heated as she hissed the words at me. I flinched under them, dipping my scrub brush back in the pail and looking for where I had missed. It was getting worse. I was making *mistakes*. The thought made me anxious, bile rising up in my throat. I *couldn't* make mistakes. I dashed some water across the floor, scrubbing at every inch I could reach, ignoring how sodden my dress was getting. I *needed* to make sure it was clean.

Ingrid thumped her boot against the floor. She was watching me with that all-knowing gaze, searing through to my core with it. She knew I would make a mistake and she was waiting for the perfect moment when I would. My back still ached from the caning I had received. I had missed clearing dishes from one of the rooms I had cleaned. A lonely cup and a spoon, tucked away, but I had missed it and I had been punished. I was sure my back was still heavily bruised. My healing was no longer existent.

"Omega..." At the taunting voice I refused to lift my head. I needed to clean the floors better because I knew she was just wanting an excuse to punish me again. I dipped the scrub brush back into my pail and before I could take it out a shattering sound had me jolting. "You missed a spot."

I slowly lifted my head at her mocking tone, a flower vase lay cracked and broken on the floor by her feet. Its contents strewn over the area I had scrubbed. My face paled and I slowly crawled towards it.

Another mess.

An Omega must never let anyone clean up an Omega's mess.

My heart hammered in my chest as I slowly started to pick up the broken pieces. I needed to clean up the mess. It was in my section, it was my mess. The mantra circled my brain, tightening the words around my skull until it ached and threatened to explode.

An Omega must never let anyone clean up an Omega's mess.

"What the hell?" At the angry voice I gave a sharp gasp turning quickly in fright to see which pack member I upset with my actions. A searing pain slashed through my palm as I completed the movement and Ingrid pushed off from the wall.

"She's a clumsy thing." Her words were bored and my eyes finally managed to land on the shifter who had spoken.

The blue eyed male glowered at Ingrid darkly. "I *watched* you drop that." He puffed himself up, his eyes growing darker with his displeasure at her actions.

Ingrid bowed her head meekly. "It was an accident." An accident. The words ran through my mind, mocking me over and over again. Ingrid was good at the deception she was playing.

"That wasn't an accident. I *watched* you do it." The male wasn't backing down, getting further into Ingrid's space, making her shrink even further into herself. She only used that position for the pack. The pack only saw her meekness and the rest of us received the cruelty she had naturally. "You're a cruel old bitch." He spat the words out at her and I quickly turned my gaze to the floor at the heavy insult. The blue-eyed male never was one to mince his words.

A throbbing in my hand made me turn my head to look and when I did I nearly threw up. My palm was gashed open, blood flowing freely from the cut I had given myself in my panic at the blue eyed male's arrival. "*Mene*!" The exclamation was heavy and the male was immediately by my side, grabbing my wrist. He ignored how I flinched as he quickly squeezed the bleeding appendage before looking around frantically.

The contact with him made me feel strange, uncomfortable. It was the same feeling as when he looked at me. It was something he did often since he had met me. Not only had he watched me but he had started finding reasons to try and speak to me. Then he had started to bring me things. He had started small, a pillow for my bed, a makeshift bed frame he had seemed so proud of that I couldn't tell him no. He had recently started to bring me flowers and small trinkets.

It was strange for me because while I enjoyed the things he did for me, my emotions were always so contradictory. Something in me shunned his attention, shunned his concern, shunned his interest. It was that same feeling that caused me to throw up after I ate, that caused me to be unable to sleep. I was *trying* to adapt, I was, but it was hard.

"Hey, hey, come back here." A hand touched my face and I reeled back, reality slamming into me. My heart thudded and I tried to stand up but my head swam with dizziness, black spots danced in my vision, and my legs gave out. He pulled me close, shushing me slowly. "It's okay. We need to get you to the doctor." I shook my head frantically, doing my best to ignore the black spots in my vision as my rapid heartbeat sent a new wave of pain over my hand and up my arm as blood pumped out of the deep cut.

"This needs stitches, Mary Mary." His voice was firm and seemed to come from far away. I blinked rapidly, swallowing convulsively as I fought back the bile that rose up to touch the back of my throat. It was bleeding too much, I could feel it dripping off my fingertips and the memories that rose up made the panic and anxiety that much worse.

I wasn't allowed to see the doctor. The doctor would *tell*. "Not the doctor." I couldn't go there. The doctor would tell and *no one* was to know.

The cut would heal, it would. I needed to remain useful. I could bandage myself up, I could tie it off and it would be okay.

"Then we're going to the Alpha. What she did was cruel." He started walking down the hall and I shook my head rapidly, trying not to follow, digging my feet into the floor in an attempt to remain unmoved.

"No!" Alpha Lawrence couldn't know. The voice in my head screamed at me loudly. He couldn't know. He couldn't know. He couldn't know. Something bad would happen if he knew. I would be sent back. I would be taken back to it.

The classroom.

A heavy shudder of icy fear ran down my spine and I felt my breathing turn even more harsh and ragged. The black spots intensified in my vision, threatening to send me to the floor.

The male stopped walking me forward but he kept his hands on me. "He needs to know." His voice was low and soothing but I shook my head, the panic robbing me of my voice. I couldn't go back to the classroom. After all these years it still haunted me, still sat as a beacon of despair and ruin. That room was like *death*. People went there to die, to cease to be. "We can't leave this." He squeezed my hand gently, sending a rolling wave of pain up my arm as it danced along my nerves.

He started walking again and I made a faint noise of protest, resisting him. He shushed me gently as if trying to soothe the heavy fear and panic that made my heart beat rapidly against my rib cage. "It's okay. We're just going to a bathroom for a first aid kit." His words filtered through the static-y haze of panic in my brain. The haze wasn't unlike the painful buzzing I got when Lucas found himself in the company of another female. I prayed that he wouldn't today. I couldn't handle that with everything else.

My hand hurt and my back ached. Despite the pain from my hand taking center stage, the bruising on my back was still there and how the male was holding me pressed against the worst of the lashes. I kept my mouth closed as I stared at the floor, carefully placing my feet on the hardwood, doing my best to focus on walking. I could ignore the pain. I *could*.

He led me into the bathroom before guiding me to sit down on the side of the tub. He grabbed a towel and pressed it to my hand. "Hold this tight, okay?" He was staring at me, I could feel his gaze against my skin but I kept my eyes downcast.

An Omega's gaze belongs on the floor.

"Yes, sir." I gave a faint nod, holding the towel close to my hand, ignoring the pain it caused and the red that was seeping through the white towel. I knew I would need to soak it to get rid of the blood. I couldn't let it get stained or Ingrid would punish me for it.

"You can call me Bennett if you want, Mary Mary." His voice was forcefully light as he said it and I glanced up as he walked towards the sink.

"Thank you, sir." He always told me to call him Bennett but I knew the mantras, I knew how much Ingrid saw. If I slipped up with him then she would know and I couldn't go back to the classroom. I couldn't do it again. As much as he wished for me to use his name I knew that lesson well. I doubted I could ever forget it.

I could hear him let out a sigh and I let my gaze fall to the floor, I could see blood spots marking a trail from me to the hallway and my heart lurched. I needed to clean it up. I went to slide off the tub when the blue eyed male returned, setting the first aid kit on the toilet as he opened it. I felt trapped as he grasped my towel wrapped hand and slowly pulled the bloody fabric away.

"I need to clean my section, sir." I couldn't look at the gash on my palm as the cold air brushed it. I knew it was bad and I knew it would make me queasy to watch it bleed, to see my skin split open like I knew it was.

"You need this to be fixed up first." He grabbed some gauze and placed it onto the wound. I stared at the floor as he did so, I didn't like him near me, I didn't like the uncomfortable feeling that made my hollow chest seem off. That feeling was terrible and I wanted it to go away. I didn't understand it and all I knew was that he made me uncomfortable when he was close.

My hand throbbed hotly with pain and I stared hard at the droplets of blood that had splattered on the floor. I would need to get used to the pain, to the strange feelings the male gave me. I would need to push harder to adapt. my stomach rolled and twisted as the throbbing pain in my hand grew worse but I fought back the nausea as best as I could.

I didn't have a choice and hope was slowly fading for me. I needed to adapt because I knew it was do or die.

FOUR

One month later

There was no adapting to my situation. The half severed bond was punishing me. It punished me every time Lucas slept with another female. The half bond we shared punishing me, not him, severely for the transgressions. It was agony. It ripped through my stomach and chest with a vengeance, waves of pain rolling over me again and again until I wanted to do nothing but scream but I forced myself to work, to function. I didn't want to be banished, this was my *home*. I wanted to stay but I was failing at my duties.

I was weak, unable to think or move quickly. I had stopped being able to eat completely a few weeks ago. Everything I ate came right back up and I was painfully aware of how many of my ribs jutted out, how my dress hung off me as if I were nothing but a coat hanger. I kept fainting at odd times during the day but I couldn't force myself to eat anything. My stomach instantly rebelled at the idea and it was terrifying. My body was starving itself and I could do nothing but watch in silent terror.

Every task I did seemed to take twice as much energy as usual and for the first time I felt physically unable to do my duties and it terrified me. I had been punished more in the past three weeks than I had in the past nine years of my life. I moved too slow, I was clumsy, I wasn't doing things right. The list of reasons Ingrid used were endless but the harsh pain from the punishments remained the same.

Even now I could barely get off the floor from where I had fallen as I tried to get out of bed. I had tried many times in the past hour but I hadn't the strength or the energy to do so. Not anymore. I had tried to adapt, I had grown used to the aching emptiness that had filled me but everything piled on me to the point I couldn't fight it anymore. My life was falling apart around me and I had no clue how to stop it.

Tears filled my eyes as I tried to force my weak arms to push my body upwards. They held me for a moment before I fell back onto the floor. I felt a sob tear through me. I was dying and I couldn't stop it.

I could hear Ingrid moving closer to my room, the vibrations of her heavy boots moving through me. They stopped by my door and she banged on it heavily. "Get up, you ungrateful little wretch!" Ingrid's voice sounded through the door and I tried hard to get up again but collapsed onto the floor once more. "Get up!" I didn't have the energy to answer before she burst into the room. "I said *get up*!" She pulled the strap from her belt and cracked it across my back. The pain was fleeting and I tried once more to get up but I collapsed again. The strap cracked against my back again and I bit my lip to keep from crying out.

I knew I was late for my rounds but I just couldn't get up. "I can't, ma'am." I barely knew my own voice. It was raspy and broken but I knew I would receive no pity from her.

"You *can't*? Oh, Alpha Lawrence will see about that." Harsh hands grasped my arm and I was yanked to my feet. My lack of weight must have surprised her because she stumbled slightly before pulling me to the door. My legs wouldn't work and she cursed in anger before her arm went around my rib cage. She half supported me and half dragged me down the hall. My eyes were on the floor, my heart pounding frantically against my rib cage. I couldn't let Alpha Lawrence know I couldn't do my job, I didn't want to be banished.

"Stupid little cow!" Her fury was palpable but I couldn't even speak in my defence. I was no longer capable of doing my duty. I was useless to the pack. You could not keep a useless omega, there was no reason for it. Ingrid pushed the door to Alpha Lawrence's office open without knocking.

"What are you doing, omega!" Beta John's voice was practically a growl and I winced slightly before I was dropped in a heap on the floor. A thick silence filled the room as I tried to push myself to sitting but like before my weak arms gave out and I lay there, heaving out laboured breaths on the floor. My heart beat thumped harshly in my chest, I could almost feel it in my ears.

"She refuses to get out of bed and do her rounds! She needs to be punished." Ingrid's voice was filled with malice and hate. She had wanted me banished since Alpha Lawrence made her switch sections with me. I had finally given her the reason she wanted. Tears filled my eyes at the look that I knew must be on their faces. Disgust for the pathetic omega who should never have been brought into the pack. "Tell him, omega! Tell him why!" Ingrid's hand yanked me to sitting and before I knew what was happening, Alpha Lawrence was around the desk and shoved the older shifter hard.

He was angry, dangerous growls exiting his chest. I forced myself to stay sitting. It made my muscles tremble but I needed to stay upright. "*Never* touch her again! Get out of my sight! Both of you!" His voice was a roar as he shoved her away, towards the door and without saying a word Beta John left just as quickly. The door clicked shut and I lifted my head to look at my livid Alpha. His face was a harsh and cold mask. There was no affection for me in his eyes and I bit back a whimper.

"Why are you not eating?" His once comforting voice was cold and I felt my bottom lip tremble. "*Answer me.*" There was a deadly quiet in the room as tears streamed down my face. I was unable to stop them.

"I can't." I croaked it out and lifted a trembling hand to my face to wipe away the tears. I wasn't sure if he would believe me, I wasn't sure if he would accept my response.

An Omega must do as an Omega is told.

"You *can't*?" His voice was hard and I gave a shaky breath and let my hand fall to my lap.

There was a harsh weakness in my limbs and body. I wanted to curl up on the floor and sleep, to give up. Fighting this was too hard. "I can't keep anything down." My voice was rough and hoarse and it came out in a hushed whisper and the tension in the room faded slightly.

"Why?" The question was asked softly and I felt a sob build in my throat before it escaped without warning. It echoed slightly in the room, such a pathetic and weak sound, I *hated* it.

"The pain is too bad." With my words there was a muted thump as Alpha Lawrence knelt down beside me. He pulled me onto his lap and wrapped his large arms around me gently, giving me the comfort I needed. Just like he did when I was a child, he let me curl up against his chest. I wanted to cling to him, to dig my fingers into the fabric of his shirt and keep him close.

"What pain? Are you hurt?" His voice was soft but it held a frantic panic, he clung to me, holding me close. I had wanted so much to be held like that, to be comforted and to be given that attention. "What is it, little one?" His tone was soft and pleading, as if he wanted me to tell him something, *anything*.

I pressed my hand to my chest. It shook and trembled with the weakness I felt. "It's in here. It never goes away and sometimes it flares up in a bright inferno because he is with someone else. I tried to do my job, I *tried* but my body isn't listening. It's not listening. It just wants me to die." Each word was like a painful sob torn from me and I clutched at him weakly.

He rubbed my bony back with soft sounds of comfort but I could feel his muscles tensing as my words registered. "When who is with someone else?" There was a faint pause as his muscles tensed. "You got rejected..." The words were a soft exhale of what sounded like despair. "Who was it?" The words were a harsh sound. He was angry but his anger was not at me but for me. Like a father's protectiveness was surging from him.

I shook my head rapidly as words wrapped around my brain and that voice screamed at me. "I can't." The words came out along with a flurry of sobs but I knew he wouldn't let up. He wouldn't abide by a pack member being hurt as I was. He would want to know by who and how. I clung to him as tightly as I could.

"Yes, you can. Tell me." It was a sharp order, a hard one that I shook at but the mantra spilled from my mouth.

"An omega must do as an omega is told." It was burned into my mind and the voice screamed it at me again and again. I couldn't forget it. I could *never* forget it.

An Omega must do as an Omega is told.

I was told to keep it a secret. I was bound by my duty to keep it that way. I would be punished if I didn't. Panic filled me at the thought of breaking the mantra, at the thought of being taken back to the classroom. I couldn't go there. I couldn't go back there.

"Tell me, that is an order." The Alpha's command in his voice made me tremble, made me feel like something was shoving down hard on my shoulders but it was enough to break through the mantra.

"Lucas." I felt relieved as the secret finally came out. Like a painful splinter had been finally removed. It didn't stop the feelings in me but it felt relieving regardless.

Alpha Lawrence rocked me slightly from side to side, rubbing my spine slowly. "Beta John's son?" He was expecting an answer but I did nothing but nod. "Why didn't you tell me? I could have done something." There was nothing he could have done. He couldn't force his beta's only son to take on an omega as a mate. It would be needlessly cruel to do so. There was little he could do with my situation.

"An omega must do as they are told. I was told not to tell." I said it quietly. The mantras had been seared into me, each one reinforced with brutal beatings in the classroom. Ingrid had been very thorough in making sure those lessons and mantras were ingrained into me. She had me for months for her lessons. My head ached as the voice screamed at me. I wasn't supposed to think about it.

"He took advantage of that." He fell silent but his arms tightened around me and I wished for a brief moment that he was actually my father. That I was his little girl and someone worthy of a mate. "I never wanted this for you, Mary Mary. You have always been the *best* thing in my life, the most precious. Never forget that." He pressed a kiss to my temple, holding it there as he shook slightly. "I'll be right back." He slowly set me back on the floor before he walked to his desk, picking up his phone.

I stared at the floor through blurry eyes. I was a useless omega and I wanted to curl up and die like my body was trying so hard to do. I wanted the aching emptiness to go away and I wanted to stop the pain I felt. His voice murmured in the background and I felt myself slumping towards the floor. I felt so exhausted. I was just so tired of it all. I just wanted it to stop, to end. I looked up as I heard Alpha Lawrence set the phone down.

He came towards me and knelt in front of me, cupping my face. He looked almost... stricken, as if he had done something, or was going to do something that pained him greatly. "I'm going to make this better. Okay, little one?" He stared at me, as if searching my eyes, trying to tell me something. His hands shook slightly as he let me go. "This will be better. I *promise*." He got up and walked out of the room.

I wasn't sure how long I stayed there. It seemed like hours before Alpha Lawrence finally returned. He wasn't alone. Ingrid and Beta John were following behind him. My gaze fell to a long red ribbon dangled from his fingers. A banishment ribbon for the useless omega. I felt my body start to tremble as he stepped forward and picked up my hand. It looked so strange next to his. The skin was so pale it was nearly white next to his slightly tanned one. He gently wrapped the ribbon around my wrist and tied it snug, leaving a fair bit trailing. I wanted to ask him how this was going to make things better, how he was going to make it better with the ribbon.

I felt tears fill my eyes, I didn't want to be banished. I wanted to stay with him, with the pack, it was the only home I knew. He picked me up and I could hear Ingrid and Beta John's sounds of protest but a sharp growl from him that rumbled through me, silenced them quickly. I felt his heart pounding harshly in his chest and it matched my fear filled rhythm. I could see Ingrid and Beta John walking in front of us and as they started down the stairs.

Alpha Lawrence bent his head down towards me. "I need you to get to the forest as quickly as you can, little one. Do not stop, do not fall. Make it there and you will be safe. Promise me you will make it to the forest's edge. Promise me you will be strong. Never forget you are the most precious thing I have in my life." The words were a faint whisper in my ear and I nodded. I wasn't sure why he wished for me to make it to the edge of the forest but he wanted my promise and I would give him that. I only ever wanted to make him proud, to repay him for taking me in at four years old and giving me a home. For showing me a kindness that not many would have shown.

Beta John pushed open the front door and I shivered at the icy breeze that came in and my eyes widened at the white snow on the ground. My feet were bare and all I wore was a white nightgown. Alpha Lawrence's shirts hidden in the pillowcase after I had been given a new nightgown. Alpha Lawrence set me on my feet and I ignored how my legs wanted me to collapse on the floor. I was pushed gently from behind and on trembling and weak legs I stepped out into the freezing cold. All of the pack was there and I kept my gaze forward as I took another step. I forced my legs to remain strong as goose bumps erupted over my body.

It was so *cold*.

"As she is unable or unwilling to do her duties as an omega to our pack. This omega is hereby banished from our pack and our lands." Alpha Lawrence's voice was strong and I bit my lip as tears fell from my eyes. They turned cold instantly on my skin and I felt my teeth start to chatter. He pushed on my back gently and I took several steps forward, the wind biting at my exposed skin. I gripped the stair railing with trembling hands as I slowly walked down the stairs. "Let this serve as a warning to you all. Remember to fulfill your duties and to do them to the best of your abilities or you too, shall end up like this omega."

There was a faint pain in my chest as I felt the separation between me and the pack. I felt a little lost as I hesitated for a brief moment, my foot lingering over the burning white snow but I let out a shuddering breath and let my foot sink into the iciness. I bit back a gasp but forced myself to let go of the railing and take another step. My feet already started to burn as I walked forward.

"Alpha, don't do this. Look at her." It was an acutely familiar voice and I glanced over to see Bennett, his blue eyes looked frantic as he glanced between me and Alpha Lawrence.

He had done much for me, had helped patch me up, gave me things I needed but Ingrid had withheld. My hand was healed thanks to him, still scarred but he had made sure it healed properly and without infection. He came to me every single day, making sure the bandages were changed and everything was okay.

"She'll *die* out there." He said it in a tone that sounded faintly like panic and I could hear a few murmurs of agreement from the rest of them but they still backed away from me, leaving a path for me to walk through. My legs wanted to buckle but I forced them to move forwards.

"Do not question your Alpha, pup!" Beta John's voice was loud as it moved over the crowd but the wind seemed almost louder as I moved forward. "If she dies, she dies. It's no longer our concern." I forced myself to take one step after another. I made a promise. I *needed* to get to the forest.

"Omegas must serve the pack and she's unable to do her duty. Banishment is the only punishment for those who are too weak to take care of the pack." Ingrid's voice was sharp with triumph, she had gotten what she wanted. I had been punished for my weakness, banished for it, and I knew she was silently gloating. She had hated me for so many years, it must have felt like a great victory for her.

"Says *you*! You can barely get your work done as it is. It should be you in the snow, you lazy old bitch!" Bennett's voice was sharp with anger and I took another shivering step forward before the cold made me freeze for a moment. "I know what you did and *you* know what you did! You better hope that Alpha doesn't turn his eyes away because I will repay you for all of it." There was a heavy growl to his voice as he threw out the threat.

I closed my eyes tightly, the wetness on my cheeks made the freezing wind that much worse. I wrapped my arms around myself trying to hold in my body heat. "*Enough*! I have already done this and it shall be as it is." Alpha Lawrence's voice was tight with a well-guarded pain but he hid it well underneath a thick coating of authority. I wanted to take another step but my strength was fading. "Keep walking, Mary Mary. Do not look back." The order was a strong one and I felt my legs move without my urging.

I lifted my gaze to look through the path the pack had created and towards the open expanse of snow that lay between me and the forest. I promised Alpha Lawrence that I would make it to the forest's edge. I promised him and I didn't want to let him down. I clutched tighter at myself as I moved forwards.

So many eyes were on me as I stumbled forward. My breaths were little puffs of fog that lingered in front of my face before they disappeared. My teeth chattered as the bone deep cold settled into my skin. A howl broke through the sudden silence and I felt a different sort of chill crawl up my spine at the haunting sound. Something was waiting for me in the forest and I wasn't sure if it was good or bad. I pushed myself forward, my body still under the order that Alpha Lawrence had given me.

"A red ribbon for banishment." The male scoffed low and I turned my head. He had moved to the edge of the crowd, closer to me. "Mary Mary, they should have tied a black one around your wrist instead. Those wolves will not be kind and you're not fit to fight them off." His eyes were angry, he thought it was unfair. I understood what he said. A black ribbon for the imminent death I was surely walking into.

As I walked past him, I locked my eyes with his vivid blue ones. Tears fell from my eyes and my teeth chattered violently. "The weak are not meant to survive." The words fell from my lips and I watched as he flinched but shook his head. I lowered my gaze before I continued forward. My toes had gone slightly numb but the rest of the exposed skin on my feet still burned hotly. "For the good of the pack, the weak must be banished." The words were rough coming from my chattering mouth and the others took up the statement.

"For the good of the pack, the weak must be banished." The words rippled through the crowd and I pushed forwards, leaving the pack members. I had only snow in front of me. A large expanse of white that brought pain with its beauty.

"You're not weak!" Bennett's voice was loud over the crowd and I didn't turn my head as I continued forward. The order was carrying me over the snow.

"Be *quiet*, boy." Beta John's voice was a deep growl and I heard someone following me before a scuffle broke out. I kept my gaze forward as I moved one foot in front of another. The wind tore at my ribbon and it snapped against the harsh and cold air moving it.

"Let me go!" The blue eye male was cursing as I knew he struggled against those who held him down. "You're *not* weak, Mary Mary!" His voice cracked slightly and I faltered at his words for a brief moment before the order forced me to move forward again.

"You aren't! You deserve better. You deserve so much more than thi-" The rest of the words were muffled and I felt another round of hot tears fall from my eyes and freeze against my skin as I continued forward. Silence fell as the wind whipped around me, tugging at my brown hair. It twisted it into knots like it was doing with my ribbon. I shivered violently but I didn't stop moving. I couldn't. Another howl sounded and I could feel everyone's unease as more joined in the chorus. "They'll kill her! Let me go! I can't just let her die!" His voice warmed me slightly. Bennett was a good male, a kind one. It was nice to have someone care for a brief moment. I could faintly hear him being dragged away.

"Enough! Everyone inside!" Alpha Lawrence's voice boomed over the crowd behind me and I resisted the urge to look back. I continued forward, my ears being assaulted by the howling of the wind and the wolves that I knew waited for me. "Remember what I said, Mary Mary. Remember!" His voice sounded faint as the trees grew closer and closer. I could feel eyes on me and I wanted to stop but I had promised.

I had promised to be strong and make it to the forest's edge. I didn't want to let him down, not when I had promised. He had said I was the best thing in his life. He had said it so no one could hear but he had still said it. He had been my only kindness in a sea of indifference.

I wanted to make him proud.

FIVE

I forced my frozen body towards the forest. Each step brought me closer to the darkness that it contained and I could barely hear anything over the chattering of my teeth. I felt like they would shatter in my mouth as they chattered loudly in my head. I swallowed against the burning air and focused on the edge of the forest. The sun was rising behind the trees and I was hidden in their shadow as I walked closer and closer.

I blinked slowly and when I opened my eyes I was at the edge of the forest. My entire body shook violently and a loud howl broke through the noise in my head and my heart thumped against my chest violently before I took another step forward. The wind couldn't reach me through the trees and there was an eerie silence as I moved further and further into the forest. My legs suddenly gave out and I crumpled to the snowy ground. I felt numb as I looked at the whiteness on the ground. My cheeks burned and my body felt numb but the shaking wouldn't stop.

The sound of snow crunching had me huddling further onto the ground. "Fuck, he sends you out in *that*? Trying to kill you, is he?" The voice was gruff, much more so than Alpha Lawrence's. The footsteps crunching against snow drew closer and I found my gaze on a pair of boots surrounded by what looked to be a cloak. "And look at you. Nothing but bones. This could very well kill you. Foolish bastard." Despite the harshness of the words there was a faint thread of affection in his voice.

The male crouched in front of me and I leaned back with wide eyes. The male looked so similar to Alpha Lawrence it was almost eerie. He shared the same face shape and the same black hair but his eyes were green instead of brown and he had a scar slashing down his forehead and across his nose and cheek. He shook out another black cloak and to my surprise he wrapped it around me. The fabric did very little to take away the cold but I appreciated the gesture, no matter how surprising it might have been.

"Well? Are you going to sit there looking like a freshly dug-up corpse or are you going to say hello to your Uncle Jace?" He smirked slightly as I blinked at him before I swallowed, trying to find my voice.

I wasn't quite sure what he meant but he wanted me to say hello. "Hello?" It came out as a slight cracking squeak and he gave a small chuckle.

"Good enough!" He quickly scooped me into his arm and wrapped his cloak around me as he did so. "Fuck, you're like a block of ice. Let's get you into the jeep where it's warm." He started moving and he frowned, I caught the look as I glanced up at him as quickly as I could. "I wouldn't worry about it too much, I'm sure there is at least *one* pack member willing to curl up with you to keep you warm. You're an awaited guest after all." His voice was still gruff but it held a note of amusement that Alpha Lawrence's never did.

"I know you're confused but trust me. Trust him." He shifted me slightly in his arms and I could hear twigs snapping around us. Several different coloured wolves appeared from the trees as if there were ghosts. I closed my eyes, I felt so cold. My teeth were chattering but I could feel the body heat from the male who called himself my Uncle Jace.

I leaned closer, trying to get closer to the heat as my eyes opened. A different hand reached towards me in my peripheral vision and I jerked my head to stare at it with wide eyes. The male who was reaching for me raised an eyebrow before he tugged up the hood of the cloak and covered my head, blocking my vision. I felt a warmth at the gesture as my face was no longer nipped by the small breeze blowing around us.

I was tired, I wanted to sleep but my mind was racing quickly. I did not know who the males around me were. I did not know who Uncle Jace was and I did not know why he labelled himself as such. My parents had died before I had the chance to remember them and as far as I knew, they did not look like Alpha Lawrence.

"Are the jeeps running?" His voice rumbled through his chest and into me and I tried to move closer to him, despite how my nerves screamed at me in pain. They were waking up and I knew it would not be pretty once they were all awake. Everything was hurting or starting to. I was used to pain but the painful aching was something that one could never truly drown out.

"Yes, Alpha Lawrence." The voice was rumbled and clipped and I lifted my head to look at the male who spoke but a large hand pressed me back to his chest.

"I know you're confused but save the questions for when your teeth aren't chattering so hard, Maricella." The name confused me. I had never heard of it before but it tugged as something inside of me. I fought it back, I couldn't remember. It wasn't allowed.

An Omega has no memories.

However the name tugged so much on my curiosity that I couldn't stop myself. "Maricella?" My voice was raspy and he let out a sigh.

"That's your name, is it not?" He sounded impatient and I tried to quell my chattering teeth.

I didn't want him to be irritated with me but I was confused. "Alpha Lawrence calls me Mary Mary sometimes but I do not recall any other name." I shivered violently and my muscles jerked without me meaning to and I frowned as my hands shook. I was starting to feel the cold again and I didn't like it. The pain was starting and I knew it would continue for hours.

"He never told you your name? What kind of fucking bullshit is that? You know what, never mind. Your name is Maricella Charlotte Lawrence. You're nineteen years old. Your birthday is June twenty-second." His voice suddenly held no more notes of amusement and I shrunk slightly, my gaze on the cloak covering me.

I didn't want him to be upset. I didn't want to but I knew those words were lies. "I am not a Lawrence. Alpha Lawrence is my Alpha, nothing more." The words were a faint whisper as tears flooded my eyes. I would have loved to be a Lawrence, to be adopted by Alpha Lawrence. The only person who had shown me kindness. Something tugged at my memories but I pushed it away, having memories hurt me. The voice screamed at me again and again.

An Omega has no memories.

A deep rumble escaped the male holding me. "That's not what his letters said." He spat the statement out as if it tasted foul and I tried to shrink further into the heavy fabric surrounding me. I did not mean to make him upset with me. I didn't want anyone to be upset with me. If they were upset then it meant I would be punished. He pressed my head back to his chest with a faint sound. *"Rest."* There was a sharp order in his voice and I snapped my mouth shut.

I clasped my bony fingers together under the cloak and hated how cold they felt. We walked in silence before the sounds of running engines filled the still forest air. I turned my head and looked forward, several battered jeeps waited in a line. A male lazily stepped out of one of the jeeps. He was wearing a heavy looking denim jacket and a small wary look on his face. He looked very similar to Alpha Lawrence and Uncle Jace. He stuffed his hands in his pockets and a chuckle rumbled out of Uncle Jace's chest.

"You can lower your guard, Davin. We've done what was requested of us. Now come and take Maricella, you and Collin are to keep her warm in the back of the jeep." He jiggled me slightly and I looked at Davin with wide eyes. My breathing was ragged as I shook harshly under the cloaks. "Or I could hand her off to Collin. My guess is he would rather enjoy snuggling with your cousin." Again the use of familial terms in regards to me. I stared up at the scarred male in confusion before I gave a small startled cry as I was pulled from Uncle Jace's arms quickly but gently.

Jace reached out and chucked me underneath my chin with an easy grin. "Easy, Maricella. You couldn't fight your way out of a wet paper bag at the moment. We'll take you far enough away that the mate bond will affect you less and your body will stop trying to kill you." I turned my face away to look up at the male who had taken me. His green eyes showed his wary agitation and his dark eyebrows were pulled low over his eyes as he carried me towards the jeep.

"I apologize, sir. For the inconvenience." The words sounded low even to my ears and he looked down at me in confusion.

"Sir? The name is Davin. Not sir." He gave me a peculiar look and I shrunk down into the cloak with a heavy feeling of panic. I didn't know what I was going to do. The banishment took me from my place in the world. I felt like I was floundering.

"I'm sorry, si-" I cut myself off before I could say it and I stared up at him as the jeep door opened. I averted my eyes, terrified he would catch me looking and punish me.

An Omega's gaze belongs on the floor.

The voice in my head screamed and howled at me, thrashing the inside of my skull with the mantras until I felt it ache terribly. "What are you apologizing for?" He set me on the seat gently before getting in as well. He was a larger male and I felt small seated next to him.

I swallowed down my fear, I wasn't allowed to address my superiors but I knew he was expecting a response. "For being an inconvenience." I knew I was an inconvenience, Ingrid had beaten it into me. I was useless unless I served the pack. The bastard child of two rogues who deserved nothing more than death and I needed to be grateful for being allowed to serve the pack.

"Family is always an inconvenience, Maricella. You just deal with it because you care for them." He sniffed slightly and I shrunk into my cloak. Everything around me was foreign. I had people claiming to be my family and claiming my name was Maricella Charlotte Lawrence. I had no recollection of any of it. Something tickled the edges of my mind and I shoved it away quickly as the panic rose up sharply.

An Omega has no memories.

"I don't have a family." I said it slowly as I glanced at him quickly and looked away. I didn't want to see the irritation marring his features. I didn't want to be punished for looking at him. I wasn't allowed to stare. I wasn't allowed to address my superiors but I was so *confused*.

"Yes you do." He startled me as he wrapped an arm around me and tugged me partially against his chest. His large hand reached inside of the cloak and started rubbing at my arm. I shivered at the heat his hand held. "Fucking Christ, you're freezing. Is your wolf helping you warm up at all?" I gave a tiny shake of my head. I didn't want to think of my wolf, she was absent, so timid she hid in the back of my mind and I had not seen her in years. The other door opened and a blonde haired male got in with a rather cheeky smile. I lowered my eyes from his face and he sat down before grabbing my legs and pulling them onto his lap.

"Try not to enjoy this too much, Collin." Davin's voice was snappish and I jerked slightly as Collin's hands grasped one of my bare feet and started rubbing it in between his hands. The feeling was weird and I resisted the urge to shake his hands off. I didn't like feeling so confused and off balance. Everyone and everything was confusing me and I just wanted to be left alone.

"She's cold." His voice was husky and I risked a glance to his face and his brown eyes were looking at my pale feet as he rubbed them gently.

He had an almost soft look on his face and Davin let out a snort. "No shit." With the tone he took I could almost imagine him rolling his eyes in irritation. I swallowed as the other male snapped his teeth together and threw a dark look towards Davin.

"No, fuck face, her feet are like ice." Collin's reply was harsh but he looked away from Davin before I watched him lift up his jacket and shirt, stuffing both my feet under it. He hissed as my feet touched his stomach and I stared at him with wide eyes through my cloak. I resisted the urge to yank my feet away and tuck them underneath myself. I didn't like that. I didn't like so much contact. The panic rolled through me and I shook violently, I wasn't sure what was causing the shaking more, the panic or the cold shivers that plagued me.

"She was forced to walk over a football field worth of snow with bare feet. Of course they're going to be cold." Davin shifted me closer and ran his hand down my arm to rub at my hand. I felt my shaking lessen slightly and then the aching started to set in. The bone deep pain set my teeth on edge. I closed my eyes tightly, going through my breathing to ignore the pain. I knew what I had to do in order to ride it through.

"What kind of shit person does that to a little female? No offence, sugar, but you're tiny." Collin patted my leg and I cracked my eyes to glance at him. He must have been waiting for it because he winked at me. I felt my face flush and his mouth curved into a smirk.

"Apparently my Uncle Andrew's pack and stop flirting with her." Davin shot out his other hand and smacked Collin's shoulder. I flinched at the action, if they were quick to hit each other I didn't even want to know what they would do to me.

"Why is she here again?" Collin looked at me in confusion and I turned my head towards Davin's chest. I was starting to get sleepy. Collin rubbed at my feet through his jacket and shirt and I slowly tried to pull my feet away from him but he grabbed my ankle, stilling my retreat instantly.

Davin rubbed at my skin, pulling me closer as if he was able to read my thoughts on pulling away from them both. The contact made me uncomfortable. That familiar feeling inside of me rolled under my skin, urging me to reject their touch and to curl away to be alone and unseen. I now knew it was the severed mate bond and it was trying to kill me but it didn't stop how much I agreed with it at the moment.

"Uncle Andrew phoned dad and told him that if he didn't come get Maricella she would end up dying because she had a mate reject her." They were both so gentle with me that I felt like I would break. I knew I wasn't in the best of shape at the moment but I had never had someone treat me like they were. Alpha Lawrence had treated me fairly and there had been moments of tenderness and affection but nothing like this. It made me anxious as to when the punishment would start. No one did something nice to omegas, it usually led up to a cruel action.

"Jackass rejected her and didn't let her accept it?" Collin's voice was a mere growl and I closed my eyes tightly. I didn't want to be on the receiving end of a punishment because of his anger. I knew if he caught me looking I would be punished.

"You got it. So now we're taking her back with us. The separation will weaken what is left of the bond, Amber will do her magic, and after a bit of time she can accept it without being near him." Despite how anxious I was to be around them, his words made sense and I was glad that Alpha Lawrence had done what he did for me. He got me away from the place that would kill me and had placed me in the care of what appeared to be gentle and friendly people. I didn't exactly trust them but they hadn't hurt me so far and I knew that if I stuck to the rules they wouldn't have a reason too.

"After that?" Collin's sounded wary and I shifted in my spot, turning slightly. I froze as Collin let out a hiss as my feet shifted on his stomach. "You have very cold feet, sugar." He grabbed them, holding them firmly so they couldn't move again. I waited for him to punish me with my heart pounding in my chest but after a few moments of nothing I felt myself relaxing.

"I don't know, Collin." Davin sounded unsure of himself and I let them continue their conversation as the cold left my bones. Their voices were a murmur that pulled me towards sleep and I yawned and stretched my arms over my head slightly, trying to get more comfortable.

"Okay, that's adorable. Just look at her cute little face." Collin's voice was coated in sweetness and I felt my cheeks blush. Davin placed my arms back into the cloak and resumed rubbing at my hands. I tried to slowly move my hands out of his reach but he merely reached further, grasping them firmly in his hands so they couldn't escape.

"What did I say about hitting on my cousin?" There was a thread of warning to his voice that reminded me of Alpha Lawrence and I felt my heart filled with love for the one person who had cared for me. He had promised me it would get better and I believed him. Despite the fact the pack connection was severed, the faintness of it barely hurt me, he was still my Alpha and I knew deep down that I loved him dearly. Tears slowly filled my eyes when I realized I didn't know if I would ever see him again. I fought back the tears, he promised me it would be better and I knew crying would only make me worse. I needed to do as Uncle Jace had said. I needed to rest.

SIX

The world came back to me slowly, the weakness still lingered in my body and I rubbed weakly at my eyes. I blinked slowly, letting my surroundings sink in. The world around me was so much more different than I remembered. I was curled up in someone's lap and I hesitantly glanced upwards to see a male with a scar across his face. Memories slowly came into my head and I lowered my gaze before risking a glance at him once more. He seemed intent on something over my head and I could faintly hear the sounds of a television.

I frowned, trying to remember his name. The voice in my head screamed at me not to use it and I swallowed thickly. "Sir?"

"It's Uncle Jace." His voice was rumbling but he didn't look down at me as he said it and I flinched slightly, waiting for the punishment to come but it didn't. I wasn't used to not receiving punishments for my wrong actions. I didn't like that I wasn't in a position I was familiar with.

I swallowed thickly, clasping my hands in my lap tightly. "Sir?" I glanced up at him quickly but he made no indication he had even heard me. Panic filled me as my body started to tremble. "Uncle Jace?" I tensed, fearing a punishment for the impropriety of my use of his name but he merely glanced down at me and a small smile crossed his face before his arm shifted around me. It felt strange having someone tuck me close to them as I slept. I wasn't really used to physical contact.

"Yes, Maricella?" He looked at me with such tenderness that I wanted to cry. I wasn't sure why he cared about me, why he looked at me like that. I was unaware of who he was, of how he knew me.

"Where am-" I couldn't get the question out as an ever familiar pain flooded my chest. I felt my breathing increase as the pain started to beat at me. It dug in deep, tightening around my chest until I felt like I couldn't breathe. "I hurt." I managed to get the words out before I clutched at my chest and breathed heavily.

Deep panting gasps filled the air and slowly a large hand rubbed at my back. It was soothing but tears flooded my eyes and I shook as the pain ran rampant through my chest and stomach. I fought the urge to throw up. There would be nothing there even if I did.

The arms around me brought me closer, tucking me closer to the large male. "I can't help you right now, Maricella, but know that we'll fix this." He rubbed my back gently, his voice soothing. It didn't help the pain and made me shake. "Amber's getting the meds ready for you. Just breathe." I could barely hear his voice through the static in my brain. I could barely force myself to breathe let alone think about what he was saying. I was rocked gently from side to side as another wave of pain crashed over me. I gave a sharp cry that faded to a whimper as it continued to beat at my body.

"Is she okay?" The new voice sounded frantic and there was a rumble from the chest I was pressed to. I couldn't focus on anything as the pain seared at new places in my body. I felt my body curl up tighter, my whimpering seemed too loud to my ears as everything was tightening with the pain. I felt like I couldn't breathe and I felt like I was going to die. "Can't we do anything? We can't just leave her like this!" I couldn't hear a response as my head throbbed painfully but I could feel the vibrations of the chest I was pressed to. I gave a pain-filled groan as I clutched at the arms holding me. I felt sorry for Uncle Jace as my nails dug deep into the muscles of his arm.

The waves grew in intensity and I struggled to breathe for what felt like hours. Sharp whimpers of pain exited my mouth and nothing around me mattered. It was like I was encased in a bubble filled with unbearable, painful static that I could never escape until it was all suddenly gone. I slumped against the large male, my chest heaving with the effort of breathing. I sounded terrible, my breath was coming out in wheezes and my entire body shuddered every so often.

"Two months of that, by *herself*? You have *got* to be fucking kidding me." The voice was pained and I rolled my head on the wide chest I lay on and saw Davin. His face was pale and he looked angry. "Why didn't you tell Uncle Andrew sooner? Why wait until you couldn't move?" His voice cracked slightly and his green eyes were narrowed. I closed my eyes against the sight and let my head roll back to its natural position.

"Don't be so hard on her, Davin." Uncle Jace squeezed me in reassurance and I felt slightly uncomfortable but at the same time I was exhausted, I couldn't find it in me to move. I lifted a shaking hand and wiped at my sweaty forehead. I could feel my hair sticking to my skin and it made me itch unpleasantly.

"I'm not. I just want to know *why*." He emphasized the word and I took in a deep breath, trying to calm the rapid pounding of my heart and to calm my wheezing breath.

"An Omega must do as an Omega is told." The familiar words fell from my mouth and there was a sudden, deadly silence in the room. I could feel Uncle Jace's muscles tighten with a sudden anger and without warning I was pulled from his arms as deadly claws emerged from the male's nail beds. Davin cradled me to his chest and I looked up slowly in confusion. He looked almost worried.

"A fucking *what*?" Uncle Jace's voice was quiet in the silence and I looked over at him. I kept my gaze on his heaving chest and slowly blinked. He was mad, furious about something but in my exhausted mind I couldn't figure out what it was.

"An Omega must do as an Omega is told. I was told to stay silent." I hated how slurred my raspy voice was and I was suddenly thirsty. The thought of cold water made me lick my dry lips.

"Oh *really*?" The way he said it made me shiver with a sudden fear. The male who had let me sleep on his lap was so far from gone it appeared as though he was on the other side of the planet. I tried to push myself closer to Davin, wanting to get further away from the angry male.

"Dad. I'm going to call Collin in to take Maricella. Stay calm, for her sake." Davin took several slow steps backwards and I leaned my head against his chest. My neck was unwilling to hold the burden any longer. I lifted a shaking hand, everything was too confusing, there was too much going on and I was so tired.

"Stay *calm*? He turned her into a fucking *omega*! After all the advice I gave him. After all of the letters he sent me, he turned her into a fucking omega! I'm going to kill him. Painfully and slowly so he knows just the reason why." He jumped to his feet and started pacing. The action looked violent and fear jumped quickly through the exhaustion, causing my heart to pound unpleasantly in my chest. I wanted to make him stop but at the same time I needed him to understand that me being an omega wasn't a bad thing.

"I am the child of rogues. I am an orphan. I was happy to have a place in the pack, no matter how low. Being an omega was better than being left to fend for myself in the wild." I stared at my hands, my voice was low as I blinked slowly. It was the one place I belonged. I didn't deserve anything else but to carry the name of omega.

"No matter how low- Are you *shitting* me right now, Maricella?" There was an edge of furious disbelief to his voice and I shrunk back towards Davin, suddenly scared that the intensity he was putting off was now aimed at me. I had tried to make it better, why had it made it worse? Everything was just getting to be too much. I wanted to go back to my pack, I wanted to be back where I knew what was going on and what I had to do to stay safe.

Davin took another step backwards. "Dad, don't be mad with her. She's just repeating what has been drilled into her for the past fifteen years. You can't fault her for this- this... *brainwashing*." Davin's tone was calm and even, as if trying to reason with the furious male. I risked a glance over to the large pacing male whose face was angular as if his wolf wished to emerge.

He stopped abruptly, running his hands through his hair as he looked at me. I quickly glanced down, not wanting to be punished for staring. "You're right. I apologize, Maricella, but that brother of mine is *never* getting his hands on you again. I swear to the fucking goddess I'll murder him before I even *think* of letting you go back there." There was a heavy venom in the words, a complete and startling promise that had me looking up at him completely with wide eyes.

I shook my head quickly. "He saved my life. He is a good Alpha." I wanted him to understand. Alpha Lawrence was a good Alpha, everything he did was for the good of the pack. He had sent me away because he had promised to make it better. He had promised me it would be better. He never broke his word. He was a *good* male.

"Well in those letters he managed to convince me he was a good father. Now I have learned he turned his daughter into an omega and you learned that he can throw you away without a thought. He had tricked us both, Maricella. He didn't even tell you your name, for Mene's sake. Your *name*." He sounded pained and I opened my mouth to say something when the blonde male sprinted into the room. I closed my mouth with a snap and immediately stared at my hands.

"Give me my sugar." I could hear the smile in the new male's voice and Davin held me a bit tighter before he reluctantly handed me over to him. I tried hard to push through the exhaustion and remember his name but it was hard. "Thank you very much." The amusement was very clear in his voice and I felt uncomfortable with him, I didn't know him. I didn't know *any* of them. It frightened me to be in a place I didn't know with people I knew even less.

"Collin, no flirting with her. Now go." There was a faint command to the words and Collin said nothing as he carried me out of the room. I clasped my hands together as tightly as I could with the exhausted weakness filling my body.

"You can put your arms around my neck. I won't bite." He was smiling as I glanced up at him and I felt my face flush slightly. I picked at my nails wondering if I should do as he said or stay like I was. These people were so confusing it made my head hurt.

"I said no flirting!" Davin's loud voice sounded from the doorway and Collin laughed loudly. The sound rumbled through me and I picked at my knuckles. The skin was slightly flaky. I knew it was from poor nutrition but I couldn't stop. I needed to do something to stop the anxiety. I could control the picking, it was the only thing I *could* control.

"Okay, sugar. What do you want to do?" He asked it so easily that I was slightly shocked for a moment. I didn't know how to answer. No one had ever asked me to do something. I was always told, I was ordered, *never* asked.

The unbearable dryness in my throat made me open my mouth. "May I please have a drink of water?" The words were a squeak and I quickly hunched my shoulders forward. I was waiting for a reprimand for speaking out of turn but Collin merely spun around with me in his arms and laughed again. The action made my head hurt slightly and I felt almost nauseous but he was enjoying himself so I didn't want to tell him to stop.

"Of *course* you may. We mustn't let you be thirsty!" With that he raced down the hall and my arms immediately went around his neck in fear of being dropped. My heart jumped into my throat, wondering if he would punish me for the action but he just made a rather ridiculous airplane sound with his mouth. "Air Sugar coming in for landing. Over." He gently set me down on a chair and I yanked my arms from around him as if he had burned me. My heart pounded in my chest with fear.

"I'm sorry!" I blurted the words out, staring at the floor. I felt terrified. I was so tired that it was making me forget my place.

"Whatever for, sugar?" He was looking at me but I refused to let myself look at him. I needed to remember my place. I was an omega and would always be an omega. Ingrid had smacked my hands with a leather strap until I could barely hold anything with my swollen fingers and beat my back bloody with a wooden cane, just to get me to remember the lesson. The voice in my head hissed the reminders at me. I would go back there because Ingrid knew everything.

"For touching you, sir." My voice shook as I said it and I looked at my hands in my lap. I was still wearing my nightgown and the red ribbon. I could hear a cupboard open and a tap turn on before shutting off.

"Sir? No, sugar, it's pronounced Collin but I can see how that might be a tad confusing. Here you go." A cold glass of water was set down in front of me and I looked at it for a brief moment before I picked it up with a shaking hand. I tried to focus on bringing the cup to my lips. I took a small sip and closed my eyes before taking a bigger drink. Before long I had drunk more than half the cup. I gave a small sigh of relief as the dryness was chased away. "You're so skinny." Collin said it casually and I heard a fridge open.

"Skinny? No, she's a walking bag of bones and demons take the motherfucker who rejected her." It was a new voice that I gave a startled jump at. The cup slipped from my hands and I watched in horror as it hit the floor and shattered.

"I'm sorry. Let me clean that up!" I quickly stood but no sooner had I taken a step my legs buckled underneath me. I fell hard to the ground with a small groan of pain as my knees slammed against the hardwood.

"Don't worry about it, sugar. Accidents happen. I'll clean it up." Collin picked me up and tears filled my eyes as he set me back on the chair. The voice screamed at me, piercing my head, causing it to ache.

An Omega must never let anyone clean up an Omega's mess.

"But I broke it. I need to clean up my mess. You shouldn't be cleaning up my mess." My voice slowly rose to a hysterical level and I started breathing heavy, looking at the broken glass. "I can clean it up. Please! Just let me clean it up!" I started hyperventilating and my heart pounded sharply in my chest. The panic was sharp and my heart pounding in my ears, nearly deafening me.

"Would it calm you to clean it up, Maricella?" Davin's voice slowly made its way through the pounding and I nodded quickly. I needed to clean up my mess.

An Omega must never let anyone clean up an Omega's mess.

He was suddenly there and he carefully picked me up and set me on the floor before letting me go. "Breathe, Maricella." I picked up chunks of glass with shaky fingers, feeling a calmness fill me at the small task. "Here's a dustpan. Put the glass in there and here's a towel." He handed me the items and I nodded, keeping my gaze on the floor as I set the large glass pieces in the dust pan. I dabbed at the water with the towel, feeling my body relax with the motion. I was useful again. I couldn't walk but I could still clean.

"What's wrong with the crazy cleaning lady?" It was the new voice again and I tried to block him out as I started to pick up the smaller chunks of glass. Cleaning it up made me relax. I was doing what I was trained to do.

"That's my cousin, you ass. She has been conditioned for the past fifteen years into thinking she's an omega." His voice was angry and I couldn't understand their anger. Being an omega, especially for me, wasn't a bad thing. I was a bastard child of rogues, it was all I was good for.

"I *am* an omega." I said the words softly. The voice hissed at me over and over again, squeezing my head so tightly until it ached unbearably.

Once an Omega, always an Omega.

"You never should have been one, Maricella. If Uncle Andrew hadn't been such a fucking dipshit with his head jammed up his own ass, he never would have let you become one." His voice shook with anger but his tone was calm. It was like he didn't want to scare me and I was grateful for the gesture.

"Alpha Lawrence is a good Alpha. He saved my life. I was happy to serve the pack." I dabbed at the rest of the water before carefully sweeping the floor with it, sending the tiny shards into the dust pan. "I was happy to serve the pack." For a brief moment I wondered if I was trying to convince them or to convince myself. That cruel little voice in my head screamed at me for the thought. I was an omega because I was supposed to be, it was the only position I was fit for.

"Sugar? You done down there?" Collin sounded completely unaffected and I nodded before setting the towel on the dustpan. It would need to be shaken out over the trash to get rid of any bits of glass sticking to it. Large hands grasped me around the waist and I was lifted to my feet. "You're so fucking tiny." He voice was low, as if he hadn't really wanted anyone to hear it.

"She's small because of the rejection. Her body is literally trying to kill itself. It still will until Amber can get the fucking meds mixed together in a timely fashion." The voice was venomous and I risked a glance up to see a dark haired male with dark eyes scowling at me. I quickly looked away and Collin wrapped an arm around my back before lifting me up completely, holding me close to his chest. I didn't like it, it made me uncomfortable.

"Ignore, Seamus. He's a bit pissy right now. Now what is it you would like to do?" He was smiling at me but I felt too off balance and stared at my hands. I started picking at the ribbon. A red ribbon for banishment.

"A male told me the ribbon should have been black for death." I could hear someone suck in a deep breath. "I understood what he told me. That it should have been black because I would never survive on my own. That they weren't banishing me, they were killing me." I tugged on the edge of the ribbon gently before looking over at Davin. I avoided his gaze and kept my eyes on his chest.

"He said I wasn't weak. He said I deserved better and tried to stop me from walking but they wouldn't let him. It was the kindest thing anyone, other than Alpha Lawrence, had ever said to me." I let my gaze fall back to my hands and I ignored how thick the silence felt. I wished I had an ability to thank Bennett. He was a good male. He had spoken out against his Alpha and beta

"Well, at least not all the members of the Tacita pack are utter assholes." Collin said it slowly and rocked me in his arms slightly. The movement made the exhaustion that much heavier in my mind.

"His eyes were really blue and he called me beautiful." I remembered the first time I saw him but I felt no embarrassment. He had repeatedly shown me kindness that should have been given to someone above my station. He had taken care of me. It was something I would never forget.

"That's a terrible line. You aren't even blushing." Collin sounded almost amused and I looked up at him with wide eyes. My gaze rested on a faint scar on his chin. I wondered for a brief moment how he got it.

"I am an omega. There is no reason to blush because I cannot have a relationship with anyone above my station." I looked away and Collin rocked me a little harder before he chuckled and spun me around again. I grimaced slightly at the action as it made my head swim unpleasantly.

"You blush at me." He was over exuberant, much like a puppy. I couldn't tell if I enjoyed it or not. Everything was a jumbled mess. I couldn't think and I just wanted to be left alone to process what was going on.

"I am uncertain of my station as of right now but I am sure I shall remain an om-"

"Do not finish that statement, Maricella. You will not be an omega because we do not have omegas in this pack." Davin's voice was sharp and I instantly rolled my shoulders forward, staring at my hands.

"Pardon, sir?" My voice shook slightly, I wasn't sure if I had heard him correctly. Every pack had omegas. Another thick silence fell and I realized what I had said. My eyes went wide and I flinched, waiting for the slap that would come.

"Call me Davin. Do not call me sir. Not here, not anywhere. I'm your cousin. We don't believe in omegas here. We do not have them in this pack. We are all equals except for dad." His voice was low and I stared at my hands as if they were the most interesting thing in the world. Collin carefully set me down on a chair. It was like he knew the conversation wasn't one he needed to be privy to. "You're family, no matter your blood.

I grew up with pictures of you and having my dad speak of you with pride. You might not have had that but I did and it hurts me deeply to see you look down at your hands, unable to look at my face because you have been twisted into something I never would have thought my uncle would allow." There was a faint pain in his voice and I winced. I never wished to cause anyone pain.

"I am sorr-"

"Don't apologize about this. This is *not* your fault. It will *never* be your fault, Maricella." He was suddenly kneeling in front of me. He was looking up at me slightly and I couldn't escape his gaze. It was either look up and come into contact with someone else's gaze or look into his eyes. I closed my eyes with a faint sigh. "Look at me." A large hand cupped my cheek and I peeked at him through my lashes.

"My father told me about you when I was seven years old. You were four. It was the first time I can remember my Uncle Andrew phoning my father. He was frantic because he had this little brown haired girl with wide grey eyes named Maricella Charlotte. A little rogue girl with no parents and he was scared because he didn't know what to do." He let out a small breath and I cracked my eyes a bit more as he closed his.

"My father explained to him that no one would want you in the pack. Being as young as you were, you had no use. He suggested that Uncle Andrew just let you go back to neutral territory. Uncle Andrew was furious." He gave a small chuckle and opened his eyes. I squinted mine again and he stroked my cheek with his thumb.

"I remember being able to hear him yelling at my dad through the phone. He said there was no way in hell he was going to do that to such a sweet little girl. So then my father told him to adopt you. The conversation ended there but a few months later my father received a letter and a photo." He let my cheek go and stood up. "Come on. I'm going to show you." He picked me up and I let my eyes open completely as he carried me through the house. We came to a room that looked like a study and he set me down on the couch gently before retrieving a large book. He sat down beside me before pulling me onto his lap. I leaned my back against his chest as he opened the book in front of me. He pointed to a photo of a smiling little girl.

"He received this photo with the letter. The letter talked about how my uncle was terrified because he had no idea how to raise a kid and how he needed help. He wrote about how sad you seemed sometimes and that your smile made him happy." As he spoke I looked at the small girl. Her brown hair was curly and her grey eyes crinkled with a smile and her chubby cheeks were rosy. I touched the photo. The picture must have been taken a very long time ago.

He tapped on another photo. "This one came with a letter telling my father that you had discovered your favourite colour was brown because it was the colour of his eyes. He said you wouldn't stop drawing on things and you were a little tornado of energy." The photo was of that same rosy cheeked little girl but she had chocolate smeared on her face. I touched that photo as well before I pulled my hand back. I couldn't remember these pictures or the memories they held. Just looking at them caused an anxious feeling to rise up in me.

"I don't have a favourite colour anymore." I swallowed as Davin went quiet at my words and slowly started turning the pages. Every photo in the book was of me growing up. An entire life that I had never seen before and couldn't really remember. Pictures of me blowing bubbles and playing with the other pack kids. I couldn't remember any of the memories. Ingrid had been quite efficient in making me forget them.

An Omega has no memories.

SEVEN

“Please excuse my bluntness but I am very tired." I wanted to curl up and sleep. I was lucky that the empty aching in my chest had almost lessened as if the distance had helped alleviate some of it.

"Of course you are. Let me take you to your room." With that I was once again cradled to his chest as he carried me down the hall and pushed open a door. The room was warm and he set me on a soft bed before turning on a bedside lamp. A cheery glow filled the space. The bed looked more comfortable than the ones the regular pack members had, even softer than Alpha Lawrence's. I felt almost hesitant to stay on it.

"Is it alright?" Davin looked uncertain and I nodded, looking at the hardwood floor.

"It is very nice, thank you. You have been very kind to me." I held my hands in my lap and Davin picked one up, feeling the rough skin with his fingers. I couldn't remember the last time they had been soft. There was a large scar on my palm from the glass vase I had slashed it on.

He brushed his thumb over the angry looking mark, looking like he wanted to ask about it before he set my hand back down. "Wait right here, alright?" He looked at me as if expecting a response but I said nothing, lowering my head as he left the room.

I smoothed my hand over the blanket, hating how my chapped skin caught on the soft fabric slightly. The door crept open and a blonde head peeked in. Collin's mischievous brown eyes twinkled as he came fully into the room. He jumped on the bed, nearly bouncing me off. He wrapped an arm around my waist to prevent me from falling off the bed. I stiffened before he removed his arm. I could feel him moving around and I quickly glanced behind me to see him staring at me with the familiar cheeky smile on his face.

"Hey, sugar. Mind sharing?" He wiggled his eyebrows before I quickly turned my face to hide my flushed face.

"Collin, get off of the bed and how many times do I have to tell you to not flirt with Maricella?" Davin was back, holding a small tin in his hand as he sat on the bed beside me. He let out a little grunt as Collin kicked him in the side. I flinched at the action but they didn't seem to notice.

"Probably a lot more and I don't want to." His voice was muffled as if he had buried his face into the pillows, The screaming voice in my head kept me from looking over to see if he had.

"Sadly, you aren't going to be able to get rid of him. He's sunk his overbearing teeth into you and he won't let go for anything." Davin spoke carefully as he opened the tin and swiped his finger through the sweet smelling paste inside of it. I felt an arm go around my waist before I was tugged to the middle of a bed. I gave a short cry of surprise at the action, my eyes wide. Collin chuckled as he sat up beside me and reached over my lap to grab the tin.

"No one likes this one because it smells too sweet." Collin took some of the paste and grabbed my hand before slowly rubbing it into my skin. "It'll work perfectly for you." He sat cross legged as he rubbed the paste into my thin fingers. Davin picked up my other hand and started rubbing the paste into the back of it. "Don't be so stiff, sugar. We aren't going to bite. We are just making your hands as soft as they should be." Collin grabbed more paste and I watched as he spread it across my palm.

"I can do it." I resisted the urge to pull my hands from their grips. It made me uncomfortable. If I believed Bennett had made me uncomfortable, this was far worse than that. He never had prolonged contact with me like they were doing.

Davin gave a small chuckle. "Even if you wanted to, Collin prides himself on being a gentleman so he would do it regardless. Probably tie you up to accomplish his task." There was a faint smile on his face and despite the feeling of being uncomfortable, I liked how his hands massaged mine. My hands had been hard at work for years, they had never really been pampered before. It was a very strange feeling but a nice one.

"Are you two going to paint her nails afterwards as well?" The voice came from the doorway and I glanced upwards. It was the same dark haired male from the kitchen, my gaze immediately left him as the voice started screaming again.

"Shut up, Seamus." Collin and Davin said it at the same time, not looking up from their task. I glanced at the dark haired male once more. His face was a scowl and I looked at his well-structured jaw, it had some stubble growing on it. I let my gaze skitter away from his face, not wanting to be punished for looking.

He moved into the room and sat at the foot of the bed. "Hey, my name's Seamus, as these assholes said before." He looked at me and I felt a bit self-conscious under his gaze. "I'm not mad at you. The scowling's for the cow fucker that rejected you." His words were confusing as he flopped backwards onto the bed, placing his arm over his eyes.

"Seamus was rejected by his mate too. He couldn't find her to accept it and ended up in a similar position as you. Except he ran away from his pack before he couldn't move. Dad found him shortly after and here he is." Davin said it calmly and I felt a pang of empathy for the male lying across the bed. Without thinking I pulled my hands away from the other two and crawled slowly across the bed on shaking arms.

I looked down at Seamus' face, even hidden under his arm he was scowling and I softly touched his cheek with my fingertips. "I'm sorry you got rejected." I sat on my knees and Davin wrapped an arm around my waist before putting me back in the same position I had been in before. My face flared bright red when I realized what I had done. I tensed at the feeling of an imminent punishment as the voice screamed at me again and again.

"Look at that. Seamus is blushing." Collin chuckled and I glanced up as Seamus sat up and ran his hand over his face. He looked at me and I focused my gaze on the neckline of his black shirt. I didn't want to look into his dark eyes, I didn't want to be caught looking at all.

An Omega's gaze belongs on the floor.

"Coming from any one of these fuckers those words mean nothing but coming from you they mean quite a bit. I'm sorry that jack rabbit molester rejected you. But I'm fairly certain he didn't deserve you anyway." He reached over and patted my foot almost awkwardly and I resisted the urge to retreat from his touch as well. I just wanted to be left alone for a bit. Left alone so I could process everything that had happened. "Just like that bitch didn't deserve me. Which is why I now have Angie." A goofy look appeared on his face for a brief moment before it was gone.

He rolled off the bed before leaving the room and I felt my heart beat frantically in my chest. "You can have more than one mate?" I looked at Davin and he jerked his head up in confusion, as if he hadn't expected me to ask him anything.

"Yah. It's based on who is the best genetic match to create good offspring. That whole 'only one mate' is bullshit. Our species would go extinct if that were true." He stared at me in confusion before he slowly turned back to my hand. I watched him rub the paste into my hands as I rolled the words over in my mind.

I blinked, hope filled me for the first time in two months. "I could have another mate?" I knew I sounded excited and the voice screamed at me but the thought of not having to deal with Lucas' rejection and the thought of having another mate was overwhelmingly exciting.

Collin gently rubbed at my palm, his fingers tracing the scar on my palm. The motion tickled and I wanted to yank my hand away. "Yes, sugar, you can have another mate. Just as soon as the rejection is complete." Collin's husky voice was soft and I jerked my gaze to his face, unable to help myself. I felt a smile spread across my face and crinkle the corner of my eyes as he looked at me. "*Mene*, I would steal a whole bushel of mates for you if it meant I could see you smile like that again." His eyes were wide and the smile was instantly gone. He looked almost crestfallen as I dropped my gaze from his. They were making me forget my place. I froze at the thought. I couldn't forget the place I no longer had. The thought almost made me panic a bit.

"You have dimples. That was the most adorably gorgeous thing I have ever seen. You should have seen it, Davin. Fucking dimples on her cheeks." He went back to massaging the sweet smelling paste on my hand, muttering about dimples and me being too gorgeous for my own good. I flushed at his words. I knew I looked terrible with my tangled hair, pale skin, and nearly skeletal frame.

"I'm going to get a brush for your hair." Davin got off the bed and I frowned at the hand he had released. My hand had never felt that soft before. I stared at it in amazement as Collin let my other hand drop.

I rubbed them together. "They are so soft." Without thinking I ran my hands up Collin's bare arm to his neck, trying to show him how soft my hands were. "See?" I reached his jaw and I looked at him with amazement. My hands had always been rough, the hot water and heavy chemicals I used to clean with, never let me have soft skin.

"I can feel that but next time you don't need an excuse to feel me up, sugar. Just go right ahead." He winked at me and I yanked my hands back quickly, my face flushed red and he chuckled.

"Sorry, sir." It was a little chirp and I tensed instinctively but he merely lay down beside me with another chuckle.

"Don't be, sugar." He reached over and placed his hand on my bare calf. His hand looked overly large on it and I stared at it for a few seconds as his thumb drew swirls on my skin. I wasn't sure if he was hitting on me or if he was just a touchy person. I wasn't used to touchy people. No omega was. We were isolated from others, from affection. I didn't like the contact but I couldn't tell him to not touch. I wasn't allowed to say no.

"Did you know that when you blush your ears turn red first? It's cute." He smirked and I looked at my hands, running them over my arms. I couldn't get over how soft they were.

"Hands off, Collin." Davin's voice held a warning and Collin patted my calf gently but removed his hand as Davin requested. I appreciated the removal, it had been making me increasingly uncomfortable.

"You should have seen her a moment ago. Feeling me up like a pro." He winked at me again and I felt another blush cross my face. I tensed once more, I didn't want to be punished. I had never been in such a position before. I wasn't sure if I liked it. At least as an omega I had rules. I had a certain schedule and everything was organized. I wasn't allowed out of a certain box and I felt safer like that. These situations never happened inside of the box.

Davin let out a small growl as he sat behind me. "Easy guard dog, she was just trying to show me how soft her hands were. She seemed quite astonished about it really." He sounded flippant and I felt Davin start to run a brush through the ends of my hair, removing the tangles. I was surprised he knew how to brush long hair. Everyone always started at the top but to get the tangles out without hurting the hair you had to start at the bottom.

"Please don't be mad. I didn't mean to." I didn't want him to hit me, I knew there were rules. A strong arm wrapped around my waist and I was gently pulled to a hard chest. I couldn't help how I tensed at the action.

He pressed a kiss to the back of my head with a faint chuckle. "I don't think I could ever be mad at you, Maricella, and I know you didn't mean to. You're too innocent to deliberately feel up Collin." He let me go and resumed brushing my hair. Collin reached over and grabbed my hand. I wanted to yank it back but he simply started to massage the appendage again and I couldn't complain. I had to accept that he wanted to touch me.

An Omega must never say no.

I tried not to hiss when Davin yanked on the knots but it was hard. I was used to doing it by myself with my fingers but having him brush my hair was soothing and my eyes started to droop.

"Look at this little picture perfect moment. Maricella, I'll have you know Davin spent close to an hour looking at how to brush and braid hair on youtube on his phone when he learned we were coming to pick you up." Uncle Jace's voice was gruff but had a softer edge to it and I glanced up at him. His green eyes were soft and Davin grunted from behind me.

"She deserves to be pampered." Collin lifted my hand up before kissing the back of it. It felt strange and I scrunched up my nose at it, my stomach rolling.

Uncle Jace laughed, the comforting and rolling sound surrounding me, before he came into the room. "Can I see your wrist, little one?" He pointed to the wrist with the ribbon and I nodded, holding it out for him. If it were possible his hands were larger than Alpha Lawrence's and my hand looked positively tiny in comparison. He fiddled with the small knot, loosening it up so he could take the ribbon off.

"Are you going to tell him she's okay?" Davin sounded so calm, I wondered if he was naturally calm or if he worked hard at sounding like the world was okay. I wished that I knew how to act like that, the anxiety was horrible, the screaming in my head was so loud.

"No." Uncle Jace's reply was gruff and I winced as Davin yanked on a knot.

He let out an apologetic noise. "Sorry, sweetie. He has a right to know, dad, despite how pissed off we are." His voice was soothing as was the brushing and I wanted to lean backwards into him but I forced myself to sit straight. That screaming voice wouldn't leave me be.

"He has no rights when it comes to Maricella, not anymore." The ribbon slipped off my wrist gently and a large hand rubbed a thumb against where my pulse fluttered under my skin. The movement made me shudder slightly.

"Send him the ribbon." Collin's voice seemed extra husky with tiredness and I opened my eyes to glance at him as he continued to massage my hand slightly. "It will smell like her. Either he will know it was you or think someone else kidnapped her. Either way you're sending him word and being petty at the same time."

"Don't give him ideas." Davin muttered it under his breath and was finally able to move the brush through my hair without running into tangles. I could hear him set the brush somewhere but I wasn't sure where as he ran his fingers through my hair. I resisted the urge to shuffle away from him. I had to get used to them touching. I wasn't allowed to say no.

"Actually that is the smartest thing I've ever heard Collin say." Uncle Jace sounded impressed and I made a small noise as I felt Davin start to braid my hair.

"I will take the back-handed compliment because I'm weak and need constant reassurance that I'm useful." Collin sounded amused as he shifted on the bed. I closed my eyes, feeling the events of the day weigh heavily on my eyelids.

"You do what you need to be happy, Collin." The amusement was back in Uncle Jace's voice. I preferred him amused, when he was amused he wasn't that terrifying angry male.

"Alpha Lawrence saved my life." I felt the sudden silence fill the air. Davin stalled in braiding my hair and Collin paused in massaging my fingers. I didn't know what Uncle Jace was doing but I could hear him breathing and could practically feel him frowning. "You may think he was punishing me but putting that ribbon around my wrist was a great kindness he gave me. It was a great kindness because it saved my life and gave me my freedom. He deserves to know I am safe because that act shows that he cared." I let the silence linger, feeling too tired to deal with the panicky thought of saying something wrong. Slowly Davin started to braid my hair again.

"This is getting a bit heavy for me, sugar. Night." Collin dropped my hand and without warning gave me a quick kiss on the cheek that both Davin and Uncle Jace growled at. "You two need to take some chill pills. It wasn't like I had my tongue shoved down her throat. Unless she would like that. Sugar?" I didn't say anything but faintly leaned away. I could hear him chuckle as he moved out the room.

"Amber should be done tomorrow. Maricella, you should get some sleep, you look ready to fall on your face." Uncle Jace kissed my forehead and I hummed at him slightly in thanks as Davin tied off the braid. I was too tired to think about the voice that had continued to scream at me. I felt ready to close my eyes and fall into unconsciousness. Davin slowly slid out from behind me, gently helping me to lay down before.

My eyes closed, my eyelids feeling so overwhelmingly heavy. I was only faintly aware of him tucking me under the covers before he shut the light off, sending my world into complete darkness.

EIGHT

“Hello, Maricella. My name is Amber. I’m the pack doctor." The blonde female smiled happily at me and I gave a small nod before looking at the white tile floor. My bare feet dangled over it. I couldn't tell if I was too small or the cot I was sitting on was too tall. I was probably too small because Uncle Jace was standing beside me and the cot didn't look to be too tall on him. "I heard you have been having some issues with a partially severed mate bond. So I’m here to check on it and give you a bit of relief for it, okay?" Her tone had an expectancy of a reply so I nodded.

I glanced up at her and her light blue eyes were kind as she moved closer. "Is it alright if I touch you? I want you to be completely comfortable here." Her voice was soft and gentle and I nodded. I didn't want them to give me a reason to not like me.

Something inside of me told me that Uncle Jace and Davin wouldn't throw me away, for some reason they liked me, *cared* for me. I tried to shake the thought from my head. They liked me because of a story in a photo album, a story about a happy little girl with grey eyes. They were protective because I had been hurt and in their eyes I was Uncle Jace's niece and Davin's cousin. As Davin said, he had grown up with me even if I never did with him.

She picked up my wrist and checked my pulse while looking at the watch on her wrist. I could see her nodding her head to the pulse. I could see several pauses in the rhythm her head was making and she frowned. When she set my wrist down I lowered my gaze, avoiding hers.

"Okay, so you have a slightly irregular heart rate. It's a bit worrisome but with the state your body is in, it's not unusual." She was looking at me but I refused to look at her. It was impossible to try and shake off the lessons I had been forced into. I had only been gone for a day and I had *years* of it branded into me. The mantras were my life. "Jace, could you set her on the scale? I know she's underweight but I need an actual weight." Large arms wrapped around me and lifted me easily off of the cot. I couldn't help how I stiffened slightly at the contact.

I still didn't have the strength to walk. Yesterday had been hard on my body and I was now feeling the effects. I had a bit of a rattle in my chest, I felt cold all the time and I spent most of the morning wrapped up in several blankets shivering while Davin, Collin, or Seamus had sat beside me on the couch. I had been allowed to watch a movie and Collin said he would take me out for movies all the time if I was that excited. Which made the excitement instantly disappear.

I wasn't sure why Ingrid made smiling or excitement seem forbidden but she did. It made him happy to see me excited about something and so the two lessons were clashing inside of me. I needed to do things that made the pack members happy but I could not show my emotions. It was enough to give me a throbbing headache.

Uncle Jace set me down carefully on the scale and I wobbled slightly, trying to stay upright on my trembling legs as Amber quickly marked my weight down. My legs shook hard and I felt like they would buckle but Uncle Jace picked me up without a word before setting me back down on the cot. My breath was coming out in pants from the exertion and I felt suddenly tired, my eyelids drooping.

"No sleeping yet. I know that was exhausting for you, Maricella, but I have a few more tests to do. Just try to stay awake, alright?" She wasn't looking at me and so I glanced upwards, taking in the lines on her face and the tight bun she had her hair pulled into. "You weigh seventy-four pounds and at the height of five foot three inches, that puts your BMI at nearly thirteen. You're severely underweight, which is something we can all clearly see." She gestured at me and I looked down at my thin wrists. I hated feeling guilty for something I didn't have any control over but I had worried people. That burden was on me.

"I'm sorry." The whisper was barely audible and I started to pick at my nails, pulling at my cuticles. Uncle Jace grasped my hands in one of his to stop the motion, my heart jumped at the motion before I tried to force it to stop. My nails were still ragged even if the skin was smoother.

Davin had rubbed more of the paste into my hand earlier, telling me it was an all-natural beeswax and herbal hand paste to help with dry and rough skin. I had been confused as to why they had it. Collin had spoken up telling me they worked rough, labour intensive jobs and didn't need bleeding or cracked hands and that I needed to stop asking questions and enjoy being pampered.

"There's nothing you need to apologize for, Maricella." His voice was low and I gave a small nod because I knew he wanted me to acknowledge his words. He squeezed my hands gently before he pulled it back. I missed the contact almost immediately. My hands were cold and his were warm. I wanted to be curled up in my little blanket nest with Davin teaching Collin and Seamus how to braid my hair. It had felt strange at first but having people gently move my hair around made me immediately sleepy and relaxed.

"I need a blood sample and then we're almost done." Amber was smiling at me, I could tell and I risked a glance upwards, her blue eyes were still kind but I let my gaze drop to the stethoscope around her neck. She went to a cupboard and I followed her movements carefully. She turned around with a needle and a small tube it was attached to, I felt my heart start to beat frantically. I never had a needle before.

Without thinking I reached out and clutched Uncle Jace's hand with my own, needing *something* to cling to.

He wrapped his large hand around mine and gave a gentle shushing sound. "It's okay, Maricella." He sat on the cot beside me and I leaned towards him. he gathered me up into his arms before settling me onto his lap. I buried my face into his chest as I held out my arm for the doctor. The TV had shown me what taking blood looked like and I scrunched my face up, closing my eyes tightly as her slightly warm hand grasped my elbow and lifted it. I bit my lip and tried not to whimper as she tapped my skin slightly.

"This is the easy part. I can see all your veins so I only need to do this once. It's okay. It will only pinch a little bit." True to her words there was a slight pinch and the feeling of something moving through my skin. I shuddered at it and clenched Uncle Jace's flannel shirt in my fist. He rubbed my back and crooned nonsense words to me as he rocked me back and forth. The feeling of panic was rising to the point where I wanted to hyperventilate but the needle was quickly gone from my skin and she pressed something soft against the spot it had gone in.

I glanced downwards, expecting to see a lot of blood but she was holding a cotton ball against my skin and she carefully untangled my hand from Uncle Jace's shirt and positioned it so I could hold the cotton ball. "Keep pressure on it, I'm going to put this in the cooler. Then I'm going to check your breathing. That rattle is worrying me." She let my arm go and I pressed the cotton ball to the small wound and I stared at it intently.

"See? That wasn't so bad was it?" The ever present thread of amusement in Uncle Jace's voice was a bit more prominent and I could hear the smile in his voice.

I found myself scowling slightly even as that voice that reminded me eerily of Ingrid screamed. "I don't like change. I don't like new things." It was the most honest I had ever been and Uncle Jace wrapped an arm around my waist as he pulled himself further onto the cot, letting me sit between his legs. He wrapped his arms around my waist and rested his chin on my head. I felt uncomfortable for a brief moment before I relaxed. He felt safe, safer than Alpha Lawrence had been and that was saying something.

"Why don't you like new things?" He kept his voice light and I frowned, trying to formulate my problem into words.

"I don't know how to deal with them. I was never allowed new things and you keep giving them to me. I don't understand them and I can't deal with them." There was a warble in my voice and I felt my bottom lip tremble. "Omegas aren't supposed to experience life outside of our station and I don't know how to function right now because everything is confusing and new. I hate new." Tears filled my eyes and I bit my lip. I sounded like a child but everything was difficult for me to process. I had been forcefully kept in the dark, like all the other omegas, having everything around me that was new and confusing and not having the ability to shut it all out was making me almost panicky.

"It's okay. Breathe and let your mind go blank." His voice was low and I took in exaggerated breaths before letting them out, trying to make the racing tornado of my brain go calm. He reached over and took the cotton ball from me and I let my hands fall into my lap.

"Maricella, I'm going to check your breathing right now. I understand you are having a bit of a panic attack but I need to make sure you don't have fluid in your lungs. With your repressed wolf I'm a little concerned you might actually have pneumonia and you don't need that right now." She didn't wait for my permission as she pressed the stethoscope to my chest as I inhaled and exhaled. I hated how my breath rattled in my chest and she hummed slightly before pulling back.

My brain finally calmed down and I felt exhausted. I leaned against Uncle Jace and closed my eyes as his arms tightened on me slightly. "There's a bit of fluid in her lungs but she doesn't have a fever yet. I'm going to put her on a rigid vitamin regime to boost her faltering immune system, as well as recommend she get a lot of fluids, I'm thinking perhaps IV for now. She should also get some rest." She moved away and Uncle Jace picked me up and carefully laid me down on the cot. I opened my eyes to look at him and he gave me a tender smile before he brushed my hair from my face.

"I'm going to talk to Amber, you stay here and rest." He pulled his hand back and I nodded, curling up on the cot. He pulled a blanket over me and I clutched it in my hands before burying my face into the pillow. "Did you mix up the medication? She hasn't had another episode but I know it's only a matter of time." I could hear them talking in low voices and I didn't want to listen because I knew, even though the subject was me, I wasn't allowed to eavesdrop. I wasn't allowed to know things that were going on around me.

"I did. I'll give her the shot soon. I have the vitamins and what not here but you have to pick up some meal replacement drinks. I want her to drink them in between her meals. She won't be able to eat a lot but the meal replacements will give her the missing nutrition and up her calorie intake. The standard drill with these cases." There was a faint silence and I could hear her give a small sigh. "I think I should examine how she is mentally." There was a faint growl.

"No. She doesn't need that right now." Uncle Jace's voice was sharp and I could hear someone moving around.

"She has been conditioned into believing an ideology and I have a feeling putting her in a different position in the pack will cause her undue stress. Davin told me she almost had a panic attack when Collin tried to clean up a cup she broke. She can't be stressed out, not while her body is focusing on repairing itself. We *need* to increase her immune response, we don't have a lot of methods to help her if she gets more ill and that means keeping her as relaxed as possible." There was a sound of angry sympathy from the doctor. "They *brainwashed* her at a *very* young age. That ideology is part of her identity but if I can figure out how to untangle it from her actual identity then we can deprogram her." The words brought a feeling of confusion. I didn't think I had been brainwashed. I had been taught my place in the pack and it was the place I was supposed to stay.

"So she wouldn't act like an omega?" His voice was low and I could hear his footsteps on the tile floor, his voice faded slightly, as if he had moved further away.

"Not really. She will probably still have some characteristics of an omega because during her formative years where she was supposed to be figuring out who she was, she was programmed to be something else. Those won't go away. She will most likely still be shy and unable to hold people's gaze for long periods of time. She will probably be timid, frighten easily and won't like people cleaning up after her but she won't panic." Amber's voice was soothing and I ignored the angry screaming of Ingrid's voice in my head and focused more on the conversation.

"Panic?" He sounded confused and there was more moving around.

"She's having panic and anxiety attacks. Omegas are put in what I like to call an isolation box." There was a louder growl and I could hear a sound of irritation from Amber. "Not an actual box, you idiot. It's a figurative box of rules. They are surrounded by rules and by things they cannot do. They have been trained that if they step outside of that box they will be punished. They have the rules literally beaten into them. She isn't scarred like some of the omegas I have seen so I take it her 'teacher' didn't want anyone to know what was going on." Her voice was closer and I rolled over and cracked my eyes, watching them. Uncle Jace's back was tight with tension and Amber's posture seemed unconcerned but she had a small frown on her face.

"Are you trying to make me want to murder my brother more than I already do?" The words were so low I could barely hear them but it made me want to shrink under the blanket. I didn't want Alpha Lawrence to be killed, especially by his own brother. He was a good Alpha. He had taken care of me.

"*No*. I'm trying to explain this to you. She's out of her box and can't get back in it." Amber stood in the room and spread out her hands outwards as she said it. Uncle Jace ran his hands over his face with a sigh.

"That's a good thing, isn't it?" He turned so I could see the profile of his face and Amber rolled her eyes as she turned to face him.

"No. She doesn't know how to process anything outside of her box. She can't retreat back into it so it's causing her to panic because her mind is expecting punishment. Everything is different for her and it's overwhelming her brain and it can't cope." She looked at the end of her patience as she sliced her hand through the air repeatedly as she talked.

"So treat her like an omega so she will feel secure?" He sounded so confused that I wanted to smile. I understood what she was trying to say and I was happy someone was able to articulate what I had been feeling or at least explain what I was feeling so even I could understand.

"*Mene*, you're thick." She muttered it out before shaking her head. "No, give her a safe place to retreat to when things get overwhelming for her. Make her a literal box, fill it with comforting items and when she starts to panic she can retreat to it to calm down. It will give her the ability to process without panicking. She can be in her safe place and watch the world around her." Amber looked like she was trying to fight between irritation and understanding.

I thought it was slightly humorous how she was being rude to the male who looked twice as wide as her. I had a feeling Uncle Jace wouldn't hurt her but it was strange watching their interactions. Everyone I had met so far had a rough presence, not physically but verbally. Their actions were brash and their words were sometimes harsh but they seemed to take everything in stride. The words didn't seem to affect them.

"What about a room?" Jace shifted his weight and Amber shook her head, rolling her eyes slightly.

"A room negates the reason for the box. If she isolates herself in her room, she won't be able to watch the world around her and understand that it's okay. It just isolates her and further cements the ideological components of being solitary that come with what I have learned of the omega training." Amber shook her head again, "She needs a small space that can be in an area that has heavy flow of traffic from the pack members so she can learn not to isolate when she needs to self-soothe."

"She's nineteen. I'm not going to put her into a box so she feels safe." Uncle Jace gestured to me and I closed my eyes, not wanting them to know I wasn't sleeping. The fear of punishment for the action was nearly overwhelming. I fought it back. Uncle Jace hadn't given me a reason to fear him. He hadn't hurt me.

That voice in my head hissed out the word yet and I tried to shove it away. He hadn't hurt me.

"She has the emotional stability of a child because of how badly she has been stunted by the abuse. She *is* a child, nineteen or not. We have to think simply with this. She has been taken from her box, give her a new one." She waved her hands as she talked and her face was pinched into a frown. "Anxiety isn't a set thing or something that you can understand without experiencing it yourself. I can guarantee that if you give her a safe place she will progress faster. The panic attacks will lessen and she will be more comfortable and well as learn to socialize appropriately." The thought of having a safe place, somewhere no one else could go was almost calming. Having a place to calm down and think about things wasn't something I thought I needed until that very moment.

"Are you sure?" He sounded uncertain and I looked at him. For a moment he looked helpless, as if he had no clue what to do to make me better. I wasn't sure why I was viewed as broken, I never felt broken before but the way everyone was acting and talking made me question that.

"I can't be sure because with these types of mental issues no one can be a hundred percent sure but it will help her process and decompress. I am eighty-nine percent certain it will help." She let out a heavy sight before rubbing her forehead.

"And the other eleven percent?" There was a sharp edge of worry in his voice and I watched as Amber paused for a moment, looking uncertain of herself.

"That's me being unsure if her anxiety is caused by the removal of her box or the fear of being punished because of it." She crossed her arms over her chest slowly and looked at Jace who looked horrified.

"I would *never-*" He didn't finish the sentence but I understood what he meant. He would never punish me. It was nice to know he wouldn't but Alpha Lawrence never punished me either and I was still punished on occasion by others. It was natural in a pack. The omegas needed behavioural correction as Ingrid called it.

"I know but she doesn't understand that. The type of conditioning omegas go through is brutal from what I have seen. She views herself as a lesser person that needs to have punishment to correct her wrong behavior." Amber shifted on her feet. Her face was sympathetic as she glanced at me. I made sure my eyes were closed enough that she couldn't see me staring. "She's scared. I would be too if I were in her position. Just keep doing what you're doing and make her the fucking box. It will help." She glanced at me again before turning towards a cupboard on the wall. There was a small silence and I opened my eyes, looking at Uncle Jace's large form.

"Maybe it would help." I blinked and Uncle Jace looked at me with a small frown. I felt a surge of slight fear at the thought he would punish me for listening when I wasn't supposed to.

"You were listening?" He didn't sound angry and I gave a timid nod. It was strange not having someone be angry at me for listening. Sometimes I got punished for listening when I hadn't been. It had been brutal because I couldn't explain anything and I knew no one would listen to me anyway as I got slapped or strapped.

"She's brainwashed, not stupid, Jace." Amber sounded amused and she winked at me slightly and I dropped my gaze from her quickly.

"Don't be rude, Amber. Do you want a box?" He didn't take his gaze off of me and I nodded again. I darted my eyes back and forth, trying to articulate what I wanted to say. Even now I had to plan my words, the thought made me wince slightly.

"Sometimes I feel like I can't escape and I want to curl up in a little ball so the world ignores me. It might help. If I am in there and everyone ignores me I might be able to understand what is going on." I lifted my gaze to his before I let it skitter away. I put my arms under my head, lifting it slightly.

"Okay. Do you want it to have cushions in it?" His face was relaxed and I scrunched up my nose at the thought of sitting in a box without something underneath me. It wouldn't be comfortable but he wouldn't have asked if he wouldn't be able to do it.

"That might make it more comfortable, Uncle Jace." I felt my face flush at my lack of propriety. I wasn't supposed to call people by their names. The voice screeched and screamed inside my head but he just smiled at me.

"Okay. I'll Send Collin and Jay to make you a box at the shop." He shifted on his feet, the smile still firmly on his face. The scar on his face made me wonder how he had gotten it but I knew better than to ask.

"Thank you." I whispered it as he came over and lifted me to sitting. He kissed my cheek with a small smile. I wanted to shy away from him. I wasn't supposed to have affection placed on me by anyone. Alpha Lawrence had been different. He had been allowed.

"You're welcome, Maricella." He smoothed my hair down and Amber came back over with a small syringe and a needle. I leaned away from her warily. The first needle has been uncomfortable and I wasn't so sure about getting a second one poked into me.

"Now that we have that covered. Maricella, this is a very important shot." She lifted the syringe slightly. "It's got a mix of sedatives and some pain killers that is going to dull your emotions a little and your nerves' reactions. It will be kind of like being in a fog but it will make it so you won't experience the pain you usually feel due to the rejection. It's also got an anti-nausea agent in it so you can eat." She lifted my arm and I closed my eyes tightly as she put the needle to my skin. I winced at the pinch and nearly right after I felt another cotton ball pressed to my skin.

"Not as bad this time. Alright, I want to see you tomorrow. I'm going to be your counsellor. We will talk about things you're feeling so I can better treat your anxiety." She was smiling and I blinked slightly before taking the cotton ball from her and pressing it to the small puncture like I had the last one.

"I never agreed to that, Amber." There was a low growl threaded into Uncle Jace's words and I watched as Amber shrugged. She was completely unfazed by his aggressive growling. I envied her slightly, I was hunching away from him slightly and the growling wasn't even aimed at me.

"It's not about what you want, Jace Lawrence. I need to try and deconstruct the intricate brainwashing they did on her. She won't get better if she doesn't have counselling." She moved away and I reached out and touched his arm. He glanced down at me, the growling stopping at the action.

"I would like to have someone to talk to about my feelings. If it isn't too much trouble." I started to pick at my nails and just like last time he covered my hands with one of his. I looked at the large, rough hand. It was a hand that had done more than shuffle papers or turn the pages of a book. It was a hard working hand, similar to my own.

"If you want to, Maricella, you can." He patted my hand gently and I looked up at him. I wanted to smile, I wanted to smile so badly but that voice was tearing at the inside of my skull. It scraped against it, tearing into it, making it hurt.

"Thank you, you are far too kind." I wanted to choke on the words as I realized something inside of me was indeed broken, not just broken but turned to dust by a greying haired female named Ingrid. I pushed it away not wanting to start panicking, when a strange feeling filled me. I blinked slowly, everything felt suddenly muffled. "What's happening?" I lifted my hands to touch my face but even that felt strange.

"Someone is about to take a very fun trip." Amber looked amused and I blinked at her slowly. "You're going to feel very funny in about four seconds. Your shot just kicked in." She held out a bottle of pills and I looked at it, trying to focus through the fog. "These are the nutritional tablets. Take one in the morning with a large glass of water." The fog seemed to almost settle for a second and I wanted to sigh in relief.

"Why am I going on a trip?" I looked over at Uncle Jace and blinked rapidly as my vision felt like it was distorting. A tiny hand pinched the bridge of his now very large nose. I wanted to laugh at it but I could still hear Ingrid in my head and the sound of the strap hitting my hands. It was enough to keep my mouth shut, even as a delightfully funny feeling filled me.

"The side effect of the shot is you experience some vivid hallucinations for about an hour or two. We couldn't get the mixture to work without them." His voice seemed to randomly change in pitch and I stared at him, trying to blink away the image. "And off she goes." He sounded funny to my ears and I watched as my vision waved and distorted again, his face slowly shifted, his chin was now huge and his forehead seemed tiny.

"Uncle Jace, your face looks weird." I went to touch him but the weird waving, almost colourful lines following my hands caught my attention. "Pretty." I waved my hands slowly through the air and I could hear Amber laughing slightly. It sounded like she was moving close to me and then far away very rapidly. I ignored it and fell backwards across the cot. The room swirled in patterns as my vision moved. I could feel the air touching my skin and embracing me.

I swirled my arms in the air above me and watched as the colourful patterns followed the movements. "So pretty. Such pretty colours." I wiggled my fingers as I blinked slowly and I could hear Amber laughing loudly, the sound was slightly distorted and I wanted to join her but an image of Ingrid popped into existence in front of me. Her mouth was moving with no sound and her face was pinched with anger. I just swished my hand through her, making her face twist and distort.

"Shut up and bother someone else, you lazy old bitch." The words echoed the ones Bennett had said and I held back a giggle. Swearing was fun. No wonder they all did it. "Ingrid is a jack rabbit molester and a cow fucker. A cranky old bat with too much time on her hands. Stomps around the house like a big, hairy beast. Everyone can hear you, Ingrid, no need to be a fuck face." I felt a wide smile on my face and I chortled happily. I needed to know more swear words. This was fun.

"She's spending way too much time with the boys. I find it weird hearing that type of filth coming from her mouth." The voice sounded demonic and I burst out laughing. Ingrid's face went pinched and I shoved my hand through her forehead wiggling my fingers. She didn't feel like she had a brain.

"Ingrid, the demon is back. You better hide before he finds out you took his job. He's going to punish you." I sang the last sentence as I laughed at her floating face. She looked so angry at me and for once I wasn't scared of what she would do to me as I poked at her eyes with my fingers.

"Maricella, come on. Let's go before this trip turns bad." The distorted demonic voice was close and I was pulled to sitting. I stared at the scarred face distorted demon that was looking at me. I let out a small coo as I touched his waving skin, which was moving in undulating patterns.

"Welcome home. You better punish Ingrid. She's been hitting me again. She is thinking mighty high of herself, let me tell you. She thinks she's above being punished. You'll show her she isn't, won't you?" I pointed at the floating face and the demon scowled. I giggled at how funny his face looked as it distorted again and again, especially when I moved.

"Where are you, Maricella?" It was a brightly lit female, the lights shining down on her seemed to make her glow and sparkle and I cooed at her, reaching for her bright aura but the demon held me back. I wanted to pout but the demon would punish me and Ingrid would laugh. I shook my head rapidly, watching the room swirl around me and change. I felt like I was in my childhood bedroom, like I had cracked open a door that had been long locked.

"Mary, Mary, quite contrary, how does your garden grow? With silver bells and cockle shells. And with lady bells all in a row." I looked at the demon and giggled. "This is a nice place." Ingrid's face floated around my head and I scowled as I tried to wave her away. I didn't want her in the room. She took all of it away from me and I hated her.

"Get out you, trumped up old hag! I don't want you here!" I scowled at her as tears filled my eyes. I didn't want her in that room. I didn't want her to touch those memories like she did the others. She took them away from me. "Get the fuck out!" I screamed the words at her face but she did nothing but smile as the world around me melted to a familiar, cold and damp room.

I felt my breath hitch in my chest before I grabbed hold of the demon and buried my face in his neck with a small cry of fear. "Take me back! Take me back!" I held onto him as tightly as I tried not to see Ingrid's gloating face.

"Back where, Maricella?" He sounded so confused and I felt a sob well up.

"Back to hell. Take me back with you." I felt tears fill my eyes and I looked up at the bright female with the sad face.

"Why?" Her voice was so melodic and I let out the sobs that had been trying to escape. I didn't want to be in the classroom again. I didn't want to be there.

"Because it's better than here." I watched with wide eyes as the female's pretty face turned to Ingrid's pinched one, a thick cane in her hand. I trembled. "I'm sorry! I'm sorry. I didn't mean to!" I stared at her advancing figure with wide eyes.

"Didn't mean to what?" Her face was a scowl and I fought against the demon's grip. I wanted to back away but I was too weak.

"Speak out of turn. Please, don't hit me again. An Omega must never speak unless an answer is required. An Omega must never speak unless an answer is required." I felt my heart in my throat as she moved even closer. The wooden cane firmly grasped in her hand. I could practically feel it slapping against my skin, hard slap after hard slap against the delicate skin of my hands. "I am sorry, ma'am. An Omega must never speak unless an answer is required." I wanted to rub at the stinging skin but I couldn't, not while she watched.

"Are you an omega?" Her eyes were glowing and I sat still, my body trembling as I stared at her with wide eyes.

"Yes, ma'am." My voice was hollow as I stared at the cane in her hands. If I spoke out of turn she would use it on my back. That hurt more than the hands. I didn't want her to do that to me, not again.

"Why?" The voice was loud and I felt the demon loosen his grip on me.

"Because I am the lowest of the low. My parents were filth and I am filth. I am lucky to be alive, ma'am." I lowered my head as was proper and stared at the classroom floor. Cold concrete I had been forced to sleep on for months.

"Who told you that?" The voice sounded so strange. It was Ingrid but then it wavered to someone else's voice. I felt my teeth chatter in fear as I stared at the floor.

"You, ma'am. You and the pack. Rogues are filth and I am the bastard child of two. It makes me worthless and insignificant. I am worth less than a pile of refuse and when Alpha Lawrence sees it, he shall tie a red ribbon around my wrist and banish me like he should have when I was little." I felt no tears at the statement. It was the truth, as a child of two rogues I was worth less than nothing. I was nothing and would always be nothing.

"Why?" She sounded so curious and it made my stomach churn with hatred. She enjoyed making me do this like she had every other lesson. I hated this classroom. I hated her. I hated what she did to me.

"Because the weak are not meant to survive and for the good of the pack, the weak must be banished." The pack would be weak if it took care of all the pathetic members, the weak members. It kept the pack healthy to banish them. I didn't want to make Alpha Lawrence's pack weak and I didn't want to be banished.

"Why are you here?" Her voice was soft and I glanced up. It was a trick and a phantom pain of a leather strap slapping me across the face startled me and I looked down just as quickly. I wanted to touch my hand to my stinging cheek but I knew better.

"So you can teach me to be a proper omega, ma'am." I bit the inside of my cheek. I hated this room. I hated the lessons and I hated her. I wanted her to suffer for taking it away from me. She took everything away from me but I couldn't move. I couldn't force myself to look at her because she would punish me.

"A proper omega? How does one become a proper omega?" Her voice was taunting me and I wanted to cry. I just wanted to leave the classroom. I wanted to escape."They have it beaten into them, ma'am." I kept my breathing even as I stared at the floor. If I cooperated she would let me leave. If I did as she asked she would let me leave.

"What is beaten into them?" I looked up slightly, eyeing the cane in her hand. She hadn't moved closer and for that I was thankful but it didn't help the sore stiffness I felt in my hands. A reminder of what happened when I disobeyed.

"The Omega's Mantra, ma'am." I swallowed. She knew the answers to the questions she was asking but this was another punishment. I knew it was to remind me of my place. To remind me of my worthlessness.

"What is that?" I hated her mocking voice and I hated her pinched face. I hated her stomping boots but I did nothing because if I didn't become an omega, I would be banished from the pack.

"A code of conduct for all omegas, ma'am." I swallowed against the dryness in my mouth. I knew what she would ask next and I hated having to remember all of them. I hated forgetting some because that meant she could punish me.

"What is in this code of conduct?" The familiar sound of a cane hitting skin filled my ears and I flinched at each strike. My back hurt, one strike of the cane for every rule.

"An Omega must do as an Omega is told. An Omega must never speak unless an answer is required. An Omega must never touch someone above their station. An Omega's gaze belongs on the floor. An Omega must not be seen nor heard. An Omega must never let anyone clean up an Omega's mess. An Omega must never show emotion. An Omega has no memories. An Omega has no family. An Omega is unworthy of attention or affection. An Omega is and always will be worthless. An Omega cannot have any type of relationship. An Omega cannot eat pack food. An Omega must be grateful to serve the pack. An Omega must take the punishment for their improper behaviour silently and without thoughts of retaliation. An Omega must never forget their place. An Omega-"

"That's enough. Have you told anyone about these lessons?" Her voice was low and filled with warning. I hated this part of the lessons the most.

"No, ma'am. Hide the bruises. Hide the hands. If I don't then you shall come and beat me proper for the disobedience because an Omega does as an Omega is told. If I tell Alpha Lawrence he shall banish me from the pack because an omega that tells is weak and for the good of the pack, the weak must be banished. Never tell, no one must ever know." I looked at my hands, not even the colourful patterns could make me smile right now. I couldn't tell because I would be banished. I loved Alpha Lawrence and I wanted to be with him.

"What the fuck?" The demon's voice was laced with low growls and I slowly turned to look at his furious face.

"Jace!" Ingrid's voice was filled with anger and I leaned against the demon once more. He would keep me safe and punish Ingrid. She had taken his job and she spoke above her station. That meant she deserved a punishment.

"Demon, can you take me back to hell? It was much nicer there." I looked at his glowing green eyes as tears finally filled mine. "It was much nicer there." I wrapped my arms around him and buried my face into his shoulder. The demon's comforting arms wrapped around me and I cried.

NINE

I stared at the small plate of food in front of me. I had stopped hallucinating an hour ago and Amber had helped me have a bath. She had been so nice and gentle as if she were afraid I would break. Her eyes were sympathetic and I wanted to ask her why. The kindness in her eyes she had before had been replaced by sympathy and I wanted to know if I had said something during my hallucinations because I couldn't remember anything. It was a blur in my mind, nothing concrete and everything hazy.

After the bath she had helped me into some clean clothes. Some flannel pants that were too big and had to be tied at the waist and a button up shirt that had the sleeves rolled all the way up to my elbows. They were warm and felt nice against my skin. I couldn't remember the last time I wore pants. It was a strange feeling but the warmth they provided made me push it all away. I had relished in the feelings but then the hunger set in. My stomach was gnawing at my spine uncomfortably. I hadn't felt hungry in a long while and it was a strange experience to have it once again clawing at my insides.

I looked at the food in front of me with a stark expression. For lunch I always had bread and a glass of milk, just like all the omegas. Breakfast was porridge, lunch was bread and milk, and supper was a tiny bit of meat and four small potatoes. I didn't even know what they had placed in front of me. I knew it was a type of noodle but I never spent any time in the kitchen besides eating my meals. I never paid attention. It wasn't my place to.

"Are you going to eat?" Davin sat down beside me and I glanced at him, swallowing against the lump in my throat. I glanced at him from the corner of my eye and swallowed again. I didn't want to ask because I knew it would upset him but I needed to know.

"What is it?" I looked at the plate and at the red sauce covered noodles. It smelled wonderful and my stomach ached to have something in it but I was worried. I didn't want to be punished for eating pack food.

An Omega cannot eat pack food.

"What do you mean? It's spaghetti and meat sauce, Maricella." He chuckled slightly and I felt ashamed at not knowing what it was or what he had told me.

"Oh." I looked at my hands in my lap and tried to blink back tears. I hadn't meant to appear that way but the memories I had in my head were painful and I wasn't supposed to know them.

He seemed to suddenly realize what I had meant with the question. "Have you... have you never had spaghetti before?" His voice sounded slightly horrified and I shook my head slowly.

"For lunch I am only allowed one slice of bread and one cup of milk." I ached for the familiarity but I knew they wouldn't give it to me. I felt my breathing increase slightly as I stared at the unfamiliar food. Amber had called them anxiety and panic attacks when I started to feel like this. The knowledge didn't stop the fact that I wasn't supposed to eat what they had given me.

An Omega cannot eat pack food.

"*Why*?" He sounded stricken at my words and I didn't like it. I knew I felt more at ease with everyone when I was so exhausted I could barely hold my eyes open. I didn't have to worry about punishment, despite how that voice screamed at me like it was doing now. I wanted to push the plate away. I didn't want to look at it. It made my head hurt.

"Because apparently omegas are not allowed to eat pack food." Uncle Jace's voice rumbled slightly and I glanced up at him, my shoulders hunching forward. He knew the rules, he would take it away like he was supposed to. "It's part of the Omega's Mantra. The brainwashing they did on her." I wasn't brainwashed. I was an omega, there was a difference. I watched as Uncle Jace picked up the plate. I sighed in relief and I looked at the table expectantly. I needed the bread and the milk.

"Collin and Jay have something they would like to show you, Maricella. Davin, could you bring her to the living room?" Uncle Jace looked at me with a slight sadness and I tried to hide my wince as my stomach growled loudly.

"She needs to eat something." Davin sounded like he wanted to argue but Uncle Jace levelled him with a bone chilling, stern look and I was picked up off the chair. I bit back the urge to tell him to not touch me. I wasn't supposed to be touched but I wasn't allowed to talk back.

An Omega must never speak unless an answer is required.

"I'll get you some food, Maricella." He whispered it in my ear as we followed Uncle Jace down the hallway and into the large living room. I glanced around and my gaze landed on Collin before darting to the handsome male who had pulled my hood up in the forest.

Collin's smile looked like it would break his face in half. "Look what we built!" He pointed to a rather large box sitting in the corner of the room. It was painted a dark colour and on the side that was facing me a very elaborate and delicate '*Sugar's Safe Place*' spiralled in swirling letters on it. It was a sweet gesture and there was a faintly familiar warmth that filled my chest as I looked at it. The aching emptiness wasn't swallowing it whole. I could barely feel it because of the drugs I had been given. I was grateful for it.

"Okay, to those of you in this room. This is Maricella's box. When she goes into the box, everyone is to ignore her and leave her alone." Uncle Jace was frowning as he looked around before his gaze landed on me. "Maricella, this is your safe place, nothing can hurt you or harm you while you are in it. If you feel overwhelmed or panicky or scared, you use the box just like Amber said, okay?" He looked at me with expectant green eyes and I nodded slowly. He walked over and handed me the plate of spaghetti. I looked at it in horror. I needed the bread and milk.

"You're going to eat this. No more bread and milk for lunch. You will eat what the pack eats." His voice was firm as he left the plate of food in my hands. I stared at it with wide eyes. I couldn't eat it. I wasn't allowed to eat pack food. I wasn't allowed but he told me to. I felt the screaming tear at the inside of my skull and the painful throbbing was instant. "Are you panicking, Maricella?" His voice was calm and I nodded quickly, my breathing was growing quicker and it felt like my chest was being squeezed as my head throbbed.

"Where do you go when you panic?" He asked the question gently and I tried to focus.

The box.

I had to go to the box if I was panicking. He told me the box was where to go if I was panicking. "The box." I gasped the words out as I held the plate with white knuckles. The box was safe. Nothing could hurt me in the box. Nothing could harm me in the box. "I need to go to my box." With my words Davin tentatively walked over and set me inside it. I sank into the soft cushions that had been placed into it and I leaned against the back, noticing Collin and Jay had put cushions on all of the sides as well.

I let my body sink into them. The box was safe, I was safe in the box. I stared at the plate in my hands and the food in it. The screaming lessened as a faint feeling of peace filled me.

Nothing could harm me in the box.

I looked around tentatively and Davin was looking over the books on the book shelf and I could hear Collin muttering about something on the couch with Uncle Jace and the male I figured was Jay. Without their eyes on me I felt what was left of the attack slip away. I stared at the plate of spaghetti with a scowl. Ingrid could not reach me here. I was safe in the box. I could hear the TV in the background and I looked around again. Davin pulled a book off the shelf and flipped it open. Uncle Jace reached across the back of the couch and slapped Collin upside the head for something he said. I flinched at the action before the plate of spaghetti once again had my attention.

My head felt silent for the first time in a long time. As an omega, I wasn't supposed to eat pack food but also as an omega I was supposed to do as I was told. Uncle Jace told me I had to eat what the pack ate. No more bread and milk for lunch. No more porridge for breakfast or tiny bits of meat and four small potatoes for supper. Davin had told me that there were no omegas in this pack and so I wasn't sure what I was to do.

"Ingrid cannot punish me here. I am safe here." I mouthed the words, trying to bolster myself. I took a deep breath before lifting my knees to my chest and resting the plate on it. I liked how it smelled and with the way my stomach was trying to eat my insides, I could tell it did as well. With a shaking hand I picked up the fork. "I am safe here. Ingrid cannot punish me for improper behaviour." I took a small scoop of the spaghetti and with my heart in my throat, I quickly shoved it into my mouth before I could second guess myself. I scrunched up my face and chewed quickly but no slap came, no angry screeching followed the action.

What did happen was the taste slammed into my mouth just as quickly as a slap would have landed on my cheek if Ingrid had seen me but it would have been well worth it. I swallowed and looked at the plate with tears in my eyes before I started crying. Small sobs shook me and I wasn't sure why, it tasted delicious, it tasted wonderful and divine. Without warning a memory I had remembered slammed into me.

"Daddy, can I have some mo?" I held up an empty plate from my high chair, the taste of the spaghetti was still in my mouth and Alpha Lawrence walked over with a big smile.

"Did you eat all of that already? My, you certainly do like spaghetti, don't you, sweetheart?" His face was soft as he looked at me as he took the plate away. "But there's no more because we have to save room for the chocolate cake we made." At his words I started clapping my hands and he laughed, a rich sound I loved. He set the plate on the big table before grabbing a cloth and cleaning my face. I wiggled in my seat, trying to escape the unwanted cleaning.

"Mary, Mary, you are quite contrary. How do we make your face glow? With bubbles a lot and heaps of wet cloths and soon clean cheeks can glow." He said the made up rhyme and I sat still, a large smile on my face before he kissed my forehead. "All done." He picked me up and I wrapped my arms around his neck and pressed a kiss to his cheek.

"I love you, daddy." I snuggled into his neck, breathing in his comforting scent.

"I love you too, my Mary Mary." The words were whispered in my ear as a large hand held the back of my head gently in a soft embrace.

I was pulled back from the memory with a small gasp before my tears renewed and I was crying again. I had eaten this before. It had been my favourite food. I could remember Alpha Lawrence's laughter as I demanded it for my breakfast. I stared at the plate of spaghetti.

How many different types of food would bring memories back to me if I tasted them? I felt cold at the thought that Ingrid and the classroom had been allowed to force me to forget my childhood. To forget what it was like not to be an omega.

With blurry, tear filled eyes I ate the rest of the spaghetti. My stomach hurt slightly at the fullness it now had but I knew nothing would come back up. I set the plate on the corner of the box and wrapped my arms around my knees.

How many other memories did that classroom steal from me? Looking at that photo album I knew it was me in the pictures but I did not have the memories that the images held. So many lost memories among the words of Omega's Mantra in my head and the sharp pain of the tools that had been used to beat them into me.

An Omega has no memories.

The thoughts and words swirled around my head. So much was going on and I didn't want to leave the box but the dirty plate was bothering me. I was still weak but the food and the shot Amber had given me had helped me a fair bit. I had scrubbed floors in this condition. I could walk in it easily. I gritted my teeth together as I managed to get myself to my feet. I wobbled slightly and braced myself on the edge of the box before stepping out of it. I hated how my muscles trembled, how they didn't wish to listen but I needed to force them.

"Do you need help, Maricella?" At Davin's voice I gave a small jump and ended up falling backwards onto the floor. The world was now looking at me again and I wanted to shrink under its gaze. "I'm sorry. I didn't mean to startle you." He grasped my hands and pulled me to standing before he bent down to lift me.

"No." I shocked myself as I said it and I instantly flinched away from him, expecting a slap to come for my outburst.

An Omega must never speak unless an answer is required.

He took a step back in surprise and his face fell slightly, his eyebrows pulled low over his eyes. "Maricella, I would never, *ever* hurt you. Not like that." His voice was low and I hunched under it. They were kind people and had shown me nothing but kindness but the voice was back inside my head. It was making things difficult for me, hissing the mantras at me, screaming about punishment.

"Can I please walk? I can't get stronger if you keep carrying me." I whispered it out and I glanced up at him. His green eyes were sad but he nodded.

"Okay." He sounded dejected. I hadn't meant to flinch from him. It wasn't his fault and I wanted him to know that.

"I'm sorry for flinching. It's just that I am used to being slapped or strapped when I speak out of turn." I sucked my bottom lip into my mouth and glanced up at him once more.

There was a pained expression on his face as he looked at me. "I know I'm not going to like the answer you're going to give me but strapped?" His expression became even more pained and I didn't want to answer because just like he said, he would not like it. I didn't like to hurt him with what I said or make him angry but he had asked me. An answer was required.

"Ingrid has a long leather strap, if you did something she did not like or that went against the Mantra, she would hit you with it. It would leave welts and bruises but it did not break skin. First time I ever spoke back to her after Alpha Lawrence returned, she slapped me across the face with it. It left a bruise. Alpha Lawrence questioned it and I had to lie. She didn't hit me across the face with it after that. It was better than being caned so I never complained." I looked up at him again and his face turned hard and severe before he nodded.

His green eyes were cold but he wasn't looking at me, he appeared to be looking somewhere else in the room. "Collin or Jay, can you help Maricella for a moment." His voice was controlled and I could see him shaking slightly. Collin was by my side instantly and just as quickly Davin was gone. I looked at his retreating back and watched as Uncle Jace followed without a word. I wondered what was going on for a brief moment before scolding myself. It wasn't my concern.

"Hey, sugar. Look at you, standing on your own two feet. Do you like it?" He gestured to the box, a wide, proud smile on his face. I looked at it and nodded. The cushions were soft and if I had a blanket in there I knew it would be a place I could fall asleep quite easily. I liked it when my brain was quiet.

"It is very wonderful, thank you very much." I glanced up at him to see a faint pink blush on his face. He absolutely glowed with pleasure at the compliment.

"I painted it and put the cushions in there." The voice came from the couch and I looked at the back of the male's head. "My name is Jay, in case you didn't figure that out from the names flying around." He looked over the back of the couch and I stared at his ear, avoiding his gaze.

"My name is Maricella." I hated how timid my voice sounded and he just chuckled.

"Is it Maricella or Sugar? I couldn't tell. Collin was quite adamant it was Sugar." He turned back to the TV and I bit my lip slightly. He was new and I had to get used to new. I looked at the box with longing but the dirty plate pulled all of my attention. I needed to clean it up before Collin tried. The thought made my breath hitch and my chest squeeze tightly.

"It's Maricella but Collin likes to call me sugar. Alpha Lawrence used to call me Mary Mary." I swallowed as I carefully picked up the empty plate and took several small steps forwards, testing my legs. They shook but they held my weight much to my relief.

"That's cute. After the nursery rhyme?" Jay wasn't looking at me and I took several more small steps. I had to take it slow. I couldn't rush after everything. Amber said my body needed time to heal.

"Yes." I nodded and glanced as Collin who was walking beside me with his hands out slightly, ready to catch me if I fell. He looked overly concerned and it unsettled me greatly.

"That's adorable, just like you." Jay turned his head and I could see the smile on his face. I felt my face heat up. I wasn't used to that type of attention. Omegas weren't allowed to be touched like that, we were considered tainted.

"Thank you." I whispered it but I knew he could hear. All shifters could hear very well, it was just something that came natural to us.

"No problem, dolly." He turned back to the TV that had the same type of game that had been on the last time I had sat on the couch.

I moved closer to the door and looked up at Collin in confusion. "Dolly? Is that another name?" I was starting to get confused almost. People kept calling me different things and it was so strange I was having a hard time following it all.

He frowned, his eyebrows drawn low over his eyes. "Yes, it's a nickname but he should know better than to flirt with you." He scowled and spoke slowly and I frowned, he flirted with me all the time despite Davin telling him not to. Or at least I believed it was flirting. I wasn't sure what that exactly entailed because I had never been subjected to it before.

"Yes because we all know that you are Collin's territory and we cannot even look at you wrong." The tone in Jay's voice was familiar and I frowned, trying to remember what it was called. I lifted my eyebrows slightly as it came to me. Sarcasm. He was being sarcastic.

"You people are so strange." The words slipped out before I could stop them and even though I flinched slightly waiting for the retaliation to my outburst, Jay laughed loudly so I found myself relaxing. He hadn't been offended so I wouldn't be punished. I tried to shake the thought off but that voice was still in my head, hissing at me.

"I take that as a compliment. Who wants to be normal?" He scoffed slightly and I felt suddenly embarrassed. I would give anything to be normal. Knowing that there was something that Ingrid had broken, had taken from me, made me wish for that more than anything.

"I do." I swallowed against the tightness in my through and Collin gently touched my lower back in comfort. I tensed against it, unable to help myself.

"Shit, sorry I didn't mean it like that." Jay looked at me from over the back of the couch, his brown eyes spelling out his apology and I shook my head slightly.

"It's okay. I know what you meant." It seemed strange but I did. Uncle Jace's pack wasn't like other packs. Jay meant he didn't want to be normal like them. He would rather be strange or weird than to be anything like them.

"You do?" Both he and Collin spoke at the same time and I bit back a small sigh before nodding.

"Normal means having omegas, having wolves above other wolves. Normal is treating people differently and not acting how you want. Normal is hiding yourself. You don't want that normal." I bit my lip in apprehension. That voice was whispering in my ear that I would be strapped for the words I spoke but it was slightly easier to push it away knowing that Ingrid couldn't hurt me, not now.

"Never let anyone say you aren't smart, sugar. Now, your legs look like they want to buckle any second so can we go to the kitchen and put that away before I have a heart attack?" Collin's voice was anxious and I nodded before continuing on my trek towards the kitchen.

Each step was hard for me but I forced myself to take each one regardless of how difficult it was. I was breathing heavily, my exhales rattling slightly, by the time I reached the kitchen and Collin's hands were so close to me I felt like he would pick me up regardless of what I wanted.

He was muttering under his breath but I ignored it as I shuffled my feet towards the sink.

"You can leave it in there. I'm sure it can get washed with the other dishes." At his words I shook my head frantically, my eyes wide.

An Omega must never let anyone clean up an Omega's mess.

"I need to clean it. It's my mess. I need to clean up my messes. No one else can do it, I have to." I was starting to get on a roll, shaking my head frantically and the words falling from my mouth without my control when Collin rubbed a hand up and down my back, making me inhale quickly in surprise and tension.

"Okay. You can clean it." At his words I instantly stopped, relief filling me as I turned on the water with shaky hands and ran the plate and fork under it to rinse it. Collin removed his hand from my back and handed me a dishcloth. I took it, grateful he had stopped touching me. It felt so strange. I scrubbed at the dish slowly making sure every bit of mess was off of it. The water was warm and I felt my eyelids lower slightly, my body finally relaxing completely.

"What are you doing?" Davin's voice was sharp but I tuned him out, rubbing the cloth over the back of the plate. There was a pleasant silence in my head that I wanted to smile at. I couldn't be punished now. I was doing what I was supposed to.

"Sugar wanted to wash her plate. You should see this. She's completely relaxed." He sounded amazed and I carefully rinsed the plate off before setting it in the dish rack and picking up the fork. I knew the pleasant silence in my head would disappear as soon as I was done with the dishes so I wanted to enjoy it.

"I told you, crazy cleaning lady." Seamus sounded amused as I carefully rubbed the tines of the fork before wiping down the handle.

"Don't make me hurt you, Seamus." Davin's voice was low with warning and with great reluctance I set the fork in the dish rack like I had the plate and wrung out the dish cloth before folding it neatly. I gave a small sigh of displeasure as the world slowly came back to me. The trembling in my legs was getting bad and I felt my heart rate increase slightly. An almost panicked awareness filled my head. I hadn't realized how much my body was doing subconsciously until it was all gone for a moment.

"Angie is back. I wanted to introduce her to Maricella." Seamus sounded nervous and I turned around to take a step when my leg buckled.

Collin caught me before I hit the ground and he gave a bark of laughter. "I fucking *knew* that was going to happen." He picked me up and sat me down on a kitchen chair. He bent down to look me in the eyes and I started at the small scar on his chin instead of meeting his gaze. "Don't push yourself past what you can handle. You need to focus on getting better."

"Collin giving sound advice? Did I enter a time warp?" It was a slightly rough, feminine voice that had amusement coating it. "What type of twilight zone is this?" I glanced from Collin's scar to the doorway where Seamus was standing beside a rather tall female with short black hair and darker, brown eyes. I looked away, my eyes landing on Davin's face for a brief moment. There was too much new.

"Hey, Angie. This is Maricella." Seamus's voice was kind and I could hear a loud snarl. The sound made me jump and I tucked my hands into my lap and stared at them quickly as my heart raced in my chest.

"*Angie*." Davin's voice held a clear warning and I swallowed, my breathing starting to increase as Collin stood up.

"I can smell the fucking rejection meds on her. Are you shitting me?" Her voice was violent and I immediately shrank in my seat. There was too much negativity flying around and I felt like I couldn't breathe. My chest was growing so tight and I felt like I needed to escape, to find a corner to curl up into until it stopped.

"Take it down a notch. You're scaring her." Davin's voice cut through the growls with a rather strong warning that surprisingly worked. I trembled in my seat slightly, staring at the wood grain on the table as if it were the most interesting thing in the world. I could hear someone let out a heavy sigh.

"Hey, sorry girly. It's just I've been there, Seamus too. I get a little testy when it comes to the big old 'R' word." Heavy boot steps came closer to me and the urge to bolt was filling me rapidly but I stayed sitting because the punishment would only be worse if I tried to run. "The name is Angie. I'm sorry for being such a bitch." A hand suddenly entered my vision and without thinking I recoiled violently in an attempt to get away. My chair tipped backwards as I sprang from it. The heavy crack of the chair hitting the floor made my heart pound hard in my chest

"Holy shit! I'm sorry. I wasn't going to hurt you." There was a heavy apology in the female's voice and I froze. I shouldn't have moved. Large arms went to go around me and I flinched heavily, expecting pain but Davin let out a heavy sigh, making me feel immediately guilty as his arms dropped.

"Just walk away, Angie. We can try this later." His voice was soft and I slowly and hesitantly stepped closer to him, pressing myself against his chest. It was an invitation for him to wrap his arms around me and he did so slowly. I was trying to focus on calming my heartbeat down. I closed my eyes and pressed my face to Davin's chest. He had a similar scent to Uncle Jace. It was almost calming to me.

"What's wrong with her?" The feminine voice belonging to Angie was low and a bit wary.

"She was an omega, babe. She even flinches with Jace. You just scared her a little bit." Seamus sounded unconcerned, for my benefit or hers I wasn't sure.

"Holy shit! I'm sorry. She looked *so* terrified. *Fuck*, I need to work on my people skills. What if she hates me?" There was a bit of panic in her voice and I winced. She hadn't meant to scare me, she wasn't trying to hit me. It wasn't her fault I reacted the way I did. The funny feeling of them being right filled me. I was broken. I was the one who was doing things wrong. I opened my eyes. I had to try and fix it.

"I'm sorry. I'm just a little jumpy with new things." I glanced at her before staring at Davin's shirt. "I don't like new things." I repeated the words I had told Uncle Jace a few hours earlier. New was complicated and confusing. I didn't like new.

"Shouldn't I apologize to you? I mean I know what they do to shifters to make them omegas. I was way out of line there. I just got a little excited. Besides Amber, I am the only female here." She was rambling. She was nervous. Why was it that everyone was nervous around me? I never understood it. I was terrified of everyone but they were always nervous around me like I was the threat.

"No, I should be able to control my reactions." I took a step away from Davin and his arms dropped to his sides before he lifted one and brushed some hair from my face as he looked at me with something akin to grief.

I should have been able to control it.

I should have.

TEN

Davin gave a soft sigh,"Maricella, you've been here two days. It's going to take more than that for you to get better. I don't know a whole lot about the mental shit but I do know that." His voice was soft and I bit the inside of my cheek, the pain making me focus.

I stared at the table, taking exaggerated breaths in and out. If I was panicking then I needed to focus on breathing. "Can I see Amber?" I wanted to talk to her. About what I wasn't sure but I wanted to talk even though the voice inside my head screamed at me over and over again.

I glanced up at him and he frowned slightly but nodded. "Okay. I'm pretty sure she's in her office. I'm not letting you walk there." He gave me a slightly stern look that reminded me of Alpha Lawrence before picking me up. I couldn't stop myself from stiffening at the contact as he cradled me to his chest. "You've exerted yourself enough today." He walked around the table, keeping it between me and Angie. I felt guilty for feeling a bit relieved at the action. I knew she wasn't trying to hurt me but nine years of sudden movements ending in pain made me jumpy and the mantras seared the inside of my skull harshly.

"Don't let that incident sour you towards Angie. She's a really sweet female. She's just... loud and boisterous sometimes. She wasn't thinking back there. We never greet new pack members like that." His voice was soft and I nodded despite the fact I couldn't understand. New members for the omegas were always a sad thing and we were never allowed to make friends. We were isolated to our sections and our quarters. It was part of the mantras and I rarely saw the other omegas other than Ingrid but she seemed to enjoy popping up randomly, as if trying to remind me of the classroom and her lessons. Always lingering around me, waiting for me to mess up.

"I understand, Davin." The name felt sour on my tongue as it did every other time I had said it but I still forced myself to do it. He had told me I had to call him by his name and I had to do as I was told. "I just need some time to reset before I meet her again." I honestly didn't want to meet her again but I wouldn't tell him that. I worried my bottom lip with my teeth as he carried me into the small infirmary.

My fear rose up in me sharply. I couldn't break the mantras but I needed to think, to let something out. "It's okay to be scared, Maricella." He kissed my temple and pushed open a door to a small room in the infirmary.

Amber looked up from her desk. "What can I help you with?" Her face was even but I could see a bit of worry at the edges of her expression. She thought one of us was hurt. I hated making her worry, I didn't want anyone to worry for me. I wanted to be invisible again, unseen.

"Maricella wanted to see you." Davin set me down on the chair across from Amber and I pulled my knees up to my chest. I wanted to escape into the fabric of the chair, to make myself disappear.

"Oh?" She looked at me and I stared at the pen holder on her desk.

"I wanted to talk." I swallowed against the lump in my throat and she suddenly relaxed, a small smile crossing her face.

"Oh. You had me worried for a second." She turned her gaze to the male who had brought me in. "Davin, you can go. I'm sure we'll be okay without you." She waved him off with a familiar gesture of dismissal. I had seen it thousands of times before at my old pack. Davin placed a hand on my shoulder and I shuddered slightly. An unfamiliar feeling washed down my spine. I didn't like the position we were in. Memories swirled around the edges of my mind.

"Call me when you are done." Davin squeezed my shoulder gently before turning and leaving the room. I relaxed as he did so before feeling guilty about it

As soon as the door closed Amber looked at me. "Are you okay?" She looked genuinely worried and I swallowed, for some strange reason I wanted to cry.

"I'm broken, aren't I?" My voice cracked slightly and she frowned. I was surprised by her reaction. I thought she would say yes without a pause but she looked confused. Everyone had claimed I was broken, that I was something that needed to be fixed.

"Broken? Why do you ask that?" She settled into her chair and I watched as she picked up a pad of paper and a pulled pen from the holder.

"Everyone keeps treating me like I'm broken. Like I need fixing." I wrapped my arms around my knees tighter and rested my chin on them. I looked at the bookcase behind her, I couldn't really see the titles but I could tell a lot of them were medical texts. I counted them, trying to silence the voice in my head. I wanted it to go away, it made my head ache.

"Do you *feel* broken?" She wrote something down on her notepad and I resisted the urge to shrug. Apprehension filled me as that voice shouted and screamed at me. The weight of the entire world seemed to shove down on my shoulders and I glanced at her.

"This is a safe place right? Nothing can hurt me here?" I didn't want to say anything unless she said it was safe. I felt a tightness in my chest as she looked at me, it was the beginnings of a panic attack. I wanted that feeling to go away. I wanted to feel *safe*.

"Yes, Maricella. This is a very safe place. This is a place where you can say and do whatever you want with no punishment." At her words I relaxed and let out a tiny sigh of relief. The tightness disappeared and I closed my eyes, swallowing. "You heard me talking to Jace this morning, right?" I nodded and cracked my eyes open, examining the room from beneath my eyelashes.

"Yes." I let my knees go and rolled down the sleeves of the too large button up shirt. They flopped over my hands and I wrapped my arms around my knees once more.

"You heard the term brainwashed then?" She tilted her head and as I looked at her through my eyelashes I felt secure. She couldn't see me looking at her.

"I did." I had heard her say it but it didn't mean I believed it. I had been trained, not brainwashed. It was my position in life, the only one for me.

"Do you believe you have been brainwashed?" The pen tapped against the pad and she looked expectant. I shook my head slowly. She didn't look shocked or even surprised by my answer. "Okay. Do you know the definition of brainwashing?" She was writing on the pad again and I frowned slightly. I understood the concept of brainwashing but I never really thought about the definition of it.

"Not really." I shifted in the chair and she looked up at me.

"Brainwashing means to make someone adopt radically different beliefs by using systematic and often forcible pressure. Would you classify the Omega's Mantra as a radically different belief?" She was looking at me, trying to gauge my reaction to her question but I shrugged. It was a very different set of beliefs and rules, I figured it could be classified as radical.

"I guess so." I grasped my right wrist with my left hand and let my eyes open a bit more.

"And your lessons, did they isolate you? Keep you separate from others, from people you cared about?" She tapped the pen against the pad gently and I blinked rapidly, thinking about the cold and damp room that I had been locked into for months at a time and slowly nodded. Ingrid told me Alpha Lawrence would never come looking and I believed her. "Did the lessons monopolize your perception of the world? Did they focus your attention on one thing and only one thing and make you question your sense of self?" I was starting to feel slightly uncomfortable but I nodded. I didn't like remembering the classroom or the lessons. I wasn't supposed to have memories.

An Omega has no memories.

"Did your lessons make you feel exhausted and debilitated or even degraded? Were threats a large part of them? And did your teacher seem to make you believe they were omnipotent and did they make you do trivial things?" She was asking a lot of questions that were bringing up very uncomfortable and slightly terrifying memories but I nodded to each of them. "You agreed to everything I said, Maricella. Everything I just asked is standard practice in brainwashing. How can you *not* be programmed into believing a radical set of beliefs when you, yourself, agreed that your lessons included all of these things?"

I froze in my chair. I didn't know what to say. My lessons were supposed to be lessons but Amber was saying that they were for the express purpose of using my mind as clay to shape what they wanted and to get me to believe whatever they said. I pressed my hands to my head as it started to throb.

"It's *normal* for victims of such abuse to not realize or deny the existence of these types of uncomfortable truths. You aren't broken, you're a *victim*. You were the victim of a heinous degree of abuse, Maricella." There was sympathy in her voice and I tried to process her words. I wasn't broken, I was simply a victim. "When you were hallucinating, you spoke of your time in something you called the classroom. Do you want to talk about it?" Her voice was soft but I shook my head frantically. I didn't want to go back there. Those were memories that I knew were best to be forgotten. They made my stomach churn and my head swim with panic.

"That's okay, we don't have to right now." Her voice was soothing and a small silence fell. It was almost uncomfortable but I preferred it to her asking me about the classroom. "Jace told me that you ate some spaghetti. How was that?" She sounded curious and I pressed my forehead to my knees slightly.

"I panicked." It was the truth, two clashing Omega's Mantras had made me panic because of uncertainty. It hadn't been fun, despite how good the spaghetti tasted. I lifted my head slightly and stared at the plaid fabric of my pants. I wondered for a moment about who used to own them.

"I heard and he said you went into your box. Did it help?" She was curious and I returned my gaze to the pen holder. There were seven pens that I could see inside of it.

"Yes." I shifted my gaze to the bookshelf behind her and started counting the number of books I could see.

"That's good and you figured out how to deal with two of your clashing mantras?" She wanted to hear that I had, she wanted to hear that my lessons weren't as deep as she feared but I knew better than to lie about it.

I shifted my gaze to the dusty potted plant in the corner. The urge to clean it made my fingers twitch. "No." I flinched at how blunt I sounded.

An Omega must never say no.

The words echoed in my mind along with that ever present angry voice. I wondered if Ingrid would ever leave my mind and memories or if she would stay there, screaming at me for everything I did wrong. Every misstep she was right there, in my head, screaming at me for it.

"Then why did you eat the spaghetti?" Amber sounded so confused and I flicked my gaze to hers before letting it fall to the thin chain she had around her neck.

"Because Ingrid couldn't hurt me and no one was looking." I wanted to shrug but I refrained. I almost wanted a nap. I seemed to tire easily and it would be nice to lie in bed, even if I didn't sleep.

"Who's Ingrid? You've mentioned her quite a bit." Amber's pen scratched across the pad and I blinked several times. There was a lump in my throat that I swallowed against.

"She was my teacher." I didn't want to talk about her. Well, I knew I wanted to talk about her and all that she did but I wanted to do it on my own. I didn't want the questions aimed at me.

"In the classroom?" Her voice was low and I nodded, tears in my eyes as I hid my face in my knees. I didn't want to remember that. "She 's the one who trained you to be an omega?" I let out a heaving sigh before thinking about how to change the subject.

"I remembered something." I lifted my head slightly and looked at Amber's mouth. I was surprised she wasn't wearing lipstick. The female pack doctor at Alpha Lawrence's had always worn lipstick. Actually, a lot of the female pack members had worn it. I didn't understand the concept of it. Why paint your lips such vibrant colours?

"Pardon?" She seemed genuinely confused by the change of subject and I felt mildly accomplished. I had succeeded in my taste of diverting the conversation.

"I remembered something after I tasted the spaghetti." I thought back on the memory and tried to ignore the tightness I felt in my throat.

"What was it?" She seemed pleasantly surprised and almost eager to hear it and I felt a small smile lift the corners of my mouth before it slid off nearly as quickly.

"Alpha Lawrence and I were in the kitchen and I had just finished a plate of spaghetti because it was my favourite. I asked for more but he said no. He told me I needed to save room for the chocolate cake him and I had made. He went to clean my face but I wasn't letting him and he sang me a silly made up rhyme to the tune of Mary, Mary, Quite Contrary." I blinked back the sudden tears and opened my mouth for a moment before closing it and swallowing. "I called him daddy and he said he loved me." I met Amber's gaze and burst into tears. I hated how emotional I was feeling. I hated how much it hurt that I couldn't remember my memories. I let myself cry for a few moments. Amber said nothing and I was grateful.

"Spaghetti was my favourite food and he was my daddy and she took it all away. She made me forget in the classroom." I pressed my hand to my mouth before a strange, unknown anger filled me almost uncontrollably. It was a hot and burning rage and I got to my feet, ignoring the shaking they had, as if the anger and rage gave me strength I didn't have prior. My chest burned and I heaved out deep breaths. Tears still streamed from my eyes but I was no longer crying. "She chained me up, my hands above my head and showed me pictures. She asked me if I remembered them and when I said I did I was whipped with a cane until my back bled. She did it over and over again until I had forgotten my daddy and I had forgotten everything she had told me to never remember."

"She took it away from me! She took *him* away from me. I hate her so much. I *hate* her and I wish she would die because she is there inside my head screaming at me for everything I do wrong. She is inside my head and I can't get her out!" I was screaming the words out and I grabbed my head and let out a loud and long scream of rage before I hit the floor. I wrapped my arms around my chest and started sobbing once more. The hurt in my chest was nearly unbearable. Nine years of bottled up anger and frustration had been pushed to the surface. Every angry thought I ever had pushed away hitting me all at once.

"What the hell is going on?" It was a loud shout as the door flew open but I held myself tighter and heaved out loud angry sobs.

"Shush!" Amber's shush almost had an order for silence and I felt the sobs subside and the burning anger returned. I looked at the ground, gritting my teeth, my body burning with the uncontrollable rage that was boiling under my skin.

"She made me forget my life and I hated him too. I *hated* him for not seeing it so I pulled away and she made it worse. Every time she saw him be nice to me, every time he tried to hug me or show me affection she would beat me with the strap until I was black and blue." I dug my fingernails into my skin. "Loving him *hurt* me. Letting him care for me *hurt* me. I couldn't let him because she punished me for it." I felt my hands shake and I bolted to my feet, my hands clenched into shaking fists against my sides. My chest was heaving as I gave another loud scream of rage. It was like I saw red as I started pacing wildly, my weakness momentarily forgotten in my adrenaline fuelled rage. The pure rage flowing through me keeping me on my feet

"She punished me for everything, even things that weren't there. She took my life away, my memories, my freedom, my will, my power, my choice, my daddy. She beat me until my mind was a blank slate that she could fucking carve up with the fucking Omega's Mantras. She carved them into me until I bled. I bled for those stupid fucking words and she had the fucking audacity to get me fucking banished. That fucking *bitch*." Without thinking I swiped everything off of Amber's desk with another scream. I grabbed my head, fisting my hair in my hands as I gave another long scream. It felt nice to finally let everything out, to let it all pour out of me in one continuous motion.

I gulped in air, "She broke more fucking mantras than anyone else. She broke them but she was never punished because she was the lord and commander of us all. She was the one that held the straps and the canes. Six months in that fucking classroom before he came back. She had me for six *fucking* months. Six months where she could beat me with everything she had before she had to rein herself in and she fucking *loved* every second of it."

My chest heaved heavily. "She is a twisted old bitch who enjoys making others feel pain." I was seething with rage as I lifted a leg and kicked the chair I had been sitting on across the room. The action felt good and I wanted to kick something else. "Someone needs to put her back into her place. Someone needs to make her bleed like she made me. Someone needs to give her the lessons she gave me and have her learn what a true Omega is. She fucking tortured me for six months before I was let out of that fucking room. Six months. I was *ten*! What *the fuck* did I ever do to deserve that? What did I do? What the fuck did I do? I didn't fucking do *anything*!" I screamed the last word before closing my mouth with a snap. A thick silence fell, the only sounds that could be heard was my laboured breathing.

"Maricella?" Uncle Jace's voice was low and I twisted my head, locking my gaze with his. He looked concerned and he held out a hand. At the gesture reality snapped into me and I felt exhausted, tears welled up in my eyes and without a word I started crying. My legs buckled underneath me and I lay on the floor, sobs shaking my entire form.

"Shhhhhh, it's okay, little one." He sat down beside me and pulled me onto his lap. I wrapped my arms around his neck, burying my face into his shoulder, crying out the hurt I felt at what I had acknowledged.

"What's going on? I heard screaming." Davin sounded concerned and I tried to muffle my sobs but it wasn't working. I needed to let it all out. It felt good to let it all out.

"Maricella left denial and jumped feet first into anger." Amber sounded slightly impressed. "I don't know what triggered it but I do know that these fits of rage might happen frequently. At least until she learns how to actually *feel* her emotions and deal with them as they arise." I tightened my grip around Uncle Jace's neck. My heart hurt, from the rejection or the fact I had been the one to push Alpha Lawrence away I wasn't sure. I had pushed him away from me, tried my hardest to break the bond because of Ingrid.

"I don't understand." He sounded confused and I took in a shaky breath before lifting my head.

"An Omega must never show emotion." I looked up at Davin through blurry, tear filled eyes. I blinked before letting out a shuddering breath and resting my cheek on Uncle Jace's shoulder. He rubbed soothing circles on my back and shifted me so he could pick me up.

"She's dismantling her isolation box, Davin. This is going to be a long process for her. She could be stuck on anger for a very long time or she could fall right into depression or she might jump between them. She has suffered severe physical and mental abuse. The scars it has left will never truly disappear but we can help her cope with them." Amber sounded almost sad and Uncle Jace held me to his chest. I could feel his heart pounding against me, I let out a small sigh and relaxed into him.

"Let's go watch TV." He muttered the words out and he carried me from the room and towards the living room. I closed my eyes but pulled my eyebrows down in a slightly frown. I needed to be where it was calm and quiet.

"May I go in my box?" I buried my face into his now damp shoulder and I could hear him let out a small sigh.

"Yes, you may. You don't have to ask for permission, Maricella. Not anymore." He pressed a kiss to my forehead before he carried me to the box and set me inside of it. I settled against the back of it and looked up at him. He looked saddened and I wiped at my sticky cheeks. I knew I must have looked terrible, tear stained face, red nose, puffy eyes and wild hair.

"May I please have a blanket?" I forced myself to hold his gaze. Nothing could hurt me in the box. I was safe there. He nodded and moved towards the couch where a fuzzy blanket lay draped over the back. He pulled it off before returning and holding it out. I took it gently. "Thank you, Uncle Jace." I pulled the blanket over me and curled up into a small ball. The blanket was soft and I pulled it up under my chin and lay my head on the side of the box. I closed my eyes and let the bone deep tiredness drag me down.

ELEVEN

Three months later

I stared at the TV, not truly watching it, as I slowly wiggled my way across the couch towards Davin. He didn't seem to notice until I was already halfway onto his lap. I didn't know if he pretended or was that engrossed in the TV show but it made me give a small smile. He let out a chuckle before wrapping an arm around me and tucking me close to his chest. He held me loosely as I relaxed against him. I wasn't sure what we were watching but I had a feeling it was a romance movie. There was too much flowery language and longing gazes for it to not be.

"Can we watch something else?" I hated romantic movies. I had discovered a lot of things I disliked since I had settled into a routine in the pack house. I hated carrot cake, romantic and scary movies. I hated it when someone larger than me placed a hand on my shoulder, the memory for that hadn't been as brutal as I thought but it still wasn't pleasant. Beta John used to come into the classroom and he would stand like that, his strong fingers digging painfully into my shoulder, trying to get me to cry out so I would be punished. I knew there was a reason I disliked the male, why I didn't like being around him.

"You're one of the only females I know who hate romantic movies. Want to watch an action movie?" He shifted slightly on the couch before I leaned forward and grabbed the remote for him before he could ask.

"Thank you." He kissed my temple and I let out a small sigh as he changed the channel, not waiting for me to reply. Action movies had good guys that beat the bad guys. I liked that about them. Good always won out in the end.

I settled into my spot a bit further. I had felt a bit more comfortable around Davin and Uncle Jace in the past few months but I still wasn't completely sure. That voice was still prominent in my head and on the odd occasion I blew up. I always felt guilty for it.

I had screamed at Collin the other day because he had left his plate on the coffee table. Seeing it there and his unconcerned attitude just made something snap in me. It was like every single thing I had wanted to say to the pack members who left messes for me bubbled up and I dumped it all on him. I had hunkered down into my box afterwards and had a nap. The outbursts of rage always seemed to drain me of all my energy. I had apologized to him afterwards and he simply smiled and kissed my cheek as if to say it was alright and he had already forgiven me.

"Collin, I know you're hanging around outside of the door." Davin picked up the gaming controller and flipped through the movies we had on the gaming system. There were running footsteps and Collin jumped over the back of the couch and bounced as he landed beside us.

He gave me a wide grin as I glanced over at him. "Hey, sugar." He leaned over and pecked me on the cheek before Davin grasped his face and pushed him away. Collin didn't seem to mind the harsh gesture, he merely winked at me in response.

"How many times do I have to tell you, Collin?" Davin's voice held an edge of amusement and I knew that he knew Collin did it just for those reactions.

"Every time." He grabbed my hand, holding it gently. "Cause Sugar pie honey bunch! You know that I love yooooooouuuu!" He held onto the last note and was deliberately singing it horribly to try and get me to smile as he held my hand. I stared at him, grimacing slightly before he let his bottom lip turn into a pout. "And not a single reaction. I need to up my game." The thought made me want to shudder but I refrained as the voice in my head screeched at me for it.

"If you do that, I will be hauling you to the roof by the scruff of your neck and throwing you off of it." Davin said it calmly and I slowly stretched my legs out. I was tentative in my actions as I looked at Collin through lowered eyelashes. He smirked at the TV but lifted my legs and placed them in his lap like I had wanted. I turned to the TV as the movie came on. Collin traced nonsense patterns into my skin and Davin ran his fingers through my hair as I slowly shifted so I was lying down.

Despite how interesting the movie seemed I felt my eyes grow heavy. I let them close and listened to the sounds around me fade away. It was something that I had learned to do. *Relax*. I had been so paranoid in Tacita that I could barely sleep at night. Now I was capable of having naps and sleeping through the night. Davin and Uncle Jace still had to come into my bedroom to calm down my nightmares but it wasn't nightly anymore. It was a relief for everyone, I knew that much. I hadn't meant to be but I was a burden on those around me at times. I didn't have to hear them say it to know it.

"Halfway through and she's almost down for the count." Collin seemed amused and I cracked an eye open. The moment for sleep was lost and I turned my gaze to the TV. I stared at it, my entire body stiffening. The male in the movie was in a dark, cement room and had his arms tied above his head, dangling from the ceiling. The position was familiar, so painfully familiar that I felt my breath hitch in my chest.

"Turn it off please." My voice barely sounded like myself. It was a weak, timid and pain filled voice that both the males reacted to. The TV went dark and I felt myself shake slightly as I sat up. For the past three months I had avoided talking about the classroom with Amber. I hadn't talked about it. I evaded questions regarding it because I thought it was better to never relive it but it seemed like no matter what I did or where I was, there were little reminders that sent me back there.

"What's wrong, sugar?" Collin sounded so concerned as I pulled my knees up to my chest and hunched forwards. I was making myself small because I knew they would be angry when I answered. I hated it when they were angry but I had promised myself to always tell them the truth.

"I didn't want to see it because Ingrid used to do that to me." My voice was quiet and I stared at the fabric of my lounge pants. Each thread was perfectly in place and I waited for their response to my statement.

"She used to do *that* to you?" Davin's voice was tight and I gave a small nod. He quickly got off the couch and I avoided looking after him. He was going to shift to release his anger away from where it could scare me. I appreciated the gesture but it always made me feel guilty.

"This Ingrid bitch seems like she needs to come down with a case of lethal strangulation." Collin's voice was just as tight as Davin's but he stayed. "You know you're safe here, right? You understand that we would never hurt you like that?" His hand touched my shoulder and I paused for a moment before slowly nodding. They were good people, in the past three months I had experienced a kindness that I had never thought could exist for a person like me. Bennett had shown me a glimpse of a world beyond being an omega and they had taken me into it fully.

"May I please have a pen and paper?" I finally pulled my gaze away from the tiny threads to look at Collin, who nodded. He didn't question my strange request, he simply pulled his hand from my shoulder and moved off of the couch to find me what I asked for. I fought back the shakiness in my limbs, I was safe no matter what the TV had shown. I was safe right where I was. The thought wasn't enough and I found myself moving off the couch and curling up in the familiar box. I wrapped the blanket around me and tried to push the world away.

The box had been a wonderful tool. I still had struggles eating the foods that were given to me. I spent most of my time eating in the box where I felt like the world couldn't see me breaking the rules. More and more memories had returned. Memories of my daddy, the male I had been forced to call Alpha Lawrence, memories of my life before the classroom. It was strange having my mind relinquish the memories Amber said it had repressed in an effort to save me. It hid the memories because I was beaten if it didn't. She said it was a coping mechanism.

There was a small sound and Collin set a pad of paper and a pen down on the corner of the box without looking at me. After a few moments I picked them up. I slid my hand across the lined sheet and held the pen in a shaky hand before I started drawing lines. I wasn't the best artist, I wasn't even good but the drawings were passable as I started sketching the room that haunted me for the past nine years. I felt like each pen stroke was pulling the pain from me. I was no longer hiding it like Ingrid had threatened me to do. I was letting it out and it felt almost cathartic.

Page after page of crude sketches filled the book as I finally let the secret leave me. The classroom had been my secret, my burden to carry. I didn't think I could stop drawing, even if I wanted to. I wanted it all out. I didn't want to stop halfway through and give up. I felt like it was important to sketch it out. To sketch out the abuse and the classroom and the tools they used to punish me.

"Hey, Maricella, it's time for your appointment with Amber." Uncle Jace walked into the room and his voice trailed off. I knew he saw me in the box and he looked away like he always did. My hand was cramping but I forced it to finish the sketch before I pulled all the pages back. I had filled the entire paper pad with my crude sketches. I wanted to burn it, as if the act of burning it would somehow make it all better. I knew it would feel good, letting the flame burn at the sketches of the classroom but I also knew Amber would like to see them. No, she *needed* to see them.

I hugged the pad to my chest and clutched at the pen tightly before I got out of the box. "Hey, you need to go see Amber." Uncle Jace was by my side almost instantly and I nodded. I did. I needed to see Amber no matter how badly the voice inside me screamed and how terrified I was about telling everything that happened. I had been conditioned to never tell, to keep my mouth shut but everything I had learned, from Amber and the others, told me I couldn't heal without letting it go.

"Hey, sugar, when you're done do you want to watch a movie with me?" Collin gave me his standard cheeky smile and I looked at him carefully. I would like to but I knew that this session with Amber would be a hard one. Ninety-one days and over a hundred hours of sessions but I knew none of them would be as hard as the one I was going to walk into.

"I don't know how long it will take." I watched him carefully but it was like the words didn't faze him as he nodded.

"That's alright but I get to monopolize your time afterwards, okay? Even if you nap, I'm going to sit there and pester you until I feel like you've repaid my hurt feelings." There was an edge of a smirk to his mouth even as he tried his hardest to pout. Any other time I would have given him a small smile but my stomach was churning unpleasantly at the thought of what was coming.

"Okay, let's get you to Amber's office." Uncle Jace pressed a hand to my back and we slowly made our way down the familiar path.

Each step seemed to resonate through me. This walk was different than the ninety-one before it. This one had everything weighing down on me, my anxiety was sky high and the paper pad felt like it weighed a thousand pounds. We reached the door and I stared at it, trying to get my mind to focus on going inside but I knew that if I did, nothing would ever be the same again.

"-cella... *Maricella.*" Uncle Jace turned me around, the action made me jump slightly and I looked up at him. "You've been staring at the door for a few minutes and I've been trying to get your attention. Are you alright?" He looked so sincere and I wanted to tell him I wasn't alright but I needed to see Amber. I knew I wouldn't find the courage a second time.

"I'm okay, Uncle. Just a little tired." It wasn't a complete lie and I knew he didn't fully believe me.

He looked at me before frowning. "Do you want me to come in with you?" It was like he had sensed my unease about entering the room and I wanted to tell him no but I found myself nodding instead. I wanted him there, for some strange reason I wanted him to be there when it finally came out. I looked up at him, holding his gaze for a moment before I found my gaze moving away, uncomfortable with the contact.

"You can't be angry." The words came out without meaning to and he gave me a strange look. "Promise me you won't be angry." I felt my body start to shake and he nodded slowly.

"I promise, Maricella." He wrapped a large hand around the door knob and turned it. The door clicked and I jumped at the sound slightly before he pushed the door inwards. I felt my heart pound in my chest. It was loud and I knew Uncle Jace could hear it. He murmured something I couldn't hear before placing a hand on my back and basically pushing me into the office.

"Jace, will you be joining us today?" Amber didn't seem surprised at him being present. Sometimes I had him come with me, especially when I was feeling especially tired or panicky. He wasn't entirely commonplace in the office but he was close to.

"I will. Maricella wanted me to be here." His voice was a low, comforting rumble. I had grown used to both him and Davin. They were comforting. True there were numerous moments when I flinched or I was scared but they never did anything to hurt me. It was hard trying to control the sharp flinching movements when that voice screamed at me about all the punishments I would receive if I said or did something against the mantras.

I walked over to my chair and curled up, mindful of the pad of paper. My hand ached from holding the pen and I leaned forward and set it on Amber's desk. She looked at it, a small crease forming between her eyebrows. She looked like she wanted to ask me why I had it before her attention was pulled to Uncle Jace closing the door. He moved towards the small, uncomfortable chair in the corner of the room by the potted plant. It was his usual spot during my sessions.

"Alright, let's start with your progress." She shuffled some papers and I knew this part was more for Uncle Jace's benefit than for mine. I was acutely aware of what my progress was, I saw Amber daily. "You've put on another six pounds in the past two weeks. That's good, that puts your total weight at a hundred and four pounds. That's still low and I know we can get it back up there but you're out of the danger of your body shutting down." She gave me a smile before looking back at the papers in her hand.

"You're still having some issues with anger but that's to be expected." She turned the page in her folder, her eyes scanning the new page for a moment. "You still aren't opening up about some of the things you are going through but agai-" She stopped talking as I tore the first page off of the pad. Her light blue eyes looked at me with curiosity as I stared at the crude drawing of the familiar room. I moved my chair closer to her desk and set the paper down on it. I watched as she looked between me and the paper before slowly reaching out and picking it up.

"That's the classroom." I choked on the words slightly. It was the cold, damp room that I had been thrown into shortly after Alpha Lawrence had left for Russia. "I spent six months chained up in that place. I was isolated from everyone and everything." I ripped the second page off and set it down on the desk. It showed the positions of the chains and I swallowed against the lump in my throat. "Two or three days after Alpha Lawrence left, Beta John came to my room early in the morning and dragged me down into the basement and threw me in there." It hurt *so* much to remember but I knew I needed to. The memories needed to come out and be seen. Abuse was perpetuated in silence and I wouldn't be silent about it anymore.

"I was confused but the confusion faded when Ingrid came. I was hung from my wrists and she beat me with canes." I tore the third and fourth page off and set it down. It showed the wall of canes, smallest to largest and a figure with its hands above its head, hanging from the ceiling. It was so poorly drawn but from the look on Amber's face as she picked it up I knew it didn't need to be perfect for her to understand what it was.

"She kept stating I was an omega and would always be an omega. After the first beating I was left alone for two or three days. I wasn't given any food or water. I wasn't allowed out to use the washroom. I was stuck in that room." I tore off more of the pages, setting them on her desk. One held a figure curled up in a corner, another held a figure banging on a door and the last one held fire.

"What is this one?" Amber's voice was quiet as she tapped the picture of the fire. I stared at it. That wasn't until later. I wanted to tell her everything in order. She needed to wait.

"After the three days. I was given a small bit of cereal but as soon as I tried to take a bite, I was hung up by my wrists and Ingrid beat me with another cane. She kept repeating '*An Omega cannot eat pack food.*' as she beat me. When I would pass out she would throw water on me to wake me up." I swallowed hard. "After what felt like hours, she let me down and gave me the bowl of cereal again. It took one more beating before I understood what she was doing. I rejected the food, thinking it would help me but she merely hung me up and beat me again. '*An Omega must never be ungrateful.*'." I ripped off some more of the pages, handing them to Amber. I noticed she had kept the fire one separate from the rest as she looked them over. I noticed a faint trembling in her hands as she shuffled through them.

"I wasn't allowed to eat for nearly two weeks and I was only allowed to because I repeated what had been beaten into me. An Omega cannot eat pack food." I remembered how Ingrid had smiled at that. A sickeningly sweet smile that showed how much she enjoyed it. "Each lesson was beat into me like that. Each mantra was forced into me through pain. After the mantras were in place, they focused on erasing everything that I had been." Tears filled my eyes and my head ached so much but I pushed forward. I knew I needed to continue.

"I had hoped that my daddy would stop them, would save me, but as time dragged on and on and the beatings continued... I couldn't hope anymore. I was so scared that I would be there forever. I was in so much pain. I was alone with no one to help me." It had been horrible, the slowly creeping time that passed and the pain that continued to wrack my body. It never stopped, it only grew less horrible before she would begin again. I sniffled as tears flooded my eyes.

"Ingrid told me he had abandoned me, that he didn't love me anymore, that he never loved me because I was the bastard child of filthy rogues." My voice trembled and I sniffled, unable to stop the tears as they fell from my eyes. "Beta John returned after awhile. He... he dragged me upstairs and outside. There was a pile of my stuff in the lawn next to a big barrel. Everything Alpha Lawrence had ever given me was there, Ingrid was too. They forced me to burn everything, they caned me while I did it. Ingrid kept repeating that an Omega has no possessions." I could still remember the acrid smoke, could still remember the pain of the words and of the caning.

"I burned my entire childhood in that barrel and they caned me for every tear that fell." I ripped off more sketches and set them down on the desk. My hands were trembling and I felt my teeth chatter slightly.

The memories that started to rip through my mind were cruel and harsh and I wanted to curl up and cry but it needed to be said. I needed to let them out. "After that, Ingrid made it her goal to remove my memories. I was once again hung by my wrists before she would show me a picture or ask me questions about my life. If I answered her, if I knew what she was talking about or if I lied, she would beat me bloody with the cane." My voice shook like I did. I felt like a trembling mess on the inside. I felt like jelly and I was nauseous, so *incredibly* nauseous.

"I started to forget things, large spans of time were simply gone. The memories that didn't disappear I pushed away. I wanted to forget because if I didn't she would beat me again and again until I did. That was the longest Mantra I had beaten into me. An Omega has no memories." It was the worst because even though she tried, I still remembered Alpha Lawrence. She couldn't make me forget so she tried her hardest to make me aware that no matter what, if she saw me near him, she would beat me bloody again. It was the not knowing that had caused me to push him away, to fall back into my routine. If he wasn't near, then she wouldn't hurt me again.

I swallowed against the bile that was trying to rise up in my throat and continued to remove more pages and set them down. "I can't remember the specific days, everything blurred together. Months of my memories are in this haze that I can't get through because I wasn't truly there. My mind had escaped that room even though my body was still trapped." Tears continued to leak from my eyes but I didn't wipe them away as I set down the paper pad, not wanting to tear any more pages out. I watched as Amber took it. Her face was pale and I looked away.

"They wouldn't let me sleep, they wouldn't let me eat. They punished me for going to the bathroom in the corners but they wouldn't let me use the washroom. They beat me for hours until my body gave up and I would go unconscious. I never scarred, for that I am lucky, but Ingrid beat me so well there is this voice inside of my head at all times. Screaming at me, reminding me what happens when I break the Mantras." I wrapped my arms around my knees and swallowed, that thin, burning film of tears covered my eyes thickly and I sniffled again. "She made me believe she knew everything. That she could tell when I was lying and would punish me. Even when I wasn't lying she would punish me. I think she liked listening to me scream, to me beg for her to stop. I think it made her feel powerful and strong." She was a sick female, her mind was not well and she enjoyed the suffering of others.

"Beta John sometimes came into the classroom to watch. He would try and make me mess up so I would be punished. I think he liked it when I was." I let out a small huff of air, halfway between a sob and a sigh. "When Alpha Lawrence came back I wasn't the same. I pulled away. I blamed him. I begged him to take me with him before he left. I *begged* him but he *left* me there... Left me to *that*. He left me and they took me. I pulled away from him because loving him brought me nothing but pain and punishment. Loving anyone, caring about anyone has only ever brought me pain." I stopped talking and a thick silence fell and I glanced over at Uncle Jace who had his face in his hands. His shoulders were shaking, from anger or sadness I did not know. There was a type of anguish to his expression I couldn't figure out.

"Maricella... thank you for sharing. It must not have been easy for you to share this." Amber's voice was slightly shaky and I looked at her. Now that I had started, everything wanted out.

"It wasn't just canes. Sometimes they would bring in some of the crueller pack warriors so they could use me as a punching bag until I stopped screaming and crying because my voice broke or they would leave me dangling above the ground for days at a time." That was the worst at times. I always felt like my sanity was slipping when they did that. "They were never consistent in the punishments or when I was punished and it made it almost worse." I shrugged slightly, it felt good to let everything out. To lay it out so everyone could see the secret I had been forced to hide.

"They told me, they beat it into me, that if I ever told, I would be banished or I would be taken back to the classroom again. I listened because I never wished to go back there again. I told no one, not even Alpha Lawrence. Six months I spent there, having them do those things to me. I never told anyone." I swallowed and slowly wiped at my cheeks. I had told but I knew this was just the beginning of the questions, of the probing into my past. I had let out the secret and I knew they needed to know everything to help me get better.

"Maricella, do you understand the reasoning behind their actions?" Amber spoke slowly and I shook my head, staring at the stack of sketches that now rested in front of her. "They were chipping away at your identity so they could replace it with what they wanted. They systematically broke you down again and again and at random to make you break so it would be easier for you to be moulded." Her hands were shaking but she hid it by linking her fingers together and resting them on the stack of sketches.

"What they did was not right, nor was it okay. You were a little girl and you need to understand that it wasn't your fault that this happened to you." Her voice was soft and I wiped at the tears that were streaming down my face. I wasn't crying, I wasn't sobbing but the tears were a steady stream regardless.

"I know." I knew my answer surprised them but I also knew the real reason I had been given to Ingrid. I had heard Beta John talking about it when he thought I knew better than to listen.

"You know what?" Amber's voice was low and confused and I looked up at her, my face even. I knew this wouldn't be good to come out but this secret was even heavier than the classroom. The reason for everything, a secret I held deep down.

"That it wasn't my fault." I swallowed and Amber gave me a tentative smile before looking down, her gaze on the sketches before she looked away with a grimace. It hadn’t been my fault, none of it had been my fault. I was a mere victim of circumstance.

"That's good." Her breath caught in her throat and I turned my gaze to Uncle Jace. His eyes were red, as if he had been trying not to cry.

His green eyes were sad as he looked at me and I blinked slowly. "It was Beta John's fault, your beta's fault." The words tumbled out without warning and he stared at me in confusion and shock.

"Excuse me?" His voice was incredulous and I blinked and stared at the dark stubble on his jaw.

"Beta John had wanted the Alpha position for the pack after your mate died but you gave it to Alpha Lawrence instead. He gave me to Ingrid because Alpha Lawrence took something he wanted away so he took something away from Alpha Lawrence, something he loved dearly. Me." I swallowed. The words lifted a weight off of my chest. Despite what had been beaten into me I knew the truth for the actions. I knew the real reason I had been forced to be an omega and it wasn't because I had been born a rogue. I had been at the wrong place, at the very wrong time. Even worse, I had been *convenient*.

Ingrid and Beta John hadn't been quiet about it. Hushed conversations where John told her to keep the wounds to a minimum and her wanting to cause scars. He would hiss that this was to punish Alpha Lawrence, that if he found out they would both be killed and for her to keep it to a minimum. It was strange, knowing the reason I had no scars was because of the same man who gave me to Ingrid to become an omega to begin with.

"I never knew that he would-"

"I don't blame you, Uncle." I shook my head. I didn't want him to feel guilty. I captured his gaze before holding out my arms. He seemed tentative but he stood up and moved close to me. I waved my arms slightly and he picked me up before sitting down on the chair, settling me in his lap. I picked at the buttons on his shirt for a moment. "Beta John is at fault. Ingrid is at fault. You couldn't have known." How could he? He grieved for his female, the mother of his son, the love of his life, his mate. He left because he had to, because he couldn't bear it. How would he have known Beta John would do that?

I picked at the fabric of his shirt. "Alpha Lawrence knew Beta John wanted his position, it's his fault too. It's everyone's fault and I was just a means to an end. I wasn't a person to Beta John. I was a punishment, a tool used to cause pain. Hurting me hurt Alpha Lawrence. There was no choice for me. I know I am not at fault for what happened but neither are you." His arms were tight around me and he had his face buried in my hair, inhaling deeply to calm himself and his wolf. He had made the mistake to trust the wrong male but that wasn't his fault. Beta John had tricked many people.

"People make choices and those choices can affect how the future turns out." I grasped his left hand and turned it over, my finger tracing the thin white line that followed his life line. A faded bonding line. I hurt for him in his loss of his mate. I knew of his pain and I hated he had to go through it. That he had to give up his place, his pack, to deal with the pain it had brought. "You did what you thought was right and you did it years before I came into the picture. You had no idea that your choice would do what it did. My parents didn't know that their choice to leave me on Tacita pack territory would lead me to the classroom. Alpha Lawrence didn't know that his choice to bring me in, to treat me like his daughter would put a target on my back. There is one person who knew what would happen. There is only one person who knew what you all did not." I felt Uncle Jace remove his face from my hair and his chest rumbled with a silent growl.

"Beta John Simmons." There was a hard steel in his growling voice that spoke and ached for vengeance and I nodded. It had always been Beta John.

"Beta John knew and he planned for years. I didn't tell because who would believe the little omega female? I was invisible and I was hurt, just like Beta John wanted. Like Ingrid wanted." I could feel him trembling and I leaned my head against his chest.

"I'll kill him." His arms were shaking and I slowly shook my head. He needed to stay with me.

"No." The word was said quietly and I bit my lip as he stiffened.

His muscles stopped shaking but he didn't relax. "What?" It was a harsh sounding word and I felt the familiar trembling begin in my limbs once more. I didn't like them angry and upset with me.

"I need you here." I swallowed against the lump in my throat. "You are the first person in a long time to care about me openly. I need you here to help me get better. I need to get better, Uncle, because sometimes I feel like I'm going to shatter in a million pieces with no way of putting me back together. All I know is I'm getting better because of you and Davin and the pack you helped create." I didn't want to see his face so I buried my face in his neck and he slowly relaxed, his arms wrapping around my trembling form gently.

"When you get better... I'm going to find him and kill him." His voice was calm and even as he ran a hand over my hair. I knew he would. Uncle Jace had stated he would do it and I knew he would follow through but he had given me time to get better. That was all I had needed, time.

"I do not mind, Uncle, as long as I am better." I turned to look at Amber. She was watching us with a strange look on her face. "May I please have the sketches?" I held out my hand and she looked hesitant before sliding them over to me.

"What do you need these things for?" Uncle Jace's voice showed his disgust for the sketches that showed my abuse and I gathered them into my hands.

I ignored his question. "Could you get a burning barrel and set it out in the yard?" I finally turned to look at him and his green eyes were confused for a brief moment before he nodded. He set me on my feet as he stood up. His figure was large but I didn't feel scared as he reached his full height. He smoothed a hand down my hair again and I looked at Amber who had also stood up. I could hear Uncle Jace leave the room and my legs trembled slightly.

"They made you burn your life so you want to burn the one they made for you." The words were low and I looked at the pages of paper in my hands. My fingers trembled as I stared at the dark lines on the white sheets. Those lines were filled with untold pain and suffering and I wanted it to be burned away.

"Yes. I want to burn it. I know it won't get rid of the memories but I think it will help." I never felt so unsure in my life and Amber walked around the desk and wrapped a gentle arm around my shoulders.

"It will. It will let you know you don't have to hold onto it anymore. That the classroom is something you can destroy, even if it is only on paper." She led me towards the door and I nodded before leaning against her slightly. I was safe and I could destroy the prison they built around me. We walked the halls towards the front door but unlike the walk I had taken before this one made me feel lighter.

I could see Collin sitting on the couch in the living room and his gaze met mine as I moved past the doorway. He frowned slightly before I turned my gaze towards the front door. I could hear him behind me as I drew closer to the front door. Amber rubbed my arm in a soothing gesture before she opened it.

The wind was cold but unlike the last time I had stepped outside in the snow, I was warm and my stomach was full. I wasn't sick. I stepped out onto the cold deck and my gaze landed on Uncle Jace who was talking to a filthy looking male with dark hair and an even darker expression on his face. I couldn't see what he truly looked like from my position. I huddled closer to Amber and she rubbed my arm again. There was a burning barrel sitting in the white snow and I ignored how the cold wood of the deck nipped at my feet. I didn't like shoes so I would put up with the cold nipping.

"That's Victor, he's a wild. He's part of the pack but he likes to live with the wild wolf pack. They're the patrol and nothing happens on the territory without him knowing it." Her words were low as she answered a question I hadn't vocalized. Without any more words she led me down to the barrel. The snow was icy on my feet but I was able to ignore it. I hated shoes, I hated the feeling of anything on my feet and after three months everyone had stopped trying to force me to wear anything on them.

Uncle Jace looked over at me and Amber and I could hear more people on the deck. I looked over my shoulder and saw that everyone was standing there. Jay, Seamus, Angie, and Collin were watching us silently. I looked forward and watched as Davin came out from the trees while tugging on a shirt. He looked surprised to see us all but he continued to move closer.

Uncle Jace walked over, leaving Victor standing in the snow. I noticed his feet were bare like mine and I smiled slightly. Uncle Jace said nothing as he picked up a small gas can and poured some of it in the barrel before pulling out a box of matches. I swallowed as he lit one and threw it in the barrel. The gasoline ignited with a whoosh and I could feel the heat of it as Amber and I stopped a few feet from the barrel. I said nothing as I grabbed a page from the stack and reached forward, letting the fire touch it and set it alight. I let it slide into the barrel before grabbing another one.

Page after page of the sketches were fed to the fire. There were no sounds in the air except for the crackle of the flames as they hungrily consumed what I fed them. Each page that burned seemed to make a tightness in my chest, that I never noticed before, loosen. I could break through the cage that the classroom had built around me. I could erase the

Mantras from my mind. I could cast that voice from my head. I watched as each page burned in the fire. The classroom couldn't hurt me anymore. I was far away from anyone that could hurt me. I let the last page slide into the fire before I looked up.

Victor stood on the other side of the fire. His face was hard but there was a harsh edge of sadness to his gaze and as I locked my gaze with him over the fire I felt my breath hitch in my chest. My grey eyes stared at me from a dirty and lined face that had high cheekbones and long, tangled hair surrounding his face. A faint memory of a different time slid into my head. A run of terror, pain, tears, a tight hug. I had been so young, so small, but I knew that face. I *knew* the male it belonged to.

"Maricella." Uncle Jace grasped my shoulder and I continued to stare at Victor.

The name tugged at that memory deep inside of me. There was another name I had been called, a soft name carried on loving tones and I opened my mouth. "Mari." I watched as Victor's hard expression softened slightly before he turned away, finally breaking from my gaze. "Call me Mari."

TWELVE

Two years later

I yipped and allowed my wolf more control as she ran from the others. The other wolves gave chase and I felt happiness grow inside of me. They may not have been shifters but the wild wolf pack was still a part of the pack and the family. I liked spending time with them. It helped me forget about everything. There was nothing like running in my wolf. After years of her being forcefully contained within me, she couldn't get enough of running around the small territory that Uncle Jace had claimed.

I felt someone nip my tail playfully and I could sense Davin among the group. I whirled around and jumped at him in playful excitement. He let me jump on his back and bite the scruff of his neck in a mock fight. I was no fighter or warrior but he pretended I could beat him to make me happy. His wolf let out a playful whine as it flopped onto its side in mock defeat.

Two years was a long time and a lot had happened during it. I had finally broken through the toughest of my mantras and once they had been broken, the easier it had been to break through the rest. There were still many I had to work around but they were easy enough to bypass or even ignore. That voice still screamed at me and there were moments when I feared punishment for breaking a mantra but the reinforcement of the punishment never coming made it easier to deal with the episodes.

Amber and I had discovered I had triggers for my panic and anxiety and on the rare occasions, shock, that Amber had attributed to acute stress disorder. It was similar to post traumatic stress disorder but it only emerged when I experienced a trigger.

Blood was a *very* big trigger for me.

The very first time it happened I walked in on the hospital and Seamus was there, he had been attacked by a cougar. He had been torn up fairly badly but the blood is what had stopped me in my tracks. The red liquid seeping from his wounds had made me instantly freeze and I wasn't in the hospital anymore. I was back in the classroom looking down at the drain at the floor watching my blood spiral down it. The coppery smell of it was overly cloying and choking as it dripped off of my toes. The red lines drawing startling lines onto my white skin.

It had taken Amber, Uncle Jace, and Davin six hours to bring me back from the memory. Six hours of my brain short circuiting and freezing. It wasn't as bad now as it had been before but I still froze and the world disappeared around me. I was usually fine if someone broke my gaze or talked me down but it was still an exhausting process that made my emotions chaotic for hours afterwards.

Even after two years I still flinched sometimes at quick movements and I still had troubles with keeping my feelings to myself. I still had troubles with eye contact and people cleaning up after me but I had made progress, even if it felt like two steps forward and one step back.

Although the biggest progress I made in the two years was finally accept the rejection that had nearly killed me. It had been such a loud cracking sound that it had startled Jay and Collin when I had done it. Angie had heard it from the kitchen and she had ran into the room before jumping on me, pulling me into a strong hug telling me how proud she was and that now she could take me 'shopping' for a mate as she called it.

I hadn't said the words to accept the rejection out loud but while sitting on the couch a flare of pain had happened and I knew he had been with someone else again. I had grown tired of it and I said the words inside of my head and apparently the bond had been weakened enough for it to work.

Collin and Jay had laughed when I told them about the pain. Jay said that it had to have been one of the best cock blocks in the world. The pain of the rejection disappeared but a strange feeling of incompleteness had filled me instead, as if I was missing something that I needed. I had told Amber about it and she had frowned slightly and told me she wasn't sure what it could be.

I was thrown out of my musings as Davin pinned me to the ground on my back, growling playfully in my face. I yipped excitedly and wiggled in the dirt. A dark brown wolf jumped on Davin, forcing him off of me. I was instantly on my feet, lowering my front end and wiggling while making excited noises. There was no feeling like playing with the others. The other wolves mimicked my movements and I watched as Victor's wolf shook Davin's scruff slightly in warning. He was protective even though Victor avoided me. I knew what he was to me and I knew he was ashamed but I tried my best to not hold it against him. It was hard though, seeing my birth father continually and have him pretend I didn't exist.

I barked before bounding over to them and nipping at Victor's tail. He let Davin go and whirled around, nipping at my nose in warning before licking my snout causing me to sneeze. A long howl filled the air and I felt my body tense and perk up at the sound. I sat down and let a howl fill my throat and released it in an answer to the call Uncle Jace had just let out.

I could hear the other wolves join me and I cut my howl off and darted for the house. I could hear the pounding of paws behind me and I knew they could outrun me but for the moment I didn't care. I was free from the weight that had held me down for over half my life and I was happy. We weren't far from the pack house and I burst from the trees, the others following me.

I saw Uncle Jace on the porch and I jumped at him, shifting as I did so. I slammed against his chest and wrapped my arms around his neck, kissing his cheek. He chuckled at the action before kissing my cheek in return. He kept his hands at his sides and did not wrap them around me. I appreciated the gesture. Despite how unconcerned I was with nudity, I still wasn't comfortable with people touching my bare skin. There were things that lingered deep within me that I knew wouldn't come out so easily.

"Hey, sugar." Collin was smirking and I looked over Uncle Jace's shoulder to where he winked at me. He held up a dress. "Give me a kiss and you can have it." He winked at me again and I let Uncle Jace go before moving over to Collin and kissing his cheek gently with a red flush on my face.

I took the dress before I pulled it over my head and looked towards Uncle Jace. He had called us back for a reason. Collin wrapped his arm around my side and I felt Jay do the same to my other side. I scrunched up my nose at the action. They were making sure I wouldn't run. The thought made my heart pound harshly in my chest because it meant Uncle Jace was going to say something that they were expecting me to react negatively to.

"Maricella, we're going back." Uncle Jace looked at me and I swallowed, my eyes grew wide when I understood what he meant. I looked at his hand and noticed a black ribbon.

A black ribbon for death.

I felt my heart lurch in my chest, my eyes on the ribbon. I tried to pull away from the arms holding me but I knew it was no use. Uncle Jace had told me two years ago that when I got to a point where Amber said I was doing better he would kill the male responsible for my abuse.

I looked from the ribbon to the steely look in his green eyes. He had two years to think about this and I knew he wouldn't turn away from his decision. I wasn't against it, I wanted Beta John to suffer, I wanted Ingrid to suffer but I did not know what would happen when I returned to that place. Here, in the house, I knew I was safe but back there, back where it all happened? I didn't know how I would react.

I felt a lump form in my stomach and I stopped fighting against Collin and Jay. "What will happen to me?" Even I could hear the fear in my tone and his eyes softened.

"Nothing, Mari. We won't let anything happen to you. You don't have to return if you don't wish to." His gaze was soft and I nodded. I didn't wish to return, not there. I had a happy life here and I didn't wish to return to where there was only pain and suffering. Dark memories lingered there and I didn't want to be brought back into the shadow of them.

"She has to, Jace. You left something there, Mari, something very important." Amber's voice was gentle but firm as she moved out of the house. I looked over my shoulder and she gave me a sympathetic look. "There's something there that you need to find." Her blue eyes were filled with confusion but she seemed firm in her decision to bring me back there.

"What is it?" I hated how my voice trembled. It reminded me of when I first arrived. Back when I was scared and weak. Back when I was trapped in the mantras. It didn't matter that I was still struggling with the effects of them on my psyche, I was better and I didn't want to ruin my progress by going back to where it all started.

"I'm not really sure but you'll know it when you find it." Her words were confusing and I heaved out a large sigh. I would not win, now that Amber had stated I had to go Uncle Jace would never let me stay.

"I do not wish to enter their territory. I was banished and I do not know how they will react to me returning. What is banished should never return." I tried to control my shaky breathing and I slowly moved away from Collin and Jay. I knew the patrols of the Tacita pack would kill me if I returned. A banishment wasn't taken lightly by any pack. Just the thought of it was enough to make my breath hitch in my chest and have fear curling slowly through my veins.

"We have the witching cloaks. They will hide our scent and we should be safe from the patrols. It's only for a short while, Mari. Just until I do what needs to be done." Uncle Jace moved closer and I felt tears in my eyes. I was scared. No. I was *terrified* of going back.

"I'm scared." I wrapped my arms around myself and he pulled me into a hug, pressing my face into his chest. It was still difficult for me to let the others know of my emotions because I still had a hard time expressing them. So many years of being told no and to keep them to myself made it so unbearably hard to show them to the world.

"I know and I'm sorry but for my sake, we need to." His voice was gruff but had an edge of pleading. I understood what he meant. Since his mate had been killed his wolf had lived for protecting his family. I was his niece and someone had harmed me greatly. It wasn't really Uncle Jace that demanded retribution and vengeance, it was his wolf and he couldn't say no.

"I understand, Uncle. Do I need to pack?" I pulled back from his embrace and he shook his head before releasing me. I ignored the chill of winter as it moved across my bare skin. I was used to the cold and I was able to remain warm. My wolf helped with that more than anything and it was something I was entirely grateful for.

"We won't be gone for very long, Mari. A day at most. We'll leave early tomorrow morning." He turned away and I nodded before pushing past Jay and Collin and heading into the house.

I found myself in the living room staring at the box. It had been converted into a chair last year. I mainly used it when I would read because with most of the difficult mantras broken I no longer needed to hide from the world's gaze. I sat down on it and wrapped the soft blanket around myself. I could hear footsteps walking towards me but I didn't lift my gaze from the corner of the chair.

"Are you alright?" Amber's voice was soft and I let out a deep breath before looking up at her. She had been correct two years ago when she said some of the omega tendencies would linger. I couldn't hold her gaze for very long.

"What if something happens? What if I go back to how I was before?" I wasn't ready to face that yet. I wasn't ready to go back. I looked at her and she shushed me gently, placing a hand on my knee.

"You'll never go back there because you're far stronger than that. By allowing that place to control your fear you are allowing it to control you. It's just a building. It's just a pack. They have nothing over you now. You're safe because they cannot possibly hurt you again." She lifted her other hand and cupped my cheek.

"You're so brave and you're so strong. This cannot possibly harm you because you will not allow it to. I believe in you, we *all* believe in you. That isn't to say you might experience some issues. The past will linger back there and you might regress for a moment or two but it's nothing to be scared of or ashamed about." She smiled at me and I looked away for a brief moment.

"What will my father say?" I choked on the words. I had remembered my childhood. I had remembered how much he loved me, how much he cared for me, I could remember how upset he had been after he returned from Russia and I pulled away, and I could not bear to disappoint him. I didn't want him to turn me away, to banish me once more. Those memories were both a blessing and a curse for me.

"I'm sure he'll be happy you're okay. He's the one who sent you here. He's the one who made sure you would stay safe. He can be nothing less than proud." She moved and sat beside me, the box chair was large enough for her and I shifted over slightly, giving her more room.

"Why do I need to go?" I wiped at the tears that fell from my eyes and she sighed. She looked uncertain of herself and I worried my bottom lip with my teeth.

"You told me that after you accepted the rejection, the empty feeling in your chest disappeared but something else took its place. You said you felt incomplete and that something was pulling you." She spoke slowly carefully, her eyes darting back and forth as if she was trying to find the words. "I think that after you were rejected you bumped into someone whose genetics complimented yours much like your other mate did. A bond was half formed. This person would have bonded to you, sensing your need of a mate but with the rejection staying incomplete they would not know and neither would you." Her words confused me and I stared at the blanket before looking over at her.

"I don't understand." It was the truth, I was confused. She was speaking as though she believed I had another mate but I could not remember anyone else bonding with me. I couldn't remember anyone who it might be.

"The bond is no longer half formed. You accepted the rejection and now you're being pulled towards the person you're now bonded to. I know this is hard to believe but was there anyone you ran into after your rejection, anyone you felt a connection to? Someone who might have felt a connection to you?" Amber looked at me, the words were spoken low and I tried to remember, I tried to think but I shook my head. "Someone who had a bond to you. Someone who was nervous around you for no reason." The words hit a chord in me and I remembered Lucas's nervous gesture as he popped his knuckles and then I remember the blue eyed male, Bennett, scuffing his foot against the floor and him shifting his weight nervously.

I felt my breath hitch in my chest. I couldn't be certain. "No." I shook my head. I could not be certain. I couldn't be certain of it. He was kind to me but he had been from a different station. I pressed my thumb into the scar across my palm. He had taken care of me, given me gifts. I wondered for a brief moment if it would have been him I needed to seek.

"You and them wouldn't have known it at the time but the bond would have been there." Her words made the memory of my walk slip into my mind. There had only been one person who had tried to stop me. One person who had tried to save me from what they thought would be an inevitable death.

"The blue eyed male." The words seemed torn from me and I stared at Amber. "There was a blue eyed male." A smile crossed her face and she held my hands gently. I felt my heart pound strangely in my chest. There was very little proof of what she was thinking but he was the only one who fit.

"Do you know his name?" She seemed earnest and I nodded once.

"Bennett. He told me to call him Bennett." Before I had believed it to be improper but despite the quiet screaming over the voice I didn't shy away from saying it.

"We can see, Mari. We can see if that's what this means." She squeezed my hands and I swallowed as I looked at her.

"I'm scared." I watched as her expression changed and she cupped the back of my head and pressed her forehead against mine.

"We all are and that's okay. We'll be okay, you most of all." With that she let me go and left. I sat with my thoughts until Collin sat down beside me. I jumped slightly and he chuckled before wrapping me in his arms. I leaned against him. He was a good friend, a great friend, much like the others who lived in the house. We were a close group, more like a family than a pack.

"It'll be okay. I'll personally murder anyone who fucks with you." He hugged me tightly and rocked me from side to side before kissing my temple. I relaxed into the comfort of his familiar embrace.

"You promise?" I smiled as he laughed. I knew he would at my words. I looked into his eyes and rested my head against his chest once more. His heartbeat was regular and strong, a comforting sound that I enjoyed. Collin was my friend, someone who continually made my smile and made sure I was happy. I didn't want to imagine my life without him. He was just too damn special to me. To us all. It was just hard because there was a sadness to him, a darkness that tugged at his edges that worried all of us.

"I promise. Now Seamus brought us back another movie. Die Hard. Apparently it's an old one but a good one." He didn't wait for my reply before he picked me up and threw me onto the couch. I laughed at the action, shaking away the nervousness I felt. I would be okay. I would be protected. I would be *safe*.

THIRTEEN

I ran through the forest, a dark figure ahead of me. A red ribbon dangled from his hand and I reached out, trying to catch him when he opened his mouth. "Mary Mary was caught unwary." The cold words echoed around me and he disappeared. I whirled around, my heart pounding so hard in my chest I thought it was trying to escape.

"No! Give her back!" I spun around before catching sight of the figure once more. I darted towards him but no matter how fast I ran he was always the same distance from me. It never grew, it never shrank.

"But where did her body go?" His voice was cold and mocking and I felt anger rise up in me. He had done this. He knew. I felt a cold breeze blow and he blew away with the wind as if he were smoke. I stopped running, my chest hurt from the icy air I was taking in as I whirled around, trying to find him, trying to catch him. "With the icy snow and the harsh winds that blow." The snow crunched under my feet and I breathed heavily. I needed to find him. I needed to find her. He was suddenly in front of me and held out the red ribbon.

"Now no one will ever know." He gave me a cold, sickening smile and I leapt at him, ready to tear him to shreds when he disappeared. The ribbon falling slowly to the white snow. I stopped, falling to my knees as I picked it up. I could smell the blood and the dirt on the damaged ribbon. The wind turned to his icy voice.

"Mary Mary was caught unwary. But where did her body go? With the icy snow and harsh winds that blow. Now no one will ever know." The words repeated again and again, echoing in the forest around me and I looked up at the moon. The bright light of it was just as cold as the words and I crumpled

the ribbon in my hand. "You can search and you can look, whelp, but you'll never find what you seek." His icy breath brushed across my ear.

"You will never find her."

My eyes opened and I exhaled heavily. It was just a dream. The same one I had been having for the past two years. I leaned my head against the cold wall and shook the bottle of whiskey I held in my hand. Only a bit of amber liquid sloshed in the bottom. There were no more bottles. I knew this because I had a hand in drinking them. I rolled my head against the wall to where my Alpha lay on the makeshift bed frame that once held a beautiful little shifter. He had drunk what I hadn't.

It was frigid in the room and my breath came out in a fog in front of my face. I lifted the bottle to my mouth and drank what was left in it. The harsh liquid burned but I welcomed the feeling. I barely felt anything anymore. The last day I felt anything was seven hundred and seventy-six days ago when I watched a nearly skeletal female walk across a field of snow in nothing but a nightgown and a red ribbon tied around her wrist to let the world know she had been banished. It was the day I lost faith in my pack and my Alpha, the day that I learned that my pack was hiding dark secrets underneath its innocent facade.

I wanted to escape it so badly but I knew if I went rogue the Hunters would be given a bounty to find me and arrest me for breaking my contract. I hadn't been strong enough to fight against the people holding me down and I knew I would not be able to survive against the Hunters that would chase my bounty. So I threw myself into training, I spent all my energy training so I could be strong enough to survive as a rogue.

The energy I didn't spend on training went to looking for the sweet, banished female called Mary Mary. Her scent led me nowhere. It was as if she had disappeared into thin air. I had wanted to help her, to help her survive but she was gone long before the first time I had searched for her. I played with the neck of the bottle.

I had searched many times for her during the first two weeks. I searched for her while on patrol. I searched for her when I was supposed to be sleeping. Two weeks into my search I had run into a wild. His dark figure was burned into my brain as he said the words that haunted me in my sleep. His sharp and cold grey eyes held no kindness only cruelty and hate.

Mary Mary was caught unwary. But where did her body go? With the icy snow and harsh winds that blow. Now no one will ever know.

A mocking parody of the nursery rhyme Alpha Lawrence had told me had been her favourite. Her damaged red ribbon had been held in his fist as he said it. He had held it out for me before dropping it and disappearing completely. I hated myself for not paying more attention to him, for not catching a scent but he was a wild, their scent blended in with the forest. He wasn't to be found anywhere. He had disappeared like smoke.

You can search and you can look, whelp, but you'll never find what you seek. You will never find her.

The words made me shiver. I had told her the ribbon should have been black because I knew she would never survive in her state. I told her and it had come true. There had been no blood on our territory. Nothing of her had shown up until the wild appeared with her tattered ribbon in his fist and his haunting message to Alpha Lawrence.

He hadn't taken the message well. The Alpha, who I had hated for banishing a sickly female who was unable to protect herself, took the message as well as I did. He tore apart his office before trying his best to kill Beta John. John had been lucky to escape with only broken ribs and several large claws marks to his belly and chest.

I never understood Alpha Lawrence's anger. I never understood his rage or sadness until I had come into her room to find him sitting on the bed I had made for her with a bottle of whiskey clutched in his hand. His eyes were bloodshot and he said nothing to me as he drank from the bottle, staring at the amber liquid as if it would solve all of his problems.

Night after night I found him in her room until I had asked him why, the word has been hissed at him the hate making the accusation clear. He did not answer my question but told me he had a hard time knowing who he could trust. He then offered me the bottle and it started our tradition of drinking in her room, breathing in her scent.

It was comforting for an odd reason. It was also the very first time I had seen my Alpha cry. He would drink until he slurred his words and then he would sob, begging someone for forgiveness. He would do it night after night until he met me in her room and handed me a photo album with the initials M. C. L. carved on the front in spiralling font.

It held pictures of a happy little girl with cocoa coloured hair and stormy grey eyes. He had drunk from his bottle of whiskey as I looked through it and when I had asked him who it was he told me the secret he had been keeping for fifteen years. The little sickly omega he had banished that day in the snow was Maricella Charlotte Lawrence, his daughter.

I had felt sickened that he had done that to her, that he had allowed her to become an omega, that he had allowed that bitch Ingrid to rule over her with such cruelty, and that he had banished her from her home. I had felt sickened until he had told me about what Beta John had done, what Ingrid had done, what he himself had unknowingly let happen and that he only banished her because she was going to die. That he had expected his brother to be there to take her to safety. The sweet little omega I had tried hard to make smile had been rejected by her mate and the bastard had been too selfish to let her break the bond fully. Alpha Lawrence had banished her to save her life, to save his daughter's life.

He had cried for a long time and for once I felt pity for the male who had no one he could trust. I felt sorry for him because his second in command, the person supposed to be his most loyal friend, had turned his adopted daughter into an omega and then his son had torn her heart from her chest. He cried as his heart broke in his chest with the thought he would never see her again. I saw him in a new light. I saw a broken male with little hope left and I found a friend among the pieces. We shared a commonality. Our lives were in tatters and we were both haunted by her.

Thoughts of her sad grey eyes that told of a harsh betrayal haunted my dreams, leaving me with no peace. My dreams were filled with her and her haunting gaze and red ribbons. I did not know why I had fixated on her, even before she had been banished I wished to be around her, to do things to make her smile. I knew many would have scoffed but seeing her with that red ribbon tied around her wrist and wearing nothing but a nightgown in the freezing winter cold made me freeze with cold dread for what was going to happen to her in the freezing and snowy woods.

The day before I had seen her scrubbing floors. I had watched as she scrubbed the floors oblivious to her surrounding her lips mouthing words I couldn't hear and the next day they were banishing her for being unable to do her duty as an omega. It made no sense, it had no fairness, it had nothing that resembled reason. I stroked the neck of the bottle before looking at the wall across from me.

It was her room. I used to come in to take in her scent, trying to memorize it for when I searched for her but now it was gone. The scent of stale alcohol, sadness and dust filled the air now. There was nothing left of her sweet smell. The smell of flowers and honey that I knew I could never shake from my mind. It was gone from her room though, replaced with my scent and the scent of my Alpha.

The makeshift bed frame I had once proudly cobbled together for the sweet female, creaked underneath the weight on it. "It's still dark out." His voice was heavy and rough with exhaustion and I nodded, pulling myself from my thoughts. I knocked the empty bottle away and hung my head slightly. A headache was building deep in my skull but I was used to the pain.

"I should go do my rounds." I knew my voice sounded just as rough as his did but I didn't care. I moved my arms to rest on my knees. Two years of intense training and the slightly muscular older juvenile I had been was no longer there. I was cold and harsh but I was strong. The only reason I stayed now was because of Alpha Lawrence. He needed someone in this pack he could trust and I knew how the knowledge of his daughter had suffered without him knowing, pained him deep to his core. An aching and terrible wound that I doubted would ever heal. I fucking *hated* this pack.

"Fuck your rounds. We need more whiskey." He coughed and rolled over onto his back, rubbing his hands over his face. His eyes were bloodshot and a scraggly beard covered his face. He sat up and I watched as he let out a heavy sigh.

"Send someone else to get it. I need to do my rounds. Also, you need a fucking shower." I didn't care that I was being disrespectful but he just waved me off. We had reached an understanding of sorts. He allowed my disrespect, I think he enjoyed it, needed it.

"You're a fine one to talk, whelp. You stink just as badly as I do." He stood up, leaning heavily against the wall. "You better get in the shower before Lucas comes looking for you." He spat the words out, his face dark with anger. I watched as he pushed off of the wall. He staggered slightly but righted himself as he walked to the door. I wasn't sure if it was exhaustion on his part or that he was still partially drunk.

"Need to stop coming in here. Her scent's gone." His muttered words didn't faze me. He said that every morning since her scent had been gone. I stood up as well, stretching my stiff muscles. "I miss her. Fuck do I miss her." He leaned against the door, pressing his face into his forearm.

His voice was thick with tears and I didn't know what to tell him. I didn't know what to say.

I hadn't known her enough to miss her, I hadn't been given the time but there was something there, binding me to her memory. I wondered if it was her large grey eyes that had seemed to look right through me and to my soul. Something about he had reached a deep part of me and refused to let go. From the very first moment I saw her, something had pulled me back to her again and again.

"It doesn't do well to dwell, Alpha." I moved over to the door and he stood up straight once again. "Take a fucking shower and be an Alpha." I pushed past him, opening the door and heading to one of the bathrooms. He didn't say anything about the disrespect and I knew he never would. I wondered if it was because he liked having someone to tell him he was wrong, to tell him that it was his fault. I knew he did what he did for a reason but she had died and that was on him.

After your shower, come to my office. His voice was sharp over the mind-link and I pushed it off. I would do as he said, I always did but he knew that I was more than willing to leave the pack for what they did. I believed that may have been another part in him not getting upset with me like he did the others. He needed me because he could trust me.

I pushed open the bathroom door and slammed it closed. The sun had yet to start to rise and I turned on the shower. I never really slept through the night, the nightmares and dreams plagued me relentlessly whenever I closed my eyes. I stripped off my clothes before stepping into the cold shower. It would warm up in a few moments but for now the icy spray was helping to shake away the cobwebs of the nightmare that plagued me.

I rubbed at my chest, over my heart. A strange pulling, incomplete sensation had filled my chest several months ago. It left me feeling agitated and my wolf feeling restless. I did not know what had caused it but it had happened shortly after Lucas Simmons had been found writhing on the floor naked and in extreme pain. He had to be restrained as he clawed at himself, his claws digging deep into his muscles.

I had watched him with cold eyes as people rushed around me and I felt a sense of justice fill me up. He had deserved those eight hours of pain. He had deserved every hour, every minute, every fucking *second* he had received for what he did to my Alpha's daughter. I didn't wish to presume to know what my Alpha thought but I knew he enjoyed it as well. We were the only two who silently rejoiced as Lucas was tied to the hospital bed to keep from tearing his own heart out.

The water warmed against my skin and I hung my head, watching it fall around me. The pounding water felt good on my stiff muscles and I held my hand against my chest, feeling my heart beat strongly against my palm. I let my fingers trace around the tattoo that rested above the strong organ. A bouquet of silver bells, lady bells, and cockle shells tied tightly with a red ribbon. It was my memorial for the banished female when everyone around me had forgotten she had even existed. A wolfsbane inked picture placed under my skin by silver needles.

I let my hand run through my hair before I went through my routine. I had no time to linger, my Alpha needed me in his office. The water became scalding but I embraced the pain, knowing that if I burned I would heal within minutes. Steam filled the bathroom as I let the burning water pound my skin. I ran my hand through my hair while I scratched as my slight beard with my other one. I turned off the shower and stepped out. I grabbed a towel and wrapped it around my waist before I used my hand to clear the fog off of the mirror. I looked at my reflection with a critical eye.

I looked tired, older than I had seven hundred and seventy-six days ago. I was twenty-six years old and I looked so much older than that. There was a cold, hard look in my eyes that never went away and I knew sometimes it mixed with disgust whenever I was dealing with the pack. None of them had stood up for her, none of them even tried.

For the good of the pack, the weak must be banished.

It had been painful for me to hear the words coming out of her dry and cracked lips. She had said it and her stormy grey eyes were filled with betrayal and tears. Everyone had taken up the words as she walked through them. They didn't reach out to stop her. They didn't offer her a jacket or anything to bring her comfort. They said those words and watched as she disappeared forever. They were not worth protecting in my eyes. They had committed a terrible crime and the Hunters should have been allowed to destroy them all.

The bathroom door opened and closed and I cursed myself for not locking it. A red haired female smiled at me before dropping the towel she had wrapped around herself. I glanced at her for a brief moment before I turned back to the mirror.

"Do you want some company?" She was beautiful there was no doubt about it but all I could think about was the ivory skin of Mary Mary the very first time I had seen her. Her thin body curving slightly in the right places before she covered it up with a threadbare nightgown that was practically see through. Brown curls fell down her back and she had looked like a fallen angel. I had been ashamed that I found her beautiful. I had been *ashamed* and I hated myself for it because wanting her should have never brought me shame.

"Get the fuck out, Linnette." The words were cold and harsh as I grasped the edge of the counter with white knuckles. I had made the mistake of fooling around with her and she never seemed to get the message that she was nothing more than a passing fuck. That she was never more than something that I used to keep my mind off of everything, off of Maricella Charlotte Lawrence.

Linnette didn't know that I sometimes imagined she had brown curls and wide grey eyes. She didn't need to know I imagined her as a certain little omega. I felt an amused smirk cross my face at the thought of her horrified face if she found out. She would be not only horrified but disgusted and if anyone else found out she would be shamed.

"Don't be like that." She reached for me and I felt a low growl build in my throat. I didn't want her touching me. It had been like that for the past few months, since the incomplete feeling has settled itself deep in my chest. I didn't want any females touching me.

"I said get the fuck out." I turned my gaze to her and she took a step back, a frown appearing on her beautiful face. "You have a group of potential mates out there. Have some decency and look for them instead of chasing someone who is disgusted by you." I meant for the words to hurt, to sting and her mouth dropped open in shock.

"You don't mean that." She sounded aghast and I stared at her, narrowing my eyes. She never got it. She never understood, much like the few others I had bedded in the past two years. I knew in their minds that if they seduced me, the pack's top warrior, that they would increase their status. They threw themselves at me in the hopes we were mates but I knew better. I knew their attention was empty, they only wanted power. It disgusted me much like Linnette did.

"You don't get to tell me what I mean with my words. I spoke the truth. You *disgust* me, Linnette. Your touch repulses me like everyone else's. Save what's left of your pride and leave." I watched as her face crumpled and she snatched the towel off the floor with shaking hands. There was the anger that let me know she finally understood. I looked back into the mirror and waited for her to leave.

"You're a fucking bastard. You can't just play with people's emotions like this." She was angry but she wasn't leaving. I slowly turned to look at her. She froze under my icy glare. I scared her but I liked that I did. If I scared her then she would leave me alone like I wanted.

"I don't have time to play games with you, Linnette. I fucked you, it was a mistake. Get over it and leave me be." I watched as she flinched under my words. I felt no guilt for cutting her down as I was doing. She brought it on herself when she insisted on bothering me.

"You're heartless." She spat the words out. She was trying to hurt me like I hurt her but that truth did not hurt. I was heartless because the little omega that had been called Mary Mary had taken that part of me when she had made that walk across the snow and to her death. My heart had died with her because the guilt smothered it. I should have told Andrew what Ingrid would do, should have told him she was growing sicker. I should have done *more* but I hadn't and that was on me.

"You're right, Linnette, I am heartless. My heart was torn out by the very pack I am forced to protect when they allowed a sick female to cross a field of ice in nothing but a nightgown and a red ribbon." I advanced on her and she shrunk under my gaze and wrapped the towel around herself. I could feel her fear and hear her heart beating loudly in her chest. "My heart was torn out by eyes filled with betrayal and a pack that held me back from saving her. My heart was torn out when a wild returned a tattered red ribbon to me that belonged to that little omega." I towered over her as she cowered against the door. I brought my face close to hers, grasping the doorknob in my hand.

"My heart was torn out because my pack sent an ill omega to her death under the guise of banishment." I watched as she shrank further away from me, her breathing speeding up. "I'm only heartless because you sick bastards made me this way." I opened the door and she stumbled backwards, landing on her ass outside of the bathroom. She scrambled to her feet, her face was pale as she clutched as the towel and I stared at her.

"You're a monster." Tears filled her eyes and I could see her bottom lip trembling. I blinked slowly. That was a new insult. I had been called many things but not a monster. Coming from her it seemed a bit hypocritical.

"If I'm a monster then I would take care to not look too closely in your mirror, Linnette, you might be horrified by the beast that stares back at you from beneath your pretty little mask." My cold words lingered in the air between us and she whirled around, her red hair flying behind her as she bolted. I closed the bathroom door, making sure to lock it before I completed my routine. I opted out of shaving my three day old stubble, not having the energy to complete the task.

I slowly cleaned the bathroom, making sure my mess had been taken care of. After Mary Mary had been banished I hadn't felt right in letting an omega clean up after me. I had started cleaning up after myself and I found a small amount of peace in the tasks. I could clean up my messes. I could make things that I had dirtied clean again. It was a simple thing to wash a dish or throw a load of my dirty clothes into the washing machine. It was easy to keep my room tidy and in order. I left everything better than how I found it.

I picked up my clothes and left the bathroom. I made my way down the stairs and towards my bedroom. I ignored the other pack warriors that were just getting up or heading to bed. They avoided me like they always did. There had been a time when I would have laughed or joked with them but that was a very long time ago. I could barely look at them without disgust. They claimed to protect the pack but were perfectly fine with letting the weakest of us die alone in the cold.

"Hey, you made my sister cry, shit stain." It was a sharp voice and I paused before I turned my head slowly towards the speaker. He shared Linnette's flaming red hair, it was her older brother Emerson. I was bigger than him but he was surrounded by his friends. He was angry and filled with false bravado, a terrible combination.

"I'm not in control of your sister's emotions. The only person who can make her cry is herself and if she cannot handle the truth then perhaps she should avoid those who speak it." I looked at him. I was calm because I knew that no matter what happened I would be the only one standing. I was the pack's top warrior and Emerson wasn't even in the top twenty.

"She told me you were playing around with her emotions. Making her care for you before you cast her off." Linnette moved fast, getting the news to her big brother before I had a chance to even get dressed. I had to admire her tenacity in trying to hurt me like I hurt her. It wouldn't work. The only person who would be hurt would be her brother, depending on how hard I decided to hit him.

"No. I fucked her. I told her that all she would ever be was a fuck and she insisted upon trying to be more than that. It's not my fault she's too stupid to listen." I blinked lazily as he started to growl. He was angry and he moved closer. I kept myself still as he advanced on me. If he wouldn't have been blinded by anger he would have felt wary, he would have thought his actions through. I wasn't the type of shifter to pick a fight with, everyone knew that now.

"That's my baby sister you're insulting." He ground the words out from between clenched teeth and I tilted my head. I watched as one of his friends grabbed his arm glancing at me warily. The smart male understood where this would be going if Emerson insisted upon an altercation. I appreciated his unwillingness to participate in the actions of fools.

"I wasn't aware the truth was an insult." I watched as he took another step before his friend pulled him away. I turned away from him before starting to walk down the hall. I needed to get dressed and then see what Alpha Lawrence required of me.

"Maybe you should go join your dead little omega bitch." His voice was mocking and despite myself I froze at his words. A cold rage filled me and I tried to push it down. I knew I wouldn't be able to hold myself back from killing him if I let it control me. "Yah, Linnette told me about your obsession with that little runt bitch. She's dead because she was weak. All she ever was, was a dumb little omega bitch and you sit there bitching and moaning about how we tore your heart out when we banished her. Good. I'm fucking glad we did. I'm glad the little bitch is dead."

I took in several deep breaths before I slowly turned around, locking my gaze with Emerson's. His eyes went slightly wide with fear before he tried to cover it up with determination mixed with confidence but I could see the fear on the edge of his expression. I slowly walked towards him. My hands clenched into fists, the one holding my clothes shook slightly.

It was because of these assholes that I hated this pack. It was because of his type of attitude that I wanted to go rogue. It was because of shitty people like him that had the audacity to speak of Maricella Charlotte

Lawrence like that, that made me want to destroy each and every one of them. Haunted and betrayed grey eyes flashed through my mind as I stopped walking. She never deserved to have that said about her. Not the poor female who had been broken for a male's pride.

I was standing close to Emerson, close enough that I could reach out and touch him but not close enough that I couldn't get a proper swing at him. "Repeat that for me." My voice was like ice and I watched him swallow. His pride wouldn't let him keep his mouth shut and I hoped to god he would repeat it. "*Please,* repeat that." I stared at him and his green eyes narrowed, he would say what I wanted him to. I watched as he slowly opened his mouth and I felt my arm muscles bunch in anticipation.

"I said-" I slammed my fist into his face cutting him off. His cheekbone cracked under the force of my fist connecting with it and I watched as he flew backwards. His eyes rolled into the back of his head and he stayed where he landed in a crumpled heap. His friends grabbed at him, trying wake him and I stared down at his prone form. My knuckles flared with pain but I ignored it, they would be healed in a few seconds, it wasn't worth thinking about the throbbing.

"I heard what you said, Emerson. I just wanted you to give me a reason." I looked around his friends. "Anyone else want to say something?" I watched as they all hunched their shoulders forward, ignoring me and unwilling to look at me. "Good. It's about fucking time someone had some fucking common sense." I gritted the words out before turning around. "If anyone mentions the word omega around me they'll be getting the same treatment." I spoke loud enough for everyone on the hall to hear me and as a quiet hush fell I made my way to my room and stepped inside.

Everything was in perfect order. My bed hadn't been slept on in months but the omegas still insisted upon washing the bedding. Even after two years of me doing my own chores I couldn't get them to stop doing the bedding or dusting the room. I threw my dirty clothes in the hamper before pulling out some clean ones. I got dressed quickly before sliding on my boots, lacing them up loosely. I closed my eyes, inhaling and exhaling slowly, trying to get the anger to slip from my limbs. The icy rage I felt wasn't unfamiliar. It was so familiar it was almost like a comforting friend but I didn't need it distracting me.

Stop punching pack members while naked. Alpha Lawrence's voice forced itself into my head and I let out a surprised bark of laughter as his words. He sounded half amused and half exasperated.

I was wearing a towel. I rolled my eyes slightly as I finished tying my boots and stood up. There was a slight pause and I waited patiently for his reply. I wasn't surprised the news had reached him as quickly as it did. People were always running to him with every little detail about what others did, as if keeping him bogged down with their little lives would make them closer to him. As if tattling on their neighbours would make him like them more.

Okay then, as long as you weren't naked. He cut the pathway off and I smirked slightly before pushing open the door. Emerson was now awake and I moved down the hall. His face was swollen and his cheek had a nasty bruise that I wanted to smile at. His cheek bone had cracked. It would take more than a few hours to heal. My bruised and sore knuckles had already healed leaving me with a phantom throbbing that would go away in a few minutes. I walked past him adjusting my shirt, rolling the sleeves up to my elbows.

"She's just a fucking omega." His words made me freeze and I closed my eyes before I turned around and stared down at him. His friends backed away from us quickly and I took several steps before I crouched down in front of him, looking into his green eyes. He was scared and I enjoyed making him feel that way.

Without a word I reached out and grabbed his throat in a tight grasp before I picked him up and slammed him against the closest wall. Pictures fell off from the force of it and he scrambled, trying to remove my hand from around his neck. I slid him down slightly keeping my gaze lazy as I brought my mouth to his ear.

"That little omega was the Alpha's daughter and if you say another fucking word I'll let him deal with you and *believe* me, you will wish to have only dealt with me after he's through with you." I whispered the words into his ear and he stopped thrashing, whimpers came from him as I let him drop to the floor. He coughed loudly as he was allowed to inhale the oxygen his pitiful body needed to live. "Run, little Emerson, and pray you don't bump into me again." He scrambled away from me, his face pale as he left without looking back. It was up to him if he believed me or not but I knew he would keep his mouth shut about it.

Strangling them now? Alpha Lawrence sounded amused and I felt my mouth twitch slightly.

I have clothes on this time. I moved down the hall, making my way to the stairs that would take me upstairs to Alpha Lawrence's office.

I don't care. I need you to get to my office. His words were sharp and I made my way up the stairs before pushing his door open.

"I'm already here." I looked over at where he was sitting. His face was shaven for once but it just accentuated how tired he looked. His skin was pale and his eyes were still bloodshot. I once again half wondered if he was still slightly drunk but with how our metabolism worked it was highly unlikely. We burned through a drunken buzz faster than house with a Christmas tree fire.

"Good." He waved me towards a chair and I closed the door before sitting down rather abruptly. The chair groaned in protest at my sudden bulk and I ignored it as I stared at him.

"You look like shit." I watched as he shrugged before a cold smirk crossed his face. He looked almost amused for a moment before the familiar emotionless mask fixed itself over his features. He wore it all the time except for when we were getting drunk in her room. It was the only time I saw him show emotion for his actions.

"I bet not as bad as Emerson looks right now." He leaned back in his chair and I blinked slowly before leaning my head back and staring at the ceiling. There was a lot I needed to do for the day. I had several hours of patrols and then several hours of training before I ran patrols again. After that was more training and there were meals sporadically through there. I never ate with the pack anymore. It was too tedious trying to keep the emotionless mask on. "I want you to challenge Beta John and take his place." I ignored his words and extended my legs as I crossed my ankles, relaxing into the chair. He did this once a week, it was starting to get tiresome.

"I don't want to be beta. I want to run away from this shitty pack." I ignored his growl and I tapped my fingers on my stomach. "Why do you think I punched Emerson? Why do you think I scared Linnette shitless? They have no respect, their attitudes are the same as everyone else's and I'm sick of it." I closed my eyes as a silence fell. I knew he understood what I was saying. He knew and he felt the same way, he had told me as much on one of our drinking binges.

"Why did you care about Maricella?" His voice was low and I felt the simmering rage flare up for a brief moment. He had no right to ask that after he was the one who banished her.

"Because what you did wasn't right and it wasn't fair." I lifted my head up and stared at him. He looked at me with a strange expression on his face. I treated her how she should have always been treated. I treated her in the way that was right. I was drawn to her, yes, but I did what was right and that was all he needed to concern himself with.

"You were the only one to stick up for her, Bennett." He shrugged slightly, his shoulder lifting and falling in an almost unconcerned gesture. I bit back a growl. I had been the only one because it had been right and no one in the Tacita pack understood what that meant. Their moral compass was broken, it would lead them straight down to the fiery pits of hell we called Mene's brothers if they continued to follow it.

"So? That doesn't make it any less of an issue. What you did was unforgivable." I glared at him and he avoided my gaze. Silence fell and the ticking of the grandfather clock filled the air. I looked away from him, staring at the dusty bookshelf behind his desk. I didn't like the turn the conversation had taken.

"Did you love her?" His voice was low and I snapped my gaze to his. The question caught me off guard and I let out a growl.

"What type of fucking question is that, Alpha? Did I love her? I did what was right. I was the only one who did in this shitty pack. You might be content to sit there with a mask on and pretend that her leaving didn't hurt you for the sake of your precious pack but I'm not." I spat the words out and he looked at me carefully as if studying my features, looking for an answer to the question he asked. I did not love Mary Mary because I did not know her and he didn't need to put those thoughts into my head. Not when she was dead, not when she was gone. Not when the thought of her suffering alone and brought me such pain.

"That wasn't a no." His words slammed into me and I narrowed my eyes before opening my mouth. He had no right to say that shit. The door slammed open, cutting my scathing remark before it could emerge. I snapped my mouth close as I stared at a paled face Beta John. "How many times do I have to tell you to fucking knock?" Alpha Lawrence's voice was filled with venom and Beta John slammed the door closed. He held out his hand before throwing a black ribbon on the desk.

THIRTEEN

I ran through the forest, a dark figure ahead of me. A red ribbon dangled from his hand and I reached out, trying to catch him when he opened his mouth. "Mary Mary was caught unwary." The cold words echoed around me and he disappeared. I whirled around, my heart pounding so hard in my chest I thought it was trying to escape.

"No! Give her back!" I spun around before catching sight of the figure once more. I darted towards him but no matter how fast I ran he was always the same distance from me. It never grew, it never shrank.

"But where did her body go?" His voice was cold and mocking and I felt anger rise up in me. He had done this. He knew. I felt a cold breeze blow and he blew away with the wind as if he were smoke. I stopped running, my chest hurt from the icy air I was taking in as I whirled around, trying to find him, trying to catch him. "With the icy snow and the harsh winds that blow." The snow crunched under my feet and I breathed heavily. I needed to find him. I needed to find her. He was suddenly in front of me and held out the red ribbon.

"Now no one will ever know." He gave me a cold, sickening smile and I leapt at him, ready to tear him to shreds when he disappeared. The ribbon falling slowly to the white snow. I stopped, falling to my knees as I picked it up. I could smell the blood and the dirt on the damaged ribbon. The wind

turned to his icy voice.

"Mary Mary was caught unwary. But where did her body go? With the icy snow and harsh winds that blow. Now no one will ever know." The words repeated again and again, echoing in the forest around me and I looked up at the moon. The bright light of it was just as cold as the words and I crumpled the ribbon in my hand. "You can search and you can look, whelp, but you'll never find what you seek." His icy breath brushed across my ear.

"You will never find her."

My eyes opened and I exhaled heavily. It was just a dream. The same one I had been having for the past two years. I leaned my head against the cold wall and shook the bottle of whiskey I held in my hand. Only a bit of amber liquid sloshed in the bottom. There were no more bottles. I knew this because I had a hand in drinking them. I rolled my head against the wall to where my Alpha lay on the makeshift bed frame that once held a beautiful little shifter. He had drunk what I hadn't.

It was frigid in the room and my breath came out in a fog in front of my face. I lifted the bottle to my mouth and drank what was left in it. The harsh liquid burned but I welcomed the feeling. I barely felt anything anymore. The last day I felt anything was seven hundred and seventy-six days ago when I watched a nearly skeletal female walk across a field of snow in nothing but a nightgown and a red ribbon tied around her wrist to let the world know she had been banished. It was the day I lost faith in my pack and my Alpha, the day that I learned that my pack was hiding dark secrets underneath its innocent facade.

I wanted to escape it so badly but I knew if I went rogue the Hunters would be given a bounty to find me and arrest me for breaking my contract. I hadn't been strong enough to fight against the people holding me down and I knew I would not be able to survive against the Hunters that would chase my bounty. So I threw myself into training, I spent all my energy training so I could be strong enough to survive as a rogue.

The energy I didn't spend on training went to looking for the sweet, banished female called Mary Mary. Her scent led me nowhere. It was as if she had disappeared into thin air. I had wanted to help her, to help her survive but she was gone long before the first time I had searched for her. I played with the neck of the bottle.

I had searched many times for her during the first two weeks. I searched for her while on patrol. I searched for her when I was supposed to be sleeping. Two weeks into my search I had run into a wild. His dark figure was burned into my brain as he said the words that haunted me in my sleep. His sharp and cold grey eyes held no kindness only cruelty and hate.

Mary Mary was caught unwary. But where did her body go? With the icy snow and harsh winds that blow. Now no one will ever know.

A mocking parody of the nursery rhyme Alpha Lawrence had told me had been her favourite. Her damaged red ribbon had been held in his fist as he said it. He had held it out for me before dropping it and disappearing completely. I hated myself for not paying more attention to him, for not catching a scent but he was a wild, their scent blended in with the forest. He wasn't to be found anywhere. He had disappeared like smoke.

You can search and you can look, whelp, but you'll never find what you seek. You will never find her.

The words made me shiver. I had told her the ribbon should have been black because I knew she would never survive in her state. I told her and it had come true. There had been no blood on our territory. Nothing of her had shown up until the wild appeared with her tattered ribbon in his fist and his haunting message to Alpha Lawrence.

He hadn't taken the message well. The Alpha, who I had hated for banishing a sickly female who was unable to protect herself, took the message as well as I did. He tore apart his office before trying his best to kill Beta John. John had been lucky to escape with only broken ribs and several large claws marks to his belly and chest.

I never understood Alpha Lawrence's anger. I never understood his rage or sadness until I had come into her room to find him sitting on the bed I had made for her with a bottle of whiskey clutched in his hand. His eyes were bloodshot and he said nothing to me as he drank from the bottle, staring at the amber liquid as if it would solve all of his problems.

Night after night I found him in her room until I had asked him why, the word has been hissed at him the hate making the accusation clear. He did not answer my question but told me he had a hard time knowing who he could trust. He then offered me the bottle and it started our tradition of drinking in her room, breathing in her scent.

It was comforting for an odd reason. It was also the very first time I had seen my Alpha cry. He would drink until he slurred his words and then he would sob, begging someone for forgiveness. He would do it night after night until he met me in her room and handed me a photo album with the initials M. C. L. carved on the front in spiralling font.

It held pictures of a happy little girl with cocoa coloured hair and stormy grey eyes. He had drunk from his bottle of whiskey as I looked through it and when I had asked him who it was he told me the secret he had been keeping for fifteen years. The little sickly omega he had banished that day in the snow was Maricella Charlotte Lawrence, his daughter.

I had felt sickened that he had done that to her, that he had allowed her to become an omega, that he had allowed that bitch Ingrid to rule over her with such cruelty, and that he had banished her from her home. I had felt sickened until he had told me about what Beta John had done, what Ingrid had done, what he himself had unknowingly let happen and that he only banished her because she was going to die. That he had expected his brother to be there to take her to safety. The sweet little omega I had tried hard to make smile had been rejected by her mate and the bastard had been too selfish to let her break the bond fully. Alpha Lawrence had banished her to save her life, to save his daughter's life.

He had cried for a long time and for once I felt pity for the male who had no one he could trust. I felt sorry for him because his second in command, the person supposed to be his most loyal friend, had turned his adopted daughter into an omega and then his son had torn her heart from her chest. He cried as his heart broke in his chest with the thought he would never see her again. I saw him in a new light. I saw a broken male with little hope left and I found a friend among the pieces. We shared a commonality. Our lives were in tatters and we were both haunted by her.

Thoughts of her sad grey eyes that told of a harsh betrayal haunted my dreams, leaving me with no peace. My dreams were filled with her and her haunting gaze and red ribbons. I did not know why I had fixated on her, even before she had been banished I wished to be around her, to do things to make her smile. I knew many would have scoffed but seeing her with that red ribbon tied around her wrist and wearing nothing but a nightgown in the freezing winter cold made me freeze with cold dread for what was going to happen to her in the freezing and snowy woods.

The day before I had seen her scrubbing floors. I had watched as she scrubbed the floors oblivious to her surrounding her lips mouthing words I couldn't hear and the next day they were banishing her for being unable to do her duty as an omega. It made no sense, it had no fairness, it had nothing that resembled reason. I stroked the neck of the bottle before looking at the wall across from me.

It was her room. I used to come in to take in her scent, trying to memorize it for when I searched for her but now it was gone. The scent of stale alcohol, sadness and dust filled the air now. There was nothing left of her sweet smell. The smell of flowers and honey that I knew I could never shake from my mind. It was gone from her room though, replaced with my scent and the scent of my Alpha.

The makeshift bed frame I had once proudly cobbled together for the sweet female, creaked underneath the weight on it. "It's still dark out." His voice was heavy and rough with exhaustion and I nodded, pulling myself from my thoughts. I knocked the empty bottle away and hung my head slightly. A headache was building deep in my skull but I was used to the pain.

"I should go do my rounds." I knew my voice sounded just as rough as his did but I didn't care. I moved my arms to rest on my knees. Two years of intense training and the slightly muscular older juvenile I had been was no longer there. I was cold and harsh but I was strong. The only reason I stayed now was because of Alpha Lawrence. He needed someone in this pack he could trust and I knew how the knowledge of his daughter had suffered without him knowing, pained him deep to his core. An aching and terrible wound that I doubted would ever heal. I fucking *hated* this pack.

"Fuck your rounds. We need more whiskey." He coughed and rolled over onto his back, rubbing his hands over his face. His eyes were bloodshot and a scraggly beard covered his face. He sat up and I watched as he let out a heavy sigh.

"Send someone else to get it. I need to do my rounds. Also, you need a fucking shower." I didn't care that I was being disrespectful but he just waved me off. We had reached an understanding of sorts. He allowed my disrespect, I think he enjoyed it, needed it.

"You're a fine one to talk, whelp. You stink just as badly as I do." He stood up, leaning heavily against the wall. "You better get in the shower before Lucas comes looking for you." He spat the words out, his face dark with anger. I watched as he pushed off of the wall. He staggered slightly but righted himself as he walked to the door. I wasn't sure if it was exhaustion on his part or that he was still partially drunk.

"Need to stop coming in here. Her scent's gone." His muttered words didn't faze me. He said that every morning since her scent had been gone. I stood up as well, stretching my stiff muscles. "I miss her. Fuck do I miss her." He leaned against the door, pressing his face into his forearm. His voice was thick with tears and I didn't know what to tell him. I didn't know what to say.

I hadn't known her enough to miss her, I hadn't been given the time but there was something there, binding me to her memory. I wondered if it was her large grey eyes that had seemed to look right through me and to my soul. Something about he had reached a deep part of me and refused to let go. From the very first moment I saw her, something had pulled me back to her again and again.

"It doesn't do well to dwell, Alpha." I moved over to the door and he stood up straight once again. "Take a fucking shower and be an Alpha." I pushed past him, opening the door and heading to one of the bathrooms. He didn't say anything about the disrespect and I knew he never would. I wondered if it was because he liked having someone to tell him he was wrong, to tell him that it was his fault. I knew he did what he did for a reason but she had died and that was on him.

After your shower, come to my office. His voice was sharp over the mind-link and I pushed it off. I would do as he said, I always did but he knew that I was more than willing to leave the pack for what they did. I believed that may have been another part in him not getting upset with me like he did the others. He needed me because he could trust me.

I pushed open the bathroom door and slammed it closed. The sun had yet to start to rise and I turned on the shower. I never really slept through the night, the nightmares and dreams plagued me relentlessly whenever I closed my eyes. I stripped off my clothes before stepping into the cold shower. It would warm up in a few moments but for now the icy spray was helping to shake away the cobwebs of the nightmare that plagued me.

I rubbed at my chest, over my heart. A strange pulling, incomplete sensation had filled my chest several months ago. It left me feeling agitated and my wolf feeling restless. I did not know what had caused it but it had happened shortly after Lucas Simmons had been found writhing on the floor naked and in extreme pain. He had to be restrained as he clawed at himself, his claws digging deep into his muscles.

I had watched him with cold eyes as people rushed around me and I felt a sense of justice fill me up. He had deserved those eight hours of pain. He had deserved every hour, every minute, every fucking *second* he had received for what he did to my Alpha's daughter. I didn't wish to presume to know what my Alpha thought but I knew he enjoyed it as well. We were the only two who silently rejoiced as Lucas was tied to the hospital bed to keep from tearing his own heart out.

The water warmed against my skin and I hung my head, watching it fall around me. The pounding water felt good on my stiff muscles and I held my hand against my chest, feeling my heart beat strongly against my palm. I let my fingers trace around the tattoo that rested above the strong organ. A bouquet of silver bells, lady bells, and cockle shells tied tightly with a red ribbon. It was my memorial for the banished female when everyone around me had forgotten she had even existed. A wolfsbane inked picture placed under my skin by silver needles.

I let my hand run through my hair before I went through my routine. I had no time to linger, my Alpha needed me in his office. The water became scalding but I embraced the pain, knowing that if I burned I would heal within minutes. Steam filled the bathroom as I let the burning water pound my skin. I ran my hand through my hair while I scratched as my slight beard with my other one. I turned off the shower and stepped out. I grabbed a towel and wrapped it around my waist before I used my hand to clear the fog off of the mirror. I looked at my reflection with a critical eye.

I looked tired, older than I had seven hundred and seventy-six days ago. I was twenty-six years old and I looked so much older than that. There was a cold, hard look in my eyes that never went away and I knew sometimes it mixed with disgust whenever I was dealing with the pack. None of them had stood up for her, none of them even tried.

For the good of the pack, the weak must be banished.

It had been painful for me to hear the words coming out of her dry and cracked lips. She had said it and her stormy grey eyes were filled with betrayal and tears. Everyone had taken up the words as she walked through them. They didn't reach out to stop her. They didn't offer her a jacket or anything to bring her comfort. They said those words and watched as she disappeared forever. They were not worth protecting in my eyes. They had committed a terrible crime and the Hunters should have been allowed to destroy them all.

The bathroom door opened and closed and I cursed myself for not locking it. A red haired female smiled at me before dropping the towel she had wrapped around herself. I glanced at her for a brief moment before I turned back to the mirror.

"Do you want some company?" She was beautiful there was no doubt about it but all I could think about was the ivory skin of Mary Mary the very first time I had seen her. Her thin body curving slightly in the right places before she covered it up with a threadbare nightgown that was practically see through. Brown curls fell down her back and she had looked like a fallen angel. I had been ashamed that I found her beautiful. I had been *ashamed* and I hated myself for it because wanting her should have never brought me shame.

"Get the fuck out, Linnette." The words were cold and harsh as I grasped the edge of the counter with white knuckles. I had made the mistake of fooling around with her and she never seemed to get the message that she was nothing more than a passing fuck. That she was never more than something that I used to keep my mind off of everything, off of Maricella Charlotte Lawrence.

Linnette didn't know that I sometimes imagined she had brown curls and wide grey eyes. She didn't need to know I imagined her as a certain little omega. I felt an amused smirk cross my face at the thought of her horrified face if she found out. She would be not only horrified but disgusted and if anyone else found out she would be shamed.

"Don't be like that." She reached for me and I felt a low growl build in my throat. I didn't want her touching me. It had been like that for the past few months, since the incomplete feeling has settled itself deep in my chest. I didn't want any females touching me.

"I said get the fuck out." I turned my gaze to her and she took a step back, a frown appearing on her beautiful face. "You have a group of potential mates out there. Have some decency and look for them instead of chasing someone who is disgusted by you." I meant for the words to hurt, to sting and her mouth dropped open in shock.

"You don't mean that." She sounded aghast and I stared at her, narrowing my eyes. She never got it. She never understood, much like the few others I had bedded in the past two years. I knew in their minds that if they seduced me, the pack's top warrior, that they would increase their status. They threw themselves at me in the hopes we were mates but I knew better. I knew their attention was empty, they only wanted power. It disgusted me much like Linnette did.

"You don't get to tell me what I mean with my words. I spoke the truth. You *disgust* me, Linnette. Your touch repulses me like everyone else's. Save what's left of your pride and leave." I watched as her face crumpled and she snatched the towel off the floor with shaking hands. There was the anger that let me know she finally understood. I looked back into the mirror and waited for her to leave.

"You're a fucking bastard. You can't just play with people's emotions like this." She was angry but she wasn't leaving. I slowly turned to look at her. She froze under my icy glare. I scared her but I liked that I did. If I scared her then she would leave me alone like I wanted.

"I don't have time to play games with you, Linnette. I fucked you, it was a mistake. Get over it and leave me be." I watched as she flinched under my words. I felt no guilt for cutting her down as I was doing. She brought it on herself when she insisted on bothering me.

"You're heartless." She spat the words out. She was trying to hurt me like I hurt her but that truth did not hurt. I was heartless because the little omega that had been called Mary Mary had taken that part of me when she had made that walk across the snow and to her death. My heart had died with her because the guilt smothered it. I should have told Andrew what Ingrid would do, should have told him she was growing sicker. I should have done *more* but I hadn't and that was on me.

"You're right, Linnette, I am heartless. My heart was torn out by the very pack I am forced to protect when they allowed a sick female to cross a field of ice in nothing but a nightgown and a red ribbon." I advanced on her and she shrunk under my gaze and wrapped the towel around herself. I could feel her fear and hear her heart beating loudly in her chest. "My heart was torn out by eyes filled with betrayal and a pack that held me back from saving her. My heart was torn out when a wild returned a tattered red ribbon to me that belonged to that little omega." I towered over her as she cowered against the door. I brought my face close to hers, grasping the doorknob in my hand.

"My heart was torn out because my pack sent an ill omega to her death under the guise of banishment." I watched as she shrank further away from me, her breathing speeding up. "I'm only heartless because you sick bastards made me this way." I opened the door and she stumbled backwards, landing on her ass outside of the bathroom. She scrambled to her feet, her face was pale as she clutched as the towel and I stared at her.

"You're a monster." Tears filled her eyes and I could see her bottom lip trembling. I blinked slowly. That was a new insult. I had been called many things but not a monster. Coming from her it seemed a bit hypocritical.

"If I'm a monster then I would take care to not look too closely in your mirror, Linnette, you might be horrified by the beast that stares back at you from beneath your pretty little mask." My cold words lingered in the air between us and she whirled around, her red hair flying behind her as she bolted. I closed the bathroom door, making sure to lock it before I completed my routine. I opted out of shaving my three day old stubble, not having the energy to complete the task.

I slowly cleaned the bathroom, making sure my mess had been taken care of. After Mary Mary had been banished I hadn't felt right in letting an omega clean up after me. I had started cleaning up after myself and I found a small amount of peace in the tasks. I could clean up my messes. I could make things that I had dirtied clean again. It was a simple thing to wash a dish or throw a load of my dirty clothes into the washing machine. It was easy to keep my room tidy and in order. I left everything better than how I found it.

I picked up my clothes and left the bathroom. I made my way down the stairs and towards my bedroom. I ignored the other pack warriors that were just getting up or heading to bed. They avoided me like they always did. There had been a time when I would have laughed or joked with them but that was a very long time ago. I could barely look at them without disgust. They claimed to protect the pack but were perfectly fine with letting the weakest of us die alone in the cold.

"Hey, you made my sister cry, shit stain." It was a sharp voice and I paused before I turned my head slowly towards the speaker. He shared Linnette's flaming red hair, it was her older brother Emerson. I was bigger than him but he was surrounded by his friends. He was angry and filled with false bravado, a terrible combination.

"I'm not in control of your sister's emotions. The only person who can make her cry is herself and if she cannot handle the truth then perhaps she should avoid those who speak it." I looked at him. I was calm because I knew that no matter what happened I would be the only one standing. I was the pack's top warrior and Emerson wasn't even in the top twenty.

"She told me you were playing around with her emotions. Making her care for you before you cast her off." Linnette moved fast, getting the news to her big brother before I had a chance to even get dressed. I had to admire her tenacity in trying to hurt me like I hurt her. It wouldn't work. The only person who would be hurt would be her brother, depending on how hard I decided to hit him.

"No. I fucked her. I told her that all she would ever be was a fuck and she insisted upon trying to be more than that. It's not my fault she's too stupid to listen." I blinked lazily as he started to growl. He was angry and he moved closer. I kept myself still as he advanced on me. If he wouldn't have been blinded by anger he would have felt wary, he would have thought his actions through. I wasn't the type of shifter to pick a fight with, everyone knew that now.

"That's my baby sister you're insulting." He ground the words out from between clenched teeth and I tilted my head. I watched as one of his friends grabbed his arm glancing at me warily. The smart male understood where this would be going if Emerson insisted upon an altercation. I appreciated his unwillingness to participate in the actions of fools.

"I wasn't aware the truth was an insult." I watched as he took another step before his friend pulled him away. I turned away from him before starting to walk down the hall. I needed to get dressed and then see what Alpha Lawrence required of me.

"Maybe you should go join your dead little omega bitch." His voice was mocking and despite myself I froze at his words. A cold rage filled me and I tried to push it down. I knew I wouldn't be able to hold myself back from killing him if I let it control me. "Yah, Linnette told me about your obsession with that little runt bitch. She's dead because she was weak. All she ever was, was a dumb little omega bitch and you sit there bitching and moaning about how we tore your heart out when we banished her. Good. I'm fucking glad we did. I'm glad the little bitch is dead."

I took in several deep breaths before I slowly turned around, locking my gaze with Emerson's. His eyes went slightly wide with fear before he tried to cover it up with determination mixed with confidence but I could see the fear on the edge of his expression. I slowly walked towards him. My hands clenched into fists, the one holding my clothes shook slightly.

It was because of these assholes that I hated this pack. It was because of his type of attitude that I wanted to go rogue. It was because of shitty people like him that had the audacity to speak of Maricella Charlotte Lawrence like that, that made me want to destroy each and every one of them. Haunted and betrayed grey eyes flashed through my mind as I stopped walking. She never deserved to have that said about her. Not the poor female who had been broken for a male's pride.

I was standing close to Emerson, close enough that I could reach out and touch him but not close enough that I couldn't get a proper swing at him. "Repeat that for me." My voice was like ice and I watched him swallow. His pride wouldn't let him keep his mouth shut and I hoped to god he would repeat it. "*Please,* repeat that." I stared at him and his green eyes narrowed, he would say what I wanted him to. I watched as he slowly opened his mouth and I felt my arm muscles bunch in anticipation.

"I said-" I slammed my fist into his face cutting him off. His cheekbone cracked under the force of my fist connecting with it and I watched as he flew backwards. His eyes rolled into the back of his head and he stayed where he landed in a crumpled heap. His friends grabbed at him, trying wake him and I stared down at his prone form. My knuckles flared with pain but I ignored it, they would be healed in a few seconds, it wasn't worth thinking about the throbbing.

"I heard what you said, Emerson. I just wanted you to give me a reason." I looked around his friends. "Anyone else want to say something?" I watched as they all hunched their shoulders forward, ignoring me and unwilling to look at me. "Good. It's about fucking time someone had some fucking common sense." I gritted the words out before turning around. "If anyone mentions the word omega around me they'll be getting the same treatment." I spoke loud enough for everyone on the hall to hear me and as a quiet hush fell I made my way to my room and stepped inside.

Everything was in perfect order. My bed hadn't been slept on in months but the omegas still insisted upon washing the bedding. Even after two years of me doing my own chores I couldn't get them to stop doing the bedding or dusting the room. I threw my dirty clothes in the hamper before pulling out some clean ones. I got dressed quickly before sliding on my boots, lacing them up loosely. I closed my eyes, inhaling and exhaling slowly, trying to get the anger to slip from my limbs. The icy rage I felt wasn't unfamiliar. It was so familiar it was almost like a comforting friend but I didn't need it distracting me.

Stop punching pack members while naked. Alpha Lawrence's voice forced itself into my head and I let out a surprised bark of laughter as his words. He sounded half amused and half exasperated.

I was wearing a towel. I rolled my eyes slightly as I finished tying my boots and stood up. There was a slight pause and I waited patiently for his reply. I wasn't surprised the news had reached him as quickly as it did. People were always running to him with every little detail about what others did, as if keeping him bogged down with their little lives would make them closer to him. As if tattling on their neighbours would make him like them more.

Okay then, as long as you weren't naked. He cut the pathway off and I smirked slightly before pushing open the door. Emerson was now awake and I moved down the hall. His face was swollen and his cheek had a nasty bruise that I wanted to smile at. His cheek bone had cracked. It would take more than a few hours to heal. My bruised and sore knuckles had already healed leaving me with a phantom throbbing that would go away in a few minutes. I walked past him adjusting my shirt, rolling the sleeves up to my elbows.

"She's just a fucking omega." His words made me freeze and I closed my eyes before I turned around and stared down at him. His friends backed away from us quickly and I took several steps before I crouched down in front of him, looking into his green eyes. He was scared and I enjoyed making him feel that way.

Without a word I reached out and grabbed his throat in a tight grasp before I picked him up and slammed him against the closest wall. Pictures fell off from the force of it and he scrambled, trying to remove my hand from around his neck. I slid him down slightly keeping my gaze lazy as I brought my mouth to his ear.

"That little omega was the Alpha's daughter and if you say another fucking word I'll let him deal with you and *believe* me, you will wish to have only dealt with me after he's through with you." I whispered the words into his ear and he stopped thrashing, whimpers came from him as I let him drop to the floor. He coughed loudly as he was allowed to inhale the oxygen his pitiful body needed to live. "Run, little Emerson, and pray you don't bump into me again." He scrambled away from me, his face pale as he left without looking back. It was up to him if he believed me or not but I knew he would keep his mouth shut about it.

Strangling them now? Alpha Lawrence sounded amused and I felt my mouth twitch slightly.

I have clothes on this time. I moved down the hall, making my way to the stairs that would take me upstairs to Alpha Lawrence's office.

I don't care. I need you to get to my office. His words were sharp and I made my way up the stairs before pushing his door open.

"I'm already here." I looked over at where he was sitting. His face was shaven for once but it just accentuated how tired he looked. His skin was pale and his eyes were still bloodshot. I once again half wondered if he was still slightly drunk but with how our metabolism worked it was highly unlikely. We burned through a drunken buzz faster than house with a Christmas tree fire.

"Good." He waved me towards a chair and I closed the door before sitting down rather abruptly. The chair groaned in protest at my sudden bulk and I ignored it as I stared at him.

"You look like shit." I watched as he shrugged before a cold smirk crossed his face. He looked almost amused for a moment before the familiar emotionless mask fixed itself over his features. He wore it all the time except for when we were getting drunk in her room. It was the only time I saw him show emotion for his actions.

"I bet not as bad as Emerson looks right now." He leaned back in his chair and I blinked slowly before leaning my head back and staring at the ceiling. There was a lot I needed to do for the day. I had several hours of patrols and then several hours of training before I ran patrols again. After that was more training and there were meals sporadically through there. I never ate with the pack anymore. It was too tedious trying to keep the emotionless mask on. "I want you to challenge Beta John and take his place." I ignored his words and extended my legs as I crossed my ankles, relaxing into the chair. He did this once a week, it was starting to get tiresome.

"I don't want to be beta. I want to run away from this shitty pack." I ignored his growl and I tapped my fingers on my stomach. "Why do you think I punched Emerson? Why do you think I scared Linnette shitless? They have no respect, their attitudes are the same as everyone else's and

I'm sick of it." I closed my eyes as a silence fell. I knew he understood what I was saying. He knew and he felt the same way, he had told me as much on one of our drinking binges.

"Why did you care about Maricella?" His voice was low and I felt the simmering rage flare up for a brief moment. He had no right to ask that after he was the one who banished her.

"Because what you did wasn't right and it wasn't fair." I lifted my head up and stared at him. He looked at me with a strange expression on his face. I treated her how she should have always been treated. I treated her in the way that was right. I was drawn to her, yes, but I did what was right and that was all he needed to concern himself with.

"You were the only one to stick up for her, Bennett." He shrugged slightly, his shoulder lifting and falling in an almost unconcerned gesture. I bit back a growl. I had been the only one because it had been right and no one in the Tacita pack understood what that meant. Their moral compass was broken, it would lead them straight down to the fiery pits of hell we called Mene's brothers if they continued to follow it.

"So? That doesn't make it any less of an issue. What you did was unforgivable." I glared at him and he avoided my gaze. Silence fell and the ticking of the grandfather clock filled the air. I looked away from him, staring at the dusty bookshelf behind his desk. I didn't like the turn the conversation had taken.

"Did you love her?" His voice was low and I snapped my gaze to his. The question caught me off guard and I let out a growl.

"What type of fucking question is that, Alpha? Did I love her? I did what was right. I was the only one who did in this shitty pack. You might be content to sit there with a mask on and pretend that her leaving didn't hurt you for the sake of your precious pack but I'm not." I spat the words out and he looked at me carefully as if studying my features, looking for an answer to the question he asked. I did not love Mary Mary because I did not know her and he didn't need to put those thoughts into my head. Not when she was dead, not when she was gone. Not when the thought of her suffering alone and brought me such pain.

"That wasn't a no." His words slammed into me and I narrowed my eyes before opening my mouth. He had no right to say that shit. The door slammed open, cutting my scathing remark before it could emerge. I snapped my mouth close as I stared at a paled face Beta John. "How many times do I have to tell you to fucking knock?" Alpha Lawrence's voice was filled with venom and Beta John slammed the door closed. He held out his hand before throwing a black ribbon on the desk.

FOURTEEN

“That was found on the porch. It has my name on it, Andrew." Beta John’s voice shook slightly as he stared at the ribbon.

Alpha Lawrence let out a thundering growl at his blatant disrespect. The sound vibrated the air and made the Beta cower. "That is *Alpha Lawrence* to you!" His anger was tangible and Beta John once again pointed to the ribbon. Black for death. I wanted to smirk. Someone had finally had enough of Beta John, it was a pleasant thought. It made my day look brighter for a brief moment.

"There are more important things than that. Someone wants to *kill* me. That is a *black ribbon* with my *name* on it!" His voice held a higher pitch of fear and I watched as he started pacing. He looked scared as he ran his hands through his hair repeatedly. His eyes darted back and forth and I wanted to laugh.

"So?" Alpha Lawrence shrugged before he used a pen and flicked the black ribbon off of his schedule book. I wanted to laugh at the action as Beta John's eyes looked like they were trying to escape his head.

"*So*, what? Someone is *threatening* me. What are you going to do about it?" He stopped pacing and threw out his hands.

I turned my gaze to my Alpha. He was looking at Beta John, his entire demeanour was calm as he watched his Beta make a spectacle of himself. "Nothing." His mouth twitched slightly and I fought hard to keep the smile off of my own face. Beta John was receiving his comeuppance for his sins. He had a juvenile female abused to get back at Alpha Lawrence for his wounded pride. This punishment was long overdue.

"Nothing. You aren't going to do *anything*?" He sounded incredulous and Alpha Lawrence shook his head, turning the page of his book, tapping it with his pen. He scanned the paper, his gaze on it and not on his Beta. I watched him carefully, as I had said before, I did not presume to know what my Alpha was thinking but I knew he enjoyed this.

"Nope." He let out a sigh and scratched something out on the book before writing something down.

I turned my gaze and watched as Beta John's face went red. "*Why*?" He spat the word out and I flicked my gaze to Alpha Lawrence who set his pen down carefully and linked his fingers together before looking at Beta John with a rather cold expression.

"I receive death threats all the time, *beta*. Only, I know who my enemies are and who my allies could be. I suggest you figure out which is which and prepare for who might be coming. If you're truly scared, stay inside for a few days." He waved his hand flippantly and I smirked at the gesture, knowing it would only anger the Beta. Stay inside. It was an insult to the male standing in front of him because only the untrained and weak stayed inside of the house when there was a threat.

"That's all you're going to say? Stay inside for a few days?" Beta John's voice screeched slightly. For a male who was supposed to be a great warrior it was damn near comical.

I lifted a hand and covered my mouth slightly, trying my hardest to hide my amusement. "It's just a ribbon, Beta John. There's nothing about a ribbon to be scared of." I looked at him and his gaze snapped to me.

His eyes narrowed in anger as he saw the smile I was trying so desperately to hide. "Watch your mouth-"

"Shut up, beta. If you are that scared, hangout with the pups for the day or better yet, go to the basement and stay there. No one goes there." There was a strange iciness to Alpha Lawrence's tone that made me want to shiver.

I watched as Beta John flinched under it but he held himself tall and swallowed. "I need you to-"

"I do *not* answer to you, beta. This threat means nothing. It's a ribbon. Just a fucking ribbon." Alpha Lawrence picked it up and froze slightly as he looked at the writing. I watched as a rather small, malicious smile crossed his face. "Oh, you have pissed off the wrong person, John Simmons. Pray that you have everything right with Mene because I cannot, nor will I, save you from who's coming." He locked gaze with the now pale faced Beta and I watched the interaction with interest.

"What?" Beta John's voice was quiet and Alpha Lawrence held the ribbon out, the name facing outwards. I looked at the strong but harsh lettering that spelled out Beta John's name in white.

"This is Jace's writing, John. Even I can't save you from him." The words were icy and I felt my heart beat harshly in my chest. Everyone knew of the prior Alpha of Tacita. The male who had given up his rightful title as Alpha after his mate had been killed in an attack. Many suspected that it had been planned, that Jace was supposed to die and not his mate but something gone wrong with it. Jace Lawrence had been left alive with his son and after he left the title of Alpha to his younger brother he left and no one had seen him since.

"You have to do something!" Beta John sounded frantic and I watched as Alpha Lawrence shook his head, that same smile on his face as he set the ribbon down. Jace Lawrence was a brutal male if rumours were to be believed and the fact his younger brother was refusing to step in to help just further cemented the fact that he wasn't someone to mess with.

"What? What can I do, beta? Jace wants you dead and there is nothing I can do to stop him. What did you do to piss him off? What did he find out? He has marked you for death and there's nothing you or I, or anyone, can do to stop it." A firm note of finality was in his tone and the smile disappeared. He was firm because everyone knew that what Jace Lawrence wanted, he got. If he wanted Beta John dead, there was nothing anyone could do to stop it.

"Put more warriors out, double the patrols. Do *something*!" John's arms waved wildly and I immediately thought of the ridiculous tube males that flailed around outside of mundane car dealerships. I bit back a laugh at the mental image and pressed my lips together tightly to prevent it from escaping.

"We're stretched thin as it is, beta. There's nothing we can do. We can hope that he comes in easy and quietly. *You* can hope he will be able to listen to reason. I will not fight my brother for you because he *will* kill me." His eyes were cold and I could see his anger at the pursuance of the subject. To him the subject was closed but Beta John wasn't listening. Even I knew better than to push his patience. I could insult him and ignore him but I did not push on a subject he was unwilling to discuss.

John narrowed his eyes. "You-"

Alpha Lawrence slammed his hands down on the desk with a loud bang and stood up. His rage seemed to fill the room and his brown eyes were icy. "I'm not willing to die for the male who gave Ingrid the order to take my daughter and convince her to be an omega! Take you punishment for the wrong you did my brother because you will have *no* help from me." He was trembling with rage and I looked at Beta John who opened and closed his mouth rapidly in shock.

"I suggest you hide with the omegas. No one will think to look for you there." My tone was mocking and he glanced at me before he snapped his mouth shut. He looked between me and Alpha Lawrence slowly. He had finally realized he had no allies in the room. It was left to be found if those that were in the room were also his enemies.

"You don't know what happened." His voice trembled with anger and Alpha Lawrence growled low in his throat.

"I know enough, Beta John. Now get the fuck out of my office." At his words John rushed out, slamming the door behind him. The walls rattled from the force of it and I let out a chuckle.

"That takes care of that problem. Now I don't have to deal with him." I looked over at my Alpha and he shook his head, a frown etched onto his face. I rolled my eyes before letting my head fall back to stare at the ceiling.

"Jace isn't killing him for the beta position. You can have it after he's dead." He sounded expectant, like he wanted me to enjoy the offer he was giving me but he and I both knew I would never take the position.

I hated this pack and putting me in a position of power would only enable me to abuse that power to make them suffer. And I *would* make them suffer. "I don't want it." I shrugged and I knew he was frustrated. I was the only person he could trust and I did not want him to trust me with that. He was surrounded by false friends and he needed me, which was the only reason I stayed.

"I'm ordering you to take it." He sounded almost petulant and I rolled my eyes, following the cracks in the ceiling with my gaze. He could not order me to take a position I did not want, especially the Beta one.

"You can't do that." I lifted my head and stared at him, narrowing my eyes slightly. He looked lost. "You said your brother was coming for him. Ask him that the fuck happened that day. Ask him why he wasn't there." I watched as anger slipped through his mask and he nodded before I let out a groan and sat in the chair properly. I rubbed at my face, scratching at my slight beard as I watched him slowly nod again.

"You're right. I need to know why he did it, why he didn't save her." His voice cracked on the last word and I stood up and stretched. With his mind on his brother and away from me taking the Beta position I was more than happy to leave him to his thoughts.

"I have patrols to run. I'll be back in several hours. Mind-link me when your brother gets here so I can watch him rip Beta John apart." I moved towards the door and Alpha Lawrence coughed slightly and I looked over my shoulder. He had a rather sad expression on his face.

"You never answered my question, Bennett, but I'm going to say this. If you loved her then you're a better male than any one of them in this pack. If you loved her enough to try and stop her, then you're more of a male than me." He said it softly and I couldn't take the look in his eyes or what he said. I left the room quickly before I could say something stupid. I hated that he had put the thought into my head, I hated how it was all I could now think about. I preferred it when he was asking me to be beta because it didn't make my heart clench with pain. I shook the thought away and focused on his previous words.

Anyone else would have been ecstatic that their Alpha wanted them to take the position but I knew the added authority would only make it harder to go rogue. He may have thought I wouldn't do it but I had made my mind up two years ago when I watched his daughter trudge bare foot through the snow. I wanted no part in a pack that did that to one of their own, that did that to *her*.

My wolf was pacing and restless. I rolled my shoulders and forced him to wait while I walked down the stairs and out the front door. The winter air was icy as I slowly stripped off my clothes and put them in a gunny sack I had grabbed from the pile by the door. I set it down and allowed the shift to move through me. I forced myself to shift slowly, my bones, snapped and shifted painfully under my skin until I was standing on four legs. I knew that if I allowed the shift to happen faster it wouldn't have been painful but I liked the pain. I embraced it because it reminded me I was alive. I shook out my fur and grabbed the gunny sack in my mouth and ran towards the tree line.

It didn't take me long to reach the edge of the trees and I moved to my usual tree and stashed the sack in the hollow under the roots. Every shifter had their own special cache for patrol and there were hundreds of regular pack ones hidden throughout the territory in case of emergencies. I shook again before I lowered my nose and breathed in deeply. My nose took in the regular scents of the forest and I started to search for abnormal scents in the air.

I allowed my wolf a bit more control as we searched large swaths of the forest. After the time I spent searching for Mary Mary, I knew the forest better than most of the pack members. I always made a large curving zig-zag pattern at the start of my patrol. It drove Beta John and his son, Lucas, crazy. They called it a waste of time but I knew it helped me get the right scents into my nose and helped my wolf become more attuned to his surroundings.

I reached the patrol meeting spot and hunkered down under a bush. If I remembered correctly, I had to deal with Lucas and several of his lackeys for patrol. They were late or was it I was early? I looked up at the sky and noticed a faint tinge of pink on the horizon. I was early.

After nearly half an hour I could hear wolves approaching and I allowed my wolf to sink further into the shadows. They were noisy, not even attempting to hide their approach. If I had been a rogue I would have been gone before they could have scented me. I had positioned myself downwind, a habit I had picked up from my wolf's instincts, they never would have been able to scent me. I could have taken down two or three of them before they got over their shock at a surprise attack. It made me want to laugh.

They were useless.

I watched as four wolves came into the small clearing, they were yipping at one another like pups and I resisted the urge to growl at their childish behaviour. That could be saved for other times. It was a patrol, a shifter needed to be on-guard at all times. Vigilant of their surroundings and always checking the air. A dark furred wolf lifted its head and let out a small growl. Lucas had noticed my supposed absence.

Bennett, it's time for patrol. Where are you? You're late. His voice was borderline aggressive in my head and I held back my wolf from growling at him. It was disrespectful to blame me for his apparent lack of brain cells. I waited several moments before sniffing the air slightly.

It's not my fault you're too distracted to notice where I am. I've been here out here for nearly forty-five minutes. I slid silently from my spot and the wolves were immediately on guard as if my sudden appearance had startled them. They relaxed slightly as I stretched and shook my head, letting the snow fall off of my fur. *Stupid children, playing when they should be working. You're going to get yourselves killed.* I ignored the raised hackles and bared teeth that appeared at my words.

Show some respect. Lucas lifted his head, trying to make his wolf appear more dominant but it made him look like a pup trying his hardest to impress a female. We were the same height but I had more bulk and he knew it.

You're not my superior, Lucas. As I'm the top warrior, that technically makes me the superior one right now. Unless you want to challenge me to take the position? I tilted my head as I sat on my haunches. I gave him a wolfy grin and I could see the want in him. He wanted to challenge me, he wanted to take the position as top warrior.

Maybe I will. He lowered down, his gaze unwavering on me as he moved back and forth, trying to entice me to attack. I waited patiently for a few brief moments before I could feel Alpha Lawrence open the pack wide mind-link.

Lucas Simmons, I do not want to go out there and tear Bennett off of your dead corpse. Do your fucking job and ignore the smart ass. Bennett, stop goading him on and ignore the immature dipshit. I don't need you taking out another patrol member. Beta John has his panties in a twist already. If he twists them anymore he's going to go full on operatic soprano on me. His words were two parts filled with authority, one part exasperated, and another part amused. I let my tongue hang out as the grin on my face grew wider. I watched as Lucas snarled at the insult and a deathly silence filled our heads. *Did you just snarl at me?* The words were low and dangerous and I laid down, the grin still firmly on my face. I rested my head on my paws and waited.

Bennett, did Lucas just fucking snarl at me, his ***Alpha****?* He was expecting a reply and I tilted my head slightly, looking at Lucas. He was cowering and I jumped to my feet. I knew where this was heading and so did the rest of the patrol.

I would enjoy this. I watched as the other three wolves backed away, their tails between their legs as they whimpered slightly. *Yes, sir.* I watched as Lucas went down to his belly and whimpered. A submissive gesture that I knew Alpha Lawrence would ignore. The disrespect had been done and he would need to firm up his position as Alpha with Lucas.

Teach him a lesson. The words were said almost lightly but filled with a strong order and I immediately let my hackles raise and my teeth bare in a threatening growl. As Alpha Lawrence was not here to punish Lucas for his disrespect I was chosen. I was *always* chosen and I enjoyed *every* instance of it.

With pleasure, Alpha Lawrence. I jumped on the smaller dark wolf and grabbed the back of his neck in my mouth, shaking him vigorously. He yelped as my teeth broke skin but I ignored it as I threw him to the side before jumping on him again. He scrambled to get away as I snarled and growled before grabbing at his front leg and biting down, forcing him onto his side. He snapped at my face frantically, trying to get me to release his leg but it only made me bite down harder. I knew that if I increased the pressure anymore his leg bone would snap like a twig.

Don't break any of his bones. There was a warning in Alpha Lawrence's voice and I released Lucas's leg before backing up and charging at him. He scrambled to his feet, trying to get away but his wounded leg made him slow. I slammed into him with enough force to send him tumbling, he yelped in pain at the action. I was on him once more, the snarling growls I let out were nearly deafening as I finally managed to pin him on his back.

I bit down on his throat, shaking him violently as he yelped, trying to claw at my belly with his back legs. He let out a high pitched whine before finally submitting. He went limp and I held him in that position for a moment longer, waiting. *Lucas, next time you disrespect me, you won't have to worry about Bennett enforcing the punishment because I will go out there and beat you bloody myself.* There was a dangerous and deadly edge to his voice and I bit down a bit more on Lucas's throat, enjoying the pain filled whine he let out before I released him. I snarled in his face as he tried to get up before I moved away. He whimpered and bared his throat to me as I stepped over his quivering form.

I didn't look back at him as I took off for my usual patrol area. I always patrolled the same five miles of the outer edge of the territory. It was next to one of the neutral highways rogues and other packs used to move from place to place. It was the only edge of our territory that was close to one. I patrolled it because from my patrol route I could plan my eventual escape from the pack. I knew where to go, which territories to stay away from and how far I would need to run every day to stay alive. All I needed to do was stay a step ahead of the people they would send after me.

I sniffed the air, something was off and it left me feeling uneasy as I started my patrol run. There weren't any tracks or any new scents but the uneasy feeling wouldn't leave me alone. *Alpha, I haven't scented anything but something has me on edge. Watch yourself.* I allowed my wolf to dash from tree to tree, taking in scents and information. I was missing something, I couldn't put my finger on it but it was there. I wasn't sure if Alpha Lawrence was in any danger but I needed to warn him anyway. I didn't wish for him to be hurt because Beta John would take his place and that would be a nightmare waiting to happen.

Thank you. I have the same feeling. Could just be my brother's message but I want you to watch yourself too. Look at the neutral territory as well. See if you can see anything out of place but don't leave the territory. I need you close in case anything happens. He closed the connection and I understood what he meant. He needed me to be close enough to protect his back if shit hit the fan. As I was the only one he trusted, he needed to keep me where I could reach him if anything happened. I moved closer to the edge of the territory, looking at the neutral highway. I couldn't see anything out of place so I continued to do my run.

Nearly an hour and a half later and I still had yet to relax. Something had me on edge and I scented the air back where I started my patrol run and I froze. There were no scents as if something had come and taken them all away. I slowly moved ten feet to the left and sniffed, the normal scents were there and when I moved back to my original position they were all gone. My wolf was immediately tense as I figured out the exact dimensions of the scent blind spot.

It was eight feet across and it lead straight towards the pack house. I knew there were no scents but the entire thing reeked of magic. I knew of witching cloaks, a cloak that had been charmed to remove the scent of the wearer by an older white witch. From how wide the path was it would have had to been nearly half a dozen people, if not more, that had moved towards the pack house. I was immediately on high alert.

Alpha Lawrence, we have intruders. I can't scent them but they're here. I sniffed at the ground, following the scentless trail. I was trying to watch my back as I tried to find any scent possible to identify the intruders I knew were on the territory.

Okay. Thank you, Bennett. I'll have to punish Lucas and the others for missing them. This is why I like you on patrol. He shut the connection down and I focused my entire attention on watching my surroundings as I followed the wide path. I ran forwards a good fifty feet before sniffing the air once more.

I froze in place. The faint scent of flowers and honey teased my nose. I sneezed, trying to shake the phantom scent from my snout. I put my nose to the ground but the scent had disappeared. I felt suddenly apprehensive as I moved forward. I didn't know why I suddenly remembering her scent. I moved forward another ten feet when the faint scent appeared again, just a slight teasing of a scent but it made my heart race. I lowered my nose but the scent wasn't on the ground, it was if it floated in the air. I followed the quickly fading scent before it disappeared quickly.

Mary Mary was caught unwary.

I shook the words from my head as I searched for the scent again. I needed to find her scent. I ignored how similar this was to my nightmare.

But where did her body go?

I ignored the wariness I felt as I moved further down the wide trail before I caught a whiff of her scent. I followed it like a wolf possessed before I abruptly stopped once more as the trail ended.

With the icy snow and the harsh winds that blow.

I darted my eyes back and forth, my entire body stilling. I waited for an ambush and when I couldn't sense one I leapt forward. My feet pounded against the earth as I tried my hardest to catch the faint scent. I hadn't smelled her scent in over a year and I wondered why it was appearing now. She was haunting me even while awake and I hated how the guilt ate at me.

Now no one will ever know.

I caught the faintest whiff of it before it was gone, the brisk winter breeze blowing it away almost cruelly. The wild's words came from around me but I wondered if it was just inside of my head as I dashed forward, my heart was pounding against my rib cage as I caught small part of it that the wind hadn't taken. They were so small that a wolf that hadn't known the scent of the territory would have missed them completely.

You can search and you can look, whelp, but you'll never find what you seek.

The scent trailed disappeared completely and after several minutes of frantically searching I found myself nearing the edge of the forest. I froze, my heart clenching in my chest. Why was my mind playing tricks on me? Had I not been punished enough?

You will never find her.

The words echoed in my head with a cruel and cold laugh as I let out a whine. I was going crazy. I couldn't handle the nightmares or the dreams. I knew it was the house, I knew it was the forest. They reminded me of her. Everything I did brought her to my mind and I was going crazy. I needed to leave. I needed to get out.

Bennett, I need you right now. So cut the panic shit out. Alpha Lawrence's voice was sharp with apprehension and I shook myself out of my slight panic. He did not sound like himself as he said it and I quickly moved to my tree and shifted. I allowed the painful shifting to focus my mind, to keep the panic from getting worse. I yanked the sack out from its hiding place and started to pull my clothes on. The snow was icy underneath my feet and I cursed as I slipped my boots on, not bothering with my socks. *Bennett. Now.* There was a frantic tone in his voice and I cursed again as I pulled my button up shirt on.

I started quickly walking across the field of snow that lay in front of the pack house. I kept my gaze down as I did up the buttons before rolling the sleeves up to my elbows. The wind nipped at my bare skin but I ignored it as I came closer to the house.

I looked up and slowed down when I saw a small figure sitting curled up on the wide steps. I drew closer and I frowned as I realized they were wearing a cloak. The memory of the wide trail of missing scents came to mind and I moved closer. I stopped a good twenty feet from them when the wind pushed against my back. I bit back an oath as the person stiffened, their head snapping up at my scent. The air left my lungs in a whoosh as beautiful grey eyes stared at me from an ethereal, almost impish face.

The eyes were wide with surprise before they turned to curiosity and I felt like I couldn't breathe. I felt like my world wasn't real because the person staring at me had died two years ago. She had died and so there was no way she was standing on that same porch she had stood on two years before. I could feel the intense pull towards her and I watched as she slowly stood up and moved down the two steps before a bare foot peeked out from beneath the cloak.

It hovered over the white snow for a moment and I shook my head. "*Don't.*" My voice was strangled as I stared at her. Even if it wasn't real I would not let her cross the snow barefoot. Not again. Not for me. I looked at her beautiful face and she looked puzzled for a moment before I moved closer to her, my movements were jerky. I wasn't sure if she had come back to haunt me once more or if she was a hallucination that my mind had constructed from my guilt.

I stopped as my boots hit the front of the bottom step. She was small, even standing on the bottom step she had to look up at me slightly. I searched her gaze trying to figure out if she was real. Her grey eyes were innocent and held a warmth to them and I scanned her face, taking in her high cheek bones and the almond shape of her eyes. I watched as her soft and full lips pulled into a small smile. I couldn't keep my gaze off of the fullness of her mouth. I felt my breathing increase and the fog from our breath mingled in the air between us. There was no way she was real. She couldn't be because I couldn't let go of my guilt that easy. This was another dream or nightmare, I couldn't tell at the moment but I knew I would wake up and she would be gone.

Alpha Lawrence's question slid into my mind. '*Did you love her?*' as I looked down at her sweet, innocent face I found the answer. I had always known it but I hadn't allowed it to come forward because of the pain it would cause.

Did I love the female I had tried to make smile with every ounce of my being after I met her?

Did I love my Alpha's daughter in those sparse moments I had where I brought her objects of comfort?

Did I love the small female who I had watched cross the snow in bare feet and nothing but a nightgown?

Did I love the female I had mourned for so long and cherished my memories of?

Did I love the omega who had been called Mary Mary?
Yes.
Yes, I did.

FIFTEEN

I felt my heart frantically beat against my rib cage as he stared at me. His blue eyes were filled with disbelief that warred with hope and longing. Their intensity caught me and I couldn't look away. He looked tired, a thick coating of stubble covered his jaw was a testament to that. His dark brown hair was unruly and longer than what may have been fashionable but to me he looked almost wild. He was chillingly handsome, something I hadn't noticed before I had been banished. He made my mouth go dry at my stark need for him. I needed him more than I needed to eat, more than I needed to sleep. I needed him more than I needed to breathe.

Without warning he lifted a hand and pressed it against my cheek, brushing my cheekbone with his thumb. I shivered at how cold it was but his rough skin against my cheek sent fire through my veins, chasing away any coldness his hand had caused. I watched as he brought his face closer before he pressed his lips to mine, his stubble scratched my cheeks lightly. The heat of the small kiss simmered under my skin and I let my eyes close before leaning into him. He pulled back slowly and I gave a small whimper at the loss of contact.

Amber had been right. I *had* left something very important. I could not imagine a life without his kiss. I couldn't imagine a life without his touch. I let my eyes flick back up to his right as all confusion and disbelief disappeared from his gaze. It was as if he had believed me to be an apparition and that small kiss had shown him he was truly in reality.

I felt my breath hitch in my chest as the hand on my cheek slid to the back of my head, his fingers tangling in my hair. Heat flooded his gaze before he brought his face down quickly and claimed my mouth for another kiss. The softness from the first kiss was gone, replaced with a fiery need that had me reaching up and grasping the collar of his shirt in my hands. I went up to my tiptoes to press my lips harder against his. A strong hand grasped my waist, pulling me closer as he slanted his mouth over mine.

I felt a faint growl of triumph rumbling through his chest as I let out a small whimper of need. I felt my need for him so sharply it was almost bordering on painful. My blue eyed male named Bennett was the hero of my story, he was my happily ever after. He had crawled into my chest and made me complete. He had given me the final piece to my puzzle. His stubble scratched at me once more as he shifted his mouth over mine again. I let myself lean against him with a sigh before he broke the kiss abruptly. My eyes snapped open and I felt myself breathing heavily. I swayed slightly, my knees felt weak.

"I'm sorry." The words were slightly pained and I let his collar go as he yanked his hands back from my waist and hair. I pressed the tips of my fingers to my lips, still feeling his pressed against mine. They tingled slightly and I looked from his chest up to his face. My face flushed heavily and I wondered for a brief moment if steam curled off of them they were so warm.

"Why?" I was confused. He kissed me like I was the only person in his world and then he apologized for it. Mates did not have to apologize for a mere kiss. I had quite enjoyed the ones he gave me, both of them.

"I shouldn't have done that. You don't need me to force myself on you. Not like that, I mean you just got back and-" He looked at a loss for words as he ran a hand through his hair in agitation. He looked lost and confused and I let my hand drop from my mouth. I shrugged. I was flattered he wanted to protect my supposed virtue but his kiss made me forget where we currently were and that was something I had needed greatly.

"That is what mates do, is it not?" I tried not to roll my shoulders forward, the house behind me felt like a lurking monster that wanted nothing more than to eat me alive. The others had gone inside and I refused to join them. My wolf had felt wary and restless just like I had at the thought of entering the place of all those memories.

"Well, yes but you just got back and we barely know each other. It doesn't seem right to just take a kiss from you, no matter how much I would like to do just that." His gaze dropped to my mouth. I could feel his want to kiss me again and I resisted the urge to bite at my lip. I darted my eyes back and forth slightly, the habit was one I couldn't break. I was trying to find the right words to say something, anything to put him at ease but his kiss still had my brain slightly muddled.

"I did not mind. It helped me forget where we are, even if it was just for a moment." I watched as his eyes went suddenly steely and hard and I shivered at the change as he looked over my shoulder to the house behind me. I focused on my breathing, the ever familiar trick Amber had taught me to help keep the panic at bay. I backed up several steps and sat down in my previous position. I tapped the step two below mine with a barefoot. "Sit." I lifted my feet to the step above that and I was surprised that he listened. He leaned his back against the railing and sat lengthwise on the step, letting one of his legs lay straight and the other to rest on the snow covered ground.

I carefully set my cold feet in his lap before leaning over and grabbing his hand, placing it on them. The warmth was nice and I felt a small smile cross my face as I grabbed his other arm and dragged it across my knees, placing it so I could lay my arm across it. I leaned my head against the railing and closed my eyes. I could feel his eyes on me and I tried my hardest to ignore him as I slowly began to draw a swirl pattern on his forearm with my fingertip. The habit was one I had gotten from Collin. He slowly started to rub my feet with his other hand and I let out a sigh of contentment.

"Where are your shoes?" His voice was rough and sinuous and I resisted the urge to shudder as the sound of it skittered across my skin almost indecently. It should have been a crime to sound that rugged and masculine. It suited him though. When I had taken my walk of banishment, he had looked like a young male just barely out of his teens. Now he was a strong, rugged, almost wild looking male that made my heart beat fast in my chest and my knees grow weak.

"I didn't wear any." I cracked my eyes open and blushed when I realized he was staring at me. His blue eyes made my heart thump nearly painfully in my chest. It wasn't an unpleasant feeling, it was just strange.

"You walked through the snow barefoot to come back *here*?" He sounded upset at the thought and I felt another slow smile cross my face at his hidden worry and slight anger. I shook my head, the smile growing wider. Collin would have teased me mercilessly about my dimples if he had seen it.

"No." I glanced over my shoulder, I couldn't really feel Uncle Jace through the pack link and it worried me slightly. "I just smiled and Uncle Jace carried me." I turned back to look at my mate and he was staring at my feet. He looked incredibly pensive as he stroked my instep with his thumb. He seemed to be a sombre type of person and I wasn't sure about how to feel about it.

"I'm afraid that if I blink I'll wake up and you'll be gone." He turned his gaze to mine and I was hit with the sheer longing and pain in his eyes. I let out a small sound of protest before I leaned forward and touched his cheek. I liked the feeling of his stubble scratching against my palm. I brushed my thumb over his lips, my heart pounding before I leaned forward and kissed him gently. His hand left my feet to immediately cup my jaw. It was a soft kiss, just like the first one he had given me.

I wanted him to realize that I was truly with him before I reluctantly pulled back, staring into his vivid eyes. "Please do not think like that." I leaned into his palm, my eyes going half lidded with pleasure at his touch as I let my hand drop from his cheek. "Not having you beside me would cause some severe panic at the moment." I let out a heavy sigh and could feel him stiffen slightly. I opened my eyes as his hand dropped from my face. He was mind-linking someone.

Mari, please come inside where it's warm. Uncle Jace's voice brought me relief that he was okay. The others had gone on a hunt for Beta John, who apparently did not want to be found, if my father was to be believed. I had no reason to doubt him but I knew Uncle Jace still had reservations about him.

Okay, Uncle. I removed my feet from Bennett's hand. He watched me silently, his expression slightly closed off. I stood on the step above where he was sitting and held out my hands for him to take. "It's Bennett right?" I waved my hands slightly and he gave a small smile before enveloping my small hands in his larger ones, letting me help him to his feet. He didn't need the help but I was happy that he let me pretend.

"Bennett Aldridge." He was close to me, his chest brushing mine and I swallowed before looking up at him. His gaze was soft and slightly sad, I felt a feeling of empathy spike through me. "You've haunted me for a very long time, over seven hundred days. You have no idea what it means to have you here. I thought you were lost forever." The words were softer than his gaze and I bit my lip, tears blurring my eyes before I slowly wrapped my arms around him and buried my face into his neck. His large arms wrapped around me in a tender embrace.

I fought back the tears, I didn't want to cry but he had said it so sweetly. He had counted the days since I had been banished. I had meant that much to him and I hadn't even realized it. I could feel his heart beating in his chest and I grasped the back of his shirt in my hands, trying to get closer to him. He was my hero, my knight in shining armour and I was terribly sorry that he had to suffer with me gone.

"I'm sorry, Bennett." I whispered the word and he shushed me gently, his arms tightening around me slightly. I didn't know what it was about his embrace but I found myself relaxing against him completely.

"Never be sorry. I would rather suffer without you for a hundred thousand days than to have had you suffering in this pack next to me for even one." He kissed my head, even though the cloak was in the way I could feel the heat of it. I shivered slightly before I pulled back to look up at him. His eyes were painted with a stark truth and I inhaled sharply at it. I started shivering and his hand rubbed at my back slightly, as if trying to warm me up.

"Uncle Jace has requested I go inside." I hated to hear the nervous quiver in my voice and Bennett let his arms drop from around me before he grabbed my hand. I looked at how he linked his fingers through mine. I shivered slightly at the action, his hand felt right against mine as heat curled through my veins once more.

"I'll be right beside you. I won't let anything hurt you, Maricella. I promise." There was a protective edge to his voice and it lingered in his eyes. They showed a swift need for retribution for anyone who would dare to hurt me. The thought of having him beside me as I made the daunting trip inside of the house that held such terrible and black memories was highly comforting.

"Okay, Bennett." I looked up at him and I watched as the corners of his mouth twitched upward slightly. It looked almost strange despite how it made my heart jump. He didn't smile often, I could tell. He took the lead and walked up the porch stairs. I followed him slowly as he led me across the familiar wooden porch and to the large front door. He pushed it open and I felt my breathing increase slightly as he stepped inside. I froze in the doorway, unable to step forward with the panic rising up.

Bennett squeezed my hand and looked over his shoulder. "I'm *right* here." His low words and his blue eyes gave me the courage I needed to step into the slightly dark interior of the front hallway. I stepped closer to him, hovering behind him. I didn't want to be scared but the past lingered in these halls. This was a big step for my progress. Theoretically, going back to the place where it all started would help me heal from the memories. It was just a house. It was just a pack, it wasn't something to be scared of.

"Mari, you really need to-" Angie's voice stopped abruptly and I slowly stepped around Bennett's wide back to stand at his side. I stayed close to him, my side touching his but he didn't seem to mind. Angie was staring at him in surprise and when she saw me her mouth dropped open. "Oh." There was a long pause as she looked between the two of us. I could see her mind working and I could feel Bennett's sudden tension. "*Ohhh*?" She looked at me carefully and I felt a shy smile flit across my face before I looked up at him with a nod.

"Oh, well. This is surprising. He's... *big*." She looked him up and down with wide eyes and I bit my lip to keep from laughing.

I leaned my head against his arm. "Bennett, this is Angie, a member of Uncle Jace's pack and a friend." I looked up at him as he shifted his gaze to me before looking back at Angie, he relaxed slightly. He made no move to greet her but he no longer held a quiet and watchful hostility.

"Well are you going to say hello?" She frowned slightly before her face brightened. "Are you mute? Is he mute? Oh goddess that would be fucking awesome. You would never have to listen to him nag you all the time. Be like a permanent off switch. Mene, I wished Seamus had one of those. He just nags me all the time. Just nag, nag, nag, nag, nag. All the fucking time. Anyway, I'm jealous of your *big* mute mate." She winked at me and I felt my face flush with embarrassment.

"You don't know me nor do you trust me. I can tell from how you're looking at me but if we don't get Mari up to the office, I just know Jace is going to flip a fucking cog. He's a little... restless." She looked almost worried and I winced before moving forward, away from Bennett slightly. His hand tightened on mine a fraction, as if he were wary of letting me go. If Uncle Jace was restless, that meant he was on the edge of snapping and it was never good when he snapped.

"Is it bad?" I watched as she grimaced before looking over her shoulder towards the stairs.

"This is worse than when Jay accidentally tripped you down the stairs." She looked at me with worried eyes and I felt my face fall. That had been brutal. Jay had to hide in the woods with Victor for nearly three weeks before Uncle Jace had cooled down enough that he could come inside. If it was worse than that then I wasn't sure if I even wanted to walk in on it.

"Oh." I worried my bottom lip with my teeth and Bennett squeezed my hand in reassurance. He was with me, he promised to be with me every step of the way. I felt comforted just by his presence and Angie looked tense.

"Yah, they're getting ready to murder each other. The office is going to look like an R rated movie if you don't hurry. Neither of them are really talking and neither are really listening. Stupid pricks, the both of them. Too similar for their own good." She muttered the last three sentences out under her breath before she scowled. "We still haven't found that fucking beta. I need to go. Seamus is asking me where I am. You need to get up there." She gave me a meaningful look before she moved into the room just off the hallway. I let Bennett's hand go and slowly pushed back my hood and unclasped the cloak. I could see the table where the other had placed theirs and I moved over to it, my feet moving silently over the wooden floor. I set it down on the others gently.

I couldn't feel Bennett behind me and I looked over my shoulder in alarm. He was staring at me with an unreadable expression but it held a fair amount of heat that made me blush. I slowly turned around, biting the inside of my lip as I fisted my hand in the fabric of my dress's skirt. It was a simple blue, it was one of my more plain ones but he was looking at me like I was the most precious thing he had ever seen. I felt my cheeks tinge pink slightly as he moved closer to me. His bulk should have been intimidating but all it brought was heat and comfort.

"You're incredibly beautiful, Maricella." He brushed some curls away from my face and I felt my mouth go dry at the sound of my name coming from his mouth. "I never thought in a million years that you could stand in front of me and be mine." He brushed his hand against my cheek and a loud crashing sound rattled the walls and the ceiling slightly.

I snapped my gaze to the stairs and with my heart in my throat I bolted. "Uncle Jace!" I couldn't help the worry that thickly coated my voice as I ran to the second floor. Another hard sounding bang happened that caused my heart to race wildly in my chest. "Dad!" I threw open the office door and felt my breath hitch in my throat as the male who raised me straddled Uncle Jace and pulled his arm back and slammed his fist into my uncle's face. I froze completely at the amount of anger and violence that they were both exhibiting.

I couldn't move as memories of similar violence entered my head. Older pack members punching my stomach and chest, anger and disgust in their eyes as I cried from the pain and begged them to stop. I felt my chest tighten and I grasped the fabric of my dress in my hands and started to tremble. I could feel Bennett behind me in the doorway right as Uncle Jace swung at my father.

"Hey!" Bennett's shout was a harsh sound as he moved around me and jumped into the fray. I felt my heart jump into my throat as he grabbed the back of my father's shirt and yanked him off of Uncle Jace. "What the fuck is wrong with you?" His voice was practically a growl and I wondered for a brief moment about the blatant disrespect he had just shown his Alpha before I watched Uncle Jace quickly get to his feet. I took a small step backwards. He was so *angry*.

"This bastard! This bastard has the audacity to stand there and give *me* shit after what he did?" The comforting timbre of my father's voice held violence and I tried to force myself from panicking but it was hard. I was stuck with the memories and I felt my bottom lip tremble. Amber had said I would be okay but watching the two males that I cared deeply for, try and kill each other was almost more than I could bear. Bennett shoved my father away before holding his arm out as if trying to stop Uncle Jace from moving forward.

"After what *I* did? What about what you did, you son of a bitch?" Uncle Jace's green eyes were murderous as he wiped at his bloody nose. I felt my hands start to shake violently as I stared at the startling red. "A fucking *omega*, Andrew! Your own fucking daughter!" There was so much hate flying through the air and I couldn't stop the fearful trembling of my limbs. I saw black spots swirling in my vision as it seemed to narrow in on the blood. I had bled too. Blood out of my nose, out of the wounds on my back and legs, and blood that I coughed up. So much red.

"Fucking stop it! Maricella, sweet one, *breathe.*" Bennett's voice cut through the dark haze surrounding me and I sucked in a deep, rasping gasp of air. The darkness instantly vanished from my vision as I started to hyperventilate. I had forgotten how to breathe in my panic.

"Shit! Mari, look at me." Uncle Jace's voice was frantic and I glanced at him, shuddering at the blood that was smeared under his nose and partly across his cheek. A haze of panic had covered everything. I wasn't sure who was safe.

He took a step forward and I took several small ones backwards. "Fuck! This is all your fault, dipshit!" His eyes narrowed dangerously at my father and I flicked my gaze to the male who raised me. His face was pale as he stared at me.

"Mary Mary?" His voice was choked and I tried to stop my chest from heaving out rapid breaths but it wasn't listening. "Is that you, sweetheart?" He took several steps before Bennett yanked him backwards almost roughly. There was a loud growl that I wanted to cover my ears at. I felt a sudden urge to bolt as I watched my father's face twist with anger. I wasn't really sure where I was, the past and present merged to the point I was confused as to what was going on. All I could feel was anger and hatred. All I could hear were loud words and harsh language and I was terrified.

"Shut the *fuck* up, Alpha. You're scaring her. Both of you." Bennett let him go before pushing past him and moving towards me. I skittered backward and he held his hands out slowly. "Shhhh, it's okay. It's okay." His voice was low and filled with comfort and I locked my gaze with his. My heart pounded frantically against my rib cage and I took a small, shaky step backwards as he continued to move towards me, murmuring low words of comfort.

I broke our gaze and darted my eyes back and forth, looking for an escape as I realized he had moved closer to me. He shushed me softly before he grasped my arms gently, cutting off any escape I would have made. I let out a large shuddering breath as he finally broke through the panicky haze in my mind. I looked up at him, my entire form shaking. Tears filled my eyes and his blue eyes were soft as he led me towards the couch and sat me down.

"Breathe, in and out." He murmured it as he sat on the coffee table in front of me. I did as he instructed, taking in deep breaths before letting them out slowly. He held my gaze as his hands moved to grasp mine. His touch was comforting and the fear retreated. He was with me, nothing would happen to me while he was there. "There we are. Okay, do you know where you are?" His voice was soothing and I gave a shaky nod as I continued to take exaggerated breaths in and out.

"Then you know that those two would never hurt you. There's no reason to be afraid of them, Mary Mary. There's no reason to be afraid because I'm right here with you." He spoke low as he leaned forward and pressed his lips to my forehead. I leaned into the contact before pulling my hands from his and wrapping my arms around his neck. I closed my eyes and he shifted so that his cheek was pressed to the top of my head. "I will always be right with you." He said it so softly I almost had troubles hearing it.

"So you didn't leave her in the forest?" My father's voice was still slightly angry but as Bennett wrapped his arms around me loosely, I wasn't afraid. No one would hurt me. I was safe, I was safe.

"What? Fuck no! She's family despite how I feel towards you at the moment." Uncle Jace sounded just as angry and rational thought came back to me slowly. I had known they would have this discussion but I should have known it would probably come to blows. They were both too stubborn and pig-headed to do anything with civility.

"What was that?" My father sounded slightly worried and I shifted my head so that my forehead was pressed to Bennett's neck, it was comforting to feel his pulse dancing underneath his skin.

"Panic attack mixed in with a heightened flight or fight reflex. Amber warned me it might happen. I just kind of figured it wouldn't be triggered by our little fight." At his words I could almost picture Uncle Jace shrugging. Nothing truly fazed him for long. He had a short fuse sometimes but it always blew over just as quickly.

"Our fight? You swung at me first, Jace." There was agitation in my father's voice and Bennett rubbed my back gently. I let out a sigh, the panic finally subsiding. I didn't want to leave his embrace but I knew the reality of my arguing relatives would intrude upon the moment.

"Because you're a fucking idiot that deserves to get hit and are we just going to stand here and ignore *that*?" Uncle Jace was agitated and I tried to ignore him but Bennett slowly pulled his arms from around me. I pulled away from him and he looked me over silently. He brushed a lock of hair from my face and placed it behind my ear. I shivered at the action and took in a few more shuddering breaths.

It was just a house, it was just a pack but I should have known I wouldn't just be okay with coming back here. I would have some setbacks because it was only natural. I had triggers and this house was one giant trigger for me. Bennett stroked my cheek with the back of his hand and I closed my eyes, letting out a heavy sigh, slumping forwards slightly.

"Ignore what? The fact my boy Bennett is getting handsy with my daughter? Yah, we are." At his words I felt my face grow slightly pink. Bennett's mouth twitched but he frowned slightly before he reached up and brushed a stray tear away. I hadn't realized it had fallen and I reached up to wipe at my eyes. I looked at my lap, feeling suddenly shy. I hadn't meant to have a full blown panic attack in front of Bennett. I wasn't sure what he now thought of me.

"No we fucking aren't. Shit stain, stop fucking touching her." Uncle Jace's voice went from agitated to angry and I closed my eyes, breathing in slowly. Bennett didn't react to the insult or the words as he took one of my hands and brushed his thumb over the back of it gently. He seemed entirely focused on me, on making sure I was alright.

"Jace, leave it alone." There was a warning note in my father's voice that I knew Uncle Jace would ignore. Being the firstborn, Uncle Jace listened to very few people when he became irrational. It was part of his charm, as Amber said, although she usually said it very sarcastically.

"He's from this pa-"

"He's the only one I would consider even letting *look* at Maricella. Feel lucky it's him. I'm not happy about it but I know when to pick my battles." There was a slight note of frustration in my father's voice and I opened my eyes to look up at Bennett, he was staring over the back of the couch to the two arguing. His face was hard and I fought the urge to shiver at the cold energy that radiated off of him.

"Are you telling me you won't fight him?" Uncle Jace sounded incredulous and I swallowed before I watched Bennett's expression. It was strange, the gentle male with the soft eyes who had helped me through a panic attack was gone and a very cold distant male had taken his place. I wondered for a brief moment if they were the same person.

"That's exactly what I'm telling you. I know better. Bennett's the pack's top warrior and he stands a very good chance at beating me if I tried, especially with her involved." The words were surprising to me and Bennett's face didn't flinch at the admission. He had blatantly disrespected my father and barely flinched at the thought of being able to beat him in a fight. I wondered who my mate was. He had changed much from the last time I had seen him. I hadn't known him then but I knew that he had not been as cold as the male sitting in front of me, nor as strong as to take down an Alpha

"With her involved? What the fuck is that supposed to mean?" Uncle Jace hissed the words out and Bennett's eyes flicked to my face, there was a slight softening around his eyes and the hard blue ice of his gaze warmed as he looked at me. I felt my breath hitch in my throat. He stood up and gently tugged on my hand until I stood as well.

"None of your fucking business is what it means." The hostility in my father's voice was making me uncomfortable and I looked over at his familiar form.

"Please stop fighting." My voice sounded timid, even to my own ears and I watched as both males snapped their gazes over. Their faces lost the edge of anger as their eyes landed on me.

My father's brown eyes filled with tears before he moved towards me. "Mary Mary." He held out his arms, there was a stark pain in his eyes as I let Bennett's hand go to move around the couch. I stepped into my father's embrace and he hugged me tightly. "I thought I had lost you. I thought I would never get to hold you like this again." He buried his face into my hair and I gently wrapped my arms around his chest. There was still comfort in his embrace and I still found contentment in his arms. The embrace brought forward so many similar moments, his arms wrapping around me bringing comfort and contentment.

Things had gone wrong but he had been young, he had come back and I had pulled away. My memories showcased him trying to make me happy. I had told him again and again that I was happy to serve the pack, that I was content, the threat of Ingrid enough to keep the truth from escaping my mouth. That and my own resentment for him not saving me, for leaving me after I had begged him to take me. So many times he had looked like he had wanted to argue before he would just nod.

"Thought you lost her?" Uncle Jace sounded confused before he laughed. "What did Victor tell you?" He sounded almost amused and my father slowly loosened his grip on me, breathing heavily, sniffling a few times. It hurt me to see him in tears, even if they were happy ones. He was supposed to be strong and I hated that when it came to me he rarely was.

"Who's Victor?" Bennett's voice was low and I turned my head so I could look at him. His expression was guarded and closed off. He looked unapproachable as he crossed his arms over his well-muscled chest. I flicked my gaze to Uncle Jace, who scowled darkly at the question.

"I wasn't speaking to you, *whelp*." Uncle Jace narrowed his green eyes, the action making his scar bunch slightly. I slowly pulled my arms from around my father and he let me go reluctantly before discreetly wiping at his eyes. I resisted the urge to clasp my hands in front of me. I had broken myself of the habit but standing in my father's office, back where it all happened, made it come back full force.

"Jesus Christ in a strip joint, Alpha. What creature crawled up your ass this morning?" Angie's perky voice sounded deliberately antagonizing and I wanted to smile at the display. Everyone liked to get on Uncle Jace's nerves. I believed they thought it was entertaining. I never saw what was entertaining about a pissed off Alpha but it made them happy and to be honest, it amused me greatly to see their ease with him.

"Your attitude, that's what. What do you want?" He snapped the words, his irritation clear and I turned to look at him as he glowered at the tall, short black haired female. Angie wouldn't be affected by the angry look, no one ever was.

"Ignore Jace, he's PMSing. Victor's the wild in our pack. He sent him to give you back Mari's banishment ribbon." She flippantly waved her hand in the air and I turned to see Bennett nod in thanks for the information. He was still but not relaxed, as if he were waiting for something to attack him at any moment. It was strange to see someone that guarded, no one in

Uncle Jace's pack was like that except for maybe Victor but he was straight up harsh and hostile with others while in human form.

"Angela, you're testing my non-existent patience." There was a low growl in Uncle Jace's voice and I let out a small sigh. Everyone was on edge and I was just plain tired. I hadn't had a panic attack in over two months and I had forgotten how draining they could be.

"What? He's hot. I was hypnotized by his stunning good looks." The sarcasm was thick in Angie's voice and I could practically feel her rolling her eyes. "He asked a fucking question. No need for you to bite his head off." I watched Uncle Jace as he held his hands out in frustration.

"He's Mari's mate." Her voice was filled with accusation and I flinched slightly at his tone. I could hear Angie tapping her foot against the floor impatiently. She didn't care. She had given Bennett her stamp of approval so she could care less what Uncle Jace thought.

"So? He's the blue eyed male." She said it as if he were stupid and I watched as Uncle Jace gritted his teeth, trying to hold his temper in. My father gently wrapped an arm around my shoulder, shifting me slightly so that if Uncle Jace lost his temper he could easily protect me. I found the gesture sweet but unneeded. Uncle Jace had never seriously hurt me and I doubted he would ever try.

"What?" His jaw tightened as he said it and his eyes held a cold confusion. I shuddered at the sound of it. I didn't need to be surrounded by angry people, by cold and distant people, especially not the ones who had helped protect me the past two years. This house was a curse on me and I never wanted to step back in it after I left.

"You know, the blue eyed male. The only other person in this shit pack besides her adopted dad that cared about her. That one?" Her tone was patronizing and my father squeezed me gently before letting his arm drop. I looked up at Uncle Jace.

"Oh. *Ohhhh*." The realization hit him and he coughed slightly before looking at Bennett with a calculating gaze. "Are you going to reject her?" My heart clenched at the thought. I didn't think I could take another rejection. I glanced at Bennett but his burning, angry gaze was on my uncle.

"I searched for her for weeks until I was led to believe she was dead. I mourned her loss for the past two years. Planned on going rogue and got a tattoo to remember her but now that I have her by my side after I thought she was lost forever, I'm going to reject her. You know, for shits and fucking giggles." His words were filled with a burning sarcasm as he rolled his eyes and I bit back laughter. Uncle Jace didn't have such qualms and laughed loudly.

"Bennett, don't be disrespectful." My father's voice was sharp and Bennett gave him a rather emotionless stare. I chewed on the inside of my cheek slightly and repressed the urge to shiver.

"Shut up, Andrew. He's going to be a good addition to the pack." There was a smirk on Uncle Jace's face and I wanted to let out a sigh of relief. Uncle Jace would not take in members who were unwilling to speak their minds against an authority figure. He liked having outspoken members. Other than me but I was different, I was family.

"You allow that kind of disrespect?" My father sounded confused and I glanced up at him, his eyes were filled with confused disbelief and Uncle Jace gave a rather impolite snort at the words.

"Disrespect? I call it lively entertainment. Everyone should be allowed to speak their minds. As long as I can hear what they think of shit that is going on, no one can stage a coup against me. I learned from my mistakes, Andrew. Oblitus isn't like Tacita." It was a low warning and I swallowed, looking at my bare feet against the wooden floor. I could hear Angie tapping her foot harder against the floor and I could feel her irritation through the pack link.

"Thanks for ignoring me. I'm only up here because we haven't had any luck in finding the dipshit." She sounded agitated and I moved away from my father. My feet moving silently across the floor as I moved behind his desk. I let my gaze roam over the dusty bookshelf. I needed to be distracted and I faintly started humming.

"I told you, he's probably hiding." My father sounded irritated and I let out a small sigh in the middle of the tune and continued it. I didn't have a memory of the sound but I had a vague understanding that someone had hummed the tune when I was very young. I had always wondered if it had been my mother.

"No shit, Sherlock." Angie's voice was harsh and my fingers trailed across the spines of the books. Many of them were encyclopedias. Some were on plants, others on animals, and at least one on shifters. I resisted the urge to pull it off the shelf before I moved towards the window.

"Order him back here, Andrew." Jace sounded just as harsh as Angie and I looked at the whiteness of the snow and let my gaze move towards the dark forest. I owed my life to those woods. They were the only part of the Tacita pack that did not hold terrible memories for me. That final walk had turned out to be the best part of my life here. There was a sudden movement on the very edge of it that caught my attention.

"It doesn't work that way. I have to at least pretend I'm protecting him." My father sounded disgusted and I watched as a dark brown wolf forced a darker, nearly black one from the trees. Its moves were aggressive and almost deadly. I felt my heart rise in my throat and I swallowed against the sudden nausea the violence caused.

SIXTEEN

“Victor has him." My voice was surprisingly calm as I watched Victor force the wolf towards the front of the house. I could almost hear the aggressive snarling and pain filled yelping from my position. I didn't like the sounds. The violence and pain within them stirred up too much within me.

"Pardon, Mari?" Uncle Jace seemed startled at my words, as if he hadn't expected me to speak on it.

I looked over my shoulder at him, my eyes wide and I swallowed against the lump in my throat that those sounds brought me. "Victor. He is dragging a wolf from the woods. He is most likely going to kill him as the wolf is most likely Beta John." At my words I watched as Uncle Jace, my father, and Angie bolted from the room. Bennett stayed in his place and I looked at him. "Aren't you going to go?" I didn't want to be alone but I did not want Bennett to lose his chance at seeing the male who hurt me so badly pay for his crimes.

"No." It was a simple word that I should have understood but I suddenly felt tears in my eyes and I locked my eyes to his blue ones. The harshness was gone and his face was gentle as he looked at me.

"Why?" The word was croaked out and he let his arms drop to his sides before he tentatively moved closer to me, as if expecting a fast movement would cause me to bolt. I could hear the snapping and snarling grow louder as did the yelping and I wanted to cover my ears. I couldn't stand the sounds. I just couldn't.

"Because I said I would be by your side and I know you don't want to see that. No matter what he did to you, I don't think you can bear to see him pay for his crimes." His voice was soft and without thinking I rushed towards him, pressing my face into his chest, my hands clutching at his shirt. His arms went around me gently and I fought the urge to sob.

"I should be happy." I hated how the words burned with truth. I should have been happy that he was getting what he deserved but I couldn't stomach seeing him ripped to shreds. I couldn't bear to see the sight of his blood pooling in the white snow.

Bennett ran his hand down my head, smoothing down my curls. The action felt wonderful and calming and I let out a shudder of relief. "You're not a person who enjoys violence. You don't need to be happy about this, Maricella. Don't try to make yourself feel what you don't want to." His words were gentle and I was once again confused as to which of the two people he was. He was gentle and sweet, kind and soft with me but around others he was cold and harsh, demanding and emotionless.

"How do you know my name?" I pressed my cheek to his chest, listening to his heart thump strong and steady in his rib cage. It was a highly comforting sound and I slowly loosened my death grip on his shirt, feeling slightly embarrassed about my reaction to what was going on outside.

"Alpha Lawrence told me a few months after you were banished." The information was surprising, my father had never told anyone other than Uncle Jace and a few people in the pack. I looked up as Bennett frowned, the expression seemed more natural on his face than a smile. "He told me about what happened to you." He glanced at me and I swallowed again, trying to rid myself of the sudden lump in my throat.

"And you stay by his side?" It was confusing, Bennett did not appear to be the type of person who would stand by an Alpha who had allowed that, an Alpha who had banished his own daughter. No matter why my father had done as he did, he had still done it. I did not know him but he did not seem like he would cater to such a person.

"It wasn't entirely his fault and he's alone without me. He has no one else he can trust. He put a lot of faith in me with his secret and I found I hated Beta John more than him, so I stay." His face had gone cold and harsh once more and I bit the inside of my cheek gently.

"How can you keep doing that?" I watched as he looked down at me in confusion, his expression softening again. It was highly confusing watching it happen and not knowing which of the two were my mate.

"What?" He looked genuinely confused and I darted my eyes back and forth, trying to find the words to explain what I needed to ask him.

"Go from kind and gentle to cold and hard. Which person are you?" I looked back up at him and he suddenly frowned. I wanted to take back the question as he reverted back to the emotionless, cold stare. I didn't like it, didn't like how it made me feel inside, like my stomach was churning.

"When you left, this was torn from my chest." He tapped at his chest, right above his heart, with two fingers and I felt my throat go dry at the gesture. "I hate this pack. It disgusts me more than anything but I have to hide it. As I'm a pack warrior, I cannot go rogue without an immediate bounty being placed on my head. So I keep everyone as far away from me as possible. I don't have friends and I do not care for their safety. I'm cold, harsh, and brutal because it's all I can be towards them, I can't be kind. It's the only way I survived living here." His expression matched the iciness in his words before he looked down at me, once again his expression going gentle as he looked at me. The iciness of his demeanour melting as his gaze met mine. I felt my breath hitch in my throat at the look of soft adoration in his brilliantly blue eyes.

"You took the heart they so carelessly tore out and you placed it back in my chest. Stitching yourself in with it. I'm soft but only for you because you're the reason my heart is back where it belongs. I cannot be cold to the female who has wrapped herself around my heart to keep it safe." He let go of my waist and brushed the backs of his fingers down my cheek. I leaned into the contact, craving his closeness. "You asked which male I am. I'm both but it's only for you that I'm soft." He cupped my cheek in his hand. "I cannot be anything but kind to you, Maricella. The thought of raising my voice against you pains me. The thought of saying or doing something careless to you is even worse." It was more of an answer than he had to give me but I felt a flame of pleasure kindle in my chest at the words. I was the only person who got to see him like this. He only did it for me and no one else.

I felt tears burn my eyes as I realized the extent of his words. He had let me into a place where no one else had been allowed. "Don't cry. I can't stand to see you in tears." He looked pained as he brushed away the tears that had fallen. His face was harsh with sharp angles and the stubble that coated his jaw. I remembered how it had brushed at my skin as he kissed me and I felt my heart jump slightly in my chest.

There was a loud howl of pain from outside and I stiffened at it immediately, remembering the reason I was in Bennett's embrace. I swallowed and pulled away from him before deliberately moving away from the window and out of the study. I did not want to hear the punishment Beta John would be receiving. I could feel Bennett walking behind me but there was a silence between us as I moved out the door and down the hall.

The further we got away from the front of the house the better it would be. There was about two feet of space between Bennett and I as I moved down the hallway. His presence filled the small space between us rather easily. I could feel his wariness and the coldness he now held but I could also feel the protective edge he had. He was watching to make sure I would be okay, to make sure no one would come out and hurt me. A familiar warmth of pleasure filled my chest at the feeling.

Memories danced along the edges of my mind but they stayed back, the silence of the house didn't trigger them. When the house was silent I had always been safe. The quiet halls held no violence or anger and it was always the best time for me to clean. There were no thoughts of punishment or Ingrid when I was allowed to clean in the silent house. I had spent so long away but now that I was back everything seemed so fresh, so close once more.

The servant's door opened and a tiny, skinny, black haired female moved out of it tentatively. Her actions were carefully planned and her gaze was on the floor as she held a laundry basket tightly in her thin arms. She was doing linens and I stopped walking as I took in her form. She was trembling with cold as she moved towards us. There was a heavy push inside to protect her, to help her. I wasn't sure where it came from but it was there all the same.

I felt tears enter my eyes as I remembered her. She had been made into an omega shortly after I had finished in the classroom. She was younger than me, but not by much. I moved towards her slowly and she gave a small cough, her breath rattling in her chest. She was getting sick, her wolf pushed down so far that her immune response was stunted.

Anger filled me for a brief moment as I remembered how I used to get sick because of the frigid quarters I had been forced to sleep in. The winter was the worst for it and we were never given any help from the pack's doctor.

I took another step towards her before I reached out and took the basket from her arms. She flinched violently and I held it carefully in my hands as she immediately clasped her hands in front of her. Her lank, black hair hung in front of her face limply. She was a few inches taller than me but I still wanted to wrap my arms around her in comfort and tuck her under my chin. However I knew first hand she wouldn't appreciate or welcome the gesture. I felt that undeniable urge to protect her fill me once more. It was strange, so very strange.

"Which room were you taking these to?" I kept my voice soft and she glanced at me quickly before her gaze was immediately lowered. I felt my heart clench in my chest as I looked at her. I had looked like that only two short years ago. So much had changed but at the time, so little as well. I felt like I had been away from there for a lifetime but at the same time I felt like it was just yesterday I took that walk.

She lifted her gaze again, her dark brown eyes wide with shock. She had recognized me. Her mouth opened before she quickly lowered her gaze with a flinch. "I am taking them to room nineteen through twenty-three before doing Alpha Lawrence's room. May I please have them back, ma'am?" She held out her thin arms, I gritted my teeth at the bruises on her pale wrists. I trembled and a strong, warm hand brushed the back of my neck in comfort.

I closed my eyes and let out a heavy sigh. "I'm going to help you." I said the words without thinking before I started towards room nineteen. I wanted to help her, to protect her. It was a strong urge that made me slightly uneasy but it was one I wasn't going to ignore.

"Pardon, ma'am?" Her voice was a frightened squeak and I paused before turning my head and looking at her. Her dark brown eyes were frightened and I blinked slowly.

"I'm going to help you with the linens." I spoke slowly and she swallowed before flicking her gaze to my face before letting it fall just as quickly.

"An Omega must never-"

"Let a pack member do their tasks. I *know*. I was an omega too. I know the mantras. I wish to help you because it will make me happy and I am not of this pack. You won't be breaking any rules." I said the last sentence softly and I watched as she shuddered in relief at the words. She could not be punished for letting me help because I wasn't a part of her pack. I turned and continued to the room and was aware of her following as I pushed open the door.

A younger male looked up from his position on his bed with a dark scowl on his face. I looked at him before moving into the room without saying anything. "What the fuck, omega?" He jumped off his bed and I could hear him gritting his teeth in anger. His voice was harsh and I set the basket down before staring at him and tilting my head. He was young and foolish. I had seen many similar pack members when I had been an omega.

"I am not an omega." I watched as his face twisted with confusion as he looked between the basket and me. I could feel the other omega lingering in the hall just outside of the door. She was too scared to come in because I had not knocked as was appropriate.

"Then why are you doing an omega's job?" He sounded so confused and I opened my mouth to reply when I could feel Bennett move to stand behind me. The young male's face went white as he stared at Bennett. There was a very dangerous aura of hostility emanating from him and it was directed completely onto the younger male.

"What did I say this morning? Have you forgotten the lesson I taught Emerson?" His tone was so icy it made me want to shiver but I repressed it as the younger male swallowed nervously. "Get the fuck out." His voice was growled and low and the other male bolted past us and out into the hallway.

I said nothing as I turned my head to see the omega peeking out from behind the door jamb. "Please, it's safe now." I gestured for her to come forward before I moved over to the bed and started stripping the covers off and folding them. I set them off to the side and before I could turn around and grab the clean blankets the omega was there, her hands shaking as she held them out. I took them with a small smile. "Thank you." I set them on the mattress before picking up the other linens.

Bennett took them from my arms and I went to protest when he kissed my forehead, the action shocking me slightly. "You worry about the clean linens. I'll deal with the dirty ones." He muttered the words against my skin before he turned and left the room. I wondered for a brief moment about how he knew where the dirty linens went before the omega took the fitted sheet from the stack. I grasped the other edge of it and we slowly slipped it onto the mattress.

"He washes his own clothes, ma'am." Her trembling voice was filled with fear. She was afraid I would strike her for speaking out of turn. I softly hummed my acknowledgement and just grabbed the other sheet and handed her one edge of it. We moved silently for a moment, smoothing the sheet out. "He cleans up his own messes too. He doesn't like it when we clean up after him." I let her talk and hummed my agreement to her words.

"Why are you helping me, ma'am? I am only an omega." Her voice was so timid that I wanted to cry but I let out a small sigh instead.

I grabbed the blanket from the stack and held a side out for her as I tried to think of why. "Because when I was an omega, I used to dream about this. Having someone help me with my tasks. Letting me relax for a moment." I shrugged slightly and looked up at her, tears filled her brown eyes and she sniffled as she smoothed down her side of the blanket. I followed suit. "I remember you. I remember seeing you a few times in the laundry room when I was here." I could hear her inhale sharply at the words before I turned away and picked up the basket. The bed was neatly made and I looked at her again.

"Why come back, ma'am? Why come back *here*?" Her voice was so tiny that I almost had troubles hearing her.

I frowned slightly, remembering why I was back in this cursed house. "My uncle came to kill Beta John for turning me into an omega. I came to find something I left. Something that was very important to me." I started towards the door with the basket tucked against my hip and I could hear her following me.

"It was him, wasn't it? The blue eyed male." Her voice had stopped trembling as much and I felt a small smile on my face as I stepped into the next room. It was empty and the linens had already been stripped off of the mattress.

"Yes." I set the basket down and the omega grasped the fitted sheet before handing me one edge with a shaking hand. I took it gently and we started putting it on.

"He is a very kind male. I fainted in the laundry room once because I had missed breakfast and lunch. He was there when it happened and he took me to his room before getting me some food." She was almost smiling, I could hear it in the voice as I grasped the second sheet and handed her one side of it. "He told me that it was safe to eat in his room because he would make sure no one knew. It was a peanut butter and jam sandwich and he let me have some cookies too." There was a faint pause that let me know her fear had suddenly returned.

"You won't tell anyone will you?" Her voice was a whisper, as if she didn't want anyone else to hear. I felt a teary smile go across my face at the thought of Bennett helping the other omegas after I had been gone. He had treated her with a kindness that I had only wished for and pride for my mate's kindness filled me.

"Thank you for trusting me with the secret and no, I won't tell anyone anything you say. I know what it is like." I grabbed the blanket and spread it over the mattress. I watched as she started to straighten her side out. "What is your name?" There was a heavy pause and I could feel her fear. "It's okay. You don't have to tell me." I felt a lump form in my throat as I turned and picked up the basket once more.

A deep sadness filled me because I knew a life outside of the omega station. I had people who had helped me break through the mantras and she was alone. I walked out of the room and towards the next one which was also empty and had a bare mattress. Bennett had moved quickly, making sure the area was ready for us.

"It's Bailey." Her voice was soft and I wanted to cry at the amount of trust she had placed in me. I looked at her with a smile.

"It's a very beautiful name." I fought back the tears as we made the bed in silence. It was a thick silence that followed us through each of the rooms as we made the beds until we reached my father's room. I looked at the interior with a faint smile. I remembered the night had given me the button up shirts to use as nightgowns. He had been trying to protect me, even then. I might not have been open to it, might not have known how to take the hand he held out to me but he had tried.

"You do not have to continue to help me, ma'am." Her voice was timid and I jumped slightly, startled at the sound of her voice. I looked at her with wide eyes before shaking my head. Now I knew how Davin and the others had felt when I had called them sir.

"I wish to help you, Bailey, and my name is Maricella but you can call me Mari." I looked at the bare mattress before grabbing the fitted sheet. "Please don't call me ma'am. It makes me think of Ingrid." We both shuddered at the same time at her name and to my surprise Bailey giggled. She clapped her hand over her mouth with fear and I smiled at her.

"I won't tell anyone, remember?" I threw the fitted sheet on the bed before turning and shutting the bedroom door firmly. Someone would have to be actively listening for us to hear any conversation. "There, now no one can hear. Does she still wear those boots?" I moved back to the side of the bed and there was no sound from Bailey as we put the sheet on. "No one ever thought to tell her to take them off." I grabbed the other sheet and we started pulling it over the bed, folding it down as we were supposed to.

"We wouldn't hear her coming if she did." Her quiet words made me giggle unexpectedly and after a few seconds she joined in. It felt nice to have her giggle with me, to have her relax enough, to trust me enough to join in on the fun.

"Better she keep them on so we can scatter when she starts coming. Stomp, stomp, stomp." I mimicked Ingrid's walk and Bailey giggled again, her hand in front of her face and her brown eyes twinkling with amusement.

"Like a beast with a sore foot." We said it at the same time and this time I clapped my hand over my mouth to smother the laughter that wanted to escape. So it hadn't just been me that had thought the same things about Ingrid. Bailey's eyes danced with the effort of holding back her laughter and I felt my shoulders shake slightly with the laughter I was hiding tight.

"Did you ever think about pushing her down the stairs?" Her eyes were wide and she looked fearful as she said it and I bit my lip as a snort of laughter escaped my mouth. I felt my eyes go wide as I slapped my hands over it. Bailey's giggled renewed and I swallowed back laughter.

"All the time. I loved thinking about her big, heavy boots flying over her head as she tumbled down the stairs." I tried my hardest to hide the smile that wanted to escape but I wasn't successful as it moved across my face. There was a snort of laughter from Bailey and I watched as her face went red with embarrassment and I breathed heavily, trying to fight the laughter bubbling up at the noise.

"And her angry squeaks as she hits each step." Bailey seemed to be having just as hard a time controlling her laughter as I was but at her words and the picture they inspired, I lost it. The laughter spilled from my mouth and I held my stomach tightly as I laughed loudly. After a few moments Bailey's chiming laughter joined mine. I felt tears in my eyes as I laughed. I hadn't laughed that loud in a long time and I tried to catch my breath but each time I did the image of Ingrid falling down the stairs, squeaking as she did so made me double over again.

I hit the floor, gasping for air as I tried to control the laughter escaping my mouth. Tears streamed down my face and I slowly crawled across the floor, trying to find Bailey. I could hear her on the floor at the foot of the bed and I joined her, leaning against the bed. Our shoulders were brushing and we were both holding our stomachs as we laughed.

How I had wished for this as an omega, how I had wished for a friend, a companion to laugh with, someone to tell my secrets too. I could feel tiny threads of friendship tying me to Bailey and I enjoyed it. I did not want to leave her with them, with Ingrid. I wanted her to come with me. The laughter died down and I felt her lay her head against my shoulder. Her entire form was relaxed and I leaned my head against hers before I reached over and grasped her hand in mine. Her skin was rough and I felt a lump in my throat.

"If I asked you to come back with me, to come stay with me in my uncle's pack, would you?" I hated how suddenly shy I felt as I gently squeezed her hand. I swallowed against the large lump as she stiffened slightly. "I don't want to leave you here, with Ingrid and the others. My uncle doesn't have omegas and Amber can help you get better. She can help you break the mantras." I hated how suddenly strangled my voice sounded and Bailey pulled away from me slightly.

"Would he let me come?" Her voice was so timid that I felt my heart turn unpleasantly in my chest but I nodded.

"If I asked him he would. He would take you in a heartbeat. I don't want to leave you here, Bailey. You deserve so much better than this." The words echoed what Bennett had shouted at me the day I had been banished. It was true, Bailey did deserve much better than a life as an omega. All omegas deserved so much more than the station they were beaten into. I wanted to help them all, I wanted to take all the omegas away from where Ingrid could hurt them but I knew we didn't have enough time or space to do so. There wasn't enough space and I hated myself for that.

"Would Alpha Lawrence let me go?" She sounded so terrified that I slowly let her cold hand go and got to my feet before walking over to my father's desk. Picture frames sat on it and I picked one up. It was a picture of me as a little girl and I carried over to Bailey before sitting down across from her. I held out the photo and watched as she took it with shaking hands.

"My father will give me anything I ask for because he wishes to make up for a great wrong that was done to me." I watched as her face went pale with the realization of who I was and her hands started shaking. "If I asked him, he would let you go. He would make it so you could leave with Uncle Jace and I." I was trembling just as bad as she was before she nodded quickly, a faint glimmer of hope on her face. Relief filled me as she handed me back to the picture. I drew my thumb over the picture of the small juvenile that I had once been with a sigh before I used my other hand to wipe away the tears that lingered on my cheeks.

"How could he give you to Ingrid?" Her voice was timid and filled with disbelief and I looked up at her. Her brown eyes met mine bravely, she looked hurt for me and I swallowed against the lump again.

"He didn't. Beta John gave me to Ingrid when my father had left. That is why my uncle came back." The words were barely a whisper and her eyes went wider, if that was possible before she whimpered and slowly moved into my lap. It was slightly surprising but with how small she was it wasn't difficult. I slowly wrapped my arms around her shaking form before she burst into tears and wrapped her thin arms around my neck, burying her face into my shoulder. I ignored the tears soaking my dress as I rubbed at her back.

Mari, where are you? Davin's voice had an edge of worry and I started to rock the smaller female side to side. I shushed her gently before starting to hum the tune that I believed my mother had hummed to me as an infant.

Helping an omega, I am safe. I ran a hand over her hair and held her tightly as the sobs seemed to get worse.

Why? He sounded curious and I didn't stop my humming as I returned to rubbing her bony back. I wondered for a brief moment about where Bennett was but as Bailey wrapped her arms around me tighter I pushed it off. She needed me more than I needed him.

Because when I was here, I wished for someone to help me. I'm bringing her home with us. I cannot leave her here. I could feel his amusement at my statement and I felt a flare of anger at it.

There was nothing funny about helping Bailey. There was nothing funny about bringing her to safety. I want to bring them all home but I can't, do not mock me for not wanting to ensure at least one of them doesn't suffer anymore.

Easy, tiger. She can come with us. After all, we are a pack of strays. He was still amused and I shut him out before Bailey pulled away from me. Her eyes were puffy and her nose was red as she wiped at her tears.

She scrambled off of my lap before letting out a tearful sigh. "I pretended. With the mantras. I didn't want her to hurt me anymore so I lied." Her words were stuttered with little gasps as she tried to control her breathing. "I just wanted to be safe. I didn't want to be there anymore. You promise to take me with you?" She looked at me with such hope that I wanted to cry.

"I won't make you stay, Bailey." I slowly got to my feet before reaching down. I helped her to her feet and lifted the hem of my skirt and wiped at her cheeks, taking the stickiness of tears away from her skin. She looked shocked at the action but I merely smiled. I wouldn't leave her to these wolves. "Come, let's finish the bed and then walk around for a bit." At her sudden stillness I frowned for a brief moment before I knew what I had done wrong.

"Or we can go to your quarters and get you ready to leave." At that she relaxed and we both moved back to the bed, pulling the blanket over the sheets and making it lay perfect. The action of making the bed was so ingrained into me it felt natural. I felt a familiar peace fill me as I did the task. The feeling had never left me even after the mantras had been broken. I enjoyed it, I enjoyed having that level of peace fill me for a moment.

There was a knock on the door and I watched as Bailey jumped before looking at the floor. My heart ached for her before I moved towards the large door. I opened it slightly and looked out of the crack.

Bennett's scent filled my lungs and I looked up at him. "Are you okay?" His voice was low and his eyes showed his concern and I nodded before opening the door wider.

I tucked a lock of hair behind my ear with a small smile. "Bailey and I are fine. We just finished and will be coming out." I looked over my shoulder and watched as Bailey picked up the laundry basket before standing straight. I could feel her nervous tension as I turned to look at Bennett. His eyes were hard to read as he reached up and cupped my cheek with his palm. His thumb brushed my skin gently and I fought the urge to shiver at the fire that raced through me at the simple touch.

"Were you crying?" The words were a low murmur and I felt a small smile flit across my face as I looked up at him.

"Laughing." I watched as his mouth twitched slightly before he stepped back, letting his hand drop from my face. I opened the door wider and stepped through with Bailey following behind me with the basket. She followed me, leaving the same amount of space that Bennett had and when I glanced over my shoulder, Bennett was following her with the same amount of space. His face was guarded but his energy spoke of protectiveness for me and Bailey. Gratitude filled me with his willingness to protect her like he did me.

I made my way to the servant's stairs and pushed the door open before slowly moving down the familiar worn steps. There was a still silence as Bailey and I moved down the stairs quietly. Bennett seemed to hesitate, not following and I wondered why and when I looked over my shoulder he was staring down the hallway.

I walked down the stairs slowly, fighting back the anxious feeling in my chest as we reached the laundry room. I pushed open the door and the sounds of the washing machines filled my ears as it had years prior. I looked around with wide eyes before stepping into the humid room. There were no omegas in there and Bailey moved around me to place the basket with the others. She brushed her hands down her grey dress and gave me a nervous, timid smile.

There was the sound of boot against concrete and we both froze at the terrifyingly familiar sound.

SEVENTEEN

The hair on the back of my neck stood up as Ingrid's boot steps made their way across the cement floor. I felt my breath hitch in my chest as they grew faster. Memories that lingered in the back of my mind grew hot and oppressive at my back, looming over me with what they held within them. So much pain and suffering accompanied the sound of her boots on the floor. I felt immobile, unable to move, once again the timid little omega as she approached.

Ingrid appeared in my peripheral vision and I flinched as she struck out. There was a sound of a hand connecting with skin but it was Bailey and not me that hit the ground from the force of the blow. I watched, unable to move, as the small black haired female whimpered on the floor, her entire body trembling as Ingrid lorded over her.

"You were supposed to be back ten minutes ago, you little cow! What were you doing?" Her voice was still that piercing screech, like metal on metal. It grated on my ears and made my wolf flash her teeth in pain. "Alpha Lawrence should banish you. Leave you to the wolves that will tear you to shreds. You are an ungrateful little *wretch*." She was shaking, her body was vibrating with her anger. It was such a familiar anger, one I had experienced again and again. Her verbally abusive tirades causing spit to fly out as her face turned red from the exertion.

I blinked, looking at Bailey as she touched her hand to the bright red mark on her face, the slap had been so harsh I could see finger marks on her pale skin. Empathy washed over me, breaking the spell that had been on me, pulling me towards her. I found myself landing on my knees in front of her to grasp her face so I could see the damage. I trailed my fingertips over the hot mark and I almost whimpered as she did. Her timid eyes met my own before they widened as she looked above me. I shifted in my spot, looking over my shoulder. I inhaled quickly in shock as Ingrid raised that familiar strap up over her head.

I didn't have time to react other than to raise my arm. The strap struck my forearm and I yelped at the searing pain as I jerked my arm back from it. It had been a *very* long time since I had felt that hot and burning brand that was unique to Ingrid.

She brought her hand up once more. I went up to my knees as she brought it down again.

I was so tired of her haunting my dreams, so tired of her *hurting* people. I didn't understand why she did it, *how* she could.

I grabbed the strap as it came down. It slapped against my palm hard but I pushed the pain away as I yanked on it. "*Stop*!" Her eyes went wide with shock or realization, I didn't know which. I yanked the strap free from her grasp and stood up. "Stop *hurting* people, stop hurting *me*!" I didn't want her to play a part in my nightmares anymore. I wanted to be *better* and I couldn't while she lorded over me with the stupid strap. I tossed it away in disgust.

"What is *wrong* with you? Why do you like *hurting* people?" There was something wrong with her, something seriously wrong with her mental state that allowed her to *enjoy* all the misery and torment she subjected others to.

"*You*!" The word was hissed out and I lifted my chin. I refused to be cowed by her anymore. I was a shaky and trembling mess on the inside but I needed to push through. I knew I could, I just needed to try. Her face twisted into a dark expression of pure hate as she looked at me. "I don't hurt people, I train miserable little *beasts* like *you*." Her face started turning that familiar red I knew and my heart lurched in my chest and the memories threatened to have my head bowing but I did my best to hold firm under the tidal wave I knew was coming.

She moved closer, looming over me once more. "I should kill you for trespassing you little *bitch*." There was a gleam in her eye, a gleeful look from her feral, blood crazed wolf, that let me know she wanted to do just that and I felt my face whiten. I wasn't a trained warrior, I barely knew how to protect myself. "You should have stayed dead." She spat the words out as she raised her hand, dark claws extended but as much as I wanted to flinch, to bow out and hunker away and wait for the nightmare to be over, I knew I couldn't. Not this time.

I lifted my chin and stared at her and I tried my hardest to tell her, to tell myself, that I wasn't going to bow down to her anymore. I had a family. One that loved me and protected me. I wasn't a ten year old juvenile anymore and I had to stand up to Ingrid for her just as much as I needed to do it to protect Bailey.

So I set my chin the same way I had seen Davin do in his defiance of anything he didn't like. I would stand strong, even if it meant I was scared the entire time. Uncle Jace had told me, his chest rumbling as he had me wrapped up tight in a blanket and tucked close to his side, that fear was natural, there would always be things that scared us but having courage and being strong didn't mean *not* being scared. It meant being scared but doing it anyway.

Her hand slashed towards me and I flinched but it never reached me. There was a sudden and dark rumbling in the room and it deepened to an almost oppressive tone and I realized Bennett had grabbed her wrist. I blinked in slight shock, I hadn't heard him come down. His eyes had darkened to a rather alarming degree and he yanked Ingrid around.

"I could snap your neck like a fucking twig and no one would say a goddamned word." His words were low and dangerous and it had my stomach rolling at the image it inspired. I turned away quickly, trying to drown out whatever he would do to her as I helped Bailey.

My muscles felt tense and tight as I hummed rather aggressively to myself, trying to drown out any noises I would hear. I helped Bailey to sitting, looking over the mark on her cheek. It was looking a little less vibrant than it had when I had first seen it but it wasn't entirely too bad. She gave a chest rattling coughing fit that had me rubbing her back, murmuring words to her in an attempt to soothe her through her coughing. She more than likely had pneumonia and it worried me.

I hunched my shoulders forward as I heard a cry of pain that sounded like Ingrid's. Bailey was looking rather blankly at the skirt of her dress. I swallowed hard and started humming once more. I felt my muscles tighten more and my wolf paced nervously, wary of everything around us. She was never this active inside of me and it made it almost worse because I didn't know how to control her.

A hand touched my shoulder and my wolf snapped her teeth together, lunging toward the person. Her action caused my body to automatically whirl around and throw a punch that I knew was poor the moment before it collided with Bennett's chin. His face turned to the side as if to absorb the blow but I was still acutely aware of the sickening pop of my ring finger dislocating as the punch connected.

My stomach lurched as I blinked in shock at my hurt hand and then Bennett who was still looking away. "I-I-I'm sorry! I didn't m-mean to *hit* you!" Nausea filled me at the thought I had actually hit him, that I had hurt the male who had done so much for me, I felt my breathing start to increase as tears filled my eyes. I wasn't sure if it was from the pain or the thought I had hurt someone I cared about.

"I both *heard* and *felt* that pop, sweet one. Let me see." Bennett's voice was tense and he immediately grasped my wrist, cradling my hand in his gently. He slowly moved it and I winced. I watched as dark bruises started to appear around the knuckle and I swallowed convulsively. The pain was sharp and aching and looking at it made it seem to be that much worse. "Don't look at it."

He grasped my chin in his hand and lifted it so I was forced to look at him. "Don't look at it, sweet one." It was a sharp order that showed his worry and I turned my head, refusing to look at what was causing me so much pain. With how my stomach felt, I wasn't entirely sure I wouldn't throw up.

"Bailey, are you able to go to your room?" He asked it and I turned my attention to the smaller omega. I knew it could help distract me. She glanced between me and him, her gaze never going above our mouths before her eyes landed on my hand and they widened just a fraction.

"Can you pack up your things?" I asked it as calmly as I could and she gave a slow nod before she glanced at me once more. I gave her a quick smile that I hoped didn't come out like a grimace. She gave one more glance to Bennett before she slowly got to her feet and left as silently as a shadow. Once I was sure she was gone I allowed myself to whimper at the pain I felt.

Bennett gently shushed me as he helped me to my feet. "It's okay. It's fine, just look at me. Don't look at your hand." He held my wrist rather tightly but it was held in such a way that my hand felt supported. I looked up at him and his dark blue eyes were filled with a rather tense worry. "I'll get you fixed up." He led me up the stairs and out onto the first floor rather quickly. Before I knew it he had me in the kitchen and grasped me around the waist and sat me on the counter. I instinctively cradled my hand to my chest, unable to help myself.

"Let me see." He reached for my hand and I shrunk away. My hand was throbbing hotly and I didn't want him prodding it. His hand went to my face, lifting up my chin gently. "Maricella, I need to make sure it's okay. *Please* do not fight me. Not on this." His words were pained and pleading and I scrunched my eyes closed before holding my hand out. He took it gently and I winced as it flared with pain. "I know, sweet one, I know it hurts." His voice was soothing and I let my eyes open as he gently ran his fingertips over the most swollen knuckle.

It looked too large and the faint touch was enough to make me whimper in pain. It was dislocated and I knew it would have to be set properly. I watched as Bennett's face twisted with pain and regret at the fact he was causing me pain.

"I'm sorry, Maricella. I'm so sorry." He looked up at me, his blue eyes wide before he used his other hand to touch my cheek. I leaned into the rough palm, taking the comfort it was giving me. Without warning his hand slid to the base of my neck before his lips were pressed against mine.

Heat flooded me and I felt another whimper build in my throat, not from pain but from need as his lips moved on mine gently. I felt a sense of rightness with him as the kiss grew more and more needy. I leaned forward, pressing closer to him as his hand bunched my hair slightly. I shivered as his stubble scratched at my skin and I went to pull my hand from my grip when he made a sharp movement with it. There was a sickening click and I felt my knuckle shift in my hand before it flared brightly with a burning pain.

I tore back from the kiss and cradled my hand to my chest. "Mother *fucker*!" The curse exploded out of my mouth without warning and tears prickled my eyes. "That fucking hurt! Jesus Christ on a stripper pole! Why does that need to hurt so badly? Goddamned, mother fucking hell and everything in between!" I whimpered, tears pooling in my eyes as I held my wrist tightly but even as I cursed the pain was starting to fade, my accelerated healing soothing the injury and mending what was needed.

Bennett kissed my face murmuring apologies, his hand on the back of my head holding me still. If I hadn't been in pain the heat the actions gave me probably would have caused me to burst into flames. "I'm sorry, sweet one. It was dislocated. I had to set it for it to heal. I'm so sorry." The words were filled with pain and I was breathing heavily, fighting back the pain.

I knew what a dislocation was, I had it happen before although last time it had been my shoulder and the finger didn't hurt nearly as badly. Besides, Amber hadn't distracted me like Bennett had. She said she was going to count to three and on one she had done it. That had been brutal but I appreciated it later, after I had finished cursing her halfway to hell and back.

"I know. I know." I muttered the words, ignoring the tears before I kissed him gently. He froze as soon as my lips touched his and I pulled back after a brief moment, missing his lips on mine almost immediately. "Thank you for distracting me." I stretched out my hand, pleased to find the sharp pain was slowly turning into a dull ache. I felt myself go pale as I remember he had a hold of Ingrid. "You didn't... you didn't *kill* her did you?" I didn't want to think about the implications of his threat and his anger, my stomach was uneasy enough as it was.

"No, I didn't kill her. I wanted to but I wouldn't, not with you there." His eyes darkened slightly before he cupped my face, brushing his lips across mine. "You're all that's good in my world. Please don't place yourself in such a position again. I don't think I could control myself or my wolf from killing that person a second time." His voice was thick and I gave a slow nod before I gave him a quick peck on the lips, my face flaring slightly red as I did so.

He backed away quickly, looking suddenly nervous. "Let me get some ice for that." He left before I could protest and I sighed. The bruising and swelling were already going down and I flexed it again. I contemplated getting off of the counter but I decided against it. It felt nice to have Bennett taking care of me like he used to.

I leaned my shoulders against the cupboards as my feet dangled. "You're going to get hurt, you know." At the new voice my gaze snapped to the doorway. A beautiful red haired female looked at me with a grimace. "I saw you kiss him." Her green eyes were filled with hurt and I frowned as she swallowed. "Something in him is broken. Missing." She gestured to her chest. "He'll only hurt you. He'll make you love him and then cast you off to break into pieces alone." There was an incredible amount of pain to her words, as if something had happened that had devastated her.

"He'll tear you down with his words." Tears filled her eyes and I tilted my head as she moved into the kitchen a bit more. Her arms wrapped around her stomach and she looked so *hurt*. "What's worse is he speaks the truth so you can't deny what he says. He finds every little thing that could tear you down and uses them against you. Please, stay away from him. You'll get hurt." There was pleading in her voice and my heart turned over in my chest for her.

"Linnette." Bennett's voice was colder than a glacier and it made me shiver. I watched as she trembled and her green eyes went wide as they landed on my mate. There was a tense silence and I looked between the two. Revulsion filled his gaze as he looked at her and it made my heart hurt to see it in his eyes. He had told me he was only soft for me but I hadn't thought as to what that meant for everyone else.

I looked between the two of them, I saw how *hurt* she was by him. "Bennett, apologize to her." I don't know why the words came out of my mouth but they did. I couldn't stand to see her so hurt. So broken. Bennett had hurt her and I wanted him to fix it because I couldn't let him be so kind to me knowing how much he had hurt her. He had to make it better.

"Maricel-" He sounded slightly irritated and I turned to him, a calmness filling me as I locked my gaze with his. I would not abide by such cruel behaviour. Not from him, not from my mate, not now, not ever.

"Please do not argue with me. *Apologize* to her." I was surprised at how firm my voice was and at the low command it held as I gestured to the scared looking red haired female. I wanted him to fix what he did with her because I could not abide by him leaving her wounds so fresh and painful. I had been subjected to cruelty in my life, I wouldn't allow my mate to act cruel to others. I couldn't stand the thought of it.

He looked like he wanted to argue but the look I must have given him must have made it die in his throat because he turned to the female he called Linnette. "What I said remains true, Linnette, but I apologize for how I said it and how it must have hurt you. I admit, hurting you was my intention but I just wished for you to leave me alone. I was not your mate and how you tried to hang off of me was growing tiresome." He shifted on his feet, his entire demeanour cold as he delivered the words.

"I apologize but you must stop feeling hurt about this. I made my intentions known to you from the start." His words were emotionless as he said them and I watched as the tears fell from her eyes. I hated how broken she seemed. I could see the pain his words caused her and I wanted to hold her tight. I wanted to let her unleash all of her hurt tears. I wanted to comfort the female who I knew had an intimate relationship with my mate. The thought did not bring me pain or hurt. I had been bonded to another, I doubted their relationship was after I had broken the bond.

"I *loved* you." Her voice was strangled and my breath caught in my throat. Oh the tangled webs our hearts may weave. I ached for her because I understood how much it hurt to love someone. I understood the punishment it could bring and the pain it could cause.

"That's your mistake, Linnette." His voice was back to being cold and I felt a flash of outrage as a sob escaped Linnette.

I glowered slightly at the side of Bennett's head as I rubbed at my bruised hand. "Love is never a mistake, Bennett. She loved you when you didn't love her back but that does not make it a mistake." I would never once believe that love, honest and *true* love, was a mistake. "The heart wants what the heart wants." I watched as his muscles tensed along his shoulders and I slowly looked towards Linnette.

"You may have put your love in the wrong male this time but that does not mean your pain is any less real." I gave a small gesture to Bennett and she looked at me, blinking in what seemed to be surprise. "You grieve for him because you know he can't be yours." That was the crux of it, she loved him and she knew she could never have him. It was a sad tale.

"It's okay, you'll find yourself another male and he will love you with a great intensity and he will erase your hurt. His touch will remove it from your memory and he will bring you only happiness." I let my gaze flick to Bennett and he was staring at me with an unreadable expression. I did not hate him for the hurt he had caused others. I understood his need to punish those he believed had done wrong, I didn't like it but I understood it.

"I'm used. No male will *ever* want me. Not now." Her jaw tensed and her face paled as if the meaning of her words had suddenly sunk into her. She looked suddenly sick before she bolted from the room. I blinked at her rapid departure before looking at Bennett.

He looked once again nervous. "I'm-"

I looked down at my hand. "I don't need the ice. My hand feels normal now." I looked up and gave him a small smile as I stretched it, as if proving my point.

He grimaced before he walked over and set a bag of frozen peas on the counter. "Linnette and I- I never meant- She-" He ran his hand through his hair and he looked lost.

I blinked slowly. "You and Linnette had a physical relationship. You didn't want anything more than that and she did." I shrugged slightly. It did not bother me. I was surprised at how much it did not bother me. I should have been jealous but the knowledge that he was mine and only mine managed to squash any jealousy that wanted to emerge. "You are worrying over nothing. I do not care about what you did with her. I cared about the fact you deliberately hurt her. That is not right, Bennett, no matter your feelings on the pack. Thank you for apologizing. I know you didn't want to." I picked up the bag of peas and held them over my knuckles needlessly.

He moved closer, his hand resting on either side of my legs, caging me in. His face was close to mine but I ignored him, letting the iciness of the frozen peas seep into my hand. "Why are you so kind? Life has been nothing but cruel to you yet you sit there give people a kindness they do not deserve." His warm breath brushed my face and I looked up, leaning backwards slightly so I could look at him properly.

"Life has not been cruel to me. People have." I swallowed before letting the frozen peas back on the counter with a sigh. "I know what rejection feels like, Bennett. I know that pain intimately. Linnette may not have suffered as I did but that does not make your words hurt her any less. I will not abide by my mate being needlessly cruel, not when I myself have been the victim of such people." I watched as he turned his face away from mine, I could see the tinges of anger in his gaze and I reached up, letting my hand slide across his jaw. I turned his face back to mine. I needed him to understand.

"I understand your need for justice but being cruel will never be justice. It will make you feel better, feel powerful, but that makes you no better than those that have hurt me." I watched as he winced openly. I could feel him tense at the words. I knew he didn't like the comparison but it was true. "You are a better male than that. Don't be like them, Bennett." I could see him warring with himself before his intense gaze met mine.

"I'm only gentle for you." The words were gritted out and I brushed my thumb across his cheek bone. He was so incredibly handsome and being so close to him made shivers erupt over me. It made me acutely aware of just how close we were.

"You do not need to be gentle or soft, just not cruel. Can you do that, for me?" I watched as his gaze finally softened before he leaned forward and rubbed his nose up and along mine. I shivered at the contact, his lips were so close to my own that I wanted to move the last few millimetres and kiss him.

"I would pull the stars from the sky if you asked it of me, Maricella." It wasn't a yes but I knew he would do as I requested. "You deserve so much more than us." He let out a heavy sigh and I closed my eyes, pressing my forehead to his slightly.

"Not from my point of view. You were my knight in shining armour two years ago and you still are now." I brushed my thumb over his skin before a faint pounding started to grow worse in my head and I felt my eyes grow wide as I realized I had blocked everyone out. I winced as I opened the connections.

Where are you? Stop shutting us out. All I could feel was fear and then nothing. Davin's voice was frantic and I closed my eyes. He was just worried but that did not mean that his emotions were giving me a headache.

I stood up to Ingrid, punched Bennett, and am getting tended to. I dislocated a knuckle. I motioned for Bennett to let me off the counter and he wrapped his arms around my waist and set me gently on the floor. I gave him a small smile before going up on my tippy toes and kissing his cheek.

"Are you mind-linking?" His voice was curious and I nodded quickly, trying to listen to Davin's incoherent rambling.

Never ever do that again, Maricella! I was worried and with everyth- wait what? He sounded stunned and I resisted the urge to roll my eyes, he wouldn't see the action anyway.

I stood up to Ingrid, punched Bennett, and dislocated a knuckle. I'm fine though. I didn't wish for him to worry and I could feel his pride at my words.

Holy shit. That's impressive. You hit someone, I guess my training wasn't all that bad. He sounded so proud that it made me feel a bit nauseous. I knew he wasn't proud of the fact I had hurt someone, it was pride for the fact I had stood up to someone who had hurt me before.

I grimaced slightly as I remembered the reason I was hiding in the pack house. *Are you guys done?* The words were quiet and I could feel his unease. He knew I did not wish to walk into a deadly fight. I did not want to see such violence.

Not quite. The pack demanded a trial before dad offed him and it just finished. He didn't elaborate and I didn't ask as I reached for Bennett's and grasped it in mine. They wouldn't be long and I hated that fact. Someone would die and it would be because of me. *Don't think like that, Maricella. John Simmons had more crimes against his name than just you.* He sounded firm before he shut the connection.

"They aren't finished yet." I hated how my voice trembled at the thought and Bennett gave a low sound in his throat before he tugged me to his side. He let my hand go and placed it on my waist. I clung to him, holding the back of his shirt in my hand.

"Do not think about it, Maricella." The words were low as he rubbed my side gently. I let myself relax into his warm embrace. He was so easily cruel to others but only to those he believed deserved it. The memory of Bailey telling me what he had done for her had my chest practically glowing in pleasure.

"You make me forget the world, Bennett." I muttered the words into his side and he just tightened his grip on me. It felt nice to be in his embrace. I felt protected from everything that may have wanted to hurt me. There was a clashing of heat and happiness as his arm held me protectively.

"Holy shit! Beta John just got his throat torn out." The loud shout came from the hall outside of the kitchen and I stiffened as I buried my face into Bennett's shoulder. I could hear the pounding of feet and I trembled. There was excitement in the air and a touch of fear. It made my stomach roll unpleasantly.

"Let's go find Bailey. I'm sure we will be leaving soon." Bennett's voice was low as he led me out of the kitchen and away from the front door. His arm never loosened on me and I held him just as tightly. I focused my breathing, taking deep and even breaths in and out. I just wanted to leave. I wanted to take Bennett and Bailey and go home. I was exhausted and just wanted the day to end.

Slowly I loosened my grip on him as we walked and he soon behind me, sliding back into the watchful protector. I ignored it as I moved closer to the servant's stairs. I watched as the door opened and Bailey came out, a small sack in her hand. Her gaze was fearful as she looked around. Her gaze latched onto my form and she walked over quickly. I could feel a building anger over the pack link and I suddenly felt rushed.

"We need to go." I didn't understand my sudden urge to leave but I reached over and grabbed her hand before whirling around. I stepped past Bennett with my heart in my throat as I pulled Bailey behind me. I was more than uneasy suddenly. I was terrified. Something bad had happened.

"Maricella!" Uncle Jace's voice boomed through the first floor of the pack house and I jumped just like Bailey did. I held her thin hand tighter as I bolted towards the front door. My heart pounded harshly in my chest and my bare feet made small slaps on the hardwood. "Get out here *now*!" There was a harsh order to his voice and I felt my breathing increase as my body was forced to obey the command of my Alpha. He was furious, *beyond* furious about something. The door came into view and I ignored Bailey's laboured breathing as I pushed it open.

"Let her go!" Uncle Jace's voice was a bellow and I watched with wide eyes as my father held Amber tightly, his face dark as she fought against his grip. My mouth went dry and I took a tentative step forward. There was so much anger and violence. I couldn't see anyone else as Uncle Jace stormed towards my father. The image of them fighting in the study jumped to the forefront of my mind.

"She is to be mine! You cannot deny me, brother!" His words were low and I finally realized what had happened. My father had found his mate in Amber and Uncle Jace was not happy about it and from how Amber was struggling, it seemed she did not approve as well.

I gripped Bailey's hand tightly, I could feel Bennett lingering close behind me and I appreciated it. My heart thudded violently in my chest as I moved forward. A floorboard creaked under my foot and at the sound everything went quiet. All eyes were on me and I glanced around before my gaze landed on a body on the white snow, a halo of blood around it. I froze, my gaze on the red halo surrounding Beta John. His head was nearly severed from his body.

My breath left in a whoosh as I became transfixed on the violent image. His head was twisted unnaturally towards me and his dead eyes stared into my own. His throat was torn out completely and his face was twisted with a violent grimace of pain. He seemed to be calling for help in his last moments. A plea for mercy that was never answered.

Blood rushed in my ears and my vision started to fade. I had never seen such brutality or violence, never in my time in the classroom had I ever been exposed to *that* type of horror. Uncle Jace and Davin always made sure to hide it away from me as well.

"Maricella, look away!" Amber's voice was sharp and everything jumped forward. My vision cleared slightly and I started to breathe rapidly. A warm hand grasped my shoulder and Bennett's calming voice sounded like it was muffled through cotton. The only things that got through were the harsh words of anger and piercing screams of the pack members.

"I can't let you take everything away from me, Jace! Maricella I understand. The omega I understand. Bennett I get but don't expect me to sit idly by while you take my mate from me!" My father sounded so angry and pained and I took a step forward, my gaze on Beta John's dead eyes. There was nothing there, he was a hollow husk of who he used to be. My breathing slowed again, my focus completely on his dead gaze. He seemed to be calling me forward, telling me to come to him. He was pleading for my help.

"Maricella, look away!" It was a sharp command and it took every iota of it to tear my gaze from the dead male's gaze to my uncle's scarred face. A curious buzzing sound in my ears as I stared at his angry face. Everything felt very far away. A poor male made a poor choice and it made for a poor fate. I was just a pawn in every game that had been played by the people around me. I had been a pawn of control for Ingrid, a pawn of destruction and hurt for Beta John, a pawn of kindness for my father, a child he never wanted but received anyway.

"Maricella, sweety!" Amber sounded frantic but it was like she was very far away and I stared at my shaking uncle, my gaze on his darkened green one. "Let me go! She's going into shock." He turned away and I slowly turned to stare at Beta John once more. The red and white was a startling contrast and I ignored the tugging on my hand as I took another step towards his dead body. I could almost hear his voice.

Help me. Maricella! Please help me.

The words floated in my head and I felt black spots dance in my vision as I took another step forward.

"No! I can't let you go!" There was a harsh snarl from my father and I froze. Beta John never gave me anything but pain and suffering. I was his pawn on a chessboard of revenge. The most important piece he could use as he wielded me across the board and trapped my father. I never had a choice. I had gone where he had made me. Still his slightly cloudy eyes called for me to come closer.

"And I can't be with an Alpha!" Amber's voice was so cold and emotionless it almost hurt my ears. I was gripped by the shoulders and shook slightly before I was grabbed none too gently by Uncle Jace. His arm went around my thighs and he lifted me without a word. My hand was torn from Bailey's and everything came back to me, all the sounds and all the emotions that had been sucked from me by Beta John's gaze. I sucked in a deep breath of air, my gaze snapping away from Beta John, searching for Bailey. I couldn't break my promise. I refused to let her stay with Ingrid, with the pack.

"Bailey!" I reached for her as Uncle Jace carried me down the steps. I watched her eyes grow wide with fear as she ran towards me. Our fingers brushed before Uncle Jace quickly jumped down the steps, taking her from my reach. "We need to get Bailey!" My heart pounded in my throat but Angie was suddenly beside the small, pale black haired female. Without a word she crouched down and pulled Bailey onto her back. Amber was quick to follow Angie away from the house and I watched as my father's face twisted with pain.

We were moving further from the pack house and I felt a sudden fear fill me. I was missing someone. "Maricella!" Bennett's voice was harsh and my gaze snapped to him before I started wiggling in Uncle Jace's grasp. I couldn't leave him. I watched as his eyes went wide with panic before rage filled them. The blue went dark as he was forced back to the porch by several pack members. I felt my breath coming in short gasps as they refused to let him pass.

"No! *No*, put me down! Bennett!" I fought to be released but Uncle Jace let out a rather nasty snarl. My heart jumped at the sound but I only fought harder. I needed to be with him. My eyes were filled with tears and the scene in front of the pack house grew blurry.

"This is how it must be!" Uncle Jace's voice was laced with growls and I felt a sob build in my throat before it burst out. I needed him. I couldn't leave him after I had just found him. I couldn't bear the thought of being apart from him.

"No! I can't leave him! Bennett! Bennett, *please*!" The shouting scratched at my throat and I coughed. "Don't do this to me! Please!" I struggled against Uncle Jace's tight grip. We were moving further and further away.

"Maricella!" His voice sounded faint and I started sobbing before I pounded on Uncle Jace's back and shoulder with my fists.

"I *need* him!" I hated how my voice screeched and he simply tightened his grip on me, refusing to let me go. I felt the sobs shake my shoulders as I looked towards the pack house. "*Bennett*!" The cry cracked at the end and I felt like there was painful stretching in my chest.

"Be *quiet*!" The command made me shut my mouth tightly, no sobs escaping as my shoulder shook violently. I still struggled. This was not the male I called Uncle Jace, this was not the male I loved like a father. This male was the one that killed without thought and I had *never* wished to meet him. I pushed and twisted against his grip, knowing it was doing nothing but giving me bruises. We moved further into the trees, my gaze of the pack house broken. Frantic fear filled me. I needed to get to Bennett. I *needed* to be with him.

"What the hell are you doing? Put her *down*!" There was a rather strong command in Davin's voice and I whimpered and breathed heavily through my nose as Uncle Jace's fingers dug deeper into my thigh. The pain was a low throbbing and I reached down, trying to pry his fingers off of my legs. A feral growl left his mouth but I ignored it as I renewed my attempts at prying his fingers off of me.

"Do *not* use that tone with me." The heavy snarl held a deadly warning and I turned to look at Davin through blurry eyes, my shoulder still shaking with sounds that I had been ordered to keep inside. I couldn't see his expression but I could feel his anger.

"Dad! I know you're pissed off but can't you see that you're fucking hurting her?" At the angry words I was dropped rather harshly. I hit the ground with a painful whimper as I slammed against the frozen earth. "*What the fuck*? Where the fuck is your promise right now? We vowed to never hurt her like they did! Maricella, sweety, are you okay?" I ignored his question, the order to be quiet was still strong. I could see hands reaching for me through my blurry eyes but I smacked them away before I scrambled to my feet.

Large angry hands grabbed my arms and I was shaken rather roughly. "Do you wish for him to be arrested with a bounty on his head? Do you?" Uncle Jace's face was twisted with rage and he shook me harshly. His fingers dug into my muscles and I froze, staring at the terrifying male in front of me. His eyes were nearly feral looking and his face was red with rage. "Stupid child! You and your father have been nothing but tests of my patience and I have had *enough*!" His voice was a roar and I let out a whimper as his fingers dug into my arms more. I felt like shrinking under the intense anger he exuded. The trust I had placed in him that I had believed to be unshakable felt very, very fragile and one wrong move would break it completely.

"Dad-" Davin sounded frantic and pained but I couldn't tear my gaze from my uncle's burning one.

"Do not question me!" His voice was an angry roar and I flinched violently away from him. The trust I had in him flew away as if it had never been there to begin with. I did not know the male standing and I certainly did not trust him. It was a scary thought and it was one that made my heart pound harshly in my chest at the close proximity of us. I wanted to escape, I wanted to curl up under the rage and hope it passed over me.

Davin was suddenly in between us, shoving his father away rather roughly. "That is *Maricella*! Your *family* that you're manhandling and for what? Because Victor took your kill? She did *nothing*!" He hissed the words out and I started shaking, staring at my uncle's fiery glare. I could feel that gaze right down deep to my bones and it left me feeling almost weak and shaky. "Walk away. *Now*." There was a harsh command to the word and much to my surprise he turned away, his long strides taking him further and further away from us.

"Are you okay, sweety?" Davin's concerned gaze met mine and I shook my head, fighting back the compulsion to be quiet. He pulled me into his arms and held me gently. "*Fuck*. He's going to be on his knees begging you for forgiveness when he gets back his sense, I hope you realize this." I nodded but I couldn't shake the fear that I had felt and my sudden lack of trust for my uncle.

I suddenly felt sick and I pushed him away, throwing up rather violently. The memory of Beta John's dead eyes making me heave everything in my stomach out until there was nothing left. I wiped at my mouth before pushing my hair back, hoping I hadn't gotten vomit in it.

He handed me a water bottle from his pack and I took a small drink with shaky hands before I swished it around my mouth and spit it out. Davin took the bottle back from me, tucking it away once more. "We should have moved the body. I'm *so* sorry. You *never* should have seen that." Davin murmured it before I was wrapped in his arms once more. "Do you want to sit here and wait for him?" He didn't specify but I knew what he was asking.

The compulsion to be quiet lessened enough for me to speak. "Yah." I whimpered as he sat down and pulled me into his lap. He opened his jacket, wrapping it around me as he held me gently. He pressed his lips to my temple.

"Victor killed John before dad could. That's why he was so angry. I'm sorry he took that out on you, Mari. He never should have done that." His words were low and filled with angry regret and I nodded. It hadn't been Uncle Jace who had been upset, it had been his wolf but I didn't know if I would be able to forgive either of them. Trust was such a fickle thing when it came to trauma.

I wasn't sure if I could ever look at him and not see the angry monster he had hidden from me.

Not now.

EIGHTEEN

I let out a cry of rage as they held me back. Maricella had disappeared into the trees, the image of her tear filled, scared, eyes as she reached for me was seared onto the inside of my mind. I couldn't let her go, not again. There were growls as I shoved forwards again. Numerous hands held me back and three or four people pushed me backwards. I could hear their grunts of exertion and my wolf howled for release. I needed to have her back in my arms. I needed her more than I needed air, more than I needed anything in my life, and if they insisted upon holding me back I couldn't be held accountable for the deaths there would be.

"Fucking *chill*! Do you understand what just happened? This pack is falling apart! It's best they're gone." Lucas grunted and I ripped free from the hands holding my arm and I used all my weight behind the punch that slammed into him. He let out a surprised yelp and I snarled, feeling the shift want to push up on me. I could feel my jaw shifting, the joints aching and popping and several people shouted, trying to force me to the ground.

"Where the fuck is Alpha Lawrence?" Someone grunted it out as I yanked against their grip. They managed to get me to my knees and I tried to rip my arms free, my eyes focused on where Maricella had been carried. I would not let her disappear again. I would rather go rogue and have a bounty on my head than never see her again.

Her uncle had been furious and the thought of how roughly he had treated her made my wolf snarl with anger. She had been shaking, her eyes on the gory scene in front of her, and he hadn't told her it was okay, *no one* had. He hadn't done anything to help her through the trauma of walking in on that.

I felt my arm bones shift under my skin and there was more shouting before I managed to force myself back to my feet. I was breathing heavily through my elongated mouth, a growl rumbled through my chest menacingly as I swung my arm out, hitting one of the pack members. My arm was grabbed by several hands and I swung with my other one but it had already been restrained. I let out a deafening growl. She had been gone for nearly ten minutes. The longer they held me the further away she got.

"Bennett, that's enough." Alpha Lawrence's command made it through the red haze in my vision but my wolf was able to shake it off. "I said *enough*." The command was intense and I immediately stood still. My face shifting back to normal as my wolf submitted under his command. I was breathing heavily and I could still feel hands on me as they pulled me backwards.

"Get over here." His voice was sharp and I turned. My burning gaze on him as I walked towards the porch. His face was stony and I refused to lower my gaze from his and as soon as I was by his side he yanked on my wrist holding it tightly. "Of all the stupid, heartless, and pointless things." His voice was icy as he spat it out. "He can take the omega, she's better off there. He can take my mate. She made it clear she wants nothing to do with me." His voice was chilling as he tied something around my wrist. I broke our gaze to look down. A red ribbon was now tied around my wrist.

A hand grabbed the back of my neck in a tight grip before he yanked me down slightly, his mouth by my ear. "But I will not allow my daughter to be without you. I can't bear for her to feel what I do now. Go." The words were a cold whisper as he tugged on the ribbon once more. I looked at it before looking up at my Alpha. His brown eyes were hard but they held a heavy pain and I reached out and grabbed his shoulder tightly, squeezing it slightly in acknowledgement.

"What's his crime?" Someone called it out from the crowd. Most of the pack members were in front of the steps, much like how it had been for Maricella's banishment.

"For the crime of claiming my daughter as his own, for choosing her over his duties, Bennett Aldridge is hereby banished from our pack and our lands." Alpha Lawrence's voice was icy as he addressed the crowd and silence fell as I made my way down the stairs. No one parted for me to pass through and I pushed forward regardless.

"Your daughter?" Another voice sounded tentative in the pack, they packed together tighter and I shoved them out of the way. There were answering murmurs rippling through the crowd.

"Maricella Lawrence, who resides in the care of my brother, your former Alpha, Jace. As Bennett Aldridge has chosen her over his duties to this pack, he is banished. Let this serve as a reminder to everyone to do your duties or his fate shall be yours." A deathly silence fell over the crowd before I heard someone cough. I shoved more people out of the way as I pushed forward, my only thought on reaching Maricella.

"That isn't worthy of banishment. She should be brought here, where she belongs." An indignant voice sounded from the left side of the crowd and there were murmurs of agreement. "Bennett is our top warrior and with our beta gone-"

"I will *not* have my daughter brought back into a pack that mistreated her! What has been done is done! Anyone against the decision will be punished by me." There was a snarl at the end of his word and I finally broke free of the pack. Snow lay between me and my destination and I moved forward quickly. My strides eating up the land between me and the forest rapidly. "Warn my brother that I will come and claim what is mine, Bennett, and I will not come alone." The warning sent a shiver down my spine as I moved further and further away from the pack that I hated and the house that had once trapped me.

I could still smell her scent and I let it draw me closer to the forest. My heart pounded in my chest. I had been banished. Alpha Lawrence had given me the escape I needed to get away from the pack, to be with Maricella. I needed to have her in my arms. I needed to make sure she was safe. Not just me but my wolf was pacing restlessly in the back of my mind at her absence. I moved quicker, trying not to panic as I reached the trees and weaved in between them as I pushed further into the forest.

A faint voice reached my ears from between the trees. "It's okay. Uncle Andrew won't force him to stay. He's not that heartless." I quickly shifted direction towards it. I could hear a faint murmur of a reply that had my heart suddenly racing. "Amber made her decision. Dad didn't give you a choice like an ass hat. Stop worrying so much." The male's voice sounded slightly amused and I could finally see their figures. A male who looked kind of like Alpha Lawrence was sitting on the snowy ground, his jacket was wrapped around the small form of my mate. I watched as he grasped her toes in a hand before burying his face into her curls. It was a tender embrace that made my wolf tense.

"Your feet are freezing. You really need to get into the habit of wearing shoes, Mari." He chuckled before kissing the top of her head, his eyes sparkling with amusement. There was a haggard look to him, as if the amusement was a facade for something else entirely.

"I hate anything on my feet. What if he doesn't though?" Her voice was small and it tugged on my heart. I took another step forward, breathing her scent in. I resisted the urge to rush over and take her from his arms.

"Then he's a jackass. Both of them. I would risk a fucking bounty to be with my mate. If he's smart he would risk death just to be able to kiss one of your toes. If he's not then he's kind of a stupid dipshit and you didn't need him anyway." At his words I realized where Maricella had gotten the rather colourful language from.

Hearing the curse words spill from her mouth had been amusing, shocking, and mildly appealing. I would have appreciated it more if I hadn't been the one to cause her the pain she needed to say them. I couldn't hold it back anymore and I moved closer, my strides purposeful as I walked towards them.

I watched as Maricella's head snapped into my direction. Her grey eyes were watery and it looked like she had been crying but relief shined brightly in them before she was immediately on her feet and bolting for me. I held out my arms and she slammed into my chest, the force of it knocking some air from my lungs. I wrapped my arms around her tightly, relishing the feeling of the rightness of her being in my arms.

"I thought you weren't coming. I thought-" Her words were trembling and the urge to protect her grew in my chest. I shushed her softly as she held me tightly. I smoothed down her curls gently. My heart rate slowed down as I held her, my wolf growing calm at her touch.

"So *you* are the mighty Bennett." The male sauntered towards us with a lazy grin. "Had me worried I might need to break into the pack house and drag you out by your tail." He was so similar to Alpha Lawrence in his appearance that it was almost alarming. He looked at me with a slightly judging expression, as if he were assessing my worth. "Angie said you weren't much of a talker and I can tell but we need to get going." He looked up to the canopy, as if judging the time of day.

"It's getting late and the patrols will start up again soon." He turned around and started walking away, as if expecting I would follow. "We forgot our cloaks in the excitement so it's going to be harder to lose them." He said it rather lazily and I released Maricella but she clung to me tightly. I reached around my back and grabbed her wrists gently. Her eyes hit me like a punch to the gut as she let out a small whimper of hurt but I simply moved her arms from around my waist to my neck before I picked her up, cradling her to my chest. She gave a low sigh of contentment before pressing her slightly cold face into my neck. I leaned my head slightly against hers as I followed after the male.

"I guess I should mention my name. I'm Davin, Maricella's cousin. Just so you don't get the wrong idea or anything." He didn't look back and I felt my wolf relax at the information. I wasn't sure why he had been tense to begin with, maybe the fact we had lost her once and seeing her taking comfort in another's arms was irritating for him. "You seem like you would have a pretty powerful wolf. You're big too. Angie did warn me about that but she thinks any shifter slightly bigger than her is large." He didn't seem like he was expecting an answer and I wasn't sure how to carry a conversation with him. I had a feeling I would probably say something to offend him because that was what I was best at. I didn't do social interactions well.

"So, mated to my cousin. The infamous blue eyed male. Got to say I expected something else. You are kind of feral looking. No offence or anything but it's the truth. Bigger than most of us too, so it makes you kind of intimidating." He walked aimlessly through the trees, looking incredibly relaxed for someone who was trespassing on another pack's territory. A pack who just had their Beta killed by his friends and would have vengeance on their mind. "So, how many females have you fucked since Maricella was banished?" The question was blunt and I felt a growl build in my throat.

"He's testing you." Maricella's voice was low and her breath brushed my neck. I shivered slightly and the growl backed off. My wolf wasn't sure if we liked the male walking in front of us so casually.

"If you tell him what I'm doing then it defeats the whole purpose of me doing it, Maricella." His voice was chiding but had an edge of amusement. "We need to get this stuff figured out." He gave a flourish with his hand. "I'm going to be easy on him. Jay too but Collin? Oh, he's going to be in for a rough time. He will be taking Collin's sugar after all and that just won't do without a full scale investigation." Davin laughed and I felt Maricella stiffen slightly.

"I'm too tired to deal with that, Davin. Please, just stop." Her voice was almost meek and I shifted her in my arms, holding her a bit tighter. I didn't like how Davin made her sound like that.

"Okay." He conceded so quickly that I was almost surprised. One plea from my mate and he was instantly done with his questioning. He looked over his shoulder, a smirk on his face. "But I'm just warning you, Maricella has a *very* big family. A lot of big brothers and a lot of father figures. You're going to have to go through them before you can get to her. So enjoy holding her while it lasts because the next time might not come so easy." He laughed once more and I could hear the jingle of keys as he pulled them from his pocket.

"Ignore him, Bennett. He's just trying to rile you up." Her soft voice brushed over my skin before she nuzzled her face closer, her arms tightening around my neck. I couldn't help but notice the slight trembling rolling through her body. She was cold and it didn't sit right with me.

"Maricella, stop taking away all the fun." He almost sounded petulant and I could feel Maricella stiffen once more in my arms. I resisted the urge to growl at him for making her feel that way.

"Davin, *please*." She pulled her face away from my neck, the word a small plea for silence and I watched as he stiffened before his shoulder slumped.

He let out a heavy sigh. "I can't say no to you." His voice was soft and he moved forward in silence. I glanced down at my mate. How could she command obedience in others with just a soft string of words? When she had demanded the apology from me, I had wanted to tell her no but the look on her face made me falter. I wanted Linnette to hurt. I wanted her to feel pain but that one look from Maricella had made my beliefs fold faster than a house of cards. Now she was commanding what appeared to be a son of an Alpha with a soft but hesitant 'please'.

"I can practically hear the gears in your head turning. No one *ever* says no to Maricella. One look of those eyes and even the most hardened warriors crack." He let out a bark of laughter and I felt, more than heard, Maricella let out a sigh.

"Davin, this story is embarrassing." Her voice was a squeak and I could feel the heat of a blush cover her cheeks.

Davin threw a grin over his shoulder, his teeth gleaming in the dimming light. "Oh no, Mari. I'm telling it." He coughed lightly as if to clear his throat. "You should have seen it. It was just perfect and hilarious. There was this one Alpha who came to try and take the territory. He wanted to absorb our pack because it was so small and make my dad give up his position as Alpha because he felt threatened by him."

He gave a flourishing gesture with his hand. "We're a small pack but we have a reputation of being tenacious and strong." He chuckled to himself for a second at the thought. "Anyway, this Alpha comes to the pack house with his goons and bangs on the door. Well, Maricella was the only one at the house at the time so she opens the door and this Alpha just starts yelling and demanding all of this shit. Like full on screaming right in her face." Maricella groaned slightly, it was an embarrassed noise that I wanted to smile at it. It was an adorable sound coming from her throat.

Davin was smiling, I didn't need to see it to know that he was. It coated his voice thickly with humour and amusement. "Now Mari's quite sensitive with shouting especially with large people doing it in her face. So she does the only thing she knows how and freezes." He gives a scoff of laughter. "Tears fill those wide grey eyes of hers and she sniffles and starts to cry. This Alpha stops mid rant, his face red and veins bulging and he looks at her in fucking terror and freaks out." Davin let out a loud bellow of laughter and it shook his shoulders. I felt a small smile curl up the corners of my mouth at the picture he was painting.

"His mouth drops open and he starts fucking apologizing to her about causing her to cry and he's standing there telling her not to cry and that is when we walked in." He threw a wide grin back at us and Maricella scowled, pressing her cold face to my neck. "There's this large Alpha practically crouching in front of Maricella begging her to stop crying and apologizing. He's frantic and he's waving his hands like an idiot and his goons are staring at him like he's lost his damn mind." He laughed again and I couldn't help the chuckle that escaped me at the image. Maricella groaned again.

"Not you too." She muttered it against my neck and I shivered at the motion, the smile still on my face.

"So of course my dad gets right pissed at the intrusion and the fact this Alpha is close to Maricella and the fact he made her cry. He damn near challenges him and things start getting heated between the two of them and she fucking starts crying again. She's not a fan of violence, as you can rightly tell." He gestured to her in a rather lazy manner. "Fight's *instantly* over and now she has two large Alphas crouching near her begging her not to cry and apologizing." Laughter was threaded through his words and I watched him lift a hand to his face, as if he was wiping away tears.

"So this Alpha, his name is Bruce by the way. Not that it matters. He starts freaking out and starts promising all of this shit to Maricella. Anyway Bruce left the pack house allied with us where our alliance is basically his pack will always have our back and will provide help whenever we need it. It's a pretty sweet alliance but the only thing they get out of this alliance is that Maricella cannot cry near Bruce because every time he caves and gives her something to make the tears go away." Davin laughed loudly once more, his entire form shaking and I felt the small smile turn into a smirk as I glanced down at Maricella whose face was bright red with embarrassment.

"I didn't mean to. He came to the door ranting and yelling and he scared me. I didn't mean to cry." Embarrassment coated her tone and I felt my heart thump slightly in my chest, warming me up. She was the sweetest, most innocent person I had ever met. I held her a bit tighter and turned to look at Davin who turned around, walking backwards. My face immediately went blank, the familiar mask settling over my features.

"Oh I know. Taught him a lesson on that one. Uncle Bruce is quite fond of our little Mari. Comes out to visit every so often with the goons that were there with him the first day. They are all very protective of her. She inspires devotion, a very *deep* devotion, in those she comes into contact with. She has the power to bring an Alpha to her knees with just a look." Davin smirked, his green eyes narrowing slightly. "Or a very strong pack warrior. She would have numerous people bring down the world if she asked it of them." The thought was almost alarming, just who was the shifter named Maricella Charlotte Lawrence? I never knew of anyone inspiring that much devotion but Davin seemed to be speaking the truth.

"He's just talking me up. Don't put any thought into his words." Her voice seemed strained and Davin's face hardened slightly as he looked at her. He didn't approve of her words and I resisted the urge to hide her from his gaze.

"Maricella has brought two non-familial Alphas to their knees without lifting a finger." His words were even and I stopped walking and he followed suit. "The reason she inspires such devotion is because of what's inside of her. She's suffered much in her time on this earth but nothing has tainted her innocent kindness. Just look at her. She has this fragility to her that begs to be protected." He jerked his hand in our direction, a frown on his face.

"Her entire manner is that of sweetness, innocence, and kindness. She wears her heart on her shirt sleeve and you can see when you hurt her and you curse every god you can think of and you need to make it better. This urge is so potent and violent that you do things you normally wouldn't." His gaze softened and I tried to process what he was saying. It made sense. I thought it had just been me. My wolf's whimpering need to apologize for the growling and for harming her. He had needed to make it go away just as badly as I did. His gaze flicked to me. "You have a lot of wolves to prove yourself to, Bennett."

Maricella shifted in my arms with a heavy sigh. "I never asked for anyone to protect me." Her tone was soft and I fought the urge to hold her tighter. She never had to ask for protection but I would give my life willingly for my small mate. Her entire demeanour demanded protection. It wasn't that she was weak, she was far from it but she had been hurt enough in her life and the need to keep her from being hurt again was overpowering.

"And that's why we do because you would never ask anything of us." Davin shrugged, the serious edge of his voice turning to slight amusement. "Dad's wolf is going to crawl back towards you on his belly with his neck bared for what he did." Despite the amusement his voice was cold. I felt a low growl build in my throat at the thought of her uncle's harsh hands on her when a howl sounded from the pack house. Davin smirked.

"Patrol's coming." He said nothing else as he turned around and bolted. I let out a small curse and adjusted Maricella before taking off after him. We were close to the edge of the territory and I saw a battered looking forest green jeep further away. Davin surged forward and I followed, mindful of my mate in my arms. We slowed down as we reached the jeep and Maricella loosened her grip around my neck.

"I'm damaged, that is what people sense when they look at me. They sense the damage and they can sense my hurt. That is why they try to protect me. I hate that I have to rely on others and I am trying my hardest to fix what damage there is." Her voice was slightly firm but I could hear the slight shakiness that it held and I couldn't resist burying my face in her soft hair, breathing in her scent deeply before looking up.

Davin opened the back door to the jeep and I set her down on the seat. She seemed hesitant before she removed her arms from around me. Her eyes were filled with something that I couldn't name before I brushed my knuckles down her soft cheek.

"I don't see any damage, all I see is perfection." I said it so only she could hear and watched as her face flushed pink at my words. I felt a swell of satisfaction fill me before I could hear an irritated growl.

"That's enough, Romeo. Get in. We need to leave." Davin grabbed my shoulder and my muscles bunched from the urge to grab his wrist and slam my other hand into his forearm, snapping the bone like a twig like my training had taught me.

I shook it off and turned to look at him. "It's best if you don't touch me." The words were cold and he raised an eyebrow before lifting his hands slightly as if in a gesture of peace.

"So he *does* speak. Alright, big guy. Get in." He jerked his thumb towards the jeep before moving around it. I looked at Maricella who looked up at me. She reached up and cupped my cheek. I felt unable to move as her small hand touched me. I resisted the urge to close my eyes and lean into her comforting touch.

"You'll always be the hero in my story." A small smile crossed her full lips and I resisted the urge to bend down and capture their fullness with my own. I brushed my knuckles down her cheek once more and she shivered before her hand dropped from my face. She shifted on the seat and I closed the door before opening the front one and settling into the seat and closing it.

"Seat belt, Mari." Davin's voice was firm and I could hear the click of her seat belt shortly after. I followed suit and Davin started the jeep. Before long we were moving through the trees, the jeep bumping around violently but there were no sounds of concern from Davin or Maricella as we were jostled around. I gripped the door with a tight grip, my knuckles growing white. I could hear Davin's faint chuckle as we bounced up onto a highway. A small hand grasped my arm from between the seats and I glanced over to see that Maricella had taken her seat belt off and was practically lying across the center console.

"*Maricella*." Davin's tone showed his exasperation and I had a feeling she did it often. Her fingertips drew patterns into my skin like when we were sitting on the porch. I tried not to stiffen at the faint touches. I wanted to shiver with faint pleasure at how comfortable she was with touching me. She was resting her cheek on her other arm, her face covered in her hair as she drew the patterns.

"Maricella, we've had this discussion." Davin reached over and grasped her wrist in a gentle hold. It didn't feel right as I watched him gently brush her skin with his thumb but I fought back the feelings that were erupting in me.

She lifted her head slightly. "I hate being in the backseat when everyone else is up front." She laid her head back down, her eyes on my arm as she trailed her fingers over my skin. I let my hand curl into a fist slightly and a small smile crossed her face, as if she liked my reaction to her touch.

I bit back a groan and resisted the urge to pull away. If she insisted upon continuing I wouldn't be able to control myself from claiming her soft mouth with mine once more. The memory of the searing kiss I had taken from her on the porch flashed through my mind. I bit back a curse and my muscles tightened more.

"I know, sweety, but it isn't safe. Here." He slipped his hand under the seat and pulled out what looked to be a beat up old ipod. He tucked it into her hand. "Listen to some music and try to sleep, you're exhausted." I watched him closely. They had a very close relationship. He was able to pick up on her nonverbal cues and her emotions without even looking at her. I glanced at Maricella who slowly moved off of the center console, her hand lingering on my arm before she pulled it away. I could hear the click of her seat belt before silence fell.

I watched as Davin checked the rear view mirror. I could hear faint music playing from Maricella's headphones and he glanced at me. "You aren't much of a talker, are you?" His voice was tight and I looked at him carefully, sizing him up. It was only natural for me. I always did it, seeing if I would be able to take the person in a fight and looking at Davin, Alpha blood or not, I would defeat him in a fight. He looked back to the road, his jaw twitching. He hadn't appreciated my assessment or my silence.

"No, and there have been six." I looked out the window, watching the trees flow by and I could sense him looking at me.

"Six what?" He sounded confused and I rolled my eyes, my hand tightening into a fist. He was the one who was asking me blunt questions and I didn't appreciate the confusion on the subject.

"Females that I've fucked since Maricella was banished." I resisted the urge to grit my teeth and for a strange reason I hated myself for every one of the indiscretions. I knew that she had still been bonded to Lucas but it didn't stop the slight guilt that I felt.

"Oh, so you *are* going to answer that?" He sounded surprised and I smothered a growl. I was going to let him do his little interrogation but there was no way I was going to put up with his inane, pointless questions. After two years of having my wolf walking on the razor's edge, I wasn't entirely on point with social etiquette.

"I just did." I spat the words out in a rather harsh tone that made me focus on Maricella in the back seat. I couldn't see her but her breathing and heart rate were normal. I didn't want her to listen to our 'discussion' because I had a feeling it could get ugly.

"Fuck you're snarky but tit for tat. You fuck any after Mari accepted the rejection?" His voice was low and harsh and I watched the clouds in the sky, the treetops racing by as we flew down the highway.

"No." I spat the word out and gritted my teeth. I could hear him doing the same. Despite the fact I wasn't in his pack, his Alpha blood didn't like being disrespected. It made me realize just how lenient Alpha Lawrence had been with me.

"Why?" His voice was snarky and I stared straight ahead. There was a lot of tension in the vehicle as our irritation and anger rose. My wolf didn't like being questioned like a common criminal because Davin thought we might harm the one person in the world that would *always* be safe from us.

"Because having them touch me disgusted me too much." I ground my teeth together tightly, my jaw aching with the pressure. My wolf snapped and snarled in my head and I felt the buildings of a headache start at the base of my skull. It was a familiar feeling but I couldn't leave the area and take a walk to calm down.

"Well, that's interesting." He went silent for a moment. "If we got into a fight, could you beat me?" I bit back a sigh. It was a matter of pride for him but I wasn't one to disguise the truth for a male's pride.

"I would win." I stated it firmly and I could sense his surprise before I looked over at him, my face blank as he glanced at me with a shocked look.

"Would?" He stared at me with surprise.

"Would." I gave a sharp nod as I said it and his eyes widened before he looked forward. I followed suit, looking out at the dark pavement. This was the furthest I had ever gotten from the pack's territory.

It was the truth. I was a damn good warrior and I had fought long and hard to become the top one in Tacita. Two years of intense training and strict rules and I had accomplished what I wanted. It had taken nearly a dozen males to hold me back when I wanted to go after Maricella. Nearly a dozen pack warriors were needed to try and subdue me and I knew that if Alpha Lawrence hadn't commanded my obedience it wouldn't have been enough.

"Oddly, that's reassuring. If you can beat me then I don't have to worry about her mate being a weak asshat." He chuckled to himself and I bristled at the insult. "How's your temper?" I felt myself gritting my teeth but the thought of being away from the pack and with Maricella made the anger fade slightly.

"It should improve." I rolled my head slightly, feeling the muscles stretch as I tried to force them to loosen. The tension in the jeep wasn't helping my anger situation. I wanted to sit in the back and hold Maricella in my arms. The thought of her small form pressed against me brought me a small amount of comfort.

"That isn't reassuring." He ground the words out and I felt myself staring at the side of his face with an icy glare. I really wasn't used to friendly conversation and his questions and comments were starting to get on my nerves.

"You try spending two years surrounded by people that cause you extreme feelings of hatred and disgust. Then we can see how you feel on the subject." I snapped the words out and I watched as his face twisted slightly, as if he had tasted something sour.

"Your manner's very harsh. It's off putting." He snapped it back before I noticed he glanced into the rear view mirror, as if checking to see if Maricella was still distracted. "Will you ever talk to her like you're talking to me?" His voice was low and I felt my eyes narrow and a growl build at his lack of faith in my ability to keep my temper in check around Maricella. I wouldn't ever speak to her as I spoke to anyone else. The thought didn't even sit right with me.

"Don't fucking growl at me. I'm only trying to protect her, now answer the damn question." His tone was low and deadly and he glanced in the rear view mirror again.

"I have never, nor will I ever, speak to Maricella as such." I narrowed my eyes at him, hating I would even need to say the words. I would never speak to Mari with anything but kindness.

"Good. Now, Mari has several close friends. Seamus, Jay, and Collin. My father and I don't count. Not that it matters with my father. He's in the shitter right now. I doubt Maricella will be willing to speak with him at all at the moment. Trauma response and all that." He turned his head slightly as he glanced at me. "There are two Alphas who come and visit who are also quite fond of her and then their top warriors and or betas. One of which has made it clear that he likes her a bit too much." Davin frowned and I felt my eye twitch slightly at the thought of someone else trying anything with her.

"How would you handle that?" His question caught me off guard. How would I handle having other males near Maricella? My first instinct would be to not let her anywhere near them but she had been so unconcerned with my own relationships that I had been confused. Her reaction to Linnette had been surprising and confusing and I felt my mouth open without meaning to.

"I wouldn't bother with the relationships until one of them hurt her. After that I would take offence." I frowned at my answer. I didn't want her hanging around other males but she had placed so much trust in me that it felt wrong not to extend the same amount of trust to her. She seemed to be just as smitten with me as I was with her. The thought of her being only mine made the jealousy fade away. Her sweet smiles and her flushed cheeks after I had kissed her cemented the thought into my mind because I knew no one could ever take her away from me.

"And what will you do if one hurts her." Davin sounded genuinely curious and I turned my head to look at him. His eyes were on the road but I could see him glancing at me every few moments.

"I'll kill the offender as a warning for the others to not make the same mistake." I shrugged, unconcerned with the direction of the conversation. I would kill the person who would hurt her and I would do so without regret or hesitation. A thick silence fell as I turned back to looking out the window. I could see Davin shifting his hand on the steering wheel.

"You're kind of terrifying. It gives me a weird feeling thinking about you being Mari's mate because all of my instincts are telling me you're too dangerous to even allow *near* her." He was speaking the truth and I inhaled sharply, grinding my teeth together. If he attempted to keep me from Maricella I would tear him to shreds. "But there's something there that's telling me that you would rather cut off your left nut then even *say* something mean to her. Let alone *do* anything to her." He seemed pained as he said it and I leaned my head against the headrest and focused on Maricella's breathing. It had grown longer and deeper and I could envision her sleeping. Her dark lashes brushing her porcelain skin in dark crescents under her eyes.

"I guess I'm giving you my stamp of approval. Look, you make me uneasy and your eyes are kind of creepy with how cold they are but she looks at you like you're the reason there are stars in her sky. She trusts you and that's enough for me and you didn't lie to me with the questions. You were honest and that counts for something." He took a deep breath and when I glanced at him, he was frowning. "Maricella is my cousin but she's more like a sister in some ways and I want to be able to trust you with her. If something happens I want to know. Taking care of her has always been a group effort and you need to participate with that." He glanced at me and I said nothing but I nodded. I understood what he was saying. They had her for over two years. They had grown attached to her and wanted to know about her ups and downs.

"I'm not planning on stealing her away. I'm a banished wolf. I have no place to go." I reached over and without hesitation I extended a claw and cut through the ribbon, taking it off of my wrist with one smooth motion. I looked at the pieces of it before crumpling them in my hand.

"So we are stuck with you then?" Davin's voice was slightly mocking and I couldn't help the small smirk that flicked across my mouth.

"You're stuck with me." I bit back a chuckle at his groan at my words. I leaned back against the headrest and closed my eyes. The tension finally left the vehicle and I could hear Maricella let out a small groan in her sleep and Davin chuckled at the sound.

"She doesn't snore but she makes every other sound imaginable. Even talks sometimes if you're lucky." There were notes of affection in his voice and I didn't acknowledge his words as I relaxed against the seat, focusing on Maricella. My arms itched to be wrapped around her but I doubted Davin would have appreciated me crawling in the back with her. "It's going to take a good four hours to reach our territory so I suggest you relax for a bit." I gave a small nod at his words, feeling slightly tired. It wasn't late in the day, it was actually fairly early but my lack of sleep and then everything that had happened made me more tired than I should have been. I let out a deep breath before I allowed my mind to drift off.

NINETEEN

I slowly woke up as the jeep slowed to a stop before it was shut off. I blinked with sleepiness as faint music filled my ears from the headphones. I yawned slightly before the door was practically ripped open. I let out a groan at the familiar scent of Collin as he yanked the door open. I was really too tired to deal with his exuberant nature at the moment.

"Gimme my sugar!" He growled it playfully before he had my seat belt off and had me in his arms, spinning me around and around. I tucked my head to his neck with another groan. The world spun around me and then suddenly stopped as Collin started rocking me back and forth.

"Collin, I'm going to be sick." I muttered the words and I could practically feel him pouting but he stopped. I felt my eyelids droop again and he shifted me slightly in his arms. I let my arm wrap around the back of his neck and I rubbed at my eyes with my other hand. I pulled out the earphones with sigh, knowing Collin would want to talk.

"Someone's tired." Collin's voice was low and I nodded. I needed more sleep, much more sleep. I rubbed at my slightly achy forehead before I wiggled slightly and Collin set me on the ground. Bits and pieces were coming back to me before a small black haired female launched at me, wrapping her arms around my chest tightly and burying her face in my shoulder. Collin let out a surprised growl and I held up a hand, cutting off the growl before tentatively wrapping my arms around Bailey. She was scared and I didn't blame her. I remembered what it had been like leaving my position at Tacita, it was terrifying. We just weren't used to it.

"Are you doing okay?" I said the words low and she didn't look up from where she had buried her face in my shoulder but she nodded. I let out a small sigh of relief, trying to ignore the cold that was permeating my bare feet. I already knew how Bailey must have been feeling. I had been in the same position with our bodies unable to regulate our temperature properly. She would need to get in the house quickly before she got frostbite or, even worse, pneumonia.

"Look at us, an entire pack of strays." Davin sounded overly cheerful as he closed the jeep's door and I closed my eyes slightly. Bailey trembled against me. I knew it was the fear of punishment that made her so scared. I had been in her place numerous times. What she suffered I had as well but I knew we were in a place where she could be better.

"It's okay, Bailey." I grasped her shoulders and gently but firmly pushed her away. She looked lost, her eyes wide and glassy as she looked at me. She looked like she wanted to bury her face into my shoulder once more to try and hide from the world. I gave her a tired smile as I blinked slowly. I looked around and saw that Bennett had gotten out of the jeep, his strong arms crossed over his wide chest. His muscles strained against his shirt and I looked away quickly, my face flushing warmly.

"Who's this new bundle of joy?" Collin sounded eager and I glanced at him, his warm eyes twinkling with excitement at the prospect of a new arrival. He reached over towards her and at the same time I pulled her out of his reach, a threatening snarl escaped Davin.

Both Bailey and I jumped at the sudden sound, Bailey immediately latching onto my side, her heart pounding frantically with fear and Collin looked confused. I slowly looked at Davin who's green eyes had darkened slightly, his gaze completely predatory on Bailey. She seemed to notice his focused gaze and squeaked before hiding her face in my shoulder again, her hands bunching the fabric at the back of my dress. I stared at Davin warily, Bennett hadn't acted like that when he had discovered we were mates. It was rather alarming coming from my usually subdued and calm cousin.

"Davin?" Collin sounded concerned and I glanced between the two and shushed Bailey gently, rubbing her back. I was tense and wary as I looked at Davin as he shook slightly. Collin shifted to a slightly defensive stance, ready to intercept Davin if he jumped at us. He looked several heartbeats away from shifting and it made my heart lurch unpleasantly in my chest.

"Don't fucking touch her." His voice was low and deadly and I took a step away from him, pulling Bailey with me and he snarled again. His muscles bunched and I flinched as he leapt forward but to my surprise he was suddenly pinned on the ground before he could get far. Bennett held him on the ground with a large hand on the back of his neck. He looked completely at ease as he pinned him down. Davin snarled and Bailey shook violently, I warily watched Davin fight against the grip holding him down. Bennett had to have some serious strength to manage that.

"Bailey was an omega. I suggest you stop your oppressive and threatening growling and snarling because you're only serving to scare your mate more than she already is." Bennett's words were low and even and I watched as Davin instantly stopped fighting. He didn't submit under the hold but it was if Bennett's calm words had made him see reason.

Bennett let him go and stood up, his gaze flicking between me and Davin, as if assessing the threat level for me. It was if his first thought was to make sure I would be safe from harm, the ever familiar warmth of happiness filled me at the thought as well as relief. I didn't know what would have happened if he hadn't been there. Just the thought of it made me uneasy.

"I'm sorry." Davin sounded a bit vulnerable as he pulled himself off of the ground and I swallowed as I looked at his remorseful eyes. "My wolf went a bit chaotic. I didn't mean anything by it." He didn't move closer but his eyes were on Bailey as he talked.

He looked pained and I swallowed hard, trying to get my heart rate under control before I nodded slightly. "Please, you need to use patience with her like you need to use with me. Mate or not, she will need time to adjust." I tightened my grip around Bailey in a small embrace before pushing her away again. I looked into her eyes before moving my hands down to grip hers gently. "Bailey, you know what Davin is to you, right?" She flicked her scared gaze from me to Davin before she gave a small nod.

"That's good. He is a very kind male. He is my cousin and he would never hurt you but I know you are very scared right now. This is all very new to you." I glanced at Davin before I looked around, my gaze landing on Amber. Her expression was severe and it looked strange on her face. I had wanted to take her to see Amber but the look on the doctor's face wasn't welcoming. "We are going to go to the infirmary and get you looked over." I swallowed again before I looked towards my cousin. "Davin, please give us some time to adjust."

He took one more lingering glance at Bailey before he nodded and turned away with a pained expression. I flicked my gaze to Bennett only to realize he had been staring at me the entire time. A hot flush burned at my ears and cheeks as I felt my gaze slide from his.

"I'm just going to go inside." I watched as he nodded, his gaze moving to Collin who seemed to finally notice him.

I watched as my friend stiffened with caution and expectation. "That's right, sugar. You brought me a chew toy. Run along and I'll be busy with him. We can watch a movie later." Collin smiled his signature cheeky smile but this time it looked cold and brittle on his face. I just nodded, unwilling to get between the two of them before leading Bailey away from the small crowd and towards the house. I gently tugged Bailey forward. I hated how much she shivered as we walked towards the house, she needed to get where it was warm.

The walk was quick as we moved up the stairs and into the warm interior of the pack house. I followed Amber towards the infirmary but stopped when she disappeared into her office. I could feel Bailey looking around warily as she clutched the back of my dress in her hand tightly. The familiar room made me relax slightly as I took Bailey to a cot and gently pulled away from her grasp. Her dark brown eyes were wide with fear and I softly patted the cot.

"Come on. You can sit here while I get everything ready." I watched as she slowly climbed up on the cot before she reached out and grasped my hand tightly once more. She was taller than me by a few inches but she was much thinner. Not as thin as I had been when I had first arrived but thin enough. I knew a bit about how to do a check-up. I could take her heart rate and blood pressure. I could check her lungs and do her weight. I could do the simple things and leave the numbers for Amber.

I gently removed my arm from Bailey's grasp, trying my hardest to ignore the scared whimper she let out as I moved away. The urge to protect her was intense and it put my wolf on the offensive. She was growling in the back of my mind at the thought of letting anyone hurt her.

It was disconcerting for me to have her make such violent sounds. My wolf had never truly growled before and it was alarming for me to have her act like that. I did my best to shake it off as I grabbed the necessary equipment and a pad of paper with a pen. It wouldn't be official but it would be enough.

Bailey took the prodding and orders better than I thought she would as I put her through the paces I was used to. She was underweight but not nearly as bad as I had been. She had a rattle in her chest that confirmed my thought that she was getting sick. Everything else was a bit low but still normal.

I let out a sigh as I finished writing down her blood pressure. I took the cuff off of her arm and gave her a small smile. "You need a bath. Do you think you could take one without help?" I watched as she nodded, her hair swaying limply around her face, her brown eyes worried. I grasped her hand and tugged on it gently, urging her to get off of the cot. As soon as her bare feet hit the floor I pulled her towards my bedroom. I needed to get her some clothes. Mine would be big on her but they would work until we got some for her.

We moved silently through the house and I pushed open my bedroom door and pulled her inside before dropping her hand. I moved to my dresser and pulled out two pairs of flannel pants, a tank top and a t-shirt. I rubbed my face with a sigh. I just wanted to sleep. I felt like every bit of energy was drained out of me since leaving Tacita. I dropped my hand and threw a smile at Bailey who was staring at the floor. She needed my help more than I needed to sleep.

"Come on. Let's get you cleaned up." I walked over to her and wrapped my arm around her shoulder, leading her towards the bathroom. I could hear voices in the house and I didn't want to deal with anyone around Bailey with how my wolf was acting. She was feeling very... unpredictable and it was upsetting for me. I wasn't used to her attitude, certainly not her acting like that.

Mari, where are you? Jay sounded concerned as I opened the bathroom door and pulled Bailey into it.

Getting Bailey cleaned up. There is no need to worry. I set the clothes on the counter and moved over to the tub. I turned on the water before putting the plug in and looking over my shoulder at Bailey. Her arms were wrapped around her stomach and she trembled.

Stay in there until we get shit calmed down. Jace and Victor are getting into it. His voice held a warning and I gritted my teeth slightly as my wolf snarled in the back of my head. I didn't know where the sudden aggression was coming from and I didn't like it. I wanted to cover my ears and do my best to drown it out. I had enough of the violence for one day.

Please, keep them out of the house. I couldn't hide the slight growl that went out with the words as my wolf's chest rumbled and I winced heavily. I didn't want Jay asking me questions I didn't have answers to. I closed my eyes and softly reprimanded my wolf, reminding her how much I didn't like such things. She growled but pulled herself further from my mind, hiding her aggression.

Are you okay? Is your wolf okay? Jay spoke slowly and I opened my eyes, ignoring him for a moment to focus on Bailey. She needed to get cleaned and dressed.

"Let's get you into the tub." I gave a half smile at Bailey but she didn't look up. I moved over, listening to the sounds of the tub filling with water. "Come on. Out of the clothes." I gestured and slowly she started pulling off the dress. I turned away to check on the water in the tub and turned it off. I looked over my shoulder at Bailey, who stood naked, her ribs stuck out slightly and I could see goosebumps covering her pale skin. I gestured her forward. She moved slowly and warily but made her way over to me. I helped her into the tub and she pulled her legs up to her chest, hiding from view.

I let out a small chuckle. "Nothing I haven't seen before, Bailey. But it's okay. I understand. The shampoo and conditioner are right here along with the body wash." I pointed out the items and she nodded slowly.

Mari, are you okay? Jay had an edge of worry to his voice and I let out a sigh as I stood up and moved over to where I placed the clothes. I grabbed the tank top and the other pair of lounge pants before pulling the sundress off.

I'm just really tired, Jay. A lot happened. I shut the connection, blocking everyone out as I slowly pulled the clothes on. I could hear Bailey moving around in the water before the sound of the shampoo bottle opening filled my ears. I gave a small smile before looking at myself in the mirror.

There was a hard edge to my face that I knew came from my wolf's aggression and I didn't like it. I wanted it gone but didn't have the energy to fight with her about it. I rubbed at my forehead and ran my hand through my hair. Dark bags hung under my eyes and I rubbed at my face, breathing out slowly. I did it several times until my tense muscles relaxed. I took a step backwards and slid down the wall, closing my eyes.

"Is he-" Bailey's small voice spoke over the sounds of her moving around in the water and I gave a small hum of acknowledgement. "Is he a good male?" Her voice was timid and I cracked an eye open. Her eyes were wide and her entire form screamed that she needed to be protected. It tugged on me and my wolf in a rather uncomfortable way.

I didn't have to ask which male she was asking about, I knew from the look in her eyes. "He's kind and sweet. He would never hurt you, Bailey, because if he did I would junk punch him so hard he would taste nuts." I heard her inhale sharply at my words before she started giggling. The sound made my wolf instantly relax and I felt a bit better, having her aggression leave us both.

"He jumped at us." Her voice was slightly shaky and I shrugged. I knew what Davin had been feeling. He had been feeling protective and slightly jealous. He had just discovered his mate and Collin, the notorious flirt, had tried to touch her.

I didn't particularly like how aggressive he had been but I understood it to an extent. "He was just surprised to meet you, Bailey. That and Collin is the world's worst flirt. He was a little jealous and possessive but I think Bennett straightened that out." The thought of how easily Bennett had pinned Davin to the ground made me shiver slightly. He was very strong. I had known that but seeing him in action made a shiver of fear or delight, I wasn't sure, run down my spine.

"Bennett is a good male. He's very kind." Her voice was soft and I nodded. I was still proud at the fact he treated the omegas as well as he did. I wanted to see him, I wanted him to wrap me up in his embrace. I wanted to bury my face in his neck and take in his musky, masculine scent that reminded me of the forest. There was a faint pressure on the inside of my mind and I sighed, letting the mind-link open.

Mari, how is she doing? Davin sounded unsure and it felt a bit strange. He had always been confident and had an answer to everything but he didn't sound like himself. He sounded wary and uncertain, he was lacking his confidence and it didn't sit well with me.

She's okay. I ran her a bath and she's getting cleaned up. I could hear the conditioner bottle open and I closed my eyes again. The urge to sleep was great but there were emotions swirling around in me that made me feel off balance. The need to find Bennett and wrap my arms around him was nearly overwhelming. The pull between us was strong, far stronger than I had been prepared for. I didn't like the separation between us and I felt almost too needy at the thought.

Tell her I'm sorry for how I acted. I didn't mean to scare her. I never wanted to scare her. He sounded pained and I nodded, despite how he couldn't see the action.

We were just discussing that. I stared at the cabinet under the sink and ran a hand through my hair. I winced at the tangles I caught on my fingers. I combed through my hair with my fingers, removing the knots as gently as I could.

What did she say? He sounded unsure and I frowned slightly at the question.

"Davin apologizes for scaring you, Bailey. He says he never wanted to scare you." I glanced at the tub and Bailey was rubbing at her arms with a washcloth. I could smell the fruit and floral scent of the body wash. Her hair was twisted up on her head, I could see the conditioner covering the black strands.

"It's okay. I just don't know what to do. Everything is new." The ways she said it made me smile. It was an echo of what I had said two years before. I had hated new and it seemed like I wasn't the only one.

She says it's okay but she doesn't know what to do. I stood up and moved towards the cabinet and opened it, taking out two towels and setting them on the toilet. I stared at myself in the mirror again. My wolf whined in the back of my head, wanting to be close to Bennett. I definitely liked her needy better than her being overly aggressive but I also didn't really like her being needy. Honestly I preferred her acting how she usually did, I didn't like deviation, didn't like change.

Okay. He didn't sound convinced and I sucked my bottom lip into my mouth, chewing on it slightly.

How's Bennett? I hadn't really wanted to ask but I felt like I needed to. I needed to know that he was okay. That everything was alright. There was an inherent need within me to make sure he was okay.

I don't honestly know. The dude has this really cold, emotionless stare that he has on that says he wants to rip out your insides if you bother him. Davin’s voice had a bit of wary amusement to it and I let my lip slide out from between my teeth. I had forgotten about that. I wasn't used to someone who was that cold with others and I felt a bit embarrassed that I had forgotten it.

Could you ask him? I hated to ask him but I wanted to know.

Are you trying to get me killed? He sounded amused and I couldn't help the smile that crossed my face at his words. There were a few moments of silence before I could feel his presence. *He nodded, didn't say anything though.*

That's alright. Thank you, Davin. I closed off the connection and rubbed at my bare arms. I glanced at Bailey who set the washcloth on the edge of the tub. She looked at me with wide eyes and I pointed at the towels.

"Those are for you. Get dried off and then I brought you some clothes. They are a bit big but they will do for now." I patted the folded t-shirt and pants before turning to the sink, looking through the drawer for a hair brush.

"You are very kind." Her voice was soft and I shrugged slightly. I was doing what was compassionate, what was normal. I had been in her position. I had people helping me like I was helping her and I wanted to make sure she was taken care of. Something about her screamed that she needed protection. I wondered for a brief moment if that is what the others felt when they looked at me.

"It's not a really big thing. I was like you, Bailey. I want to help you like everyone else here helped me. I wanted to help the others too, rescue all of them but I couldn’t." I found the brush and I could see her from the corner of my eyes stepping out of the bath and wrapping a towel around herself. I turned and smiled before moving over and passed her to drain the tub. She shivered slightly and I grabbed the second towel and put it over her head before starting to dry her hair. Silence fell between us as I towel dried her hair gently.

"Who is the male with the scar on his face?" Her voice was shaky and I paused slightly, wincing at the thought of Uncle Jace. I knew whose face it had been but the person wearing the mask was no one that I had known. My stomach twisted unpleasantly at the reminder of what had happened in the forest, a faint note of panic striking through me.

"That was my uncle but when you saw him, I can honestly say I have no clue who that male was." My voice was slightly choked with fear as my heart thumped in my chest at the reminder. I breathed deeply, pushing it away as I pulled the towel away from her hair and gently placed it on the towel rack. I couldn't think about that right now. I moved around her and grabbed the clothes. I stared at them for a second. "I forgot to get you some underwear. I'll be right back, okay?" I watched as she nodded and took the clothes that I held out before I left the bathroom.

The voices downstairs had quieted down some but I could hear faint murmurs outside as I ducked into my room and quickly grabbed some underwear for Bailey. I moved back into the hallway and flinched when I could hear Uncle Jace cursing downstairs. His voice was booming and I froze for a moment, the panic saturating me in remembrance of how he yelled at me, how hard he had held me, shook me, before I dashed towards the bathroom.

My wolf huddled in the back of my head with a low growl rattling in her throat. She was scared of him, which made me so sad because I never once thought it was possible to be scared of him. Bailey looked at me with frightened eyes as she clutched at her towel. I tried my best to give her a comforting smile but it felt strained. I held out the underwear and she took it with shaking hands. I turned around, giving her privacy to change.

I could still hear him cursing downstairs and it made my wolf's hackles rise up and I rolled my head, trying to get rid of the sudden tenseness I felt in my muscles. I didn't like how wary and on edge that my wolf and I were feeling. I hated that my happy little life had been thrown into disarray because of Tacita. I sighed and rubbed my hands over my face, I wanted everything to go back to being normal. Tears pricked at my eyes as I realized it might take a very long time before that happened. I was getting better but that didn't mean my issues disappeared or stopped, it just meant I was a bit better at navigating them. They would still be there, they would *always* be there.

"I'm finished-" Bailey stopped herself from speaking and I turned around. She was dressed and I forced myself to smile, even as she stared at the ground with her hands clasped in front of her.

"They are a bit big on you but I figured they would be." I held out my hand before reaching over and grabbing the hairbrush. "Let's get you into my room so I can brush your hair." Bailey hesitated before tentatively reaching out and taking my hand in hers. I opened the bathroom door, my hearing highly tuned to where Uncle Jace was downstairs as I led Bailey to my room.

Once safely inside I gestured for her to sit on the bed as I closed the door and locked it. I ignored her curious stare as I drug a chair over and jammed it under the door handle. My wolf was still antsy at the thought of being in the same house with Uncle Jace and I honestly didn't blame her. The anger he was letting off was grating and palpable to both of us. It made me shake slightly. I knew if I wasn't a shifter, my thighs would have still held the finger shaped marks that he had left on them. Even without them, it was a harsh reminder of what happened when he was angry. I slowly moved onto the bed behind Bailey before running the brush through her hair. As I pulled the brush through her hair I could feel her relaxing.

Time slipped by as I gently brushed Bailey's hair, removing tangles and years of stress that had bunched her muscles tightly. After a few more minutes Bailey slumped backwards, her breathing even and slow. I smiled slightly before setting the brush down and adjusting her on the bed. I pulled the covers over her form and my wolf paced restlessly. I frowned as she battered at me, demanding to be released from her confinement. I thought I could ignore her but she just grew more violent, forcing me so much my joints ached and popped heavily. With a touch of fear at her aggression I got off the bed and quickly stripped before I shifted.

My wolf growled low in her throat before jumping on the bed and lying beside Bailey protectively. Despite how tired we both were she didn't move her gaze from the bedroom door. In wolf form the scents were much sharper, as were the sounds. I could feel my wolf focusing solely on Uncle Jace's position in the house. I let out a sigh and curled up in the back of her mind, closing off everything around me. She wasn't in a mood to be trusting and the fact she practically forced the change on me made that abundantly clear.

She was hyper aware of his exact location in the house and she was completely attuned to his voice, the changes in pitch to let her know his mood. All that we could discern was he was still pissed off but the waves of anger had faded slightly. Time slipped by as we focused on him moving around. I was unsure as to how long we stayed there until my wolf immediately went on the defensive as we sensed him slowly moving up the stairs. My wolf uncured from her ball and slowly stood above Bailey's sleeping form, her hackles rising in warning.

He moved down the hall and my wolf lowered her head, baring her teeth, a low growl emanating from her throat. She didn't want him to come anywhere near us or Bailey. A preemptive strike against a person who she feared.

The sun was starting to descend in the sky and despite the window it was slightly dark without the lights on. She snapped her jaws together, that low rumble growing. I curled up tighter in the back of her head, I didn't want to hear her snarls or her growls. I didn't like them.

"Maricella." Uncle Jace spoke softly and the door knob turned slightly. My wolf's reaction was instant. She let out a deadly snarl, the growling growing in intensity as she licked at her bared teeth. Bailey gave a small cry of fear as the sounds woke her up. It only served to make my wolf more aggressive as Uncle Jace jiggled the handle. "Maricella, sweety." My wolf once again snarled loudly, Bailey curled into a tight, terrified ball underneath us and trembled. My wolf's growling grew louder and I felt her need to start pacing restlessly but she didn't want to leave Bailey unprotected.

"Dad, if you can't tell by the growls, she doesn't fucking want you anywhere near her right now. And to be honest, I don't want you near Bailey. Go somewhere else." Davin's voice was sharp and I could feel Uncle Jace's hesitation. My wolf snarled again and Bailey's small hand reached out and grasped one of our legs, her fingers trembling as she clutched at us. It only served to bolster our need to protect her more.

"I need-"

"You need to leave. You won't find a timid Maricella behind that door. You will find a very aggressive, dangerous wild animal that distrusts you and I don't blame her for distrusting you." Davin's voice gradually grew a bit softer and I could feel Uncle Jace's regret and hurt but my wolf did nothing but growl louder, the sound bouncing off the walls of my room. She didn't relax until Uncle Jace's presence went back downstairs and close to his office. Bailey's fingers tangled in our fur and my wolf carefully stepped over her and padded softly towards the chair blocking the door before nudging it out of the way. It landed on the floor with a clatter that she ignored.

We were aware of Bailey watching us as my wolf used her nose and nudged at the old fashioned turn lock. My wolf's thought process was simple, Bailey was scared and her mate could help. I resisted the urge to protest because I knew it would need to be done at some point. As soon as the click of the lock was heard she moved us back towards the bed and jumped on it. With a huffing groan she lay down beside Bailey, her head on Bailey's trembling lap. With hesitant fingers Bailey started to scratch at our ears. My wolf didn't much care for our sensitive ears being touched but she allowed it for Bailey's sake.

The door cracked open and my wolf stared at it intently. "I take it you unlocked the door because you wanted me to come in." Davin kept his voice soft as he slowly slipped inside and closed the door. "You aren't going to eat me, are you?" He looked at my wolf warily and when he took a step towards the bed a rumbling growl filled our chest. A soft warning for him to keep his distance. Davin held up his hands and grabbed the chair my wolf had knocked over and set it up right before sitting in it. Bailey's hand froze mid-scratch and her entire form stiffened slightly.

"Hey, I'm Davin." He was looking intently at Bailey and my wolf nudged her slightly with her nose. Bailey resumed her rubbing and scratching. "Look, I didn't mean to scare you like that but my wolf got a little freaked out. You were scared and Collin was reaching for you. I'm sorry, it's no excuse. I should have had some control over his behaviour." The words came out in a rush and my wolf let a grin appear on her face as her eyes closed. She wanted to nip at Bailey to get her to stop rubbing at her ears but she refrained. She didn't want Bailey scared any more than I did.

"I suggest you stop playing with her ears. She's getting irritated with it. Rub between her eyes and on her cheeks. She likes that." Davin's voice was soft and Bailey's hands stilled on our ears before she did as Davin suggested and my wolf let out a content groan at the contact. "See? She likes that better. Her ears are sensitive." I could feel Bailey's satisfaction at making my wolf happy. It was easy and safe to make people happy for an omega.

"My name is Bailey." Her voice was soft and her eyes were on her hands as she trailed them through our fur on the sides of our face.

"That's a beautiful name." Davin's voice was slightly choked and he gave a small sound to clear his throat.

To both our surprise Bailey laughed softly under her breath. "That is what she said too." Her fingers tapped down our nose and my wolf sneezed at the weird feeling, causing Bailey to laugh softly once more.

"Maricella?" Davin seemed to be enjoying the small bit of conversation and my wolf cracked an eye open. He looked eager. His gaze was filled with pleasure and satisfaction at his interaction with his shy and timid mate.

"Yes, she is a very kind female." She returned to stroking our cheeks and my wolf groaned, turning her head so Bailey could reach an itchy spot close to our chin.

"One of the best ones I know." He sounded tentative but it was if Bailey did not sense his unease or uncertainty. It was strange for both my wolf and I to see him without his usual easy confidence. Who knew all it took to throw Davin Theo Lawrence into uncertainty and fumbled words was one tiny omega?

"She wants to protect me." There was a thread of pleasure in Bailey's voice, as if the thought of us wanting to protect her made her happy. My wolf grinned again before lifting her head and licking Bailey's chin with a whine. Bailey giggled, a smile spreading across her face as she scratched under our chin.

"I can understand that." There was a hidden meaning to his words and even my wolf understood his need to protect his mate with his life.

"Who will protect her? That male wasn't nice to her." Bailey's voice trembled with fear and my wolf whined slightly, nuzzling her neck and licking at her chin again in comfort. My wolf wanted to shake with fear as well but she felt safer with Davin around. Jace wasn't there and Davin was. He would protect us.

"That male's a fool and from the fact that it's Mari's wolf sitting with us and not Mari. I'm guessing she doesn't need too much protecting." Davin was smiling and my wolf tilted her head at him, cocking an ear. She was pleased that Davin believed she could protect us.

"Bennett will protect her. He used to protect me in the pack house. When others would pick on me or call me names he would order them off and ask me if I was okay. I knew he did the same for the other omegas. He showed us a great kindness when Ingrid couldn't see." Bailey sounded happy and the words put my wolf on edge for what Davin would say.

"Why-"

If Ingrid had seen, Bailey would be punished for it. Bennett made sure she wouldn't be caught or punished for his kindness. I forced my wolf back to say it before I let her have the control back. She didn't fight me, understanding my need to explain it so Bailey wouldn't be frightened by the questions. There was a sudden silence and Davin coughed slightly.

"He is a good male, Davin. A kind male." Bailey's voice was soft as she wrapped her thin arms around our neck and buried her face into our fur, the conversation over as she shook slightly. The interaction took a lot out of her, I could tell because I had been there as well. Even the shortest conversations always took a lot out of us omegas when we were first pulled from the position.

"Okay. I'm going to go but if you need anything, don't hesitate to ask, Bailey. I'm here for you, for anything you need or want." He sounded strained and I knew that he didn't want to leave his mate, his wolf must have been protesting. My wolf bared her teeth and growled menacingly and Davin lifted his hands. "I got it. I got it. I'm going." He left and she relaxed, rolling onto her back, wiggling on Bailey's lap happily. She giggled and scratched at our chin. I pushed forward and to my surprise my wolf allowed me to shift back.

I looked up at Bailey in human form, her hand was tangled in my hair and I burst into laughter at the shocked look on her face. I felt tears in my eyes as I laughed loudly. I rolled over, curling up as I tried to cover myself slightly. Not long after, Bailey started laughing with me. She flopped backwards on the bed as we both snorted as tears streamed down our faces. I slowly crawled off the bed, wiping at my eyes as I gathered my discarded clothes and tugging them on.

"Is she always so pushy with you?" Bailey's voice was threaded with laughter. I could hear her rolling over to look at me as I tugged my tank-top on.

"My wolf? Never but I'm guessing today was just too much for her." I looked over my shoulder before adjusting my hair, pulling it out of the tank top.

"Davin is very handsome." She flushed bright red as she picked at the bed spread and I felt a large smile cross my face at the thought of Davin's reaction to hearing her say that.

"I am not going to tell him you said that because his ego is too big as it is." I watched as a small smile crossed her face. I sat on the edge of the bed and covered her hands with one of my own. "He's absolutely taken with you, Bailey. There is *nothing* he wouldn't do for you. He's talked about his mate for so long." I smiled slightly. It wasn't a lie. Davin had always wanted someone for himself. He wanted the same bond that Seamus and Angie shared.

"We are a reclusive pack. Never really get out and see others so I am lucky he saw you. I don't know what I would do with a pushy, mean mate to my cousin. I like you much better." I squeezed her hands before patting them gently. I let out a small sigh. "It's safe here, no one can hurt you. Do you want to talk?" She started picking at the blanket once more but I could see her nod. Silence fell but I waited patiently, I knew she would start talking when she was ready.

"I was given to Ingrid when I was seven. My mum and dad died and my uncle didn't want to deal with me. He said he didn't have time for a pup so he gave me to her. I spent... I think it was four months in the classroom." Her voice was small, as if she didn't want to be heard. "All I did was cry because I missed my parents but now I can't even remember their faces. I can't remember what they sound like because she took them away from me." Her voice wavered and I nodded slowly. It was the same for every omega. We stood in solidarity because we suffered the same.

"I told the truth when I said I lied about the Mantras. I lied so she wouldn't hurt me anymore." She sounded pained and I shrugged slightly. I had done the opposite. I had fought and struggled for months before I had finally given in.

"I didn't. I fought her at every turn and it was the worst thing I ever did. She beat me so bad there was a voice always with me, taunting me in my head, screaming at me for everything I did wrong. Is it in your head too?" I looked over at her and she tilted her head at me slightly, a small frown marring her features.

"No. I get phantom feelings. A cane to the back, a leather strap on my hands or a slap to the face." She lowered her gaze with a shaky sigh and

I nodded. I knew those as well. I shifted further onto the bed and stared at my hands. "How are you so okay?" Her words made me scoff slightly.

There were many things that I was but okay wasn't one of them. I was getting better but I wasn't simply okay and I knew it would take a long road to reach that point. "I have nightmares and troubles with panic attacks. I have serious anxiety. I flinch away from people I know won't hurt me. I am a minefield of triggers for shock and attacks. I suffer from mild post-traumatic stress disorder. I am prone to fits of rage and depression that have been called manic. I cannot look people in the eyes for too long. I have episodes where I cannot stand to see dirt and so I obsessively clean until my hands are raw and bleeding." I stopped and looked at Bailey, her face was pale.

"I am not okay but I am getting better. This is a long road, Bailey. I have been on it for over two years and I am still not okay but I am better than when I started." I kept my tone soft and I reached over and grabbed her hand gently, ignoring how she flinched slightly at the sudden movement.

"My favourite word is 'better'. Things will be better now. You will get better. Things are better and I am feeling better. It is a very positive word. It indicates progress." I squeezed her hand gently with a sigh. "The road out of being an omega is a long and hard one. You will have Davin with you and that will help immensely. I hope his love will serve as a guide to lead you to an easier life and as a rock you can cling to when everything threatens to drown you. I can only hope that he will help you get *better*." I looked at her as she brushed at her cheeks, wiping away tears I hadn't realized filled her eyes.

"I don't know how to trust him." She glanced at me, a lost look on her face. She didn't know what to do and it hurt me to see it on her face because I was so used to seeing it on my own.

"I don't know how to trust Bennett either but I know he won't intentionally hurt me." I was confident in that fact. He hadn't shown me anything to question that and I doubted he ever would.

"I want to be near him but I'm *scared*." Her voice trembled and I said nothing as I shifted closer to her before wrapping her in my arms. She sobbed quietly in my arms. I let her cry, knowing that the emotional release was good for her, it would help her to express her emotions. I had a feeling that her road to recovery would be much quicker than mine was. I smoothed down her hair and murmured soft comforting words in her ears.

She would be better, I would make sure of it.

TWENTY

I wasn't sure how long we stayed like that until her stomach growled loudly, startling us both. She giggled slightly and I pushed her hands from her face as I wiped her tears for her. She was my cousin's mate, a cousin who was more like a brother. I wanted to make sure she was safe and cared for because she meant the world to him. That and the fact that the instant I had seen her I had wanted to protect her. It had been a bone deep urge for me that I had been incapable of ignoring. Which was weird and I didn't understand.

"Are you hungry?" I cupped her face in my hands and she gave a small nod and I nodded in agreement. Even without my wolf I could sense Uncle Jace downstairs. I didn't want to walk down into that, not when the fear of him still lingered. My wolf was more than tense at the thought and with her pushing me around I didn't want to risk it.

I let my hands drop from her face. *Davin, your mate is hungry and would like something to eat.* I could feel his eagerness over the mindlink and chuckled softly. An ache entered my chest when I realized how eager I would be to help Bennett with something. I needed to see him. *Bring Bennett with you*. I felt his hesitation at that and I wanted to roll my eyes but refrained.

His hesitance disappeared rather quickly. *Does Bailey want anything in particular?* His voice was almost tentative as he asked it and I honestly wasn't sure how to respond to it.

I frowned slightly as I turned to look at Bailey, who was back to picking at the comforter. I thought back to what she had eaten previous and a smile tugged at my mouth as Bennett inadvertently provided the answer. *A peanut butter and jam sandwich, cookies, and a large glass of milk. Bring enough for four people.* I wanted to laugh at his confusion but I didn't as I flopped backwards onto my bed.

I don't understand. He was frowning but I could hear the faint sounds of cupboards opening in the kitchen from my place on the bed. He must not have been too confused because he was making the food anyway.

You and Bennett are going to eat with us. I could feel his immediate excitement at my words and I chuckled slightly. Even my wolf was amused at his childlike glee at the thought of spending more time with his mate.

"Bennett and Davin are going to eat with us. Is that okay, Bailey?" I turned my head to look at her and she glanced at me before looking back at the blanket she was trying her best to mangle with her short fingernails.

"Yes, ma'am." Her tone was timid and I wrinkled my nose at the title. I seriously didn't like being called that, it brought to mind Ingrid.

"It's Mari. I don't want to overwhelm you with new things all at once. Just let me know if you are tired or uncomfortable." I looked back at the ceiling with a sigh. Everything felt different. *I* felt different. There was something in me that had changed or snapped loose. It was strange and a bit alarming for me.

"I wish I was as strong as you." Bailey's voice was soft and I scoffed lightly before looking at her.

"You are." I watched as she met my gaze with an incredulous look on her pixie-like face.

"No. Your wolf challenged your *Alpha*." She sounded so disbelieving, as if unwilling to believe that someone could have done that and to be honest, two years ago I would have felt the same way.

"Yes but he scared me and was acting like kind of a dick." I gave a slight chuckle at the choking squeak she let out at my words. My face went a slight red, I wasn't really used to calling him names but he did deserve it. How he acted had been wrong, regardless of how upset she had been, he shouldn't have taken it out on me. I knew that our relationship would be strained. My trauma responses had been triggered by him and that would take time to work through.

"Uncle Jace expects people to call him names or insult him and if he ever deserved to be called a name, it would be today. He was cruel and unkind." I frowned at the thought of my uncle, the panic rose up into my throat and I pushed it away as a knock sounded on the door. I could smell Bennett and both I and my wolf perked up at the scent. Without waiting for an answer the door opened and Davin walked in with a plate of sandwiches and cookies. I watched as Bailey's face lit up at the sight, her stomach growling once more.

She had eaten it before, that was why I asked for it. She didn't need to have the Mantras pulling her in two, not for her first meal with us. I went up onto my elbows and watched as Bennett walked through the door before closing it behind him. He had a pitcher of milk in his hand and four cups stacked in his other. His gaze burned into mine and I felt a flush cross my face as I sat up completely before sliding off the bed and sitting on the floor. I reached up and grabbed Bailey's foot, tugging on it gently.

After a few moments she slid off the bed to sit beside me. She tucked close to me and I reached over and took a sandwich from the plate Davin had set on the floor. He and Bennett sat down across from us and I tore the sandwich in half, handing the other half to Bailey. My wolf was slightly on edge but she wasn't afraid for Bailey's safety, just wary of how Bailey would react. I gave a small smile as she took the half of the sandwich from me. I took a bite out of my half and glanced at Bennett who was looking at me intently. My wolf urged me to move closer to him but I refrained to stay next to Bailey.

"I'm happy that you're protecting her, Mari." Davin's voice was soft and I felt Bailey stiffen slightly.

I shook the sudden urge to growl off as I smiled at Davin. I needed to stop reacting so strongly to Bailey's every movement. It was odd and disconcerting. "She's family." I shrugged slightly before snagging two cookies and handing one to Bailey. Without thinking I broke the other cookie in half, gesturing for Bennett to take it. He took it with a small nod that caused my face to flare red. I realized what I had done when I could sense Davin's slight pang of hurt through the pack bond.

I had always shared my food with him first and I had inadvertently hurt him slightly with the action. I wanted to take it back but from the corner of my eyes I watched as Bailey broke her cookie in half. With a small moment of hesitation she held half out for Davin and there was a slight pause before he took it. I could see the happiness radiating off of him even as Bailey buried her bright red face into my arm in embarrassment.

"Thank you, Bailey." He kept his tone soft and Bailey pressed closer to me and I gave a slightly amused smile before taking another bite of my sandwich. I watched Bennett through half closed eyes as he poured the milk into the cups. He was a fine male and I was just reminded of how strong he was as his muscles ripple across his shoulders and down his arms.

"I remember this meal. I gave it to you the day you fainted in the laundry room, didn't I?" Bennett's voice was soft and gentle as he handed out the cups and I glanced at Davin warily as he stiffened slightly.

Bailey pulled her face away from my arm with a nod. "Yes, but you brought me oatmeal cookies instead of these." Her tone showed her nervous energy but she trusted Bennett and I resisted the urge to smile at him.

"You're right and it was mixed berry jam instead of strawberry. This is still good though." He took a bite of his sandwich and I followed suit. I took the cup he had set in front of me before taking a long drink. I closed my eyes completely. It felt nice to just be near Bennett. I liked how his tone was gentle with Bailey as if he knew not to act aggressive or violent in front of her.

"Yes, it is. Thank you for bringing it up here. You didn't have to." Bailey was growing bolder as she stopped tucking close to my body. She was still close but she had put some space between us. I felt proud of her. Baby steps were still progress no matter how small a distance they seemed to cover.

"I wanted to see Maricella and I'm currently on supervised visitation." There was an edge of amusement, as if he were just playing along with what the others had said to do to humour them. As if he knew that they wouldn't be able to stop him from being with me if he truly wanted to be by my side. I bit back a smile at the thought. My mate was a very strong shifter and my wolf approved of him greatly as did I.

"Hey man, as you can clearly see Mari currently has me on supervised visitation as well. Don't take it personally." Davin said as if defending himself against the accusation and I cracked my eyes open and took another bite of my sandwich, finishing the half off. I wiped my fingers on my pants and grabbed the cup before dunking the chocolate chip cookie into it.

"I didn't aggressively jump at Maricella when I discovered she was my mate. You did." Bennett's voice was even, his face impassive but I could see the upwards twitch of his mouth. It wasn't significant but I could still see it. The memory of what he *had* done when he first found me made me want to melt into a warm, gooey puddle on the floor as my cheeks heated up considerately. Bennett's eyes flicked over to me for a brief moment as if he had sensed what I had been thinking about. It only served to make my face grow even hotter.

"He didn't mean to." Bailey's words were quick and I watched as her face went bright red again and Davin's smile grew with pride as he glanced at his mate.

"Yah, Bennett, I didn't mean to." He taunted Bennett slightly and I rolled my eyes before finishing off the cookie and the milk, setting the empty cup on the floor.

"You're blushing, Davin. I'd say your little mate already has you wrapped around her finger." Bennett's tone was mocking and I fought against a smile as Bailey stiffened with indignation. It seemed like they were getting along quite well.

"I do not." She sat straighter and I chuckled. It was the truth. I was learning I could trust Bennett to tell the truth, blunt or not he would always speak the truth.

"Bailey, if you told him to yodel on the roof, he would probably ask you what pitch. He's fallen head over heels for you... *Well*, I'd say Bennett gave him a bit of help in that department." It took a second before my words registered and Bailey burst out laughing. She clapped her hands over her mouth in surprise. Her eyes were wide and I couldn't help but laugh softly at the look on her face as Davin pointed at me.

"Low blow, Mari. That's just mean." He frowned at me, a small pout on his lips but I just shook my head slightly, a smile planted firmly on my face as I shrugged.

"I've never seen someone eat dirt that quickly." I smirked at him and Davin clutched at his chest as if in pain.

"Bailey, help me. I'm dying here!" He looked at her imploring for help and I watched as she bit her lip slightly, her cheeks turning pinker by the second.

"Well, it *was* funny." Her head was down but I could tell her gaze was on Davin as he gave a choked sound, looking pained.

"Oh you wound me deep!" He gave a dramatic groan that had Bailey giggling, her head coming up and her eyes shining as she watched him. "Oh the pain! It's just too much." He flopped back onto the floor and I watched as Bailey shifted closer to him, as if trying to look at his face.

"I didn't mean it. It's just that Bennett is very strong and you didn't stand a chance." At her words I burst into laughter as Davin lifted his head and gave his mate a disbelieving stare. She had been slowly moving closer and I watched as she reached out and touched his hand before brushing her hair behind her ear shyly. "It's okay. I still like you." Her smile was nearly dazzling and I watched as Davin slowly sat up as she settled beside him, looking at him as if he were her entire world. He probably was for her, I knew I felt that way about Bennett.

Without warning I had a large arm wrapped around my waist and I was pulled onto an equally large lap, my back against Bennett's chest as he buried his face into my neck. He didn't loosen his grip from around me as if he was afraid I would run. I relaxed into him, unable to help myself. His presence was comforting and relaxing. I felt safe and protected, *enveloped* by him.

I watched as Bailey let Davin hold her hand and I felt the sight tug on my heart strings. Davin was the perfect mate for her. "Could I show you around? You don't have to if you don't want to." He looked at her with such hope that it made my chest ache.

I watched as Bailey glanced at me, her form uneasy with the suggestion. Not uneasy with Davin but not wanting to let go of what she felt was familiar and safe. "He won't let anything happen to you, Bailey. He knows better." I flicked my gaze to Davin's.

My wolf suddenly surged forward for a moment, looking through my eyes and I watched as he nodded slightly in shock. I had never been so aggressive but my wolf had an insatiable need to make sure Bailey was safe and protected at all times. I didn't like the change in myself. I wasn't an aggressive person but she immediately calmed down as Bennett nuzzled my neck softly, taking my scent in.

Bailey grabbed the plate of sandwiches and cookies and took a deep breath in. "Can you show me the kitchen?" She hugged the plate close to her chest and Davin nodded before he picked up the cups and the now empty pitcher.

"Yes, I can. Stay close to me. I promise nothing will harm you when I'm around." He gave her such a truthful look that I was surprised at it before he slowly led her out the door, leaving me with Bennett.

"You know, they couldn't keep me away from you if I really wanted you in my arms." His hot breath brushed the sensitive skin of my neck, sending goosebumps erupting across my flesh.

"I know." It was the truth. He was a highly trained warrior and he was strong. One of the strongest warriors I had ever seen. Once again my wolf was pleased at the choice of mate. She sent me images of strong pups and a feeling of pride and I shook her away, a deep flush burning my ears and cheeks. The only way to have children with Bennett was sex and I was still very much not ready in regards to that. I knew what it meant but the thought made me squirm uncomfortably.

"Your friend, Collin, is a handful." He sounded amused but there was an edge to it. I knew Collin would react violently to my mate, not out of jealousy but a need to protect me. He was just more protective over me than a mother bear.

"How many times did you let him hit you?" I phrased it carefully and he let out a small grunt of annoyance as he pulled away from my neck, his arm tightening on my waist slightly. Bennett wouldn't be caught unwary, he would have to physically allow another person to hit him.

"Twice before I pinned him." He buried his face into my hair and I was surprised at his response. I had expected an extended and violent fight.

"You didn't hit him back?" My question was quiet and he wrapped her other arm around me, letting his hand rest on my thigh. I shivered at the feeling of its heat sinking through my clothes and into my skin. It felt like fire was licking at my nerves.

"I didn't think you would appreciate it." The response rumbled through his chest and I resisted the urge to groan at the feeling it caused. Just being in his presence made every fibre of my being attuned to his presence. I could feel the pull to be near him, our bond demanding our closeness for the sake of the future generation. Having him touch me made my nerves tingle pleasantly and fire to race through my veins.

"Thank you." It sounded breathless and I cleared my throat. I was slightly afraid about how much he meant to me but at the same time I was elated. It was confusing and I felt the strange, uncontrollable aggression slowly leave my body at his presence and as a result I felt shyer, more timid.

"He said his piece, as did Jay and a male named, Seamus. Although Angie told him off and slapped the back of his head for, and I quote, '*acting like a father even though you haven't pumped me full of any pups. If I don't have babies. You can't pseudo parent Mari*.' She's definitely an interesting female." There was a clear amusement that laced his words and I felt a silent chuckle rumble through my back from his chest. Angie would say something that crass but then again the conversation I had with Bailey had been equally crass.

My wolf whined at me, as if trying to get me to understand something. "Are you alright, sweet one?" Bennett spoke it into my ear and I frowned, trying to figure out what my wolf had wanted to tell me.

She kept sending me images of standing up to Ingrid, the images moving slower and slower, as she replayed them for me. I closed my eyes trying hard to understand what she was trying to say. Everyone in the Oblitus pack relied on their wolf's instincts and intuition. We trained to be as close to one with our wolf as we could without going wild. She froze the image on the moment when I stood up to Ingrid before she sent me an image of things breaking. I rubbed at my forehead as it throbbed. I couldn't quite grasp what she was saying.

"Maricella." Bennett sounded concerned and I shook my head. He needed to be quiet in order for me to focus. I wasn't nearly as good at interpreting my wolf's messages as the others. It was usually instinctual, growing up with a wolf made it easy but I had gotten her just before being given to Ingrid. She had been forced into the back of my mind, subservient to everyone. I hadn't bonded or grew with her as others had. I had to learn things that should have come naturally to me.

"Hush, Bennett. She's trying to tell me something." I closed my eyes tighter, trying to shut everything out and listen to my wolf who was growing restless at our inability to properly communicate. She threw the images at me but focused on a specific memory from the classroom. Being let down from the chains.

I winced at the memory but she played the moment of being let down over and over again, the relief of being let down swamping me before she combined the two memories. The memory playing out to the moment the strap made contact with my hand as I grabbed it, she switched it to the other memory, the freeing release of chains. She played it a few more times but she slowly replaced me in the chains with a wolf, with herself.

That was it.

"Oh." I understood what she was telling me and it wasn't entirely good.

"What is it?" Bennett sounded worried but I simply smiled. It had taken me a minute or five but I had figured out the message.

"When I stood up to Ingrid, I allowed my wolf to break free of what the Mantras had done to her. That is why I am suddenly feeling so strange." I shifted on his lap, looking at his face. His blue eyes were guarded as he looked at me but I could feel his confusion. "My wolf no longer has to fear her so she is able to be a bit more pushy with me. That is why she forced me to shift, that is why she is acting more aggressive. She is influencing me. Unintentionally, of course, but I have a more submissive presence and she is now a bit more aggressive than me." I watched as he frowned slightly.

"That can cause some issues." He loosened his grip on me slightly and I understood what he was saying, having a shifter who could not control their wolf was not a good thing. I knew my wolf would not intentionally push me away but if I wasn't careful her personality traits would alter my own, my own rather shy and timid personality being replaced with her brash and aggressive one.

"I know. We have training for dealing with our wolves. Although I doubt Jay has seen something like this before." It was the truth, Jay taught all of us but I knew he had very little knowledge on omegas and our wolves. The same with Amber, I knew she was writing some journals for the Hunters about it but we were all learning as we went. As it was my personality was more subdued due to the trauma but my wolf, now unleashed by my actions, was more aggressive and she would start pushing or testing the limits of my control over her. It actually sounded tedious and I wasn't looking forward to it.

"Like what?" He actually sounded curious as he looked at me. I avoided meeting his gaze, feeling my face heat up slightly. With my wolf pulling back on her brashness I was shyer, feeling more normal and like myself.

"A wolf suddenly having a more aggressive personality while unintentionally pushing the more submissive human side away or altering its personality." I shrugged slightly and Bennett wrapped his other arm around me, hugging me slightly. I relaxed into his embrace

"You're so incredibly intelligent, Maricella." He murmured the words into my hair and I shivered slightly. I wanted so much from him but at the same time I was terrified because I didn't truly know what it was that I wanted. The bond between us was confusing and exhilarating at the same time.

"This bond is so confusing. It keeps making me feel things that I am not truly feeling and that is odd." I swallowed as Bennett started to chuckle. It rumbled through his chest and into me and I fought the urge to inhale sharply at it.

"A mate bond is made to keep you off balance and so that your mate is the only one who can keep you even and balanced. It forces you to rely on them so you may form an emotional bond or a physical one. It's to ensure the survival of the species." At his words I let out a heaving sigh. I knew that but I hadn't realized it would be so intense or contradictory. "Do you not like it?" There was a slight pause in his voice, like he was worried about what I would answer.

I shook my head slightly. "I *like* having a bond with you, Bennett, I just *hate* how confusing it is. I should not feel fear and joy together. I should not feel embarrassed and bold at the same time. This is frustrating." I frowned and Bennett chuckled, a rumbling, throaty sound that sent shivers through my body. I would die happy if I died hearing him chuckle like that. It trailed off and he pressed his face against my shoulder, the feeling of his stubble scratching my skin made even more shivers erupt through my body.

"Maricella... I doubt I could ever meet a more delightful creature. Our bond frustrates you, not many female shifters would claim that." He sounded amused and I resisted the urge to cross my arms and pout. I wasn't a child despite how tempting the action was.

"That is because they are lying. This is frustrating." I frowned and chewed on the inside of my bottom lip. I truly disliked how frustrating it was for me. I wanted everything to be simple because simple was something I could process. I hated things when I couldn't process them in a rational and normal way. When they confused me and I couldn't figure them out it agitated me.

"She also hates romance movies. Only female I truly know that does." Collin's voice was even and I looked over at him with a wide smile. His mask stayed on for a brief moment before he caved, a cheeky smile crossing his face. "I told you I would get you a whole bushel of mates if you smiled at me like that. Sadly, I've allowed you only one. I don't think my knuckles could take punching more of them." He rubbed at them and Bennett stiffened slightly.

"Your mate has a thick skull." He pointed at him and I looked at Bennett before turning to look at Collin again. He was wary and on guard as he looked at me. "Also, I'm extremely uncomfortable with him holding you like that. It looks like you're trying to escape and he's not letting you." At the words Bennett growled, the sound skittering across my skin and into the air.

Collin's jaw tensed immediately at that and I blinked slowly. "Collin, Bennett would never hurt me just like you would never hurt me." I said each word slowly but he didn't relax and he aggressively ran a hand through his blond hair.

"He's fucking terrifying, Mari. *Look* at him!" He jerked his arm out and I looked at Bennett, taking in the harsh angles of his face and the cold emotionless mask he had on. Yes, he looked slightly terrifying but his thumb brushed my thigh gently and I felt no fear.

"He's my mate. That is all I see, Collin. A male who I am bound to from now until the day I die." I forced myself not to look away as Bennett's gaze met my own. I smiled at him and everything faded away. He was my sole reason for existing as strange as it sounded. If he was gone or if he died I would lose a huge part of who I was.

The bond between us was strong. It had lasted through two years apart and had somehow pulled us together with the force of it. Bennett rested his forehead against mine, exhaling heavily. I reached up and touched his cheek as I looked into his eyes. The bond felt like a tangible thing between us, a living thing that beat with our hearts, matching the rhythms and keeping us completely synchronized.

"I take back what I said. He's a fucking teddy bear with you." Collin sounded amused and I broke my gaze with Bennett to look at him with a frown. Collin's brown eyes twinkled with mischief and I let my frown deepen. Maybe Bennett should have been allowed to smack him one.

"Is there a reason you're intruding, Collin?" The coldness was back in Bennett's voice and I shivered slightly against it but he simply squeezed my thigh and resumed brushing his thumb over it. I shivered for a completely different reason, one that had Collin's eyes narrowing.

"Making sure you're keeping to the hands off policy but I can see that's already broken. Bribing Davin with his mate was low, Mari, but I concede that point because I respect underhanded tactics and I do approve." He pointed at me before grimacing. "However, I don't want to be an uncle because I am *way* too young for that so I'm going to ask that you please step away from your giant, terrifying mate for a few minutes... or *years*." He looked pained and disgusted at the same time and I felt a small smile cross my face at his words. Of course he would be worried about me having babies and him being an uncle of all things.

Bennett's arm tightened around me before he slowly stood up, taking me with him. I let out a little squeak of shock at the action before he set me down on my feet. His arm stayed around my waist as he bent down and pressed his face into my shoulder for a brief moment. I could feel him breathing in, taking in my scent once more before he let me go a bit reluctantly. I hated the sudden coldness that filled me as he stepped away. I resisted the urge to shiver and wrap my arms around myself.

"Mari, you look exhausted. You should probably get some sleep. Davin will bring Bailey back up after they are done with their little tour." Collin gave me a small smile and I nodded before slowly moving over to my bed.

I looked over at Bennett who gave me an unreadable look before he walked over and cupped the back of my head with a large hand. "I'm not going to be far." With that he kissed my forehead, his lips lingering on my skin for several heartbeats and let me go, strolling out of my room seemingly without a care.

Collin shook his head slowly. "Seriously, he puts the good guy get-up on for you but the rest of us are getting frostbite every time he looks at us." He muttered it as he walked over and shut my curtains before shutting off the light and closing the door.

I lay down in my bed, curling up in a tight ball, trying to ignore the instincts that were screaming at me to go back to Bennett. I craved his touch more than I had anything else. I hadn't been bonded to Lucas long before he rejected me. I did not blame him but I never felt the soul tearing pull towards him like I did for Bennett.

Maybe the bond grew stronger the longer one had it. That and Lucas had never touched me so maybe every little touch made it harder and harder to stay away. Mene was urging us to bind our lifelines together with a cut of silver, to clasp hands in front of her eyes and succumb to the bond that would be forged in blood between us.

I shivered at the thought, looking at the life line on my left hand that would become a scar. It seemed a simple thing but it held much more than that. It was a bond that was made for life and not to be taken lightly. We had been given the choice to reject those we were incompatible with but you could not reject your mate once the ceremony was complete.

Well I wasn't sure if you could but I knew that if a mate dying could drive the other to madness then a rejection would be horrible, tearing your souls apart cruelly and harshly after you bound yourself tightly to your mate. The thought made me feel slightly sick, the feeling of your soul being torn away from the one you had promised the moon, Mene, to love and cherish for the rest of your life. Even the thought made me feel the phantom pain of my own rejection and I vowed to never let Bennett or myself go through that.

I curled up tighter under the blankets, trying to shake myself from the thoughts of rejection. Collin was right, I was more than tired, I was weary. I was exhausted and worn down. The events of the day dragging me down to where I should have been able to sleep but I was held back, something in me refusing to let my body just shut down.

I was awake when Bailey came back to my room. I was awake when she let Davin kiss her cheek goodnight. I was awake when she crawled into bed beside me and curled under the covers and fell fast asleep. I was awake when the house fell silent and when the moon hung high in the sky. I was awake because something inside of me would not let me sleep. It kept pulling me towards the inevitable and I let out a heavy sigh as the pulling gave me a harsh tug.

I looked at Bailey's sleeping form before I got out of the bed and left my room. Everyone was asleep as I moved down the stairs, my bare feet making no sounds on the hardwood as I followed Bennett's scent. I walked down the basement stairs and found myself standing in front of the door to the guest bedroom where he was staying. I wouldn't be able to sleep without being close to him, the bond was pulling me too incessantly. I hesitated, wondering if I should knock before I took a deep breath and simply opened the door, slipping inside and closing it quietly.

There was silence in the room but Bennett's breathing relaxed me slightly as did his scent as I crept over to his bed. His large form looked almost too big for the bed and I worried my bottom lip lightly before it took whatever courage I had and slid onto the bed beside him. I tried my hardest to relax but he rolled over and I could feel him staring at me. I blushed heavily, thanking Mene that it was too dark to see my face.

"You're lucky. I was going to go up to your room and crawl into bed with you." His voice was slightly husky with tiredness and I wanted to squirm under the intensity of the gaze he had on me. A large hand grasped my waist and I was pulled closer. I let out a small squeak at the action and he chuckled. "I'm not going to do anything, sweet one. I just need you close to me." His hand wrapped around my waist to rest on my back, pulling me even closer. I could feel a sheet separating us and it helped calm my suddenly pounding heart. Despite myself, I found myself relaxing as he slowly rubbed my back with firm fingers.

I felt the sleepiness fill me once more. His scent surrounded me and I could almost feel the heat of his chest. The bond stopped its tugging and I suddenly felt all the exhaustion hit me at once. I let out a small sigh and couldn't help it as I reached out and touched my fingers to Bennett's bare chest. The small contact burned my fingertips pleasantly but for some reason I needed it before my body let me go limp and sleep.

TWENTY-ONE

I wasn't able to sleep for the whole night, only for a few hours after Maricella had joined me. The environment was too different and both my wolf and I were on edge because of it. We couldn't protect Maricella when we didn't know the area or the people in it. I knew that no one would hurt her but much like with her need to protect Bailey, I had an even more oppressive urge to protect her. My wolf was paranoid. We had lost her once and he didn't want to ever lose her again. I agreed with him and I was half surprised when I had awoken to her in my arms, I had expected it to be a dream.

I had expected everything to be a vivid dream but then I had woken up after several hours of sleep to her still in my arms. She had moved closer to me, nearly touching my chest with her own. She was curled up in a small ball but her fingertips were still touching me. The small contact was one that shook me. Even in the midst of her dreams, when her mind was far away from her body, she still needed contact with me.

I hadn't lied to her when I said I would have come and gotten her from her bed. My arms had almost physically ached to hold her and I had been at the very edge of my control snapping when she had snuck into my room. Just her scent had made the ache lessen in my muscles. I looked down at her sleeping face as she let out a small sound of contentment, her fingers twitching slightly against my chest. I felt the iciness and rage I held so tightly for so long dissipate as I watched her.

I brought my hand up and brushed some hair from her face, letting my knuckles linger against her skin. She was a truly beautiful female. I couldn't believe I had thought any female had been beautiful before her. I knew it was partly because of the bond but I truly believed she was the most magnificent female I had ever seen. Maricella's beauty seemed more earthy, more... *real* than the others I had dealt with before.

From her almond shaped eyes, her high cheekbones that told a story of her heritage, the delicate line of her jaw and nose to her fuller mouth. She was everything I could have possibly asked for in a mate. I pulled my hand back, not wanting to get carried away with touching her.

The sound of creaking floorboards drew my attention. Someone was walking into the house from the front door. I stiffened slightly before brushing Maricella's cheek with a kiss. I bit back a smile as she muttered something happily under her breath before snuggling closer to her pillow. I slowly slid off the bed and listened as I moved silently towards the door to my room. I could barely hear the whisper of bare feet on hardwood as the person moved towards the stairs.

Bailey was upstairs by herself. The thought had my wolf make up my mind for me. Bailey could not be left unprotected. Maricella would never forgive me and despite my feelings, Davin was a good male and I wouldn't allow his mate to be hurt. I slipped out of the room and slowly made my way to the stairs, listening for the intruder. To my relief the footsteps bypassed the stairs and went down the hall towards the office.

I had made sure to get the layout of the house figured out while Maricella was upstairs in her room. I quietly made my way to the first floor and could hear the low tones of talking in Jace's office. He wasn't my Alpha but I wasn't quite sure what to call him. Alpha Lawrence seemed too strange for me considering where I had left but I shook the thoughts away. I needed to make sure Maricella and Bailey were safe from whoever was in the house.

I slipped down the hall, listening to the voices rise slightly. The office door was closed and I could scent Jace and the scent of wild and forest. I frowned slightly before I lifted my hand and knocked. The loud voices were silenced and I tried to keep my uneasiness under wraps.

Jace was a formidable opponent and looking at him I knew I would not be able to take him down in a fight, his wolf was too unpredictable and he had the advantage of size. I didn't like being on his territory without having a place in his pack. It felt wrong for some reason. The entire situation felt wrong to me. I needed to have a place in the pack, I needed structure to function. It was how I always lived my life. I was pulled out of my thoughts as the door opened.

A tired, angry looking Alpha ripped the door open and his eyes narrowed slightly as he looked me over. He tilted his head and I stared at him, unwilling to lower my gaze to an Alpha who had not accepted me into his pack. He let out a heavy sigh before running his hand through his hair. He looked suddenly uncertain and it was a strange expression for an Alpha to have.

"Come in, Bennett. I forgot about you." He let out another sigh and opened the door wider. I nodded at him and stepped inside when my eyes landed on a chillingly familiar form. The wild hadn't looked any different than the last time I had seen him and I felt a growl erupt out of my chest without warning. My wolf was immediately on the offensive as we looked at him.

"This is Vic-"

"I know this shifter. He's the one who told me Maricella was dead." The words were low and so icy I was almost surprised. I had a lot of sleepless nights because of this wild bastard.

"Never said she was dead." His voice was harsh, as if he wasn't used to speaking in mixed company, or at all.

"Well you fucking well didn't state she was living, now did you?" I ground my teeth together, the icy rage swirling up through my body and into my limbs. I wanted to hurt him like he had hurt me. *Over* two years I had spent in mourning, over *two years* of having guilt and anger eat away at me because of his actions and words.

"Don't disrespect me, whelp." He sneered the words out and I cracked my neck slightly as I looked at him, breathing heavily. I wanted to hurt him for what he did.

"Victor, be quiet." Jace's voice was tight with anger and I glanced at him as he ran his hand over his face. He looked like he hadn't slept at all.

"Oh so you're on his side?" Victor snapped the words out and I felt my wolf stiffen and I straightened my spine, staring at the male, assessing how badly I could hurt him in a fight. Even him being wild I would do some damage, he wasn't big enough to be able to throw me around. My wolf liked the thought.

"He's her mate. What the fuck do you expect me to do? I hurt him, I hurt her." Jace looked frustrated and I bit back a growl at the fact that they were ignoring me. Anger crackled in the air as the two of them stared at one another.

"Do *something*." Victor spat it out and Jace's face went stony.

"Like you did?" His voice was tight and accusing and Victor's expression turned blank. I kept shifting my gaze between the two of them. I knew when to pick my battles and jumping between these two was not one I wanted to get involved in. My anger was pushed away for wariness as I watched them.

"I did what I had to." Victor was gritting his teeth as he stated the words, his grey eyes hard like flint.

Jace slammed his fist onto his desk. "You took what was *mine*." He was seething and I forced myself to step back, letting them have room if they decided to fight. I didn't want to get trapped between them. Both of these males were unpredictable and their wolves were even more so. I was a warrior but I wasn't a fucking mind reader, I also had Maricella to think about.

"You don't think it was mine as well?" Victor's words were confusing but Jace slammed his first down again, making the various items on his desk jump.

"You had *no* right!" His voice was booming and I looked at the open door, wondering if anyone woke up because of the shouting.

"I had *every* right! He killed her, Jace! He fucking killed her!" Once again Victor's words were confusing me. According to tradition, the one who sent the black ribbon had the right to the kill, no one else.

"Oh, just because you fucked her mother, it gives you the right to take my kill." At Jace's statement I wanted to choke. I stared at Victor, studying his dirty face, underneath the dirt I could see structuring that was similar to my little mate's, the high cheek bones, the eye shape, and the realization floored me as I stared at his eyes. The wild was Maricella's father, her *biological* father. His skin was a bit darker than her own but the resemblance was there.

"Don't you fucking dare bring that up." He leaned forward, his hands clenched at his sides and I blinked rapidly. Did Maricella know he was her father? From what Alpha Lawrence had told me, her parents were supposedly both dead, obviously her father survived his injuries but did she know that he did?

"*What*, Victor? Still lying to yourself about it?" There was an ugly look of mocking on Jace's face. His anger seemed to have no limit to it. "Still *pretending* that you don't see your mate in *everything* she does?" Jace's words were made to wound and even I felt a bit of disgust for them. Poking fun at a dead mate was cruel and so low that even most rogues wouldn't go there.

"I'm warning you, Jace. You don't *know*! You don't know what happened, what I had to do!" Victor growled deep in his chest, his entire form shaking as he tried to hold back his wolf. I could see his face turning more harsh, more angular and I shifted back towards the door just a fraction. I wouldn't be left in the room with no escape when he decided to wolf out on Jace.

"Why? Can't handle the truth that you left her there? Can't handle the fact you failed your mate and your little girl?" Jace had a rather ugly sneer on his face and it made him look even more formidable than usual.

Victor tilted his head, his long, tangled hair falling over one shoulder as his neck cracked ominously. "Jace-"

Jace cleared off his desk with a heavy snarl. "No! I'm sick and tired of this bullshit, Victor! Either you toe the fucking line or you get the fuck out!" A vein throbbed in his forehead as he shouted the words.

"Bennett, what are you doing?" At Maricella's soft voice the office fell instantly silent and I turned my head so quickly my neck cracked slightly. Her brown curls were a mess of tangles and she was wiping at her tired grey eyes but she was still beautiful, even as a sleepy mused female with bedhead. "Come back to bed. I'm tired." She yawned and I felt two sets of angry eyes land on me at her words and I kept my face blank. That wasn't something I needed to explain to them.

"Excuse me?" Jace's voice was icy and I refused to let myself look at him. I could feel his gaze drilling into the side of my head. I didn't particularly need two father figures lecturing me on my relationship with Maricella after I had three brotherly figures do it earlier.

"Bennett, please. I'm tired." She ignored the males in the office as she shuffled her way into the room and grasped my hand in hers. I looked down at it and she took a step towards the office door, tugging me with her.

"You aren't going anywhere with him." Jace's tone was icy and forbidding and I tensed at his words. My wolf didn't like being told to keep away from our mate. I forced down a growl as Maricella stiffened, her entire body on point before she sunk close to me, seeking my protection, her tired eyes wary as they looked at him.

"What the hell is going on?" Davin came into the room, rubbing his face with a dark scowl. So Jace *had* woken other people up with his shouting. I wondered just who else might join us.

Jace gestured to me and Maricella. "I'm gunna tell you what is going on. Bennett is sleeping with Maricella." He spat the words out and Mari grasped at my stomach and back, trying to cling to me. I wrapped an arm around her, holding her close as I looked between the two males

"*So*? I doubt they are doing anything improper." Davin's scowl deepened as he looked over at us. "She looks exhausted. I *highly* doubt she would want to try anything and Bennett is too honourable to do anything without permission." I was surprised he was defending us but I appreciated it. I didn't want anyone thinking I would take advantage of her.

"I won't stand for this." Jace bared his teeth as a deep growl rumbled out of his chest. The sound of it made Maricella sink further towards me with a low growl and Davin snapped his teeth together as he noticed.

"And what are you going to do about it?" Davin's tone was icy. "Scream in her face, shake her, leave bruises like you did last time?" Jace actually had the grace to look ashamed at that and I felt Mari's chest rumble at the words. The low growl made me more than aware that Maricella was having issues with controlling her wolf. I squeezed her hand gently. She was trembling and I knew her wolf was trying to push forward but I was impressed at how long she was lasting in keeping her in check.

"Davin, please calm down." Victor spoke carefully as he looked at the bristling male and I glanced at him. He looked pained but his focus was on his daughter and how she shook.

"That's *rich* coming from you. You're the reason for all of it. You couldn't reign in your instincts for three seconds, could you? You just had to fuck everything up." Davin's voice was low and accusing as he turned to look at the wild.

Victor turned his full attention to Maricella as if looking for an ally. "I don't think it is a good idea for you and him to be in the same room right now."

A deep growl came out of Maricella's chest at that, her control over her wolf was fraying with all the tension. All eyes snapped to her in surprise at that. "You don't get to parent me. You gave that right up when you left me on Tacita territory when I was four years old." At her words there was a thick and still silence and I looked between her and Victor. Whatever colour he had in his face before was now completely gone. I should have placed my bets on her knowing. She was too intelligent not to have figured it out.

He swallowed hard and looked down at the floor, shame radiating off of him. Davin crossed his arms over his chest as he looked at the wild. "She has a point. Did you think we didn't figure it out? Did you think *she* wouldn't figure it out?"

Jace's gaze immediately snapped towards Davin with a sharp growl."You don't get to bring that into this, Davin." There was a heavy censure to Jace's voice that had Davin giving a cold laugh.

"You didn't seem to mind throwing it into *Mari's* face when you were busy screaming at her. They share DNA that doesn't make *her* responsible for *his* fuck ups." Davin jabbed his finger at the wild, his green eyes narrowing dangerously. I didn't like how he was between me and getting Maricella to safety. I needed a clear exit and he was blocking it. "Do you like her acting like this? She's *terrified* of you to the point her wolf is aggressive with you. Do you like that you did that to her?" Davin gestured to where Maricella was clinging to me, scared and aggressive growls rumbling her chest as her wolf fought against her control to protect her.

"Davin." Jace's tone was sharp and Davin moved further into the room as he scoffed.

"Don't *Davin* me." He jerked his finger towards his father. "We made her a promise and you broke your promise. It could take her months to get rid of that fear and work through that trauma response. *Months*." The scarred Alpha stared down at his desk, his mouth pressed into a thin line. As if sensing a break in the tension Davin looked at me. "Take her back to bed, she needs the sleep." I looked down at her and her grey eyes were glassy with tears and exhaustion carved deep lines into her face.

I nodded at Davin before I started towards the door, keeping my body between her and the three males in the room. Once safely out I lead her back to the basement stairs. That had been a little too intense. There had been a lot of fear and aggression in her and my wolf wanted to make sure she was okay. We slowly made our way back to my room and I opened the door before pulling her inside and shutting it. I pulled her to the bed and sat her down on it.

"Are you okay?" I crouched down in front of her and at my words I could see her crumbling. She raised a trembling hand up to her mouth and she started crying. My wolf was instantly tense, not knowing what to do as her entire form shook as she cried. "Sweet one, it's okay." The panicky feeling started to fill my body and I sat down beside her and pulled her onto my lap, trying to get the tears to stop. I couldn't stand seeing her cry. I held her tightly, trying to fight the constricting feeling surrounding my chest at the sound of her soft sobs.

Her arms wrapped around my neck and she pressed her tear stained face into my shoulder as her chest heaved out the hurt she was keeping inside. I felt frozen. I wanted the tears to stop. I needed her to stop crying because each sob was tearing at me viciously. I held her a bit tighter and shifted further back on the bed before laying her down. I brushed her hair from her face as she removed her arms from my neck and covered her face with her hands. I shushed her gently, trying to stop the panic from encasing me.

I hated that she was crying and I hated how useless I was with getting her to stop. I could deal with crying females, I *could,* but Maricella was different. Her happiness was more important to me and my wolf than anything so seeing her so hurt with nothing we could do was causing us both to panic.

I rubbed at her back, holding her close as she continued her breakdown. After a few minutes her sobs slowed down and I felt the tightness in my chest loosen as I murmured to her softly. I didn't exactly know what I was saying. I was just hoping the sound of my voice would help calm her down.

"Don't leave me, okay? I woke up and you were gone and I thought everything was a dream." She sniffled as she pulled her hands from her face and I made a sound in the back of my throat before I pressed my forehead to hers.

I brushed her sticky cheek with the back of my hand before cupping it and wiping away her tears with my thumb. "I'm sorry, sweet one. I won't leave. I promise." I was relieved to hear that someone felt the same way about our situation.

"Okay. Can we sleep now?" Her voice was soft and despite her sniffles I could hear how tired she was. I nodded before kissing her forehead and pulling the blanket over both of us. She snuggled closer, sniffling a few times before wiping at her cheeks. It didn't take her long to fall back asleep but I knew I was too wired from the intensity in the office. I couldn't hear anymore talking or walking around so either they were all dead or decided to call a temporary truce.

I watched Maricella sleep and couldn't help myself as I brushed my thumb over her eyebrow. I honestly felt a bit off-kilter about our bond. Not a bad feeling but everything with Maricella was changing how I usually dealt with people. I was cold to the people around me but she had fallen into a different category completely. I felt like a different person with her only to be yanked back into the cold persona I had worn for so long whenever I dealt with someone else. I didn't mind it. I loved it when I made her smile but having to switch between the two personalities so often and quickly made me think I had a split personality disorder.

It was a terrible habit but I would be willing to endure pretty much anything for Maricella. I hadn't lied when I told her I would pull the stars from the sky if she asked. I let out a heavy sigh and closed my eyes. I knew I wouldn't be able to sleep but I wanted to stay with her until she woke up. I didn't want her to feel like I had left her again.

I winced at the thought of the males I had to deal with in the house. Only three females, not including Bailey. Oblitus was a small pack, only nine members. Not large enough to qualify as a pack at all but Jace seemed to not care about those rules. Once you hit fifteen members you were allowed to name your pack, *if* you had a territory. Jace had a territory but not fifteen members but I wasn't going to argue with him and I doubted anyone else was either.

Oblitus didn't have a normal pack dynamic either. It seemed like they were a bunch of broken people who had used each other to build themselves back up. Davin had told me that nearly twice as many people had come through the pack but hadn't stayed. He had stated it was where the forgotten dregs of shifter society would go. Half broken mate bonds were a specialty of the Oblitus pack doctor, Amber.

I winced at the thought of Maricella going through that. I wanted to hurt Lucas for causing her pain but a sense of justice filled me at the memory of him trying to tear out his own heart. I was glad I got to witness the punishment Mene had inflicted upon him for the pain he had given Maricella. I didn't get to watch Beta John's punishment but I was content in the fact I had watched Lucas'.

Maricella shifted beside me, her cold fingers reaching out and touching my bare chest again. I smirked a little at the action. She needed to touch me like I needed to touch her. I was proud that our bond was so strong. Very few shifters could say their mate bond survived a half severed bond and two years separation. I sucked in a breath at the realization that I would do it all over again if it resulted in having her beside me like she was.

As strange as it was, she was everything to me. My allegiances to my pack had meant nothing. I was willing to leave it all behind just to be with her. I didn't care who I was aligned with as long as I had her by my side. I wanted her to be happy and I wanted her to be safe. I wanted those two things above everything and I wasn't even certain if it was just the bond that was making me feel that way or if the innumerable days I spent loving her memory that made me feel like that.

I found myself absently tracing patterns into the soft skin of her side and I froze, not realizing I had slipped my hand under her tank top. I slowly pulled my hand away from her warm skin and tugged her shirt down. It didn't do well to have any form of temptation where Maricella was concerned. I pushed away the thoughts of our kiss on the porch. I didn't need to be reminded of that when her face was so close to mine. I meant it when I told her it wasn't right to just take a kiss. I looked at her slightly parted lips with a faint groan. No matter how much I wanted too.

I pulled my gaze from her lips with difficulty and stared at the wall. It would be difficult. Every instinct was telling me to make her mine, to shower her with affection and love but despite what I had told her, you could see the jagged edges she was trying so hard to hold together. She had done well for herself. She truly had but I could tell it was starting to take a toll on her.

I wanted to take her burdens from her, to ease her mind and let her relax. Although I had a feeling that it would be a bit longer coming than I would have liked. Teaching a shifter how to overcome their wolf was a big challenge. Especially considering Maricella's wolf was hell bent on making sure she was protected against everything. An aggressive, scared wolf didn't work well with others.

I rubbed a hand over my face and rolled onto my back, hating how her fingertips left my bare skin. The spot seemed cold now but I ignored the feeling as I stared at the ceiling. I wanted to be there for her for the rest of her life. I wanted to watch her hair turn grey and I wanted to watch as she got laugh lines from smiling at our children. I wanted to be there for her until we both grew old. The want was like a physical ache and I closed my eyes and inhaled deeply, her scent calming my rolling thoughts. Soft and feminine, just like her.

I let it sink into me and I felt my muscles relaxing. There would never be a day that went by where I did not know her scent. It was so ingrained into my mind that it was practically a part of who I was. I slid an arm behind my head and rested my other one on my stomach. Maricella grumbled something under her breath and I bit back a smile. Davin had been right, she made quite a few noises in her sleep. I stiffened slightly as she shifted over on the bed, wiggling her head onto my arm and sliding her arm across my chest. She muttered something under her breath, a ghost of a smile crossing her lips.

I relaxed and let the feeling of her so close to me sink in. It was very hard to not be affected by her touch, even as innocent as it was. My nerves came to life when she touched me. Fire burned through my veins, sinking into me, demanding more and more until I felt like I was going to turn to ash. I stared hard at the ceiling, swallowing as I did so. I couldn't push with her. I didn't want to scare her off.

"Bennett, I can hear you thinking." Her voice was mumbled with sleep and she shifted slightly to look up at me and I could do nothing but smirk at her. She was so adorable when she was half asleep. I felt a strange softening in my chest as she blinked sleepily at me. Her grey eyes half lidded as she looked at me.

"Hush, Maricella. Sleep." I said it softly before taking my hand out from beneath my head and wrapping it around her gently.

"I can hear you thinking and it's distracting." She yawned loudly before shifting again, resting her head on my chest with a sigh.

"You can't possibly hear me thinking." I chuckled slightly and she let out a groan before rubbing at her eyes with her hand. We hadn't claimed our bond, there was no way the connection was there.

"I can. It's like a murmur of your voice in the back of my head. Too far away to hear fully but it's there." At her words I stiffened slightly. Our bond was a lot stronger than I had thought. Mates didn't usually hear each other's thoughts until they were bound and fully mated. I liked that she could hear my voice in her mind, even if it was unintelligible and in murmurs. "Stop it. I'm never going to be able to sleep if you keep doing that." She was frowning, I didn't need to look at her face to know she was.

"I'm sorry, sweet one." I bent my head and kissed the top of hers gently, letting my lips linger as I took in her scent.

"'S okay." She muttered it out before nuzzling my chest and letting out a small sigh, letting her arm wrap around me once more. I relaxed into her embrace. It felt right to have her in my arms. Everything about her felt right to me. I closed my eyes and willed all thoughts away. She needed sleep and if my inner musings were keeping her awake, I would try my best to stop thinking so much. I let myself sink into the comfort she provided. I still knew I wouldn't be able to sleep but I would try to stop thinking.

Her small arm tightened on me slightly and she let out a small sigh of contentment. I looked down at her before letting my hand tangle in her curls. She was so much healthier than the day of the banishment or any of the time I had seen her while she was at Tacita. Her body had filled out nicely with good care and her hair was soft and no longer hung around her face limply. She was so beautiful that it made my chest ache before I wanted to grab her and push her against the closest hard surface. The thought of being between her legs as I kissed her hungr-

"Stop thinking like *that*." Her voice was a small squeak and she glanced at me, her face red. I could see it despite the fact it was very much dark in the room.

"I'm sorry. I can't help it." I bit back a chuckle as she sat up slightly and glowered at me.

"You aren't the least bit sorry and I want to be mad at you for thinking *anything* right now but your previous train of thought has derailed my wolf from annoyance into raging, hormonal desire." Her eyes went wide and she slapped her hand over her mouth as she realized what she said.

I raised an eyebrow. "Oh *really*?" I smirked and brought my face closer to her as I locked my gaze with hers. The thought that her wolf had approved of my train of thought made my wolf very happy. I could see him grinning in the back of my head.

"*No*. You don't get to look at me like you are the big bad wolf and I am *not* little red riding hood. It's not allowed." All tiredness was gone from her voice as she narrowed her eyes as she pointed at me. I couldn't help it and laughed softly at her reaction.

I wrapped my arm around her waist and tugged her to my chest, ignoring the adorable squeak she let out. "I'm not going to do anything you aren't ready for, Maricella. However, my thoughts are terribly dirty and you should not venture there." I couldn't help but grin as she gave a sound of protest before pushing on my chest slightly to look at me through narrowed eyes.

"You think I can help it? Your thoughts are little whispers in the back of my head." She pointed to her head and hissed the words out accusingly as if it was my fault she could almost hear my thoughts.

"I'm not apologizing for, nor am I going to stop, thinking about every little thing I want to do to you every time I see you." I let some heat into my words and she inhaled sharply before narrowing her grey eyes at me.

"I'm sorry but I get to see vague images of all the things my wolf wants to do to you. I do not need your thoughts in my head as well. I'll go insane." She lifted her head defiantly despite the blush staining her cheeks. I couldn't help myself and laughed once more. She softly hit my chest with a closed fist. "It's *not* funny!" I could see her trying her hardest not to smile as my laughter turned to chuckles after a few moments.

"I think your wolf and I will get along fine." My grin stayed firmly on my face and she made a sound of irritation mixed with disgust.

"Don't encourage her bad behaviour." A smile was frantically trying to spread across her face but she was admirably forcing it away. She couldn't stop the amused twinkle in her grey eyes, the colour lightening significantly even in the dark. Her eyes were remarkable and I wanted nothing more than to watch them change from her moods but I could still see the dark bags that hung under them. She needed sleep.

"As much as I would like to encourage your wolf's bad behaviour, you need to sleep, sweet one." I pressed a kiss to her forehead and pulled her to my chest once more.

"I like it when you call me that." Embarrassment coated her quiet voice and I smiled in pleasure. I liked that I made her happy, even if it was just for a name.

"I'm glad. Now *sleep*, Maricella. You clearly need it." I didn't like how she was still exhausted after sleeping for most of the day. Anyone would have been good after a nap but she spent the entire afternoon in her room, lying in her bed with Bailey. I just wanted her to be healthy and her not sleeping wasn't helping with that. I closed my eyes, willing my thoughts away. I thought of nothing as I tried my hardest not to disturb her as she settled onto my chest, trying to find a comfortable spot to sleep on.

She let out a small sigh and relaxed against me. I forced myself to stop thinking, to not feel anything so that I did not distract her from her sleep. Without our bond being completed, she would have no way of stopping my thoughts whispering in the back of her head. I didn't like that she couldn't shut it out enough to sleep but at the same time I liked that I was there with her, letting her know she wasn't alone.

I never wanted to have her be alone again.

"Be *quiet*, Bennett." Her voice was low and I couldn't help but chuckle as I tightened my arm around her once more.

TWENTY-TWO

I stared hard at the phone on the desk. Bennett had grabbed my hand at the breakfast table and had hastily written something on my palm before he was off with the others to do his tests. It was a phone number and I bit my lip slightly as I looked at the phone. Bailey was currently napping in my chair in the living room and I had snuck off to phone whoever it was that Bennett wanted me to call. I hesitantly picked up the handset and dialed the numbers with a shaky hand.

It rang twice before I heard someone pick up the other end. "Hello?" It was a deep voice that tugged on my memory slightly but I pushed it away quickly out of habit.

"Hi?" It came out in a rather startled squeak that I wanted to groan at. My face flared red with slight embarrassment as a silence fell from the other end of the line.

"Who is this?" There was a faint hint of suspension to the tone and I swallowed hard. "This line is a private line-"

"Lucas! Get the fuck out of my office and stop answering my phone!" The booming voice in the background was more than familiar and I felt a large smile spread across my face. I could hear the phone being exchanged and I couldn't help but feel happiness radiating out of my chest at the gift

Bennett had given me. "This is Alpha Lawrence." His voice was gruff in my ear and I pressed the phone closer to me as if it would bring me closer to him.

"Hi, daddy." I knew I was too old to call him that but I couldn't help it, I had missed so much with him that I felt like I was reverting back to my childhood when I heard him speak.

I could almost hear his shock through the phone but it didn't last long. "Maricella?" There was a sudden softness to his voice and happiness threaded through the words.

"It's me. How are you?" I swallowed quickly before sitting down in Uncle Jace's chair. I settled myself into the well worn chair as I clutched the phone in my hand tightly.

"Hey, sweetheart. I'm hanging in there." His voice immediately softened to the tone I remembered as a child and I felt tears prick at my eyes. We had *so* many years stolen from us. "All of my favourite people are gone, so I'm not having too much fun at the moment." He sounded sad and I winced, thinking of Amber and him. She didn't reject him but she had walked away and that must have hurt just as badly. "I don't want to sound like I don't want to talk to you but how did you get this number?" He sounded genuinely curious and I smiled brightly

"Bennett gave it to me." Pleasure spread through my chest and limbs at the gift he had given me. A way to reach out to my father, a way to talk to him. His gift couldn't be repaid and I swallowed against the sudden lump in my throat. I honestly didn't deserve him or his warmth. He was a male without equal in my eyes.

"Is he treating you alright?" His voice went back to being gruff for a moment, letting his stern, fatherly side show that he still cared about my well being.

Even in those moments when I had been an omega I could still remember that tone, still remember the faint pleading as he secretly begged me to tell him the truth, to tell him something, *anything*, he could use to save me. The voice in my head had always drowned him out. He had made some poor decisions but he had been *so* young and he had trusted people he thought he could and they had taken advantage of that.

"Yes, he's a gentleman." Nothing but that, he was perfect in every way when it came to his treatment of me. I could sense that it eased his mind and he paused slightly.

"And the omega, Bailey, I think her name was. How is she?" He asked it softly and I could tell he was genuinely curious to know about her and how she was doing and I truly appreciated that he cared enough to ask.

"She's going to get better. She's actually Davin's mate so there is that." A silence fell and I waited for him to speak. I could sense he needed too.

"And how's Amber?" There was a hitch in his voice and I wanted to be there to give him the comfort I knew he needed. I knew how hard it was to be separated from a mate, being away from Bennett for those achingly long minutes had been almost more than I could bear. I couldn't imagine what it would feel like to have him all but reject me before he left me of his own volition.

I swallowed hard, trying to shove those thoughts from my head. "To be honest she's moping in her office. She's not happy." I wanted him to know that he wasn't the only one affected. That her decision hurt her as well. She didn't state it but I could see it in her behaviour, in how she held herself and picked at her food. This was a decision that cut her just as deeply as it must have cut him.

"Oh." There was a pause. "Could... could you tell me about her?" There was a hurt longing in his voice and I felt my heart ache for him. I knew what it felt like to know nothing about a mate, I knew that feeling intimately and I didn't want him to suffer that.

"I can." I nodded even though I knew he couldn't see me. "Her name is Amber June Blanche. She is, I *think*, forty some years old. She has been a pack doctor for over twenty years." I frowned slightly, quickly thinking it over in my head, trying to get the details right. "Her favourite colour is mint green, like the ice cream colour and not the plant." My frown deepened as I tried to remember more details for him. "She is very work orientated and very opinionated. Her and Uncle Jace get into a lot of arguments that she usually wins. She is very passionate about everything she puts her heart into." I paused again, the rest of the knowledge escaping me for the moment. It was slightly aggravating to have happen. I wanted to help him more.

"Has..." He paused as well, his voice pained. "Has she said anything about me?" His voice was wary and I hated how I had to tell him the truth.

"Not really. She's hurting but I think she's scared too. She's not a fan of Alphas." I knew she wasn't. She had alluded to that fact numerous times but I had never pried before. I wanted to know why but she sometimes had a haunted look in her eyes that made me never want to ask and I wasn't about to start now. I knew that sometimes someone else's burdens could negatively affect your own and I knew that she would never tell me based on that in particular.

"Why?" The words came out like a defeated sigh.

"I'm not sure. She barely tolerates Uncle Jace but that is only because he lets her speak her mind and doesn't give her trouble for it. I would ask her for you but I...I-" I wanted to make him happy, I wanted him to be happy. He was my father. The young male who raised me, who cleaned my chocolate covered face and kissed my injuries no matter how minor they were but I couldn't find it in me to say I would pry into Amber's life like that. I didn't want to drudge up any of those memories for her.

"Don't worry about it, little one." He said it quickly as if he could sense my internal dilemma and I felt a wave of relief as it made my shoulder slump. "Can you tell me anything else?" He was making his tone lighter, trying to shake the heaviness that had settled over our conversation.

"Well, she hates onions and cannot cook at all. Last time she tried she literally set the stove on fire. Everyone has banned her from the kitchen." I listened as he laughed loudly at my words. "She loves reading tedious medical books. The newer the version the better and she has this habit of twirling a chunk of hair around her finger and yanking on it when she is thinking." I tilted my head slightly. "She's a *very* kind female, she loves helping people. She has been with me since I came here. She would make a great mother one day." I thought about them having kids and I smiled wider. I wanted siblings. Shifters aged differently than humans, our lifespans were much longer so they could have children well into their seventies if they wanted.

"She cares about you a lot." He sounded pleased at the thought but a bit hurt as well. I could only imagine him wondering why she couldn't care for him like that.

"She's my therapist. She knows everything that I went through." I could almost hear his wince on the other end of the line and I wanted to hit myself for bringing it up.

There was a tense pause before I heard him let out a heavy sigh. "I'm *so* sorry I wasn't there for you, Maricella." He choked it out, "I wanted to bring you with me… to Russia. I wanted to bring you so *badly* that it hurt but I listened to John." His voice shook with his anger and something like anguish and I felt my breath catch in my throat. John had done so many terrible things to so many people. "I listened to him and *you* paid the price." Shame and regret coated his voice thickly and I felt my heart twist harshly in my chest. "I was *so* stupid. I knew something was wrong the moment I came back but I let myself be deceived. I *knew* there was something wrong, that you were hiding something, but I didn't- I didn't push."

He cut himself off and let out a shaky breath. "I should have been there for you. Should have done something, *anything*, to make sure you were okay. I failed you in the worst possible way and when I finally figured it out-" There was a thick pause, "You were… I was so scared that if I pulled you out of it it would somehow make things worse."

His voice trembled slightly and I felt a returning burn in my eyes. "*Don't*, dad. Don't beat yourself up about it." I made my tone firm so he wouldn't continue. I didn't need to have him listen to me cry into the phone. I didn't want the moment tainted by that. I wanted it to be happy.

"*Someone* has to, Maricella. I failed you as a father and I failed as an Alpha. I *let* those things happen." His tone was sharp with anger towards himself and I could practically *feel* his self-loathing and it hurt my heart. "I didn't question anything and I blindly trusted others. I *need* to be held accountable for that." His tone was sharp, the same tone I had heard him use before when he signalled the end of a conversation but despite how my stomach twisted at the thought of defying him in his words, I knew my feelings needed to be said.

"You were young." I darted my eyes back and forth despite the nerves in my stomach as he gave a low sound in his throat.

"Enou-"

"Dad… let me say this." I winced as I cut him off but as the silence continued I cleared my throat. "You were young. Only twenty-one when Jace threw the pack at you. You weren't trained for the position, you didn't have any knowledge about what you needed to do to keep it or to keep the pack running." I took a deep breath. "You relied on who you thought you could trust. John was Jace's beta, why *wouldn't* you trust him?" He had no one and nothing to help him. He would have relied on anyone. He was so *young*. Jace had told her what had happened and she *ached* for the young male who had been tossed into that position with no preparation.

"And then when I came along you were only twenty-two, not nearly ready enough to take care of a child, but you did your best anyway and the memories I have of you show the kindest and most loving father who just wanted me to be happy." I paused and there was nothing from his end so I pushed on. "You made a mistake, you relied on someone you thought you could trust and I got hurt."

"You deserve to hate me for that. I let them do those things to you, let them *hurt* you." His voice hitched slightly. "My little girl."

The truth burned me but I knew that the feelings had to be released or they would fester. "I did resent you. When I was getting the memories back I resented you a lot for letting me stay there." I didn't need to hear him to feel his shame and self-loathing and I hated that I put it there. "But I also remembered that on some level what you were doing was trying to protect me. Not showing me open affection, silently begging me to tell you what was going on. You threw me as many life lines as you could but my mind prohibited me from taking them. You were young and you made a mistake." It was what I held onto. I had made mistakes as well. I had done things or said things I regretted, it was part of having humanity.

"I could have done *more*." His voice was clipped and hard and I bit back a sigh. "I should have taken you from that position. I should have done it."

"No you couldn't have...My mind... it was broken." I knew that now. I had learned so much over the years and where I had been when I first came to Oblitus. There had definitely been an aspect of my mental state that had been fractured. "You would have caused me more harm if you had done that and didn't have the appropriate tools to fix me." I couldn't even imagine how I would have turned out if I hadn't had the resources I had access to.

“It was just...” I swallowed hard, “It was just a mess that neither of us were ready for or could cope with.” That was the barest truth of it, it was such a *mess*.

There was another thick silence and he cleared his throat, "Does Jace know you called me?" His voice was back to being slightly gruff as he changed the subject.

"No." I pinched my lips together as my wolf growled, baring her teeth in anger as the fear churned my stomach.

"Alright, little one. I won't tell if you won't." There was a conspiratorial edge to his tone as he said it that had me smiling but after a moment he let out a sigh. "I'm trying my hardest to be able to come there. I am. In a few months hopefully. You can't tell anyone though. I can't risk it getting out." His tone was serious and I tried to hide the hope that soared through me at his words.

A few months and he would be with me again. I hated how badly our relationship had been twisted and torn. I just wanted my father. My *real* father. Victor was my biological father but he was never my dad. It was always apparent when I caught his gaze, his face a blank emotionless slate before he looked away. It hurt, being ignored like that, having him pretend to not see me, to know me. I was getting used to it, I had a long time to get used to it, and that was the saddest part.

"Okay." I nodded, I wanted him to trust me. I wanted that trust back so badly that I hurt with it.

"I can trust you, right? You aren't going to run to Jace and tell on me are you?" His serious tone had faded to lightly teasing. I remembered that tone from when we used to make a mess in the kitchen. Him asking me if I would tell the cook on him and my childish giggles as I vehemently refused to turn him in.

"We currently aren't on speaking terms. I can barely stomach being in the same room as him right now. Your secrets are safe with me." The words felt sour on my tongue but they were the truth. I was just too... scared. My mind was a strange place and sometimes it showed, a traumatized mind didn't always work the way one thought it should and what happened had triggered something inside of my psyche and now it was all a mess.

"You put my big, bad brother in the dog house. I wish I could be there to see that." There was a small silence on the other end of the line before he sighed heavily once more. "I have to go, little one. I have some things to do. I am always here if you want someone to talk to. Just pick up the phone and give me a call. I love you and stay safe, okay?" I could hear the hurt in his voice. He didn't want to say goodbye and neither did I. I missed my father. I missed him so much it hurt.

"Okay. I love you too." I felt my heart lurch in my chest. "Can you say it for me? Please?" I was pleading but I needed to hear the stupid nursery rhyme from him. I needed to refresh the comfort the words had always brought me. There was a silence that made my heart jump into my throat but he chuckled faintly.

"Mary, Mary, quite contrary." His comforting voice brought tears to my eyes and I held the phone tightly, pressing it harder to my ear. "How does your garden grow? With silver bells, and cockle shells, and pretty ladies all in a row." I sniffled against the feeling the words brought. It had been too long since I had heard my father say the rhyme to me. I felt like a small child again back when everything was right in my world.

"Thank you, daddy." I whispered the words and willed the tears not to fall.

"You're welcome, my darling girl. I love you." The line went dead and I set the phone back in its cradle. I felt a bit lighter but saddened that the call couldn't last longer. I let out a heavy sigh and wiped at my eyes. I had hated how little I had been allowed to speak to him on Tacita pack territory. I looked at the number on the palm and I felt panic rise in me as I saw the numbers had smudged slightly. I frantically searched for a pen and a chunk of paper on Uncle Jace's desk.

Are you okay? I can feel your panic. It was Uncle Jace and I winced at the threatening growl my wolf sent through my head even as the fear and panic bloomed in my stomach. I focused on shutting down his connection, barricading it strongly. I didn't like how it made me feel and Amber always told me to avoid what scared me until I was ready to safely deal with it. I found a pen and paper and quickly jotted down the number and clasped it in my hand tightly before I left the study.

Maricella, dad is freaking out right now. Are you okay? Davin sounded exasperated and I rolled my eyes.

I'm fine. I just... I just can't have him in my head right now. I made my way to the living room and felt relieved to see Bailey sleeping. She needed the sleep and would for the next few weeks. I smiled slightly when I remembered finding Davin sleeping in front of my door after Bennett couldn't keep his mind quiet. I could still feel his whispered murmurings in my head but it was currently comforting rather than irritating.

I can't blame you but the next time he asks you something just send it to one of us so he doesn't blow a gasket. He doesn't like how he doesn't have a way to communicate with you. He sounded amused and I shrugged slightly. I could deal with that even though the entire situation made my feelings go into complete and utter turmoil.

Okay. My wolf doesn't want anything to do with him. I leaned against the door jamb and watched as Bailey snuggled deeper into the chair and the blanket.

What about you? He sounded genuinely curious about how I felt about the situation but I also knew he wouldn't like the answer.

To be honest? I'm terrified of him. I rubbed at my face, I felt guilty for it but I knew I didn't have control over that. What happened was traumatizing and my trauma response wasn't something I could just shut off. I couldn't change how I responded. *I don't know if he's going to flip out again. I don't want to be around him and be focused on every move he makes because I don't trust him not to hurt me again. It's that or have my wolf attack him. I can't do either so it's better to avoid him.* I could feel a stillness from Davin and I sighed. I didn't want to strain his relationship with his father.

How's Bailey? His change of subject was much appreciated as I looked at his mate.

She's currently sleeping in my chair. She's doing okay though. She can only get better from here. She has you after all. I kept my tone light and could feel his sudden relief at my words. He was worried and I wondered for a moment about Bennett.

As if sensing my sudden change of thought Davin let out a sigh along the mind link. He's not saying anything but he keeps glancing towards the house. He's probably worried about you. Especially since dad let it slip Luka was coming down today. At Davin's words I let out a small excited squeal.

Alpha Sterling, or Luka as we liked to call him, was a close family friend. Jace and his father had been close friends before everything had gone down with Uncle Jace's mate. He was like a brother to Davin more than anything else. Especially since he had come out every month or so to train with Uncle Jace since he had been forced into the Alpha position five years ago.

He was family to me as well. I loved Luka dearly. He was a soft spoken male and his calm and soothing energy had helped me quite a bit through my transition from being an omega. I had felt comfortable around him, certainly more than the others. He was non-threatening but in a very good way. We were good friends and he was more like a brother to me than anything. It had been a long time since I had seen him. I felt a happy smile slowly cross my face. I needed to see some normality, something normal in the chaos that was now my life.

I wandered around the living room, keeping myself busy tidying up the various messes I found. It was like a compulsion when I saw something out of place. Amber told me I would probably always be like that. I didn't mind it, cleaning always made me feel better, calmer and more peaceful.

I wasn't sure how long I had cleaned for but the living room was completely tidy and in order when I realized what I was doing. I glanced at Bailey before moving over and tucking the blanket around her tighter. It would do her good to nap.

There was a scratching at the front door and high pitched whining that made my heart race and a smile break out on my face. I tore my gaze from Bailey and bolted for the door, my feet making small thuds on the floor as I tore the front door open to see two dirty looking black wolves. Scars cross-crossed their bodies and one had a deep scar that went over his left eye and down his cheek. I had always wondered how Ezekiel hadn't gone blind from the wound.

As soon as they saw me they were immediately pushing me around, weaving around my legs, taking in my scent and marking theirs in a friendly greeting. I cooed at them as I touched whatever parts of the large wolves that I could. Michael nipped at my fingers gently before licking my hand.

"Hey, how far is Luka?" I smiled as he tilted his head to the left like a puppy. On the rather intimidating looking wolf it was comical. Ezekiel nudged the back of my leg with his snout before licking my other hand. I scratched at the ever itchy spot above his left eye. The right side of the scar always seemed itchy for him.

I can scent something unfamiliar heading to the house. I'm guessing wilds. Angie's voice held warning as she said it through the pack wide link and I rubbed between Ezekiel's eyes. I could feel everyone's sudden tension at the words, their presence focusing on me, pushing on the walls of my mind to make sure I was alright.

I know. Michael and Ezekiel are here. Luka shouldn't be too long. I spun around and grabbed Michael's face roughly and shook his head back and forth with a playful growl. With that he leapt backwards and dropped his front end and barked at me. The sound was loud but I didn't care as I lunged at him, intent on trying to best him. I knew I never would. He was a well-trained shifter and a wild as well so his instincts and reflexes were trying for even the best opponents. True to his training he kept out of my reach almost like he was taunting my slower reflexes as he nipped at me gently.

I could hear Ezekiel let out a huffing groan and his heavy body hit the floor as he flopped down. He was always the serious one between the two of them. I let out a small battle cry and changed targets, sprawling on his vulnerable form. He let out a huff of air but let me straddle his prone form in a pretend victory.

"I have bested the warrior! None are as strong as me." I tilted my head back and cheered loudly. Michael nudged me roughly, sending me tumbling off Ezekiel. I glowered at him as I wiped some pretend dirt off my pants. "Another challenger? I shall defeat you as well!" He gave me a wolfy grin that made him look even more intimidating before he barked at me rapidly. I jumped at him and let out a growl, resisting the urge to shift and let my wolf have fun with them. Despite being wild, they were as much family as Luka.

Before I knew it Michael had me on my back, pinning me on the floor while growling playfully in my face. As playful as a large, dangerous, scarred wolf could look. I just scrunched my face up at him. He snapped the air in front of my nose playfully and there was a terrified scream from the hallway. Michael and Ezekiel were instantly on the offensive. Their hackles raised almost in perfect synchronization as they eyed the newcomer. I rolled over onto my stomach and could see Bailey's pant legs and I could hear her heart beating frantically.

"Stand down you smelly pups. That's Bailey." I got to my feet and smiled at her brightly. Her face was pale and her eyes were wide as she stared at the two wolves who had sat down at my words, their tongues hanging out, all aggression instantly gone. "Hey, Bailey. Did we wake you?" I rubbed the back of my neck sheepishly. I had forgotten about her in my excitement from seeing them.

"He was attacking you." Her voice was a terrified whisper and I laughed at her words and shook her head. I moved over to her and grasped her hand before gently tugging her forward. She dug her feet in slightly and I smiled at the action.

"No he wasn't. Bailey. This is Ezekiel and Michael." I pointed them out and at their names they bowed their heads, humanity glinting out for just a fraction of a moment. "They're Alpha Sterling's loyal guards. Also, the world's best playmates. Well Michael is. Ezekiel has always been a stick in the mud." I stuck my tongue out at his low growl and Michael bumped his wide shoulder against his companion with a strange huffing sound that reminded me of laughter. Bailey giggled at the movement.

Omegas always took better to wolves than human forms. It was so much easier to deal with wolves than people. I pulled her closer and Michael let out a whine before slowly wiggling onto the floor and rolling onto his back, showing her his belly. Bailey wasted no time in going on her knees and scratching at his chest vigorously. I bit back a laugh as his back foot started kicking frantically. Ezekiel watched them with disinterest before he leaned over and licked Bailey's face gently.

I clasped my hands together in contentment. They liked her and with that came their protection and companionship. I could always count on them when they were around and that had meant a lot to me when I had first started my transition to normalcy.

"Hey, Bailey. I bet it has been a very long time since your wolf has come out." I watched as she stiffened slightly before ceasing all movement. "Do you want to play a bit?" I watched as she turned her head to look at me with wide eyes. She nodded vigorously, a bright and wide smile on her face before she started stripping. I followed suit as I headed outside. I ignored the nudity, as did Ezekiel and Michael as they left out the open front door. I grabbed Bailey's hand and tugged her towards the door. I pulled off my shirt, kicked out of my jeans, and once I hit the porch I allowed the shift to happen.

It was almost comforting to hear my bones shifting and rearranging in my body. It was over quickly and I shook my fur out and looked over my shoulder to see a smaller black wolf looking around timidly. I barked at her happily before I bounded towards Michael. Ezekiel never wanted to play with us but I never minded because he was always watching. Michael stood still, his head lowered as he looked at Bailey.

I whirled around and pranced towards her. I barked in her face before jumping backwards. I whined and nipped at her until she nipped back at me. I barked before retreating and after a few moments of teasing she jumped at me. Her small form wasn't very heavy but I allowed her to push me over as she yipped excitedly. With another excited yip she started bolting around the yard in wide circles. Michael joined her and as soon as I shook off the grass I followed him.

Despite her previous exhaustion, Bailey's wolf was full of energy as she zipped back and forth, even giving Michael a hard time in trying to catch her. I fell back and laid down watching the two of them run around, burning off Bailey's excessive energy. I glanced at Ezekiel before slowly belly crawling towards him. His eyes were closed but I knew he could sense my approach. I wiggled slightly as I crawled forward more. I wanted to play with him, despite knowing he would never let his guard down enough for that. Michael did but Ezekiel was always wary and never forgot his instincts.

I paused as Ezekiel's eyes cracked open, the dark green eyes of the wolf focusing on me. I let out a huff of irritation before bounding the rest of the way to him and grabbing the scruff of his neck, shaking my head vigorously with playful growls. He suffered the shaking for longer than I thought he would before he had me on the ground, the earth pressing into my ribs. He didn't growl at me but instead flopped on me, pinning me down. My wolf hated the feeling of his heavy weight on us. She wanted to play and I growled at him, squirming under his dead weight. I wanted out of his rather unorthodox pin. I knew he had done it because my wolf wouldn't be able to escape it or retaliate.

I whined pathetically as I tried harder to wiggle free. He was always a wet blanket. A heavy, oppressively warm, wet blanket that didn't like fun. I finally ceased struggling and let out a huff of air, trying to focus on breathing despite his heavyweight trying its hardest to crush me. I wheezed out a breath and struggled to inhale before Ezekiel was torn rather roughly off my frame. Michael nudged me gently while Bailey barked frantically in worry. I huffed out a sigh of irritation before standing up and shaking myself off.

The movement letting them know I was alright before I shifted. I stretched in human form while Bailey and Michael went back to playing. I went back to the porch and my discarded clothes. I pulled them on quickly before sitting down on the porch. I closed my eyes and could hear something approaching and I bit back a smile as a large head gently placed itself in my lap. I kept my eyes closed as I slowly swirled my fingers in Ezekiel's fur. He let out a rumbling groan and relaxed into my touch.

A peaceful feeling filled me as I absently scratched his head and listened to Michael and Bailey playing in the yard. Her yipping was growing less exuberant and I was pleased to know that Michael had tired her wolf out. Once Bailey would go to sleep she and her wolf would bond closer together and begin to heal. The more time she spent in wolf form, the faster her healing would be. It would also mitigate any illness that might be brewing inside her.

I had been the same way but I hadn't gone into wolf form until I had been at the house for over six months. It had been hard to reconnect with something Ingrid had nearly beaten out of me. Bailey was lucky to still have the connection with her wolf. It had taken me a long time to find mine hiding in the back of my head.

Cowering and fearful of even me but I had learned that was only because she wished to protect me. She had wanted to attack Ingrid but punishment was always swift when one even thought to strike Ingrid back. She hid herself away to protect me from her impulsive actions.

The road back to normalcy was not an easy one. It was fraught with problems, pit-falls, and setbacks. No one truly knew how it would go or if I or Bailey would be a hundred percent okay. Things still clung to me tightly and I wondered if the emotional and mental abuse would ever truly let me forget. Some of the most painful wounds were the ones you couldn't see, the ones that would never be visible to the naked eye.

I shivered slightly and Ezekiel shifted his head in my lap slightly with a faint whine as if sensing my mild distress. I patted his head gently before scratching around his scar. I wanted to ask him how he had gotten it but I had never actually met him in human form. He was a wild, more of a wild than Victor. Luka never told me how he had come into contact with the two wilds in the first place and I never pried. Although he did let me know that other than his mother, Michael and Ezekiel were the only people he trusted.

I knew it was hard for him. He wasn't meant to be the Alpha of Fortis. He was the third born son. He never had to worry about Alpha duties or training. He didn't have the power the birthright would have given him. That was until the car accident that killed his father and his two brothers. It had been a fluke accident, a semi had lost control and in that moment it had ripped everything Luka had known and thrown him into a world he was completely unprepared for. He had been thrust into the Alpha position at the age of twenty-two. His life as he knew it had been over and he had contacted Uncle Jace in a panic pleading for help.

That had been five years ago and I could still see a young male floundering in a world he felt he didn't truly belong to. Luka was like an older brother to me and seeing him struggling so hard and so alone made my heart squeeze unpleasantly in my chest. I let out a heavy sigh and opened my eyes. Bailey was still running back and forth on the lawn and Michael's speed had slowed down significantly and I smirked when I realized Bailey had actually tired him out.

I could hear a car pulling up the lane way and I perked up at the same time as Ezekiel and Michael did. They moved in eerie synchronization and moved to sit beside the parking spot. Bailey bolted for me and her claws skittered on the wooden stairs as she moved to hide behind me. "It's okay, it's just Luka. Go ahead and get dressed." I stood up and could hear her shifting as a beat up looking car pulled into the parking spot.

I watched as a tall male got out. His form was lean but it still held strength. He just wasn't bulky like most other Alphas. His face was slightly scruffy and he rubbed at his eyes slightly, his thick framed glasses moving with the action. I could practically see the stress radiating off of him and I bolted.

"Luka!" At my shout his face lightened considerably and he smiled at me, holding out his arms. I leapt at him with a laugh, wrapping my arms around him tightly.

"Hey, kiddo." He hugged me tightly and I squeezed him harder before letting go and smiling at him. The stress seemed to fall away for a moment. His soft grey eyes flicked to something at the house before he looked back at me. "Who's the shy, little creature hiding behind the pillar?" His voice was low, a near whisper as he looked at me expectantly and I smiled once more.

"That's Bailey. She's Davin's mate." I watched as his face went still for a moment before his entire form relaxed into the soft, gentle aura that I had come to know well.

"She was an omega as well." He didn't ask it but I still nodded. I looked over my shoulder to see Bailey peeking around the pillar.

"Let's get you inside before the others come. Bailey is probably hungry." I didn't want to admit it but I was also hungry. I smiled when I realized there was left over bacon in the fridge. Enough for all of us to have a BLT. I grabbed Luka's hand and practically dragged him to the house. I ignored his chuckles as I went up the stairs. I smiled at Bailey and grabbed her hand.

"Bailey, this is Alpha Sterling, better known as Luka. He's like family." I could feel her apprehension but I ignored it as I drug them both into the house and into the kitchen. I pushed Luka to a stool in front of the island and I pulled Bailey around the large island and handed her a knife and cutting board. She would relax better with a task.

I could hear the clicking of claws against the hardwood floor and I moved to the freezer. I pulled out two meaty leg bones. I occasionally went to the nearby meat processing plant and got some bones from their scrap bins. I usually fed them to the wild wolf pack but I kept the better ones for Michael and Ezekiel.

I could sense them behind me and I turned around, holding out the bones for them. They didn't hesitate and took them from me gently before moving to the hallways where they could see the door. I could hear their teeth scraping on the frozen bones before I moved to the sink and washed my hands.

"She spoils you two rotten." Luka's voice was amused as he watched his two guardians as they enjoyed their bones, keeping an ever watchful eye on the kitchen and the front door. I pulled out the ingredients for the sandwiches and Bailey seemed to understand what we were doing and started to slice the tomatoes. "I take it you are from Tacita as well, Bailey?" Luka's tone was soft and Bailey stiffened slightly before nodding. Her entire attention on getting the tomatoes sliced into perfectly even portions.

"It makes sense. Tacita has a certain knack for Omegas. They have a certain smell. Maricella smelled strongly of it when she came here. She still smells like it slightly. It's almost a sour smell. It's repugnant." His tone never wavered in its soft and even tone and I focused on putting the bread in the toaster. "Not you, though. The scent of an omega is. It's repugnant because the entire practice is repulsive. Wolves lording above others is wrong." I pulled the toast from the toaster and spread a thin layer of mayo over it, listening to Luka's words carefully.

"But you are an Alpha." Bailey's voice shook as she moved to the lettuce, carefully pulling leaves off, making sure they were the right size. She was becoming bolder, becoming relaxed as she did the task. Just like I knew she would. I placed more bread in the toaster and started to construct the sandwiches.

"Not by choice, tiny, just like you I was forced into my position. You, however, were able to escape your prison. I'm still trapped." His tone was soothing but I could feel his caginess about the subject. He wouldn't tell her to leave it alone but he didn't like discussing it. He never did.

"But you are an Alpha." Bailey's confusion was apparent, it hung heavily in the air.

"A gilded cage is still a cage, tiny." Luka's tone was softer than before and I glanced over my shoulder to look at him but his eyes were on Bailey, his expression unreadable.

"My name is Bailey." Her reprimand was quiet but firm and I smiled brightly at her. She would make a good Alpha Female. She was already coming out of her shell, despite how shaky her voice had been she had put her foot down, however small of an action it was, she still did it.

Luka looked amused and he shifted on the chair, the tension leaving the room with his smile. "I know that but you're also tiny."

He had a point and I turned back to the toaster and pulled the toast out. "He gives everyone a nickname, Bailey. He calls me kiddo." I put some more bread in it and moved to the fridge, pulling out the plate of bacon. I spread some mayo over the bread and finished two sandwiches before starting on another two.

"That I do." He was smiling, I didn't have to see his face to know he was. When he first met me that was the first word that came out of his mouth. He didn't give anyone a chance to introduce us, I was simply kiddo and that was all he cared about and now it seemed like Bailey was to be called tiny. The toaster popped and before I could move over to it Bailey was already switching it out and spreading the mayo on the toast.

I started to put together more sandwiches. "How is everything with Fortis?" I placed the sandwich I just finished making onto the plate with the others and a stillness filled the air.

"Not good." He didn't elaborate and I didn't push the question. He didn't want me burdened down with his pack's problems. At least that is what he had told me whenever I tried to pry.

"Packs are named after the traits the first members had." Bailey's voice was quiet as she pulled the toast out of the toaster and replaced it with more bread. "But as the years go by, the pack members start to emulate the name. Tacita means silence. We keep quiet, we do not speak of ourselves to others. Oblitus means forgotten because the people here are the ones that the world forgot. Fortis means brave and steadfast." Her small speech surprised me and I tilted my head at her.

"You're very perceptive, tiny, and correct. The pack name has power, it does influence those it's tied to." He let out a long sigh. "But with bravery comes stupidity and rashness, with silence comes secrets and divisions and with the forgotten comes pain and misery. The name influences the behaviours. Which is why a pack is supposed to change the name with each new Alpha." Luka gave a lazy gesture as he spoke. "A new Alpha, a new start but we are still entrenched in the Old Ways as a society so we leave our packs to fight against the compulsion of their pack name. The longer the name is there, the stronger that compulsion becomes." A silence fell and I finished a sandwich and placed it on a plate before turning and giving it to Luka.

"You are a good Alpha, Luka. Don't forget it." I winked at him and he just shook his head with a small smile but took a bite out of the sandwich anyway.

TWENTY-THREE

My body felt sore but I didn't mind. It felt good to be put through my paces and I had heard Jace Lawrence wasn't one to go easy and he hadn't. He had certainly proved why he was an Alpha. His power was smooth but it had the edge of savageness to him that Alpha Lawrence never had. The edge of ferality to him and his wolf that made him rather impossible to predict. We walked through the trees and back to the house. Collin, Seamus, and Angie were running patrols with Victor and the wild wolf pack. Everyone else, excluding Bailey and Maricella, had come to watch me prove my worth.

"You're in peak physical shape." Amber's voice was sharp over the chatter and I simply nodded at her, acknowledging her words but not speaking. I didn't even know what to say to her otherwise. She had basically dumped my previous Alpha rather coldly and besides that interaction, I wasn't sure what the hell I could even say to the female.

"That he is. He'll do good as a pack warrior. Perhaps he can help train those that wander through the territory, if they so choose." Jace's voice was low and I let my eyebrow rise in slight surprise. I hadn't been aware that Jace had allowed rogues or any other sort of shifters onto his territory to be trained.

I looked around, Jay and Davin were walking through the trees as if they had no concerns about the area around them but I could tell they weren't as relaxed as they looked. No one was. They all had an edge of wariness to them that I approved of. It was okay to let your guard down but only when you knew you wouldn't be caught off guard by an attack.

"How much do you want to bet that Mari is making Luka something to eat right now?" Jay's voice filtered into my ears and I hid a grimace. I didn't want to ruin Maricella's relationships, not with her friends but it was difficult because we had not been bound together and my wolf was paranoid we would lose her again. Not to mention we didn't know who this Luka was and it made us agitated to not be there to make sure she was safe.

I had found that having a paranoid wolf and an incomplete mate bond was not a very fun combination. I struggled between claiming her fully and hiding her from everyone until the time she was ready to be claimed. I ran my hand through my sweaty hair and tugged on it slightly. My wolf was pacing restlessly in the back of my head and I hated how possessive he was getting. Maricella didn't need to be possessed, not the way my wolf wanted to possess her. It wouldn't be fair and it would terrify her.

"Collin says Luka's here and is most likely inside with the girls." Jay's voice was calm and I glanced at Davin to see his shoulders tensing. His wolf must have been battering at him just as strongly as mine. The urge to bond to what was ours was stronger in males than in females sometimes but that was not saying some females didn't get jealous. I had seen my share of jealous females attacking other unmated females for looking at their mates. It was just stronger for males because we knew we had competition and that an unclaimed bond could be broken as easily as the next. It was ingrained into us to claim our mates to further our bloodlines, to extend the future for our species, plus the testosterone didn't help.

"Hopefully those two are behaving." There was a wary tone in Amber's voice and I glanced at her from the corner of my eye. She had a steely, pained look in her eyes ever since we had left Tacita but currently wariness and worry had replaced it instead. It made my wolf grow unnervingly still.

"Michael and Ezekiel don't ever leave wolf form. They wouldn't hurt anyone close to Luka. You know this." There was a soft edge of reprimand to Jace's voice and I watched as Amber stiffened from the words or the reprimand, I wasn't sure.

"They're *wild*. We barely know how they'll behave. They follow the whims of their wolves and there's a chance they could snap." Her tone was firm as if he hadn't just reprimanded her. My wolf growled low in my head. He didn't like the thought of a wild near Maricella. Victor was different, he was her father, but having two others we didn't know around her was worrisome for both my wolf and I.

"And their wolves view Maricella as part of the pack." Jace was being reasonable but I could see Amber's hesitation. A wild was highly unpredictable and truly did follow the whims of their wolves. They were buried so deep within themselves that they had no control over their wolves and just let them roam as they pleased. However if they viewed Maricella as a pack member then it negated a large portion of the danger. It still didn't mean she was completely safe as a wild animal was always unpredictable.

"But not Bailey." At her words I looked at Davin whose entire form stiffened and he walked faster, pulling ahead of Jay and the rest of us. His wolf was more than likely demanding to see to the protection of his mate. Mine was as well but I forced him back, refusing to let him dictate Maricella's friends. I would not be foolish enough to pull her away from her support system. She was better than she was before but that didn't mean she didn't need to progress further.

"Maricella wouldn't let anything hurt her." Jace was gritting his teeth slightly but he didn't snap at her like I expected him to. It was like he respected her too much or maybe he just needed her too much to just snap at her. She didn't seem too inclined on Alphas from what I had heard from her words to Alpha Lawrence. I almost winced at that. I wouldn't have wished that on anyone.

"Maricella *isn't* a fighter! She barely knows fighting forms or moves." Her voice was sharp and I could hear her worry. She cared for Maricella deeply, a bond had been forged between them. "All she knows is what she learned in mock attempts to play warrior." That edge carried through heavy to the last of her words. She was agitated and worried and that didn't make for a good combination.

"Mari's wolf knows. It's all instinct and Collin has informed me that Mari is now having troubles distinguishing between her wolf's more dominant personality and her own subservient one." Jay's tone was light and he paused slightly. "She wouldn't win by any means but she would do some damage." He shrugged slightly and we breached the trees. I could see an unfamiliar rusty looking car parked in the driveway and the urge to go to Maricella was nearly overwhelming.

I watched as Davin jumped up the stairs to the porch and I pushed forward, incapable of stopping myself from speeding up. I could faintly hear conversation in the kitchen and I could smell food. My stomach rumbled slightly and I quickly jumped up the stairs as Davin had and walked into the open door.

I walked forward and could hear bones crunching between powerful jaws and I looked over to see two large black wolves. They were covered in scars, their fur only tufts in some places. They had a savage aura of power around them as they chewed on what looked to be beef bones. As if sensing my presence they looked at me at the same time before jumping to their feet, their hackles rising all the way down their back.

"Michael, Ezekiel. Stand down and enjoy your treat before kiddo takes it away." The voice was soft and calm and I watched as the wolves instantly went back to chewing on their bones, seemingly without a care in the world. I walked forward, ever watchful of the two wilds that were mangling the beef leg bones in the hallway.

"You can't tell them I would take it away, Luka. They can tell it's an empty threat." Maricella's voice was amused and I could hear the sounds of cupboards opening as I stepped into the opening for the kitchen. A slimmer male was sitting at the island with his back to me, his black hair was cut short to his head and he had a very gentle presence about him. I felt my eyes slide to Maricella and as if sensing my presence she looked over her shoulder. A wide, heart stopping smile crossed her face, dimples appeared on her cheeks and her eyes crinkled in the corners.

She turned around fully and held out a plate. "I figured you guys would be hungry. Bailey and I made sandwiches." A BLT sat on the plate and I moved into the kitchen and around the island to take the plate from her. She gave me that heart stopping smile once more before reaching out and touching my arm. The contact burned my nerves but I could see her relax.

"Mates?" The male's voice was curious and Maricella nodded softly. He was wearing glasses and looked exhausted. To be honest he didn't look like an Alpha, far from it in fact. His energy was soft and calm and lacked the very clear dominance that usually came with the Alphas title. I looked around, Bailey and Davin were gone and I could faintly hear voices in the living room. Bailey was clearly safe and in good hands.

"This is Bennett. Bennett, this is Luka. He's like my big brother." She looked between the two of us, as if wanting my approval and I set the sandwich down before reaching a hand out to the Alpha named Luka.

He shook it with a partial smile as he glanced between Maricella and I. The smile grew almost wistful before it faded into seriousness. I knew where it was going. "You hurt her an-"

"And you'll kill me?" I couldn't help the snap my tone had. I was tired of being questioned about my ability to hurt Maricella. I would never do so and both me and my wolf were tired of people assuming I would.

"No, I would never take a kill from Michael or Ezekiel." He gave a lazy gesture to the wilds who stilled in their eating to pointedly stare at me, their chests rumbling. "I, myself, wouldn't do much damage to you before you ripped me apart but when you come between a wild and its pack members... well it's not pretty." He shrugged slightly and I was almost floored at his admission of not being able to beat me. Alphas were prideful creatures. They would never truly state someone could beat them because that just opened doors for challengers.

"Don't look at me like that." There was a faint edge of an Alpha command to his voice and I shook my head slightly before looking at the sandwich Maricella made for me. I bent my head and kissed the top of hers.

"It looks good." I let the sincerity fill my tone and watched as her cheeks flushed red at the compliment before I bent my head lower and kissed her cheek. Her cheeks went nearly scarlet at the action and I turned to the sandwich and took a large bite. It was good. I hummed my approval and Maricella grabbed my wrist and tugged the sandwich towards her before she took a bite.

I quirked an eyebrow and she covered her mouth as she chewed. "You can share, right?" She looked up at me and I smirked slightly before nodding. She leaned against me, her hand still gripping my wrist. My wolf liked the contact, no matter how small it was. He settled down in my head and I could feel his love for her radiating out of every inch of him. He was smitten with our mate, even more than I was. I took another bite of the sandwich. It really was tasty.

There were sounds from the front door and Luka perked up slightly. "Is that Jace I hear?" He looked over his shoulder before turning on the stool, leaning an elbow on the island. I could feel Maricella tensing like an over-torqued spring. My wolf became suddenly protective and surged to the front of my mind as she pressed herself closer to me as if trying to hide herself.

"Luka, my boy! How have you been?" Jace's voice boomed through the house and Maricella jumped and I could hear her heart rate increase as the tension in her seemed to wind tighter. It would be the first time she would be in the same room as him since last night and she had been so tired last night that I doubted she really appropriately reacted.

"Better now that I'm here." Luka sounded sincere but my gaze was on the doorway. My wolf wanted us to keep an eye on Jace. He was soon to be my Alpha but my wolf and I hated how much he frightened her. Even his voice made the fear roll off of her. It was small waves but as he moved into view it grew in intensity. She shifted closer to me, trying to put herself between my frame and the island. I moved back a fraction and she took the invitation. Her back pressed tightly against my chest and I could feel her trembling as Jace walked over and hugged Luka tightly.

"It smells great in here! I hope there's enough for everyone." Jace didn't say it to anyone in particular but Maricella stiffened anyway. The scent of her fear was riling up my wolf and I set the sandwich on the plate gently, trying not to make any sudden movements. Jace moved around the island heading for the food and Maricella's grip tightened around my wrist. Her grip grew to being at the borderline of pain as her knuckles white while she trembled against his presence.

She was *terrified* and I fought the urge to remove the source of her fear. "I see you two are getting cozy." I could feel him staring at me and I could feel Maricella's breath hitch in her chest as she stopped breathing entirely, her heart pounding frantically in her chest.

"None of your concern." I placed my hands on the island and leaned forward slightly, caging Maricella away from his view. Her heart pounded so harshly I could feel it thumping against my chest. I silently urged her to breathe before she passed out.

"She's my niece, she's always my concern." He leaned against the counter beside me and I shifted my shoulder, obstructing his view of her. The fear was rippling off her so intensely it made me want to gag. It was thick and sour and my wolf battered against my defences, wanting to remove the threat from our mate.

"Jace, I need to talk to you." Luka sounded firm and I glanced at him. There was a frown on his face as he looked between Maricella's shaking form and her uncle.

"Not now." Jace snapped it out and I could feel him staring at me.

"Okay, pleasantry over. You need to back off." Luka's voice vibrated with an Alpha command but it wasn't strong. It would do nothing against Jace.

"Luka, you're an Alpha but your command is still weak." His words were harsh and I looked up at Luka who sighed, the frown deepening on his face.

"Can't say I didn't warn you, Jace." He snapped his fingers and two loud snarls came from the hallway. Before anyone could react the two scarred black wolves were in the kitchen.

One leapt onto the island, driving Jace away from Maricella and I. I leaned back slightly as it scattered several plates and cups, my sandwich included. Its claws were scrambling on the smooth surface and the other one brushed roughly past my legs, driving Jace around the corner of island towards the snapping jaws of the wolf standing in front of Maricella and I. I could hear Maricella's audible inhale and I sent out a silent thanks to Mene that she was now remembering to breathe.

"Fucking *really*, Luka?" Jace bellowed as he dodged their pointed attacks. The one on the island jumped onto the dining table. Its claws dug deep into the wood and it snapped and snarled at the irritated Alpha.

"They are my command, Jace. You're *terrifying* her. How do you expect them to react?" Luka shrugged, looking unconcerned for the wilds he had just set on Jace. "You don't come between a wild and their pack." He gave me a rather pointed look and I heard the message loud and clear as the second wolf rounded the table, sending Jace closer to the doorway as he fended off the wolf snarling in his face.

"Call them off before they get hurt." At Jace's words I could see a faint smirk on Luka's face. He took a large bite out of the sandwich in front of him before setting it down again.

"This is really good, kiddo. I need to get you to cook for me more often." He winked at her as Jace let out another curse as the wolves drove him from the kitchen and down the hallway. "I need to go talk to Jace and find out what the hell is going on here." He leaned over the island and kissed Maricella's forehead, ignoring me completely.

He leaned back and grabbed his sandwich, winking at her as he did so. "Ezekiel, don't let him run too far." He bounded out of the room and I could feel Maricella instantly relax. I didn't and kept my body caged around hers. My wolf was a hair's width from tearing through my skin and bones if I moved an inch I knew he would do just that "Michael, stop biting so hard!" At Luka's frustrated voice I bit back a chuckle. I leaned down and breathed in her scent, letting it soothe the wolf within me. She was safe.

"Fucking Tacita." Amber's voice was a low grumble. "Mari, I want to see you in my office." Her words were soft and Maricella slowly let go of my wrist. Red marks marred my skin and I wrapped an arm around her waist, burying my face into her hair. My wolf was still restless but it was better now that the fear wasn't rolling off of her so intensely. I didn't want to let her go so easily. My wolf wasn't budging on the position I had taken.

"I'm not going to hurt her, Bennett. I just need to help her work through some things with her. If I don't she's going to have a breakdown." Her voice was firm but soft as she moved closer towards up, I felt a growl build in my chest. The vibrations rumbling through me and into Maricella, instead of pulling away like I feared she seemed to sink back into me. Her hand wrapped around my wrist again, her fingers tracing patterns into my skin. I shivered slightly at the contact, trying to ignore the goosebumps that covered my skin. "Mari, please reason with him." Amber gestured at me with a bit of frustration.

"I want him to come with me." Her voice was clear and I watched as she lifted her head to look at the doctor. The female doctor frowned. "Bennett needs to know about my diagnosis so he can better help me with my episodes." There was something hidden in her voice that I couldn't figure out but I watched as Amber looked ready to argue but her shoulders slumped instead.

She let out a long sigh before looking at me with burning blue eyes. "If you tear apart my office in a rage, I will sedate you, *remove* your balls, *pickle* them, and display them proudly on my new desk." Something about how she was looking at me told me she wasn't joking and I nodded slowly.

"Deal." I watched as she walked out of the kitchen. Maricella wiggled out from between me and the island but held onto my wrist as we followed the blond female. I felt cold without her pressed against me and I ignored the urge to shiver at the feeling it left me. We walked down the hall, passing the office. I wondered for a brief moment if Maricella had phoned Alpha Lawrence.

"Thank you." She squeezed my wrist slightly as she gestured at the door. I wondered if the murmurings in her mind were loud enough for her to hear my train of thought. "It was nice to talk to him again. I didn't talk to him a lot while we were at Tacita." Her voice was small and I simply nodded. It made me and my wolf happy to see that we had done something to bring her joy.

We moved into the infirmary and I watched as Amber pushed open a door to a smaller room. I hated the sterile smell of the infirmary. I always had but I ignored it as Maricella pulled me towards the open door. I could see it was an office and when we stepped inside it felt a lot smaller than it looked.

I felt almost cramped in the space and Maricella pulled me towards a chair before gesturing for me to sit as she moved to the corner of the room. I watched as she pulled out another chair that had been hiding behind a healthy looking potted plant. She set it beside my chair before sitting in it, curling her legs up to her chest. She looked small and lost in that position and I reached over and placed a hand on her knee, trying to send her comfort.

"This is her file." Amber's voice was sharp as she set a rather thick file down on the desk. She flipped it open and pulled out a stack of papers. "This is a basic rundown of her... *issues*. The rest are detailed and I don't want you reading them all at once. You're free to read them at Maricella's discretion of course but you aren't to speak of it outside of the Oblitus. We're forgotten and it's for a reason. No one needs to know what goes on here with our members. It's not their business." She waved the papers and I leaned forward and took them in my hand before I carefully and hesitantly took my hand away from Maricella's knee. I liked the contact and didn't want it to end. Just touching her soothed the wolf that was always pacing inside of me.

Each page was numbered and I could see dates beside certain paragraphs. There was a lot of writing on the pages and I frowned, most of it was typed but there was handwriting as well. It seemed organized but the first few pages seemed more hectic than the rest. I looked at the date. It was the day after Maricella had been banished. November eighteenth. My eyes scanned the words that had been jotted down in pen.

Maricella's weight is worrisome. She is severely underweight, I would say a starvation period of about eight to nine weeks would be needed to reach the point she is at right now. She is very weak and her heartbeat is slightly irregular, which coincides with severe starvation. Another two weeks or three weeks and her body would have started to shut down, her heart probably would have been the first to go. As with every other rejected bond I have seen, it is literally killing her.

I felt a hot rage fill me as I read it. Lucas had nearly killed her in his selfish stupidity. I hadn't realized just how close she had been to death that day. The unpleasant taste of self-loathing coated my tongue. If I had fought harder, I hadn't been weak, I could have helped her. She could have died, she *would* have died if her uncle hadn't been there. I jolted slightly as Maricella gripped my wrist, trailing her fingers over my skin. I felt some of the ugly feelings leave me as I turned back to the page.

As with previous bonds, the medication given should dull her senses enough for the bond to weaken naturally without allowing it to try and kill her body. However during her hallucinations she believed me to be a female named Ingrid and was convinced she was in the place called 'the classroom'. It seemed as though she had regressed through her memories and became stuck in that certain memory or grouping of memories. I managed to coax some information from her. It appears most of her abuse came from the classroom and that is where they 'trained' her to become an omega. She referred to something called the Omega's Mantra. A list of rules used to confine a shifter into the lowest parts of a pack.

I blinked before skipping several paragraphs that talked about what the Mantras were. I didn't need to know the specific rules. I knew enough of them from the two years I spent around the omegas of Tacita. They were constantly muttering them as they did their work or if anyone interrupted them. It was a sad state to see them in, they were broken creatures.

Maricella is showing signs of an intense and brutal brainwashing. These 'Mantras' are ingrained into her to the point where if she even comes close to thinking about breaking them it sends her into a panic attack. These attacks are quite frequent and I have seen some edges of anxiety among the panic and if I am correct she has severe anxiety as well.

Despite how Jace is reacting to her condition, I am afraid that her symptoms are completely natural for the trauma I am certain she has suffered as an omega. I am very much aware of the Old Way practice of creating omegas and I am surprised to see she has no scars. Although I am positive that has to do with the fact her father, Andrew Lawrence, would be returning to see her and the abuse would need to be hidden from sight while under his watch.

I scanned the rest of the page but it held nothing of significance. The date changed to the twenty-ninth and I started reading once more.

Maricella came to me asking if she was broken and I prodded her about the mantras, Ingrid, and the classroom but she refused to speak of them. She did however manage to eat some food. One of the mantras was that omegas must never eat pack food and she was terrified to break it.

Jace took my advice and had a box built for her and it seems as though it is helping her cope with the new changes in her life. She said she couldn't deal with the mantras tearing her in two so she ate in the box because no one could see her breaking the rules.

With this came a startling revelation that she had remembered her father. A memory of eating spaghetti with the male that had raised her and treated her as his beloved child. I cannot dive deeper into those memories yet as Maricella is still coping with the sudden changes around her. I still do not understand if she is scared as she doesn't have a place or if she is terrified of being punished for not having the place she had been forced into as a child.

She was discussing losing her memories and we had a breakthrough. Maricella became angry at the female named Ingrid for 'taking away her memories'. She ranted and raged, screaming uncontrollably about what had happened to her until she collapsed into sobs. An Omega must not feel emotions. She broke another mantra and completely on her own volition. If we can deconstruct the cage this Ingrid had built around her then perhaps we can bring out the female that she should have been.

I flipped the page and read more about her health and weight. I fought back the anger I felt at reading about the mysterious but severe abuse that Amber was certain Maricella had gone through. It made a hard knot of anxiousness build in my stomach. I knew Maricella hadn't been treated well as an omega but I wasn't even sure if I was okay with reading about what had happened. I *had* to know what she went through but I didn't know if I could control my wolf while learning about it.

Maricella squeezed my wrist gently and continued her trailing designs on my skin. I resisted the urge to shudder but I focused on her touch. Despite the heat the actions caused, it was more than relaxing. I let out a deep breath and looked back at the papers. The next few days written down were similar to the first few. They recounted Maricella's numerous panic attacks and her nightmares. I was shocked at the amount she had. On one day alone she managed to have over thirty panic attacks and fourteen nightmares. I wondered how she managed to sleep at all.

I read how she continued to struggle with flinching at sudden movements, panic attacks mixed with anxiety, trusting people, and eating normal food. She caught pneumonia despite the antibiotics that had been given her. Her immune system was compromised from the malnutrition and neglect. It took a huge weakness of our bodies to even get a bit sick so the fact she had managed to get pneumonia was shocking and alarming. The words serious emotional, physical, and mental trauma were common and I hated each use of them, knowing what it meant.

I flipped through page after page, feeling both sick and angry that they had managed to hide it. I had never known how we had gotten omegas. One day they would show up, always young ones. No one above sixteen or seventeen and I had never thought much on it and I hated myself for it. They had been doing to others what they had done to Maricella and no one had stopped it. I took another deep breath and continued to read.

Maricella still refused to talk directly about the abuse she endured. She would make offhand remarks about it but never directly spoke about it. I read about how fidgety she would become and how evasive she would become when asked about it. She had more and more memories emerge as well as more episodes of uncontrollable rage where one or more of the pack members would be at the brunt of her vocal fury. I frowned. There was no mention of her wolf in any of the paragraphs I had read. I scanned the page several times but I still couldn't find any mention of her wolf.

"I couldn't find her. My wolf. I shifted six months after I arrived. First time I had in years. Omegas aren't allowed to shift often or at all. It's why we get sick and don't heal as well as others. Without our wolves, we are simply *less*." Her voice drifted into my thoughts and I looked over at her, she gave me a small smile. "My wolf was trying to hide to protect me from Ingrid. She is quite vindictive when she wants to be and I always got punished for her actions." She shrugged slightly before staring at my wrist as she continued to make her designs.

"It's common for abuse victims to hide in their own mind. Mari's wolf was just doing what was natural to protect her. She hid away from everything. Mari's shifting six months into her stay had been the first one in nearly five years." Amber's voice was soft and I glanced up at her. "We never had to deal with omegas before. Rejection, yes. Deprogramming omegas? That was a completely new concept." Amer slowly and gently gestured to Maricella. "Maricella was our guinea pig. She still is. Everything she is going through is new for us. Omegas aren't supposed to exit their station, ever." She laced her fingers together and stared at me with a small frown.

"I honestly never thought they could. Maricella, and now Bailey, are test subjects. Oblitus takes care of those the world has forgotten about. Omegas are now to be included into that." She paused for a brief moment. "People come in and out of this pack regularly. We provide help to those who seek it. They are drawn by our name. The forgotten. Mari was just another person our world has forgotten. We all were but we still have a lot to learn about all of this. I'm hoping that if I get enough evidence we can do something about it."

She gestured to the papers in my hand. "That's what we needed to learn. The mantras are ingrained deeply into every omega, beaten into them mercilessly. These people are brainwashed heavily and it is sickening that so many packs still practice this barbaric tradition." She scowled darkly and I swallowed against the lump in my throat. I couldn't believe I hadn't known about what the omegas truly meant. How they came to be. "I hope, that with this research and evidence, we can get some reform done with the Hunters. The thing we want most is to extend protections for omegas to get them out of these situations and protect others from being forced into these... *torture* camps." I couldn't argue with her, I agreed. If it was this bad for the rest, they needed to be protected, however we could protect them.

"Do you want to read about what happened or do you want me to tell you?" Maricella looked at me, her beautiful eyes locking onto my own and I thought for a moment.

"Please tell me." I wanted to hear from her. I didn't want a piece of paper to coldly outline her abuse. I wanted to hear it from her.

"They took me when I was ten, when my father went away for six months to deal with some issues with the Sol Warrior uprising in Russia. There is a concrete room in the basement of the Tacita pack house, far enough away that no one would come looking for it. That is where it happened. Ingrid called it the classroom." She paused and seemed to search for the appropriate words. "I was forcibly isolated, starved, and beaten to the point of unconsciousness. Every day for six months." She said it bluntly and I inhaled, clenching my hands into fists. My wolf slammed against me again and again. He wanted to tear something apart. He wanted to destroy those who had hurt his mate. Her hand slid up my arm, my wolf instantly focused on action. I shivered at the heat the motion caused.

"I was hung from the ceiling by my wrists. I was usually caned or strapped. For hours until my skin broke and bled. Until I stopped screaming. Thankfully I healed well enough and didn't scar. I knew if they really wanted me to scar, I would have but that's beside the point." She frowned again and I focused on her tracing patterns on my skin. I needed to focus on that before I tore apart the room and headed back to Tacita and killed Ingrid. "Sometimes Ingrid would allow some older, more cruel pack members in to... *relieve* tension or anger." The vagueness made me grip the arm of the chair until the wood splintered. All I could see was red.

"Pickled, Bennett. *Pickled.*" Amber's voice was low with warning and I pushed my wolf back, trying not to piss the good doctor off.

"I wasn't... I wasn't assaulted, Bennett, at least not sexually." Maricella's sweet voice made the red haze disappear as her words registered. I hated that I was thankful, I hated that I was thankful that she was given one brutality over another but the thought of anyone harming her like that was beyond enraging. "Thankfully I was saved that fate. They just beat me. The punishments were never consistent or similar, other than the caning that is. I was forced to endure six months of such punishments until I finally gave in. I became what they wanted me to be. I was an omega and that was all I would ever be. Then I came here and I've been getting better."

She reached over and tapped the pages. "I've got issues with episodes of rage. I've got depression and I'm dealing with sometimes crippling anxiety. I have moments of mania where I clean until my hands bleed. I have a lot of triggers for panic and anxiety attacks. You saw two of them. Violence and blood. Blood is a bad one." She let out a sigh and I wanted to wrap her in my arms and never let her go. My wolf whined in my head to do just that, he wanted me to comfort our mate. "But I'm getting *better*. I'm better now than I was before. I just want you to know what you are getting into. I'm going to have issues. I'll most likely flinch away from you at some point. I'll wake up screaming from a nightmare and refuse your touch and you will probably make me cry." I opened my mouth to disagree but she held up her hand and looked at me, a small, sad smile on her face.

"It won't be you. That is on *me*. My mind is a minefield and you will find some of them explode without reason and that will never be your fault. If I flinch from you, it is not because I don't trust you but because I have been conditioned to flinch at movements. I will sometimes refuse your touch, not because I do not want it but for the reason I will need time to calm down and recover. You will make me cry because everything makes me cry sometimes." She looked determined as she looked at me. "These are my issues so never blame yourself for something that I will do. I just want you to know that this will not be easy or fair for you." She looked at me as if she expected me to turn away from her and I felt my heart twist unpleasantly in my chest.

"You are the reason I existed for the past two years. Your memory has kept me alive and driven me forward when I felt like I couldn't continue." I turned and grasped her face firmly in my hands. I searched her eyes with my own. "I never asked for something easy or fair. All I want is *you*, Maricella. That is all I will ever require." I wanted her to see the truth of my words. I would never willingly give her up. She was my mate, the mother to my future children, and I wouldn't let her fight her problems on her own, not anymore. Her burdens were mine to shoulder as well.

"I just want you to understand-" I cut her off, pressing my lips to hers like I had wanted to do so many times before. It was just as sweet and fiery as the ones I had taken from her on the porch. The need to claim her was pounding at my temples and through my veins but I pushed it away. I wanted to enjoy the moment. I wanted to enjoy being with her, moving my lips against hers. I pulled away from her soft lips reluctantly and her cheeks flushed prettily as she blinked almost as if in a daze.

"All I need to understand is that you're my *mate*. We will deal with this together." I pressed my forehead to hers and closed my eyes. "You're the only thing I have, Maricella. Don't expect me to give you up because it might be hard. Life will *always* be hard but this bond we have ensures we can deal with it *together*. Do not expect me to give it, or you, up for anything."

TWENTY-FOUR

I wanted to cry, to let out deep heaving sobs as Bennett threaded his hand through my hair, his other hand sliding down my cheek and neck to rest on my shoulder. His words were like a punch to the stomach and I felt like I couldn't breathe. I had expected him to hear what I went through, to see all the progress I still had to make and to run the other way. I didn't want him to but I knew it was a high probability that he could.

I had been broken, shattered into pieces, and no one wanted to deal with the issues that came with that but he *wanted* to deal with it with me. He wanted to be with me as I dealt with everything. He was more than I ever could have hoped for. I took in a shuddering breath, the urge to cry was still heavy and I reached over and grasped at his neck, holding the back of it tightly. I never wanted to let him go.

"Don't start crying. Please." There was a faint thread of panic in his voice and I couldn't help the wet sounding chuckle that escaped my mouth.

"What do you expect, Bennett? You can't tell a female that kind of thing and not expect tears." Amber sounded amused and I pulled away from Bennett, letting him go as I looked at my doctor. She had an edge of sadness around her and I felt guilty for revelling in my bond with my mate in front of her. It felt like I was rubbing salt into an open wound in front of her. I opened my mouth and she held up a hand. "Don't say what I think you're going to say, Mari. It was my choice." She shook her head slightly and I frowned. She was too observant for her own good sometimes.

"I'm going to go somewhere else and finish reading these, okay?" Bennett waved the papers in his hand and I nodded. He kissed my forehead before leaving, gently closing the door behind him. He had taken everything better than I thought he would but that didn't mean he wasn't upset about it. I could feel his rage, at that moment the whispers were dark and angry. It made for a heavy feeling in the back of my head.

"Now what's going on?" Amber's voice had an edge to it and I knew exactly what she was asking about. I winced slightly, shifting my eyes back and forth, trying to formulate the right words.

"Uncle Jace is-"

"No. The amount of sheer terror you put off is surpassing the amount you used to put off when you first came here. Now tell me." Her tone left me no room for argument or deflection. It was hard and stern, it had no bent or give and I let out a sigh. I had told Davin how I felt but Amber hadn't been there. She hadn't seen what had happened.

"He terrifies me. I don't think I can trust him anymore. He was... *aggressive* with me." I grimaced at how her eyes narrowed. There was an edge to her that made me almost wary. It was like her wolf was peeking out to look at me and I didn't like the feeling.

"How aggressive?" Her tone was low and deadly and I swallowed. Uncle Jace was in trouble, more trouble than he was with me,

"H-He yelled at me and shook me." I swallowed hard before my eyes landed on my lap. "He... he had been rough carrying me and-and he left some bruises and h-"

"That *son of a bitch*!" Amber shouted it out, effectively cutting me off. I jumped as she slammed her hands onto her desk, my gaze snapping to her slowly reddening face. "Two fucking *years* we've been establishing trust between pack members and your wolf and he fucking blows it!" She got to her feet breathing heavily. Anger hung off of her form and I watched with wide eyes as claws emerged from her fingertips and dug deep grooves into the wood of her desk. Her eyes grew darker and she bolted, kicking open her office door.

I stared after her with wide eyes before I realized what she was doing. "Shit!" The curse slipped out as I jumped out of the chair and raced after her. She was already halfway down the hallway by the time I exited the infirmary.

"Jace!" Her voice was a bellow and I felt my heart pound in my chest as I tried to catch up to her. No matter what Jace did to me I didn't want him hurt. My mind was a tetchy place at times and just because I didn't trust him it didn't mean that I didn't love him.

"Amber, please think this through!" I shouted it out as she raced out the front door. I skidded to a stop in the doorway and watched with horrified eyes as she took three steps onto the lawn and slammed her fist into Uncle Jace's jaw. The sound of flesh hitting flesh was sickening as Jace stumbled and fell over from the force of the hit.

"You fucking bastard!" Amber's face was red and she clenched her fists tightly, her knuckles turning white. "Do you know what you have done? Do you?" She looked like she was half a second away from shifting as her body vibrated with the anger she wore like an armour.

Jace's face went from shocked to livid as he jumped to his feet. "*Don't* challenge me, Amber! Back off!" He straightened himself out to his intimidating height that, despite the distance between us, had me cowering slightly. I looked around, Luka was backing away from them, his two guardians following him but keeping their gazes on the two angry shifters.

"You piece of shit! You left her with bruises? Fucking *bruises*?" Amber's voice was choked with rage as she trembled. "My little Maricella? My little girl?" Her words were confusing and I watched as all the colour drained from my uncle's face, except for the dark, ugly bruise that was blooming on his jaw. It would have been comical except for the fact he looked utterly terrified of the willowy doctor.

"Oh fuck." He said it so quietly I could barely hear the words before he bolted for the trees. Amber bolted after him, a loud snarl escaping her mouth as she shifted. Her wolf chased after him, following him into the tree line as she snarled. I could hear faint snarls and growls coming from the tree-line and I shrunk back into the house. Nothing good was happening in the woods.

"Well, that's an... *interesting* development." Luka sounded curious as he lightly jogged up the steps to stand in front of me. "Was it Victor or Andrew she bonded to?" He tilted his head, his grey eyes slightly probing.

"Andrew." I frowned at him as I backed away from the doorway and let him enter. He held out a hand behind him in a gesture to Michael and Ezekiel. I watched as they laid down, looking to the trees and I felt a bit safer with them keeping watch.

"Makes sense." He closed the door and stared at me. His piercing gaze was almost making me uncomfortable.

"Not really. Why did she call me her little girl?" I could always trust Luka to tell me the truth, no matter what it was. He tilted his head, a small smile tugging at his mouth.

"Wolves are very strange creatures. Shifters even more so." He gestured to me. "Your father, Andrew, adopted you, creating a familial bond that some say will block out the mating bond until you're of a certain age." My confused expression must have showed on my face because he gave a lazy gesture as if waving it away. "Don't ask me why, I don't know. I don't even know if it's true." He crossed his arms over his chest as he continued to look at me with that pointedly interested expression.

"So Andrew, free to have a mate bond, bumps into Amber and a bond is formed." He let his arms drop as walked past me and towards the kitchen. I followed after him, unsure of what else to do. "Now, your father's wolf has a very strong bond with you, as do most parents with their children, but now Amber's in the equation. Her wolf can sense the bond between you and Andrew, her mate. Not to mention her wolf has formed her own bond with you. So, now Amber has a wolf that's bound to your father *and* you." He pulled a cup from the cupboard and filled it with water before handing it to me. His words were still confusing but I was grasping what he was saying, just not why.

"This still isn't making any sense." I took a drink of the water and watched as he leaned on the island.

"You're Amber's mate's child. That means, by proxy, you're *her* child. Jace didn't harm or break trust with one of her patients. Jace hurt her *child*. It doesn't matter that she walked away from Andrew. That doesn't matter because her wolf already views you as her offspring. The future. Jace threatened that future." He shrugged and I paled slightly and blinked. "Never come between a mother wolf and her pups. *Ever*." He chuckled and I tried to process the mind breaking information. Amber was my mother or at least her wolf viewed herself as that due to her bond with my father.

"Jace knew he fucked up as soon as he Amber labelled you as hers. He harmed her pup, he scared her pup, and she will deal with the threat accordingly." He shrugged again but I could see a hint of smug satisfaction in his expression. He saw it as justice being served and all I could see was blood and possibility for death.

"She won't... *kill* him, will she?" I swallowed against the sudden lump in my throat and he jolted slightly before frowning.

"Probably not. Drag him back here by the scruff of his neck and make him apologize and beg for your forgiveness is the more likely scenario." Luka scratched at his slight scruff and I took another drink of water. "Your mate is feral looking. Not very sophisticated. I like him." I choked on the water and coughed loudly, trying to get my breathing under control. I had not been expecting that. At all.

Luka laughed slightly before taking the glass of water away from me. I stared at him and he wrinkled his nose at me. "Don't give me that look. I have a type of person I like." He crossed his arms and leaned on them, his grey eyes narrowed behind his glasses. He looked slightly thoughtful. "The Alpha Gathering brings in all the Alphas it can from all sorts of different areas. I have found that the more sophisticated an Alpha is, the more entrenched into the Old Ways they are. Whereas the more savage and untameable they are, the more I'm inclined that they treat their mates with respect."

I frowned at that. "Why do you say that?" I tilted my head and sat on the stool in front of the island.

"The Old Ways demand that a mate be broken and forced to heel to their new masters. They are forced to submit and punished when they do not. They're claimed by force, not the way it's done now. Their mates bite their shoulders or neck but they are not allowed to mark them back and females are considered to be nothing but brood mares." Luka was gritting his teeth as he said it and I felt my stomach roll at the thought of the entire process. I had known very little of the Old Ways, just enough to know it was never a good thing and females were constantly urged to reject mates that were raised with such ideals.

"I know. Sickening, right? I hate dealing with them but that's beside the point." He seemed to gather his thoughts for a moment. "The savage and untameable Alphas, the Alphas from the packs far into the mountains where there is nothing but cold, snow, and death. The *Mountain* Alphas.

They do it differently. Females are not claimed by force but are instead picked based on their strength. The females are a force to be reckoned with, they are warriors in their own right." He looked rather intrigued by that line of thought as if it was a practice he highly respected and coveted.

"The mountain shifters respect power and the more power a person has, the more respect that is earned. Male or female it doesn't matter, strength does. The sexes are equals because sex has no basis in power and strength." He seemed lost in thought and I looked at him intently. It was rare he shared his knowledge like he was doing. I liked it when Luka told me of the world outside of Oblitus.

His face darkened slightly. "The people who follow the Old Ways are like a snake, smooth and refined, a calculating animal waiting to strike to take you down efficiently. You never turn your back on them because they will seize the chance to take you and your title." He gestured slightly with his left hand, his face lightening from its previous dark expression. "The Mountain Alphas are like the mountains themselves. Rugged and dangerous but if you know how to move around them, how to conquer them, how to live with them, then you're safe with them. Your mate reminds me of them." He gave me a small smile.

"He's rugged and dangerous but he would never claim you by force, he would never break you. His feral presence lets others know to back off but much like the Mountain Alphas, he softens for you." Luka chuckled as he looked at me, a small smile on his face. "I have seen savage, powerful males go limp under their mate's gaze. Their bonds are intense and wild. They claim the same as the Old Ways but they share in the pain, the mates mark each other." He had a faint tinge of longing in his voice and I reached over and took my cup of water back from him.

"You respect the Mountain Alphas." It wasn't a question and he nodded. I took another drink and set the cup down in front of me.

"They're on to something. They've birthed a culture out of necessity from their way of life but it seems to be a better one. It goes against everything in the Old Ways and I like that. The Old Ways will destroy us all if we continue to let it run rampant." He frowned with a small sigh. "There is so much going on in this world, Maricella. Not all of it is good. The Old Ways are clinging to the edge of oblivion, refusing to let go, to progress with us. And then the Mountain Alphas are growing in size and strength. You should see some of them. Three times as wide as me and another foot on me at least. They are *huge*." He seemed impressed and I smiled at his faintly hidden excitement. It was clear he respected them immensely and it felt like he wanted to follow their teachings.

"Which is another reason I say your mate is like them. He's big." He shrugged and looked at me lazily and I flushed with pride at Luka's notice of my mate's size and strength. He was big enough to remind him of the Mountain Alphas and I found it to be a wonderful compliment.

"He was the top pack warrior for Tacita." I stated it proudly and Luka chuckled.

"I can see why. I was informed that he took Davin out when he arrived and forced Collin to submit under him. If he truly wanted, he could be an Alpha. The raw power he puts off is astounding for someone who isn't of Alpha blood." Luke narrowed his eyes in contemplation and I smiled smugly. "Alpha Thorn would like him." He tilted his head before a bright smile crossed his face.

"Actually a *lot* of the Mountain Alphas would like him. Strong, calm, and an expression colder than the mountains they live on. However the most important part is that he knows that he can soften for you." He gestured to me again. "Mountain Alphas pride themselves on providing and being caring for their mates and their children. Their families always come first and Bennett has shown that no matter what, you come first. He would have their respect." Luka straightened, his back cracking in several spots. The more I heard about the Mountain Alphas, the more I liked them and their ways.

"Thank you." I finished off my glass of water and Luka frowned in confusion.

"For what, kiddo?" He frowned at me, his grey eyes darkening slightly. I smiled at him softly.

"For telling me the truth." I appreciated it, I always did. I had a tendency of being kept in the dark with a lot of things but Luka never lied to me. If something didn't need to be discussed or was too sensitive to discuss he was always sure to tell me so and I respected him more each time he did so.

"So what the fuck is Amber doing to dad?" Davin sounded irritated as he leaned against the door jamb. He crossed his arms and looked between me and Luka.

"Amber found out he wasn't very nice to her pup. She and her wolf didn't take kindly to that so he's being punished for his aggressive behaviour." Luka shrugged and Davin raised an eyebrow in disbelief.

"You expect me to believe that?" He stared at Luka and I cleared my throat slightly and levelled Davin with a look.

"Davin, Amber mated to my father." I watched as he looked at me. He scowled as his green eyes locked onto mine. "She is mated to my *father*." I waited for the recognition but he looked irritated and confused.

"Mene, you're thick, Davin. Amber is mated to kiddo's daddy making her kiddo's mommy." Luka's tone was patronizing and anger flashed in Davin's gaze as his eyes snapped over to Luka before the words registered. His mouth dropped open. "Yah. Jace threatened and bruised Maricella, who happens to be Amber's wolf's new pup."

"Oh. She won't kill him, will she?" Davin's face was slightly pale at the information and Luka let out a sound of frustration.

"Why do you people ask these things?" He looked pointedly at me and then Davin. I shrugged slightly, trying to hide a smirk at Luka's frustration. "You guys must have something in the water or kiddo is spending too much time hanging out with you guys. She should come stay with me for a few months so she can go back to normal. You guys are all weirdos." I laughed lightly at his mild insult and Davin scowled.

"We're weirdos? You're the one who made two wilds his betas. They've never come out of wolf form since I've met them." His face was hard and Luka merely shrugged, unconcerned for the words Davin had said.

"I trust them and that's enough for me. I don't care that they never leave their wolf forms." Luka winked at me and I smiled, catching onto his little game.

"Yah, Davin. Michael and Ezekiel are just as capable as any other wolf." I looked at my cousin and he narrowed his eyes at me. I liked playing games with Luka, it was the only time I ever really got to tease anyone. I didn't feel comfortable doing it by myself. I was trying to learn but it was still very difficult for me.

"I know what you two are doing and I don't appreciate it." He pointed his finger at me before moving it to Luka. "You two do this every time Luka comes over and I always end up looking like a bumbling idiot."

His expression darkened and I bit my lip to keep from grinning at the look on his face.

I looked towards Luka, who was smirking slightly. "Davin... it doesn't take me and kiddo to make you look like a bumbling idiot. You do that well enough on your own." At the sharp insult Davin's mouth dropped open.

"Oh fuck you. Now come here so I can beat your face in." Davin advanced on Luka who simply laughed and jerked his head at the doorway.

"Go watch a movie with tiny." He winked at me, "I have a bumbling idiot to beat up. He did insult my betas after all." I laughed at his words before leaving the kitchen and heading for the living room. The two males followed after me before passing the open living room doorway and out the back door. I stepped into the quiet room, looking around. Bailey was once again curled up in my chair sleeping and Jay was sitting on the couch watching a nearly silent television.

"I didn't want to wake her up." He didn't look at me as he gestured to the TV and I nodded before moving around the couch to sit beside him. "Davin would kill me if I so much as breathed near her." I couldn't argue that fact. Davin was very territorial and protective over his small and shy mate.

I moved closer and leaned against Jay with a sigh. "He's busy killing Luka right now." I looked up at him and he chuckled before draping an arm over my shoulder.

"Okay." He made a low humming sound in his throat. "She's cute. In a kicked puppy sort of way." He stated it with a faint grimace and I absently smacked his chest with the back of my hand. "I didn't mean anything by it, dolly. It's just you get your mate, then Davin gets his." There was a faint tone in his voice that I couldn't distinguish.

"Are you jealous?" I made sure to keep my tone serious. I wanted to know so I would know to keep my bond with Bennett minimal when around him. I didn't want to make him uncomfortable or hurt him in any way.

"*Longing* is a better word. I've been rejected, Mari, and seeing you and Davin so happy with your mates makes me wish I had one." He let out a sigh that sounded on the very edge of wistful and I thought for a moment.

"You could always go to a gathering." At my words he let out a choked laugh.

"No thanks. After what happened with the last one I went to, I'll just stick here or to the Hunter checkpoints. Always a beautiful rogue female there." He winked at me and I giggled slightly before looking at the TV. It was football and I let out a small groan. I never understood the appeal of the game. I could get into it because of the guys but I was never excited about it like they were.

"You'll get a good mate, Jay. You deserve one. We just tend to be a bit anti-social." I shrugged and he laughed loudly before he cut it off, looking over his shoulder to the chair with wide eyes, checking to see if Bailey was still sleeping.

"A bit? You're funny." He squeezed me gently before looking at the TV once more. I relaxed into him. I was happy that not all of my world had been thrown into disarray by Tacita. Collin and Jay seemed to be normal as well as Seamus and Angie but the rest of my little family was going crazy. The ones I needed most had gone insane. Amber was becoming a protective mother, Uncle Jace terrified me with the monster he had hidden under a facade and Davin was completely wrapped up with his mate.

I needed normalcy. I needed something or someone normal to cling to so I could weather the storm I was now enduring. The faint mutterings in my head became nearly oppressive and I winced and rubbed at my forehead. Bennett wasn't happy with what he was reading. The rage was palpable and it made my wolf whine with a need to go and calm him down, however there was a part of my mind that balked at the idea of seeing him that upset and angry.

"It'll be okay, Mari. We'll make sure it will be." Jay kissed my temple and I let out a sigh as I nodded. It would be okay, it just needed time and everything seemed jumbled. I knew time would help sort through the mess that had been created.

I could faintly hear Luka and Davin fighting outside. Their grunts and shouts were barely there but still audible. I knew they wouldn't be satisfied with the sparring until one or both of them were bleeding. It was just how they were. They were closer to each other than I was to either of them. They were like brothers, they had grown together. Something I hadn't been allowed as a child. The thought pained me and I pushed it away. I couldn't change the past, I could only work with the future so it didn't do well to dwell.

Maricella, come outside right now. Amber's voice was firm and I shrunk closer to Jay. I didn't want to go outside. Outside meant her and Uncle Jace had finished with their fight and she would be making him apologize.

"Ignoring her isn't going to make her go away. She told me to take you outside." Jay stood up, taking me with him as he wrapped an arm around my waist and picked me up. I let out a groan of protest, yanking on his arm but it stayed firm around my waist. I hung dejectedly as he carried me out of the living room.

"Jay, I can walk." I knew I was pouting but I couldn't help it as my heartbeat increased at the thought of being anywhere near my uncle. Bennett wasn't beside me to protect me and it made the anxiety that much worse.

"Yes, I know you can but we both know you will walk the *other* way." He chuckled as he carried me towards the door. I groaned and briefly thought about pressing my feet against the door or tripping him but I knew I would never get halfway through the actions before Jay would counter them. There was a reason he helped train. He didn't have a size advantage but he had speed and he was capable of using an opponent's own momentum against them. I had seen him take down shifters nearly twice his size before.

He shifted me slightly before he opened the door and carried me outside. I looked at the wooden boards of the front porch, refusing to look up to see what was going on. I could hear well enough. Davin and Luka were still fighting behind the house and I could hear the panting of another wolf but I knew it wasn't Michael or Ezekiel. I winced when I realized it was probably Jace.

"You can go now, Jay." Amber's voice was firm and Jay merely grunted his acknowledgement before setting me on my feet. After a moment's hesitation he removed his arms from my waist and kissed the side of my head before he was gone, the door clicking shut as he closed it. I stared hard at the wooden boards, afraid to look up and see what was there waiting for me. There was a loud whine and I flinched when I realized who it came from. "Maricella, come here. Jace has something to say to you." I stood frozen in the spot, my eyes wide and fearful, my heart beating erratically fast in my chest. "Come, child. Don't be afraid." Her voice was low and soothing and I felt compelled to move towards her.

The new bond that was forged between us wasn't old but it was strong. I felt safer with her near, much like I had with my father. They were my parents, as messed up as it seemed to be. Not one of them blood and the one walking away from the other in a pseudo rejection but the wolf in me recognized the parental bonds that had been forged and she trusted them.

I swallowed thickly, keeping my head down as I slowly and hesitantly made my way to Amber. My wolf was whimpering in fear and it matched my own. Sure there had been times when she lashed out at Uncle Jace but underneath it all she was terrified of him like I was. A cornered animal would always lash out in an attempt of control or escape. That is what I was with Uncle Jace, a cornered animal.

A gentle and soft hand grasped my arm and I was pulled partially behind Amber. A protective stance that made me relax a fraction and glance upwards. Amber was nude and covered in dirt and streaks of blood. There were several leaking bite marks on her skin that seemed to be healing fine and her blond hair was flowing freely, if a bit tangled.

I nearly winced when I saw a battered black wolf lying on the ground in front of her. Despite its dark fur I could tell that he had the worst of the wounds. He hadn't submitted to Amber but it was more like he had accepted the punishment for his behaviour. He allowed her to tear into him, allowed her to drag him back to the house and allowed her to seemingly force an apology.

He looked at me, his eyes filled with remorse as he slowly started to crawl towards me and I grasped Amber's arm before hiding behind her. I hated how much I did not trust him. I hated it with all that I was but I knew there was little I could do to control it. It was how my brain was, as flawed and difficult as it was. I couldn't control my trauma response anymore than I could control gravity.

Amber let out a threatening growl, her form stiffening at my sudden fear. The need to protect her new pup ran deep in her wolf and that was what was at the forefront of her mind, I knew that. The human nature being pushed aside for the natural instincts of the wolf, at least until the bond settled into place. She would be protective and nurturing but also firm. I was twenty-one years old, far too old for a new parent in the eyes of the mundanes but with wolves, family was everything and the fact I now had a mother was disconcerting but not strange.

I would cling to her as a child would to their parents, forcing the bond to grow stronger until it was deep within us both. We would rely on each other until our wolves settled and functioned as a family unit. It didn't matter that she and Andrew were not my birth parents because I had been so young and my wolf had not come till later. Yes, Victor and the mother I couldn't remember and did not know were my birth parents and the human side of me mourned them but the wolf in me knew only Andrew and now Amber. Victor had given me life but Andrew had given me his love and that was the bond that my wolf cared for more than anything.

I peeked around her and watched as my uncle bared his throat in an act of apology but not submission. I knew this would be grating for him. Alphas did not apologize to others. It was more than likely a heavy blow to his and his wolf's ego and pride but I hoped that the remorse and regret he felt would drown out his wounded pride. He was trying to salvage the tattered parts of our relationship, trying to mend what he had destroyed in his rash anger. I understood that but it didn't stop me from reacting how I did.

I didn't know what to feel. I was still scared, terrified really, but the action lessened it slightly. He whined and whimpered, crawling towards me on his belly, his fur lying completely flat, making himself appear smaller and less threatening. I watched him with wariness and Amber growled low in her throat, a warning to him to be careful. I slowly crouched down, hiding behind Amber. Not willing to leave the protection or safety she provided me with. I peeked around her leg and held out a shaking hand towards the wolf.

I closed my eyes but could hear him whining as he approached. I wrapped my other arm around Amber's leg, unwilling to do it by myself. My actions were child-like but it is how the bonds were forged. My wolf would act like a pup for Amber until the bond was forged with her own wolf. It was a delicate balance between wild instincts and the human side. I would need to appear defenceless and in need of constant protection for Amber's wolf to accept me and mine as her own. It was just how it was done.

I felt fur on the tips of my fingers and I yanked them back, my heart thumping painfully in my chest. Amber snarled, the sound reverberating the air around me but it didn't scare me. A loud whimper came from Uncle Jace's wolf and I took a deep breath and stuck my hand out again, keeping my eyes closed tightly. A warm tongue slid across my fingertips and a large head bumped against my palm. The fear was nearly overpowering but Amber's presence and his submissive posture kept it from overwhelming me completely. My heart beat so loudly in my chest it almost hurt.

I took in deep rasping breaths before Amber grabbed my wrist and pulled me to standing. "That's enough for today." Her tone left no room for argument as she backed away from the wolf, forcing me to move as well. I let my eyes open as she turned us. Uncle Jace's wolf was whining as he lay his head down on his large paws. His gaze was on me as Amber ushered me up the stairs and to the front door. "Need to clean up and put something on." She muttered it to herself more than anything as I opened the door and entered the house. Bailey looked at me from the entrance to the living room. She rubbed her eyes and gave me a half smile.

I smiled back and moved towards her before wrapping my arms around her, trying to stop the harsh pounding of my heart. She gripped the sides of my shirt tightly in her hands and she pressed her face into my shoulder, searching for comfort. I liked how quickly she was progressing, perhaps when she pretended with the Mantras it hadn't been beaten into her as badly as they had been me. I sighed slightly, feeling the tension leave my body as I released Bailey from my embrace.

Everything felt off-kilter and strange. My body wasn't sure which bond to deal with first and it was both exhausting and confusing. First the mate bond with Bennett, then the protective bond I had formed with Bailey and finally the familial bond to Amber. That didn't include the issues I was having with Uncle Jace. Everything was so overwhelming and I was hit with a sudden urge to cry. I couldn't process everything that was happening and it was bombarding me relentlessly without me actually knowing what to do with it all.

I felt my bottom lip tremble and I sniffled, breathing heavily. I ignored Bailey's frown and tried my hardest to smile for her. She didn't look convinced and I gently turned her around, letting the smile slide off my face. I tried to force the trembling to stop.

"Davin is in the backyard. You should go see him." I deliberately kept my tone light and she nodded before hurrying towards the backdoor. I could practically feel the happiness radiating off of her as she moved away. I pressed a hand to my mouth and leaned against the wall. I couldn't deal with everything that was going on. I didn't know what to do and I didn't know who to talk to about it. My head started to pound as my eyes watered. I had cried last night but it hadn't been enough. Everything was snowballing into a situation I couldn't control. Amber's words filtered into my racing mind.

I just need to help her work through some things. If I don't she's going to have a breakdown.

I wanted to laugh. I hadn't worked through anything and now I was breaking. I slid down the wall and let the sobs shake my form. I couldn't control anything anymore. My life was being torn into so many different directions that I felt like I was going to be shredded into a million pieces. I pulled my knees up to my chest and buried my face into my arms. My heart hurt so much. There was so much fear, images of everything that happened flickered through my head as the emotions started to overwhelm me.

It was hard to breathe. Every inhale I managed was just forced out with a sob. I had no control over anything and I wasn't as okay as I pretended. I tried my hardest to be strong for the people around me but I was failing miserably. Each sob tore through me with a vengeance and the pounding in my head felt like it had gotten worse. My temples throbbed and I pressed my hands to the sides of my head whimpering in pain through the sobs.

Images were flashing through my head but I couldn't concentrate with the skull splitting pain I was experiencing. I felt the sobs disappear slightly as I breathed through my teeth, the pain becoming nearly unbearable before all I could see was red. My mind went instantly still as the red spilled across a white background. I was no longer inside my own body.

If things are left too long, they sometimes hit us when we do not expect them. I like to call them memory bombs.

Amber's words seemed almost taunting as the red spilled across my vision and the image of pleading dead eyes caused me to freeze.

Memory bombs aren't good, Maricella. That's why we need to deal with things as they come instead of hiding them.

I stared into the dead eyes of Beta John, the male who turned me into an Omega. I stared into them and could see hellfire. The phantom pain of a cane hitting my back made me gasp. Blood was sliding down my pale skin and I could hear it dripping onto the floor, letting me know that I was still alive. The pain was throbbing and I wanted to cry but I knew I would be punished if I did. I stared down. My skinny, pale legs had crimson lines drawn on them as my blood lazily followed the path gravity made for it.

There was always so much blood when Ingrid was done. So much blood. I stared down at my legs once more, watching the blood drip off my toes and slowly make its way to the drain on the floor. Not even the pain of the caning could make me tear my gaze away from the red liquid swirling down and away from the room they had destroyed me in.

Memory bombs are dangerous, Maricella, because sometimes they can suck you in and refuse to let you go.

I felt reality slip from my grasp as clearly as I heard the classroom door close behind me.

TWENTY-FIVE

My lungs burned as I ran through the trees. After I had read the file my wolf and I had decided it was best to get away from everyone to release the rage that was boiling in our veins. Maricella, my mate, as a ten year old girl was abused and tortured for some sick idea of revenge. I had known that. Alpha Lawrence had given me the concept of it but he never gave me details.

The details in the file had been vague, very basic, but had just been enough so that I could imagine what she had to go through and each image that was constructed made the rage boil worse and worse until I could feel my limbs bending and aching from the pressure of the shift that would have been forced onto me if I hadn't left.

I had been running for hours, trying to run off the rage or at least run my wolf and I to the point of exhaustion. It seemed like that was the only option that was working. Our legs burned as we patrolled the small territory. The wild wolf pack that was living in the area with Victor had avoided me, feeling the waves of dangerous rage that rolled off me. I appreciated the avoidance, I hadn't wanted to hurt any of them. They were part of Maricella's family and she never would have forgiven me for hurting them. I didn't know her a lot but I knew that much.

I finished my sprint around the territory before turning back to the house. My tongue hung out and my wolf was silent, too exhausted to even whine. I had pushed myself harder than I should have but I needed to. I needed to drive myself to the point of exhaustion because if I didn't I would have taken off after Tacita. I would have taken off to kill those responsible for her abuse.

I had a vague understanding about which pack warriors would have been cruel enough to beat a little girl and then there was Ingrid. There was very little I didn't want to do to her. I wanted her to feel every little thing she ever did to Maricella and the omegas before and after her. I wanted to break her down until there was nothing left and only when she begged for death or mercy would I give her that only kindness she had deserved.

Despite my exhaustion, rage flared up once more but I pushed it away. I couldn't allow myself to get out of control, not around Maricella, she deserved more than that. I ignored the rage that demanded I destroy everything in my path and focused on Maricella. I pushed everything away as I raced towards her. I needed her in my arms, to make sure she was okay. I wasn't paying attention and nearly slammed into Alpha Sterling. I felt my claws dig into the earth as I came to a stop. It was strange how he was in the middle of the forest, so far from the house.

"Shift." He held out a pair of what looked to be shorts and I did as he requested. I took the shorts with a small nod before looking at him. His face was pale and he looked haggard. "I need your help." There seemed to be something in his tone and I narrowed my eyes as I pulled the shorts on. Something wasn't right. Something was going on.

"Can't it wait?" I couldn't help the aggressive tone I had taken. I needed to be with Maricella, something wasn't right. The need to be with her was growing and I stiffened slightly at the thought of his sudden appearance and my apprehension. Something was going on and I didn't like it.

"No. I wouldn't be asking you if I didn't need the help. Maricella told me to ask you." He was lying and it didn't sit right with me. I narrowed my eyes more and tilted my head. I needed to figure out what he was lying about and why. "Stop looking at me like that. I'm a weak Alpha. I have people who wish to challenge me but hold back because of Ezekiel and Michael but this situation is bad." He ran a hand through his hair and looked frazzled for lack of a better word.

"My pack is splintering, Bennett, and I can do nothing to stop it. I'm a shit Alpha. I know it, Jace knows it and my pack knows it." His words floored me. His brutal honesty struck a chord deep in my chest. This male had found some of my respect. An Alpha who was willing to admit his shortcomings was one I could respect. "I can't run a pack. I can barely use an Alpha Command. I'm *fucked*." He let out a sigh that seemed to make the air around us heavier.

"How does this involve me?" I crossed my arms over my chest as I looked at him. I narrowed my eyes, despite the new found respect, he was hiding something from me and I didn't like being lied to.

"I need your help. There are some dissenters in my pack and I want them gone. I can't command Ezekiel or Michael to do it because they would kill anyone who even remotely insults me. I need someone who has a bit more control." He looked me up and down and then met my gaze. His grey eyes were similar to Maricella's but a bit darker, more slate grey than cloudy. "Just for a few days and then you can come back. I need you to help me instill fear into my pack." His words were almost sour in the air. Running a pack through fear wasn't always the right route to go.

"That isn't the best way to run a pack." I said the words coldly but he didn't even flinch against my tone, he simply nodded his head as if agreeing with me.

"I know but it's the only way I can. If they refuse to give me respect, I need to force them to fear me." He ran his hands through his hair. "It's my last chance. If I can get them to fear me then I can control them for at least a year, until I find something that can give me the power I need to gain their respect. I need to do this. I'm at the end of my rope, Bennett. I promise you this isn't going to be how I run my brother's pack." He spat the words out and I felt an eyebrow rise slightly.

"It's your pack. You're the Alpha." I watched as he let out a bitter laugh.

"Not by *choice*, Bennett. I'm playing at a job that my brothers trained for their entire lives. Sadly, they're buried six feet in the ground next to my father and my mother is too psychologically damaged to run a pack. So that leaves *me*." Bitterness hung off of him heavily and I looked at him carefully. He truly looked like he had no options left. He wasn't born to be an Alpha, it showed in his aura. He lacked the power a firstborn, and even a second born, would have had.

"Shitty but if you excuse me." I let my arms drop to my sides and I took a step forward.

"I was sent out here to distract you. To convince you or con you into leaving with me for a few days." He tilted his head and I froze. The burning rage instantly went icy at the thought of someone scheming against me or attempting to separate me from Maricella. I stared at Luka, my gaze cold and he shrugged. "Honestly, I was against it. So it probably would have worked better to *not* send me out here but they did. Now what I'm going to do is distract you and help you burn off some rage before you go back to the house." He shifted on his feet, putting his hands into his jean pockets as he looked at me expectantly.

"Do you want to go for a walk with me while I tell you what's going on?" He tilted his head the other way and despite the rage that had filled me, I could see the hand he was extending. He was *helping* me. He was going against those he knew to help me and most likely Maricella. I had underestimated him as a person. He wasn't a strong Alpha, I knew that but he had conviction, a steel back bone, and a sense of justice and that wasn't something I had expected from the soft spoken male.

I forced the rage down until it was back to a simmer, the feeling of anxiety quickly filled the spaces it left. I had been right in thinking something was wrong with Maricella. If they didn't want me to see her then something had happened. I felt like I had failed her.

"What happened?" My voice was tight with worry and Luka started walking through the trees. I fell into step beside him.

"Maricella has this issue. It's similar to PTSD but Amber says it hits a bit harder and happens a lot quicker. It's set to very traumatic triggers." He hunched his shoulders forward. "Amber calls it *Acute Stress Disorder*. Essentially it means Maricella goes into a sort of psychological coma. Her brain freezes and she is stuck somewhere inside of her head until she can dislodge herself." I knew what he was speaking of. I had read in the notes that the most serious trigger had been blood and I winced.

"This happened because of yesterday, didn't it? Because she saw Beta John?" I wanted to kick myself. I should have known. I should have made sure she was okay. Everyone should have but instead she had been forgotten, as if the incident had never happened.

"More than likely that *and* during those ten minutes she was forcibly removed from her mate, had a person she trusted more than anything tear that trust to pieces before he left her with bruises. It was a highly emotional and traumatic event." He scuffed ground with his foot and I felt the ever familiar feeling of self-loathing fill me. I hadn't been there for her. I was supposed to protect her and I had failed her. "Her mind is a strange thing but Amber should have known this would have happened. It was like a bomb and shortly after you left the house or it was sometime when she was alone. We don't actually know. It exploded." He let out a heavy sigh.

"She's completely unresponsive. They have been trying for the past six hours to get her mind to release her but nothing is working. They wanted me to take you away so you wouldn't go ballistic on them but I have a feeling that the only way this is going to get better is with you." Luka looked at me and I felt my chest tightened painfully. I glanced through the trees in the direction of the house. I needed to be with her. "Don't go there just yet. Walk with me for a bit." He continued forward and I hesitated before following. I wanted to be with Maricella but I trusted that Luka wouldn't lie to me, not about Maricella's safety.

"I'm a shitty mate." The words burned but they were honest and Luka let out a sharp bark of laughter.

"And I'm a shitty Alpha. We make quite the pair." He chuckled for a brief moment before shaking his head. "You aren't a shitty mate. You protect her, even from those close to her. You didn't think I would notice how you were ready to rip Jace's throat out for frightening her? Not many mates would go as far as to challenge an Alpha for their mates." He stepped over a fallen log and I followed suit.

"I should have been there. Instead I was running around like a child." I was kicking myself for it. I should have been with her and the fact I wasn't burned me deep inside as the bond tore at my nerves and skin, raking it with a faint and throbbing pain.

"Been there to what? See her mind crumple and hide her deep in the recesses of her memories? It would have happened, Bennett. Only if you had been there you would now be saying how shitty of a mate you were for not doing more to stop it." He sighed, "You ran off to hide your rage. You did it to wear yourself out, to make sure you were in complete control. That speaks of a great maturity. I've seen Alphas that don't have that level of forethought. You're a surprise, Bennett." Luka stopped walking and I stared at him. Ignoring the way my body itched at me to take off to the house. I needed to be calm before I went back. It was difficult with the guilt and anxiety eating me from the inside out.

"You obviously don't know me." I ran my hand through my hair, shaking out the long strands. It was getting almost too long and I would need to take a pair of scissors to it.

"I know enough." He frowned and crossed his arms over his chest. "I was serious about you coming to help me out with my pack. Not now, after all of this shit is over. I need help." I felt a pang of irritation at his words. I wasn't some sort of guard dog and I was definitely unwilling to leave Maricella.

"What do I get in return?" I did not do anything in the realm of guard dog without serious compensation.

"My heartfelt appreciation and thanks?" At his words I levelled him with a cold glare that he seemed completely unfazed by. "I'm kidding. You get to bring Maricella, meet some new people and have a holiday for about a week. Oblitus can be a bit much for the first few months." He gestured around lazily and I couldn't find it in me to disagree with him on that paint. Oblitus was a... *different* sort of pack.

However my frown deepened. "And you honestly think Maricella would like-"

"She would love to come for a visit. She doesn't get out enough." Luka's tone turned a bit bitter. "She's *stuck* in that house in this territory. She *never* goes anywhere and I honestly hate it. I can't convince Jace to let me take her but if you're going he wouldn't have a choice but let her go." He shrugged again before walking once more.

"Besides I think it's best if she gets away from this whole Jace thing. With her here, Amber's going to be constantly at Jace's throat. They will need a week or so to sort everything out." He gave another shrug and I had to admit it would be easier for everyone, Maricella included, if we went somewhere else for at least a week. Let her settle her emotions and mind and relax for a few days.

"So? What do you say?" Luka looked over at me and I frowned. I didn't want to promise anything to him until I was sure Maricella was okay.

"I would like to but currently my entire focus is on Maricella." I glanced at him and he nodded in understanding.

"No worries. I don't blame you. I'm staying for a few days to train anyway so it can wait until I need to leave or later." He shrugged and I silently agreed with him. It could wait a few days. I glanced in the direction of the house. "No looking over there." His voice was sharp and the Alpha Command was still weak but it was stronger. I levelled him with a stare that he ignored.

"Don't look at me like that. We need to keep you distracted for a bit longer. Five more minutes, Bennett." He said it as if I were a child and I glowered at him coldly. He simply smirked. "So how is a mate bond?" His face went serious as he looked at me.

"Strange." It was the only way I could explain the feelings I had.

He rolled his eyes at me. "I need details." I didn't understand why he needed to even ask.

I found a deep scowl on my face as I walked forward. "Why?" I snapped it out and he let out an all-suffering sigh.

"I got rejected by a female and refuse to find another one to take her place. I'm trying to live vicariously through you. So just answer my question." He sounded irritated and I winced. I hadn't realized that he had been rejected.

"I'm sor-"

"I don't need that. She was a power hungry bitch but she made some valid points about my lack of power and inability to control my pack. So, how is a mate bond?" He waved me off before throwing me a lazy smile. I wanted to frown but resisted the urge, this male could switch emotions like it was nothing.

I also didn't like how friendly he was being with me. I didn't do friendly with others. Thinly veiled hostility was more my style but I thought on the bond I had with Maricella to appease his curiosity. "I need to protect her. It's bone deep and it's all-consuming. She's constantly on my mind. I worry about her excessively and the need to claim our bond runs through me fiercely. It's like being in a box and the sides are pushing in on you until you do what it requires." I frowned as Luka made a noise of surprise.

"Is it enjoyable?" His entire presence was calming and I couldn't help but relax slightly. I could see why Maricella liked spending time with him. For an omega, it would have been incredibly easy to be around him.

"Maricella calls it frustrating." I had to smile a fraction as he laughed at the words.

"Kiddo has *always* been a strange one. Only she would claim it was frustrating." His chuckles faded off and a silence fell between us as we moved through the dark forest.

The moon hung high in the sky, looking down at us as she bathed the world in her light and I let out a sigh. "A bond is different for everyone. Just remember that." I looked at Luka from the corner of my eye and he shrugged.

"I don't care. Last thing I need is to get rejected again." He gave a strained laugh. "I'm a free male. No brothers, no girlfriend, no mate, barely any parents. I can do whatever I want unless it's what I *actually* want." He shoved his hand through his hair with a jerky and agitated motion. "Sometimes I just want to fucking run and never stop. I never signed up for any of this shit. I'm a fucking thirdborn son." He snapped his mouth shut, his jaw tensing. It was obvious he didn't mean to say that much.

"Third born or not. You're an Alpha. Act like it." I stopped and stared towards the house. The urge to go to Maricella was nearly overpowering. My wolf was whining and scratching in the back of my mind and Luka looked in the same direction.

"How does one act like an Alpha when their entire life they have been told they will never be one? I was never meant to be an Alpha." He spoke slowly and evenly as if it would help me understand his positioning.

I shrugged before gesturing at him. "Yet here you stand." He was an Alpha and he should have gotten used to that.

"Here I stand." There was a bitterness to his voice, making a slight face as if able to taste the words he spat out. "I think you should be okay to go back. I'm going to stay out here a bit longer." He looked at me and I moved past him. His hand grabbed my arm quickly, the movement making me freeze. He looked me over and I glanced down at his hand and then back up at him. The urge to break his arm was growing rather quickly. "I think you might need this." His voice was soft before handing me a long thin case. It looked strange but he simply handed it over to me before he let me go and whistled. The two wilds seemed to melt from the shadows to walk beside him.

"Come on, boys. Let's go for a run." He said it calmly as he shifted almost violently before taking off, his black fur glinting slightly in the patches of moonlight. I was surprised at the force and speed of his shift. One second he had been standing there and the next second he was standing on four legs. I had never seen anyone shift that quickly before. There had to be a lot of repressed rage there for the shift to happen that quick and violent.

I looked after him before I turned my gaze to the box he had given me. I opened it and my eyes went wide at the silver dirk that rested in the soft interior. The handle was wrapped intricately with cloth to prevent the wielder from getting burns. It wasn't a fancy blade but seemed to have an ethereal feeling to it. I closed the box quickly, my heart thudding in my chest. It was a blade used to claim a bond. I held it tightly in my hand before running towards the house. I needed to make sure Maricella was okay.

It didn't take me long to reach the front lawn and I didn't hesitate before I bounded across it and up the stairs. I shoved open the front door and sniffed the air. Maricella's scent was faint but I followed it. I found myself in front of the infirmary where her scent was thicker. I opened the door slowly, trying to ignore the harsh pounding of my heart.

"What the fuck *can* we do, Amber? It's been over six hours!" Jace's voice was booming and there was a loud snarl.

"Don’t speak to me like that and take that tone elsewhere. For all we know it could be *you* causing her to stay in her own mind." The accusation was heavy in the doctor's voice and I stepped inside of the door and looked between the two. It seemed everyone but Bailey and Davin were in the infirmary. I could see Maricella sitting on one of the cots. I ignored everyone and moved towards her.

"What the fuck are you doing here?" Jace reached for me and I couldn't help the warning growl that escaped me.

"Don't. Let me be with my mate." I spoke it as calmly as I could given the rage that was filling me before I sidestepped him and made my way to the cot. Maricella's usually expressive eyes were empty as she stared straight forward. If I couldn't hear her heartbeat I would have thought she was lifeless. A growl rumbled through my chest as I got onto the cot beside her and pulled her onto my lap, wrapping my arms around her.

I tucked her close, resting my chin on her head. Holding her calmed me but even my wolf could sense there was something wrong and the rumbling growl in my chest didn't stop. Someone moved closer and the growl became a snarl. I narrowed my eyes at Collin and he glared right back. I held her protectively as a red haze started filtering in on the corners of my vision. Both my wolf and I on the very edge of control as we held our broken mate.

"What the fuck was Luka thinking?" Jace practically spat it out and I shifted my gaze to him. He was the biggest threat in the room and the rumbling in my chest grew deeper and louder, warning him to back off. His eyes narrowed at me and I clenched my jaw tightly, trying to stop my jaw bone from shifting.

"He was thinking, that out of all of you, I would have the best chance at bringing her back. Thanks for that by the way. Separate the new mates and see what the fuck that gets you." My words were low and growled, my wolf and I speaking as one. We didn't take kindly to his plan and I narrowed my eyes further as he growled at my disrespect. The red haze darkened slightly and I bared my teeth, the growl sounding louder at the action. All the people around us who had plotted to take her away from me were making it incredibly hard to hold onto the last bits of my control.

"Don't, Jace. He has a point. As her mate, he’s closer to her than we are. He would have a better chance to reach her." Angie's voice was calm and I looked at her, the rumbling in my chest growing even louder. "*Don't* growl at me. I'm on your side. I didn't want them to separate you. You obviously would never hurt her." She looked away, crossing her arms over her chest. As her words registered the rumbling grew less, my wolf and I no longer viewing her as a threat to our bond or mate.

Amber walked towards the cot and my gaze immediately snapped to her. "Bennett, I need you to please let her go. I have to check her over." The doctor's voice was low and I snarled at her, unable to help myself. I held Maricella's waist tightly with one hand and leaned over, pressing my other hand onto the cot, effectively caging Maricella with my body.

My wolf preferred the position. No one would take her away from me. She needed to be protected and I could feel my wolf fuelling my actions, both of us feeling the burning need to protect her, to make sure she was safe. The red haze grew darker over my vision as I looked at the blond doctor. She was a threat.

"I think you guys should go." Davin's voice came from the doorway and I turned to look at him, assessing the newest threat. The haze was growing even darker and I felt my bones ache with a need to shift. I held Maricella tighter to my chest, the rumbling loud enough to almost shake the air in the room. I could see Jay and Collin shift uncomfortably before slowly moving to stand between me and Jace, an unconscious action to protect their Alpha. I snarled at their movements, snapping my gaze to their forms.

"You're just making him worse." I snapped my gaze back to Davin as he spoke and narrowed my eyes at him as he came into the room. My gaze quickly moved to Bailey as she peeked around him. The red haze faded slightly as she looked around shyly and hid behind him as the rest of the people in the room slowly left.

Jace and Amber looked at us and I snarled at their hesitation. "Davin, if he hurts her in any way that is on you." Jace's words were cold and Davin shrugged, as if unconcerned. My wolf and I still weren't ready to trust him in our state. Our mate was hurt and unable to protect herself and we were going to be forced into separation. It had driven our rage into a frenzy to protect her against anything and everything.

"She's his mate. She's safe." At his words Jace slammed the door and my rumbling lessened. I felt my body relax slightly but I still kept my gaze on Davin. Bailey slowly moved out from behind his back, a brush was clutched in her hands and Davin said nothing as she slowly moved across the infirmary. I growled at her, the haze growing but she simply gave me a small smile and tilted her neck slightly. The submissive gesture shocked me and my wolf enough that the rumbling stopped completely.

She said nothing as she slowly moved closer. My gaze was on her intently as she reached the cot. As soon as her hand touched it the red haze returned with a vengeance and I snarled at her. I knew I would regret the action later but at the moment I needed to keep Maricella safe.

"Easy, Bennett." Her voice was shaky but firm as she slowly crawled onto the cot. I let out a deep rumbling growl, my hand tightening the sheets of the cot, tearing the fabric, but she simply shushed me gently, cooing calming words as she moved to sit beside me. "I'm not hurting her." She slowly settled beside me as if completely unconcerned with my aggressive stance. She lifted her hand to touch Maricella and I snarled at her, moving my mate away from her hand. Bailey blinked at me before repeating the gesture.

My wolf and I were confused and the haze started to lessen as we watched as she touched Maricella's hair, the rumbling grew but we made no move to pull our mate away from the small omega. We watched her actions with wariness and a pointed stillness as she gently lifted the brush and started to brush Maricella's hair. The action of her grooming our mate pushed the rest of the red haze from our vision. My wolf pulled back a fraction, knowing our mate was safe. I watched Bailey carefully as she gently removed the various tangles from Maricella's curls.

Maricella stared blankly forward, showing no signs of acknowledgement to the actions and it made my wolf whine. She was missing, her body was there but her mind was gone. I released my grip on the sheets and wrapped my arm around her, holding her to my chest tightly, trying to ignore the feeling of tears burning my eyes.

"She will be okay." Bailey's voice was a low murmur and I looked at her intently. She gave me that same shy smile. "She has you and that will be enough to make her okay." Despite how her voice trembled the words brought me comfort, as did the gentle way she brushed Maricella's hair. Bailey would never hurt her just like I never would. I watched her intently as she methodically brushed her curls until they shone. She set the brush down before grasping Maricella's hair in her hand, running her fingers through it.

"You need to come back, Mari. Everyone is worried about you. I'm worried about you. You are my first friend, my hero. You need to come back." Bailey's words wavered with tears but she continued her motions. I tuned out her words as I focused on trying my hardest to reach Maricella through our bond. It was impossible as the bond was only partially formed. It wasn't claimed, it wasn't complete but I still wanted to try for her, to try to bring her back to me.

"Is this right?" Bailey's words filtered through and I watched as she stared at the mess she had made of Maricella's hair. She frowned, an adorably sweet expression on her face before she looked over her shoulder to Davin.

I snarled when I realized he had moved closer and he simply ignored me and sat on the cot behind Bailey, pulling her into his lap. He reached around her and trailed his hands down her arms. I watched as Bailey shivered at the motions as he nuzzled his way to her ear.

"No, love, you have too many strands." He helped her gently remove the knots she had accidentally placed in Maricella's hair. I wanted to growl at him but as he gently murmured instructions in Bailey's ear, his face shining with adoration, I couldn't. I wanted to push him away but as he moved his hands deftly in Maricella's hair her eyes fluttered closed and she slumped down in my arms. I shot up in alarm, my arms tightening around her but Davin simply chuckled. "She always falls asleep when someone plays with her hair. Hopefully sleep with relax her enough to come back." He grasped Bailey's hands gently and pulled them away from Maricella. He wrapped his arms around her and I shifted away from him. Listening to Maricella's soft and even breathing. She was asleep, she was safe.

"What if she doesn't?" The words escaped before I could stop them. I hated showing them my vulnerability. I hated it but I had said it. Davin let out a sigh before reaching behind me slightly.

"She's strong but if she isn't strong enough. There's always the second option." He set the thin box beside me, his eyes slightly pained. I felt my heart turn over in my chest. That was something I didn't even want to think about.

"I won't take that decision from her." I never wanted to force her into this bond, to force her into *anything*. Claiming a bond was a *huge* decision that needed to be discussed between *both* parties.

"You might not have a choice in the matter. She has never been in there for so long. You might be the only person who can reach her even if it's through the claiming of your bond." He turned back to Bailey, leaving the box by my knee. My wolf whined in the back of my head, even he didn't want to force that decision onto our mate. The claiming of a bond was a serious thing, it was a decision that both mates needed to agree too. My wolf and I weren't of the Old Ways, we didn't claim by force.

"She'll be okay, Bennett." A small hand touched my arm and I bristled at the contact. I resisted the urge to growl with every fibre of my being.

Davin gently grasped her hand and pulled it away. I relaxed as soon as the contact was gone. "No touching, Bailey. Bennett doesn't like touching." There was a touch of amusement to his slight chastisement and Bailey blinked slightly in worry.

"I'm sorry, Bennett." Her voice was soft and I gave a slight grunt of acknowledgement as I shifted Maricella on my lap, cradling her in my arms, leaning my cheek against her head. We could still feel she wasn't right, we could still feel that she wasn't truly there but it was enough for now. I ignored how painful it was to have her in my arms but not truly with me.

I wouldn't be sleeping, I knew that and I resigned myself to it. Maricella needed me more than I needed sleep. It was ingrained into me to make sure my mate was safe and healthy, just as it was ingrained into Maricella. The bond was very much adamant about how it forced shifters together. People had even called it the living entity of fate and future. Everything the bond demanded of us was for the sake of the future generation, the continuation of our species.

I closed my eyes and tried to fight back the emotions that were crashing over me. The bond was rewarding me for our closeness but punishing me for her state. I felt like I was being torn in two and I barely paid attention as Bailey cooed and murmured soft comforting words into the air. The few times I cracked my eyes I had seen her gently touching Maricella, her eyes filling with tears as she pleaded for her friend to return to reality. I was aware when her soft pleas grew quieter and she fell asleep, her hand gripping Maricella's shirt. I looked down at her and felt a surge of affection for the small omega who had called to my mate, trying to bring her back from her mind. Her breathing was coming in soft, even puffs, just like Maricella's.

"Thank you, Bailey." I reached out and smoothed down her hair gently, patting it softly before returning to Maricella. Davin was staring at me. I could feel his eyes on the side of my head. My wolf and I didn't like his pointed staring and a low rumble came from my throat, a faint warning to him. He lowered his gaze and gently scooped Bailey up. I stared at him and he simply shrugged before placing her on the cot next to mine. He lay down beside her, pulling her close before tucking a blanket over her small form.

"I don't want to sleep on the floor again. One night was enough." He didn't seem like he was expecting a response but his words made a brief flare of amusement appear before it died out. I shifted my position on the cot, placing my back against the metal headboard. I shifted Maricella so her head was on my shoulder. I let her warm breath blow across my skin and it brought me a semblance of comfort. I kissed the top of her head.

"Come back to me. Don't deal with this alone." I murmured the words in her ear, hoping she heard me but fearing she never would.

TWENTY-SIX

I had held her in my arms the entire night. Not once did she move and not once did I falter in my sombre vigil over her. By the time the sun crested the horizon my wolf and I were worn out. I hoped fervently and prayed to the moon a hundred thousand times that she would wake up and be there once more but her absence was still palpable to us. She hadn't returned in her sleep, she was still trapped wherever it was that her mind had her.

I ignored the sounds in the house as the rest of the pack members woke up. I ignored my hunger, my feelings did not matter as long as Maricella was stuck within herself. I ignored Davin as he slowly rolled off of the cot, picking Bailey up in his arms.

"I'll keep them out, Bennett. You try to get her to come back." He spoke in a low voice as he shifted his sleeping mate and I said nothing as my hand slowly rubbed Maricella's back. I knew the action soothed me more than it did her but I couldn't stop it. It had almost become automatic, mechanical even. He left the room and I stared at the wall on the other side of the infirmary.

Maricella shifted slightly on my lap, her form straightening and I watched as her eyes opened. The eerie blankness was ever present and I simply wrapped her in my arms, whispering into her ear. I told her of my hopes and dreams for her, for us.

Hours passed and no one entered the room as I spoke to her, my voice slowly going hoarse from the constant stream of words coming from my mouth. I was trying *everything* I could to reach her in a place I couldn't follow. It burned at me that she was with me but she wasn't truly there. I promised myself I would be there for her but now she was so far away. Her mind had escaped to a place I couldn't follow.

I bent my head, pressing my lips to her hair before I stiffened and snarled as the door flew open to reveal a red faced doctor. Her eyes landed on Maricella and I shifted her, blocking the female's gaze. She let out a threatening snarl as she advanced. I felt a red haze cover my entire being as the rage surged forward. She was a threat and would try to take our mate from us. I returned her snarl with one of my own.

"Bennett, calm down! She needs to see her pup!" Davin's voice was booming but I had my entire focus on the blond doctor who was growling just as violently as me. My wolf and I wanted her, and everyone else, far away from our mate.

"Mine!" Her voice was low and growled and I snarled at her as she took another step forwards. "My pup." Her blue eyes faded to pain filled confusion before she ran her hands through her hair bunching the blond strands in her fists. Her entire demeanour went defeated and she whimpered. "I failed her, my pup. I should have done more. I should have done *something*." Her voice cracked as she looked towards Maricella and I found the rage lessening as I watched her crumble with guilt and fear. "What would An-Andrew say?" She faltered on his name and tears filled her eyes.

"I couldn't protect our pup." She whispered it out and crouched down, tugging on her hair, sobbing harshly. I, and my wolf, were uncomfortable with how the interaction was going. We could sense the familial bond and we knew its importance and with a heavy and great reluctance I set Maricella on the cot before moving to the sobbing female. I said nothing as I picked her up, placing her on the cot beside Maricella. The sobbing did not stop but Amber wrapped her arms around my unresponsive mate and cried into her shoulder.

I didn't want to leave her alone, not with how she was but I knew how important the bond between her and Amber was. Amber needed to see to her child, her wolf demanded it of her intensely. I left the infirmary, ignoring Davin as I closed the door and stood guard beside it. It was as far as I was allowing myself to go.

Davin let out a sigh and leaned against the wall beside me. A thick silence fell as I tried my hardest to hear what was going on inside of the infirmary. "It's past noon. Do you want anything to eat?" He asked it quietly and I shook my head, not trusting my voice to work. My throat was sore from the constant stream of pleas and hopes that I had spoken. I ran my hand over my face and tried to force myself to think of a solution that wasn't claiming our bond.

"Just keep trying, Bennett. Something's bound to get through." He reached out before hesitating, his arm hanging in the air before he let out a sigh and patted my shoulder gently. I tensed at the contact but we could sense what he was doing, offering sympathy and friendship. "I don't know what I would do if it were Bailey. She's my everything." He sounded pained and I simply nodded.

"You're doing good with her. Maricella would be proud of how your bond has progressed." My voice was rough and hoarse but it was the truth. Bailey was timid and shy, as were all omegas, but she was embracing her bond with Davin. He was good with her, he was what she needed to get better. I had wanted that for Maricella, I wanted to be that for her but I had no clue how. Not now. It was easy when she was with me and could communicate but having her simply gone, locked away in her own mind, prevented me from even knowing where to begin.

"It's okay to miss her. Whenever she got like this I always missed her. It was like a hole in my chest that wouldn't go away." He patted my shoulder again, ignoring how I stiffened. His words were true, despite everything. It felt like I had a giant hole punched into my chest somewhere in the vicinity of my heart. "I'm surprised you left her with Amber."

I pinched the bridge of my nose, I had a headache building deep in my skull but I knew it didn't matter. Not when Maricella was stuck how she was. "Amber's soon to be her mother. That bond is important." I honestly didn't want to talk anymore but Davin had extended several gestures of friendship towards me and I wasn't going to throw that back in his face. I owed him a lot when it came to Maricella.

"Your wolf must be going insane." He stated it almost offhandedly and I shrugged.

"He understands." He understood but he didn't like it. He wanted us to be back where we could see our mate. I wanted to open the door and check in on them but I knew Amber needed time. Their bond was new and it was fragile. The strain of Maricella's condition would throw Amber's emotions into chaos. I wondered for a brief moment if Andrew could feel it. If he could feel his daughter's absence and his mate's chaotic emotional state. If it would show him just a fraction of the upheaval of their lives. He deserved to know, to see it himself.

"You should do something. Have a shower, eat something, go for a walk." It came out casual and I stiffened, a growl building in my throat.

"And give them an opportunity to keep me from her?" I levelled him with a deadly stare. There was no way I was going to leave her side and allow them a chance to bar me from seeing her, being with her. The thought made my wolf bristle as his teeth barred in a deadly warning.

Davin slowly shook his head, looking at the floor as he shoved his hands in his pockets. "Amber isn't going to let anyone in and neither will I. No one's going to separate you two, I'll make sure of it. I just need to make sure you're in top shape. So eat something, have a shower., make sure you are healthy for her." He didn't command me, it was more of a suggestion but I didn't want to leave my position at the door. He glanced at me before he rolled his eyes. "There's a bathroom with a shower literally *right* there." He pointed to a door part way down the hall.

"I'll get someone to make you something to eat." He moved to the other side of the door and stood guard before waving me off. "I won't move. I *promise*." He looked at me, his expression was sombre but I could see the truth in his eyes.

I gave a slow nod before slowly moving towards the bathroom. Every fibre of my being was refusing me to move forward but I pushed through it. It did Maricella no good for me to let myself get into a state where I couldn't protect her. The thought was enough to enforce the strict control I had on myself. I moved to the bathroom and slipped inside, locking the door behind me.

I ignored the mirror and slipped off the shorts and turned on the shower. I stepped into the freezing water. I hissed slightly, feeling instantly awake but I barely cared as I washed up. I was done everything before the water even had a chance to turn warm. My skin was covered in goosebumps but I ignored it as I grabbed a towel and dried off.

A knock sounded at the door and I couldn't help the snarl that escaped. "Easy, big boy. I have some clothes for you so either you open the door so I can hand them to you or I pop the lock and see you in all your naked glory." Angie's voice was taunting and I scowled at the wood of the door before walking over, unlocking it and opening the door a fraction. A pale hand reached into the crack with a set of clothes. "Shame. Not even allowed a peek." She muttered as I took the clothes.

"Angela!" Seamus' voice was almost booming with agitation and I hesitated in closing the door, wanting to hear their little fight. It was distracting and at the moment I needed something distracting.

"*What*, Seamus? I'm stuck with you for the rest of my life. I get sick and tired of your face sometimes, okay! If I want to look, I'll take a peek now and then."

"Oh *hell* no, Angie." There was an edge of a snarl to his voice but there was no fear from his mate. I almost smiled at her attitude towards her mate. Despite her words there was a deep edge of affection for him. It was clear that she poked and prodded at him but she loved him, deeply and truly.

"You look at other females." She said it like it was simple.

"*What other females*? There are like four females in this house and I'm mated to one of them! I only have eyes for you and I expect the same in return."

"Oh, did I hurt the poor baby's feelings? No worries, honey, you're all the male I can handle."

"Your condescending attitude is not helping. Time to show you just how much of a *real* male I can be." His voice was low and growling and I could hear Angie squeak before she giggled. Seamus' heavy footsteps walked away and I pulled on the clothes as I opened the door wider and stepped out. I could faintly hear Angie's laughter from somewhere in the house and I couldn't help it as my mouth twitched. She had gotten what she had wanted from her little display.

I ran my hand through my hair and looked towards the infirmary. True to his words, Davin was still standing where I had left him. I took my position back up and he shook his head. "You took like ten minutes. Your food isn't even ready." He stared at me and I grunted, a scowl deeply embedded on my face. My wolf was crawling up the walls of my mind, needing to see Maricella. "So talkative but I don't blame you. I want you to eat something before you go in there." Despite myself, I was hungry and I just nodded, looking at my bare feet. I heaved out a sigh and rubbed at my temples.

"Shits tough, bro." Davin shoved his hands in his pockets and I nodded as I continued to rub my temples. Everything was fucking difficult but I would endure anything for Maricella.

We stood in silence for a few moments before Collin walked down the hall. "I didn't make anything fucking fancy." He scowled, his face was pale and he looked like he hadn't slept either. In fact nearly everyone looked like that. The situation must have been hard on the entire pack. He held out a bowl of mac and cheese and I took it with a small nod. I slowly ate, despite how my stomach seemed to want to rebel against the food. I forced myself to finish what was in the bowl before Davin nodded and jerked his head towards the door.

I held out the bowl towards Collin who grunted in annoyance but took it anyway. I pushed open the infirmary door. Amber was writing on a clipboard, all evidence of her meltdown gone as she slipped into her role as pack doctor.

"No change in her but she's stable physically. However the fact she has been stuck in there for more than twelve hours isn't good, nor is it healthy. But the fact her mental stability has always been a little shaky, the emotional traumas she suffered means this is an expected reaction to it." Her voice was calm and even but I could almost hear it tremble. "There's little we can do but wait it out and hope for the best." I could hear her reluctance at the words and it matched the one in me. I couldn't wait it out. I didn't know if waiting it out would do anything for my mate. I moved towards the bed and once more wrapped her in my arms, setting her on my lap.

"Your touch and voice should help her find something to fight towards. That's all I can recommend as a doctor but as someone who cares about her, greatly. If drastic measures need to be taken, take them to bring her back." She lifted the slim box and I winced at the look of it before she set it on the cot beside me. I stared at it as she moved away. I shook my head slightly before looking at Maricella. She looked the same, her condition had not improved or changed in my short absence. I pressed my face into her hair and simply held her.

I had never felt more useless in my life. My mate was stuck in some hellish purgatory of her mind's creation and I had no ability to help her out of it. I rocked her back and forth, pressing my lips to her temple. I wished with all of my heart that she would snap out of the stupor she was in. That she would embrace me back.

Hours passed and there were no changes in her condition. The blankness remained as the night descended and the moon rose into the sky. People came and went through the infirmary. I was too focused on Maricella to pay attention to who they were. My nerves were frayed as the house fell silent, the others more than likely collapsing into their beds.

Everything was eerily quiet and I couldn't stand it. I looked at Maricella, taking in the ethereal beauty of her face. She was perfect in my eyes, she was my *entire* world. There wasn't anything I wouldn't do for her but I knew I had no other options left. I was on the edge with everything and I knew there was no other choice left.

The harsh truth was, I was completely lost without her. I didn't know how I had managed without her at Tacita. She was my due north on my internal compass, I would always need her but now she was gone and I was left confused and lost. I closed my eyes and pressed my face into her hair, breathing in her scent. I didn't want to go through life without her. I refused to do that to myself and her.

I looked at the thin box that hadn't moved from where Amber had set it. A bitter taste coated my tongue at the thought of what I was going to do and tears filled my eyes. I never wanted to take the choice from her. What I was going to do needed to be discussed first, to be agreed upon, and I was taking that away from my sweet one. My Maricella.

I would carry that guilt as a heavy burden for the rest of my life. It would eat away at me and I knew it would but I had to bring her back, my wolf and I could not take any more of it. I reached out and picked up the box before standing on shaking legs and slipping it into my back pocket. I picked Maricella up and held her to my chest tightly as I left the infirmary and took her outside.

The moon hung, a waxing crescent hanging in the sky, as if waiting for what I was about to do. Her cold beauty made the front lawn glow slightly and I walked towards the center of it before setting Maricella down and sitting across from her. I grasped her hands in mine and kissed her knuckles reverently.

"Forgive me, Maricella. Forgive me for taking this choice from you." I whispered the words before I looked up to the silver crescent. "Forgive me, Mene. Forgive me for this." Tears flooded my eyes once more as I pulled the box from my pocket. A lump formed in my throat as I set it down. I couldn't even look at it as rolling disgust filled me.

I turned my focus to Maricella and cupped her face in my hands. "I love you with all that I am and all that I will be and I'm so sorry." I kissed her cheeks and her chin. I kissed her nose and her forehead, trying to remember the feeling of her skin on my lips because I knew that she might not let me touch her for a long time after this and she would be well within her rights. I opened the box and grasped the dirk in my hand before placing it on my left palm. The silver burned my skin as I sliced open a large gash across my palm, following the lifeline.

My heart beat frantically in my chest as I watched the blood pool rapidly. I turned away and gently grasped Maricella's left hand and cut her life line with a wince. There was no reaction from her as the blade cut her skin. I threw the dirk away, unable to touch it anymore before I turned to Maricella.

"Come back to me, my sweet one." I lifted her hand and lined it up with mine. Tears fell from my eyes unrestrained. I didn't want to do it but I knew it was the only way that we could guarantee to have her back. "Come back to me." I pressed a chaste kiss to her lips before I pressed our hands together.

TWENTY-SEVEN

The classroom was dark and damp. I wasn't sure how long I had hung there for but it felt like an eternity. The wounds on my back never closed. They never ceased bleeding but there were never any new ones. Ingrid was still missing but I could still feel the cane every so often as it continually reminded me of where I was. As I hung there I wondered how on earth things had gotten as bad as they had.

I couldn't even comprehend life away from the small concrete room but I was aware there was one there. Faint murmurings that felt muffled and small seemed to come from the door behind me but I could never grasp what they were saying or who was saying them.

Every time I tried to remembered all I could see and feel was anger and blood, there was nothing that told me of what had happened. I felt stuck and unable to move. I closed my eyes in defeat and that was when the first pulse hit me. It was like pure burning energy moving through my body in tune to my heartbeat.

I gasped and my eyes snapped open. The room around me pulsed and wavered with each energy wave that seemed to come from outside of the room and from inside of me at the same time. I gasped at each one that struck me. There was no pain with them and I felt almost comforted at their rhythmic pulsating.

The pulses were like a living entity, their entire form one giant heartbeat that shook the foundations of who I was and who I would be. I felt suddenly frightened as the walls around me pulsed violently, the solid concrete bending and waving like paper. I yanked against the chains around my wrists, the fear rolling through me insistently.

I swallowed hard and gave up as the chains refused to move, refused to budge even a fraction. I held my breath as the pulsing grew faster and faster until it was like a constant hum through my body. I gasped loudly as I watched the world around me vanish into darkness. The walls tore down without a sound and the room disappeared as the ever brilliant red of my blood faded like smoke.

I floated in the dark abyss with the humming singing through my body before I was yanked forwards. I flew faster and faster, as if being pulled by an invisible tether. I felt myself swirling around and around, dizziness became all-consuming before I realized I was becoming conscious. I grew more and more dizzy and a heavy feeling descended upon me as I felt a myriad of different emotions and sensations bombard me violently.

Panic filled me, I couldn't control the emotions I was experiencing as I snapped my eyes open in the first time in I didn't know how long. Bennett sat across from me on the dark lawn, his shadowed face was sombre. Confusion wracked my brain, I had a breakdown in the hallway and now I was sitting on the lawn with my mate. The humming seemed to grow more powerful and I snapped my eyes to our hands.

His large left hand was pressed to my smaller one and a jolt of sheer panic filled me as I realized what it meant. I took in a deep rasping gasp as the pulsing stopped completely before I yanked away, scrambling to my feet and bolting. My heart pounded in my chest violently and emotions swirled around me. I couldn't focus as I bolted through the dark forest that surrounded the house. I needed to get out, needed to escape. I couldn't focus on anything but that.

Escape

Escape

Escape

Escape

The word thundered in my head, pushing me forward, it was the only thing I could focused on. So I ran like the hounds of Hades were chasing me. My heart felt like it was pounding hard enough to escape my chest and the emotions swirling inside of me were violent and intense. I ran until I was forced to stop, gasping for air as I leaned against a tree as I felt my chest tighten painfully. I took in short gasping breaths, feeling like I wasn't getting enough oxygen into my body as the foreign emotions bombarded me mercilessly. I slumped down, wrapping my arms around my stomach and trying to suck in the air I needed to live.

I couldn't sort through the feelings and sensations that were running through my body and it was becoming too overwhelming and I started to sob. Deep heaving sobs that made it even more difficult to breathe. I couldn't stop them even if I wanted to as I let the terrified confusion roll over me.

I was, I didn’t remember what was happening and then Bennett had claimed me without my consent, without asking me, and now everything was pressing down on me, overwhelming me to the point I couldn't breathe. The panic was just as intense as the terrified confusion and I didn't know how to gather myself together, how to sort out my emotions.

There was a whining noise and a cold nose brushed my cheek but I couldn't respond as I sobbed out the emotions that were swarming me relentlessly and without end. I couldn't get a break, couldn't gather my bearings underneath it all. The sound of cracking and shifting bones barely registered before I was wrapped up in huge arms and cradled to an equally large chest.

The person sat down in my spot with a faint grunt. I couldn't stop the sobbing as the unknown person simply held me. There were no movements of comfort, no shushing sounds, just deep, even breaths and the calm, steady pounding of a heart next to my cheek. Despite myself, the sounds the person did make were comforting but it didn't stop the chest heaving sobs.

"Hey." It was a familiar voice and I turned my head to see a figure, blurred by tears, standing in front of me as I sobbed. "Okay, okay." Silence fell and the figure moved closer and rough hands cupped my face. "Maricella, you need to breathe, you’re having a panic attack and we cannot explain things if you’re like this." His voice was calm and soothing and I tried to take bigger breaths in but they stuttered out in sobs.

"This isn't working, Kiel." There was a pause as I continued my panicky, overwhelmed sobbing. "Maricella, there is a spot of calm in you. You need to find it. *Find it*." There was an order to the familiar voice that my overwhelmed and panicky brain clung to. I searched until I wanted to scream, I couldn't find it. There was no center of calm in my raging mind. There was nothing in the panic I was feeling that I could count as calm.

The steady thumping of the chest I was cradled to broke through everything and I focused on the sound. Steady and calm. I found myself trying to match my frantic, pounding heart to the calm rhythm that the unknown person had. I took in deep heaving breaths, the sobbing lessening but the shuddering of my breathing remained the same.

"Okay, good." The hands left my face and I quickly wiped at my eyes, wanting to know who it was that was holding me. The tears were relentless but I could somewhat see as I turned my head and looked up. My breath caught in my throat at the savage and feral looking male that was holding me. His face was filthy as was his long black hair and he had numerous scars criss-crossing his chest and neck but the one that slashed down the left side of his face caught my attention, as did his eyes. They were green and familiar but the colour was lighter, *off*. The colour made them seem more... *human*.

"E-Eze-kiel?" The word came out stuttered as I tried to calm my heaving chest. The feral looking male gave a simple nod before he leaned down, his face close to mine. I held my breath unsure of what he was doing, his harsh looking face was shadowed and he looked deadly. He held my gaze intently before he nuzzled my forehead with his nose. The gesture was so familiar that it had an unexpected, hiccuping giggle escaping from my mouth. He pulled back, a faint smile on his mouth before I turned to look at the other person.

Luka smiled down at me. He was wearing a pair of shorts and nothing else as he sat down. "Ezekiel scented you out. Now we need to fix the problem we made." He shifted slightly, glancing at the male holding me. "Bear with me. Kiel isn't very good with words so I'm going to need so have some time to interpret the pictures he's sending me." Luka's eyes darted back and forth rapidly.

I felt my breath hitch in my chest as the emotions started pushing down on my once more but I closed my eyes quickly. I focused on the sound of Ezekiel's steady heartbeat and everything faded away. The calm was addicting as my body wanted to break down into tears once more. I didn't want to deal with the explosion of emotions that rested outside of the calm.

"You're probably feeling very overwhelmed right now, Maricella. That's regrettable, as is this entire situation but know that it wasn't Bennett's choice to claim the bond by force. I told him he might need to." At Luka's words my eyes snapped open and anger flared hot and bright in my chest. My wolf growled low in the back of my head and he held up a hand. "You were gone for over twenty-four hours, Maricella." The words alone were enough to shock me and send tears to my eyes.

Over a full day I had been locked in my own mind.

I had never been gone that long. I felt my stomach churn suddenly at that and as if Ezekiel sensed what was going to happen he shifted me as I turned and heaved. There was nothing in my stomach to throw up but Ezekiel merely rubbed my back as I retched. They were full body heaves that seized all my muscles and made me feel weak and shaky as nothing but bile escaped.

Images filtered into my mind, Beta John's frozen and twisted face and the red of his blood that had leaked from his torn throat. Uncle Jace's twisted face as he screamed at me, his hand and fingers digging deeply into my flesh as he shook me hard for the actions of another.

I pressed a trembling hand to my forehead after I finished my heaving before I slumped against Ezekiel's chest. I shook violently, feeling tired and achy and weak. The large and feral male simply stroked me from the top of my head to my lower back in calm and even strokes. There was another whining sound before I slowly opened my eyes. Micheal dropped a bottle of water beside Ezekiel and nosed it towards me, his dark eyes shining as he gave another small whine.

Luka reached out and picked the bottle up, opening it before he held it to my mouth. "Easy, kiddo." I took a small mouthful and swished it around before I spit it out. The acrid taste lingered in my mouth and when he offered me another sip I took it quickly, rinsing the taste away completely. He let out another sigh as I swished the water around in my mouth. "Nothing was working and we only suggested it as a last resort to bring you back. It isn't ideal, what you're going through. The emotions would have been less if you had been able to adequately prepare for the claiming." He spoke slowly and I spit the water out before I wiped at my eyes. I couldn't help the small shaking sobs that escaped.

A full day. I had been gone a *full* day. Everyone must have been freaking out. I thought being gone for six hours was bad enough. "The emotions you feel aren't truly yours. You've had your soul bound without your consent so everything has been thrown into chaos at the moment. This is okay."

Tears fell from my eyes and I glared at him slightly as I trembled. "H-how is th-this o-kay?" The words were stuttered by sobs and I felt a dull throbbing fill my head from the pressure of trying to keep the emotions from bombarding me.

"It's okay because you're safe and it's okay because we can deal with it." His voice was soft and the anger roared through me, my wolf was demanding vengeance for the forceful claiming. I didn't like her anger in the rolling chaos of everything else. I didn't want to deal with her but I didn't have the strength to push her away.

"Y-you don't ha-have to deal with ja-jack shit, Lu-ka!" I found it difficult to shout while still sobbing and Luka made a pained noise in his throat.

"I'm sorry. This is my fault, Maricella. I know. Find the calm spot." At his words I growled and lunged for him.

"Fuck your calm spot, Luka!" My wolf was pissed and Luka was the target. She wanted blood for the forced bonding and she wanted it immediately. Ezekiel simply held us tight to his chest, his arms unmoving and he was seemingly unconcerned with our growling or wiggling attempts to escape.

"Easy." The word was hoarse and more of a growl than anything and the hairs on the back of my neck stood up. I froze as I slowly turned and Ezekiel's eyes had narrowed a tiny fraction and I instantly cowered in his grip. All fight gone from me and my wolf. The amount of power he had hanging off of him was terrifying and having just his irritation on us was enough to make us want to become invisible and tiny. Our submission was both complete and absolute.

"Your wolf is going to be highly upset, Maricella. As is her right. This isn't how a claiming is supposed to work. There's supposed to be love and acceptance with a claiming, yours had only fear and panic and confusion. It will bring complications and your emotions will not settle and be intense for quite some time. A few weeks or more." He sounded pained and I couldn't take my eyes off of Ezekiel's face, even though he had looked towards Luka.

There was a faint moment of time before Luka cleared his throat. "Ezekiel... I think you broke her." Luka sounded concerned and let out a small eep as Ezekiel turned his gaze back to me once more. I shrunk further into his grip, trying to melt away into nothingness. He lowered his face closer to mine before tilting his head, the motion reminiscent of his wolf. Tears filled my eyes as the fear coursed through my veins. It was hot and burning and left a bitter taste in the back of my throat.

He tilted his head the other way before a small smile crossed his face and he shifted his arms around me and pulled me even closer to his chest. He tightened his arms slightly and gave me a hug, pressing his cheek to the top of my head. He rocked me from side to side for a few moments until the fear and tension slowly left my bones and muscles and I relaxed into him.

It was oddly strange that a terrifying, deadly male hugged me to make me relax simply because he scared me. He nuzzled my hair gently before relaxing his grip. I was more than aware he could have nearly broken my bones with the hug but he had restrained himself.

"Now that's an image that I never want to disappear from my head. Ezekiel *hugging* someone." Luka sounded amused and Ezekiel made no indication he even heard the words as he settled me back in the position I was in before. "Okay, so your emotions are going to be out of control for a while, Maricella. Luckily if you're around Bennett they will settle some. Ezekiel isn't sure, he only knows what he has experienced and seen." Luka looked lost and filled with regret.

Micheal whined and nudged Luka's arm with his nose and Luka absently patted his head. "I just wanted you safe. We *all* wanted you safe. This should never have been forced on you, Maricella. A claiming is meant to be beautiful and wonderful or some shit like that and we ruined it for you. It's like mundane females and their weddings. We trashed your pretty white wedding like huge giant assholes because we were scared." Luka sniffled slightly and I looked at him in shock. "I fucked it up for you, Maricella." His voice was quiet and I felt a huge surge of guilt.

"You were just trying to help." I sniffled and he shook his head, his hand falling to Michael's head.

"Your relationship with your mate will now be strained and it's my fault." He sounded like a small child and I just wanted to wrap my arms around him. Despite everything bombarding me, he just wanted to help me. A rumbling moved through me from the large chest, making me tense but the rough, rasping chuckles coming from Ezekiel's mouth were more than shocking. "Don't laugh at me, Ezekiel." There was a hint of an Alpha Command to Luka's voice but even I could tell it was half-hearted.

"Sap." The word was raspy and growled like the previous one he had said and I watched as Luka simply smiled at his guardian.

"Shut up. I'm allowed to be emotional at times. We can't all be robots, Ezekiel." He childishly stuck his tongue out at his companion as he looked at him.

"Beep." The raspy chuckle returned and Luka let out a laugh at the word.

"Fuck, Kiel. You're a cheeky bastard." He shook his head as Micheal barked at the words, shoving his face into Luka's as the male laughed. Luka did his best to push the large wolf away as he laughed harder. "Do you see this, Maricella? I have to deal with this every day. Such disrespect." His voice was teasing and I smiled slightly at their antics. There was an intense sense of camaraderie between him and his guardians. I felt a pang in my heart, I didn't have friendships like that.

A silence fell and I leaned my head against Ezekiel's chest, listening to his steady and strong heartbeat. It was the only thing keeping the emotions from tearing me apart and leaving me a sobbing mess. I let out a sigh and closed my eyes. I was tired and still slightly confused.

"Don't be mad at Bennett, okay? If you need to be mad at anyone. Be mad at me." Luka sounded sincere and I looked at him carefully.

"I don't know what I'm feeling right now. I'm pleasantly calm. Thank you for that, Ezekiel. Your heartbeat is very calming." I looked up at him and he gave me a small nod of acknowledgement.

"That's... weird." Luka gave me a strange look and I shrugged slightly.

"You told me to find a calm spot." I was starting to feel a bit better, the trembling had lessened slightly even though the emotions were just as intense and overwhelming as they hung right outside of my reach.

"Yah but I didn't think it would be Ezekiel." The strange look faded to a frown and I scoffed lightly.

"It's not Ezekiel. It's his heartbeat. It's even and strong. It drowns everything out." I was slightly irritated and Luka nodded, his frown disappearing before his eyes started to dart back and forth.

"Ezekiel says that bonds are complicated and can be confusing. He understands how much you dislike being confused but he says it's unavoidable. You need to be closer to Bennett. He will help transition you. Your soul is connected to his and your entire mind is in upheaval because you're connecting with another person on a very personal, intimate level. You're both going to need each other until it levels out." He relayed the information calmly and looked at me. I lowered my gaze, my stomach in knots. I reached up to run my hand through my hair when I saw my scar. The line I thought would be white was a red colour and it felt warm. I touched it with my fingers and winced as a sudden pain flared through it.

Ezekiel moved one of his arms and grasped my wrist. His hand was so large it took up nearly half of my forearm as well. He stared intently at the scar before he let my wrist go and shook his head. He showed me his palm and I bit back a gasp. He had a line similar to mine but it was a much darker red and it looked like it had black veins running from it to the rest of his hand and up his arm. It looked like it was severely infected and painful.

I let out a noise of sympathy before grasping his giant hand in mine and staring at the brutal mark. "What happened?" I looked up at him. His lips pressed together in a thin line and he remained silent. I turned to Luka and he looked away, as if not wanting to speak about what happened to his Beta.

"Happen. After." Ezekiel spoke like he wasn't used to using words. He set me down on his lap and used his other hand to grasp my hand and tap on the scar. "Mate. Reject." He thumped his chest with a closed fist and I stared at him, realization filling me.

His mate rejected him after they had claimed the bond. I felt my bottom lip tremble. I couldn't help myself and threw my arms around his neck. I ignored how dirty he was and squeezed tightly. I had briefly thought on what would happen if someone was rejected after the claiming but I never thought someone would be callous enough to do it and to someone I cared for deeply.

"I'm sorry." I felt guilty for bringing it up, for his mate being heartless enough to do that to him. He gently pulled me away from his neck and stood up. He set me on the ground and I became aware of how enormous he truly was. I came up to maybe the middle of his sternum and he was easily twice as wide as I was.

He bent down slightly, grasped my hand and pointed to the moon. "Thinks." He pointed to me. "Reject mate." I felt all the colour drain from my face and tears welled up. I hadn't meant to make Mene think I had rejected my mate. I hadn't meant for that. I would *never* reject Bennett.

"She should get back to the house." Luka stood up as well, Michael close behind him and I felt my bottom lip tremble again. I felt suddenly small and lost. If Bennett thought I rejected him would he forgive me?

I took a small step backwards and tears burned my eyes. "I don't want to go alone." The thought of Bennett pushing me away was soul wrenching and I didn't want to be alone for that. I felt my breath quicken in panic before Ezekiel grasped my small hand in his much larger one. His hand completely engulfed mine and I looked up at his intimidatingly bulky frame. He said nothing but gave me a small, tiny smile that turned up the corners of his mouth slightly before he started pulling me forward. I felt my face flare red when I realized that despite how filthy he was, he was most definitely naked.

Luka chuckled from behind me. "Another great image. Naked Ezekiel holding hands with kiddo who had only just realized he is, in fact, naked." He sounded amused and I looked at the forest floor as Michael gave a huffing sound that sounded suspiciously like laughter.

The earth was cold on my bare feet but it was nearing April so it was expected, despite the snow that had melted a few days ago. I clung to Ezekiel's hand tightly, my discomfort with his nudity sliding to the fear that Bennett would turn away from me. It made my palms sweat and my heart thump frantically in my chest. I didn't want him to hate me. I didn't want him to push me away but the fear was nearly consuming me as we moved closer and closer to my mate.

"Easy." The raspiness was starting to leave his voice and the low and growled tone was very much still there but the small word comforted me. Ezekiel was still Ezekiel, whether wolf or human. He was aloof with brief moments of tenderness that let me know he cared.

"I'm part of your pack right?" I looked up at him and he tilted his head as he stared at me before he flashed me a toothy grin with a glint in his eyes. "If Bennett r-rejects me. Can I stay with you guys?" I knew I didn't want to be near anyone else if my mate rejected me and with Ezekiel already knowing how to deal with a rejection after a claiming he would be able to help.

The grin didn't fade from his face instead it turned almost malicious. "Silly female. Mate reject." He pointed at me with his other hand before he thumped his chest. "I kill'm." He looked pleased with himself and I felt an odd combination of terror and sweetness at his words as he continued to walk me to the house. I felt like a child walking beside the giant of a male. When in wolf form you knew he was powerful but I also knew that the power was more easily seen on the human side. He felt like he wouldn't have any difficulties taking down Uncle Jace, as if he ate Alphas like him for breakfast. I was happy that Luka had someone that strong to take care of him.

My breath came out in little white puffs of air and I tried to continue to push back against the emotions that threatened to crush me under their intensity and my headache was growing worse. I bit the inside of my bottom lip hard, trying to use the pain to make my brain focus but it only served to hurt.

The house was growing closer and closer and my panic was only building. I knew it was cowardly but I just wanted to hide away from the situation I was going to walk into. I never was one for confrontation and the fact it would be with Bennett had me shaking in my nonexistent boots. I felt like a huge coward but it didn't stop me from dragging my feet. Ezekiel only chuckled and tugged me forward slightly.

My eyes went wide as I stumbled from the strength of it. "Easy, Ezekiel. Not all of us are built like the incredible hulk." I stared at him and his mouth twitched slightly and he looked down at me with undisguised affection. It made his light green eyes twinkle and I couldn't help but smile up at him. He tilted his head and chuckled before looking forward once more. The interaction eased my panic slightly as the house came into view.

I froze as I caught sight of Bennett sitting on the porch stairs, his arms on his knees and his head down. Ezekiel didn't seem to appreciate my sudden lack of movement because he tugged me forward once more, his long legs eating up the ground so quickly I had to take three steps to his one.

I truly felt like a child as I practically had to run to keep up with him. My hand was clasped tightly in his and I tried to ignore how my body trembled as we neared Bennett. His scent soothed me and the emotions swirling around me but almost made the fear that much worse. I was a coward. A big coward that wanted to tuck tail and run. Ezekiel stopped moving and gently pulled me in front of him and disentangled his hand from my death grip.

I didn't want to look up. I didn't want to see the anger in Bennett's eyes. I couldn't do it but Ezekiel didn't seem to care as he placed both of his large hands on my shoulders and gently pushed me forward.

"Yours." His voice was low and rough, making the word nearly indecipherable in his growling voice. I let out a small squeak as my gaze snapped to Bennett's form. He didn't look up and Ezekiel let out a rather dominating growl. "Whelp." There was a demand to the word that had Bennett looking up, a dark scowl on his face. He froze when he saw me.

Ezekiel pushed me forward once more. "Yours." With that he dropped his hands from my shoulder and shifted, the cracking of his bones echoing slightly in the quiet night. His large nose poked my lower back before he rubbed against the back of my legs and took off for the forest once more.

I slowly turned my gaze back to Bennett. His face was stony as he stared at me and I felt tears spring to my eyes as a thick silence fell around us. It felt uncomfortable, so highly uncomfortable that I wanted to disappear into nothingness. His blue eyes were guarded and he made no move to stand up or touch me and it tore at me deep inside. I opened my mouth and closed it quickly. I swallowed thickly and tried to breathe through the panic that was now covering me. Ezekiel's heartbeat had been my calm spot and now it was gone.

"Please don't reject me! I know it was childish and stupid to run away but I was scared and panicking and I was so overwhelmed. Everything was hitting me all at once and it was too much and I needed to get away from it all. I just needed to go and hide and I know that it was stupid and you probably hate me and want to reject me but please, Bennett. Everything is so confusing and overwhelming." I inhaled deeply as the words ended. They had been ripped from me, pulled out of me as they pulled the air from my lungs. "Please don't reject me." I felt my chin tremble as I practically panted and I tried to remain strong as he stood up. I hugged my arms around my stomach, feeling suddenly nauseous.

"Reject you? *Maricella*." He spoke softly and the dam broke, the emotions swarmed me once more and I was sobbing again. Ugly and harsh sobs that made it nearly impossible for me to breathe. I was wrapped up in

Bennett's arms and I clung to him tightly. A feeling of peace and serenity filled me, the newly claimed bond rewarding us for the closeness we were sharing. The heavy, oppressive emotions were forced back and I buried my face into his chest. "Who was that?" He sounded curious but on the very edge of concern.

I gave a choked laugh, my sobs dying off as the peaceful feeling seemed to fill my bones. "Eze-kiel." I pulled away slightly, wiped at me eyes, trying to get my breathing under control as the sobs disappeared completely.

"He's terrifying." At his words I nodded. Ezekiel in human form was enough to terrify anyone. I let out several shuddering breath, pressing my cheek to Bennett's chest, letting his heartbeat calm me as Ezekiel's had. He rubbed my back as he slowly stiffened before his shoulders slumped. "I know you're mad at me, Maricella." His voice was low and the corners of my mouth turned down slightly. I was too content to truly frown.

"I'm mad at Luka, as is my wolf. It was his idea. You just did what you thought was best for us." I nuzzled closer to him, holding his shirt tightly in my hands. The relief I felt was immeasurable. He wanted me, he wasn't going to reject me. I felt stupid and silly for panicking before, for feeling like a coward. Bennett had only shown me acceptance but I had let the overwhelming emotions rule my thoughts and actions.

"That doesn't change what I did. I claimed our bond by force, without your consent. You have no-"

"It was implied." I shrugged slightly as he let out a small choked sound in the back of his throat.

"What?" He sounded utterly confused and I fought back my irritation. I didn't want to be irritated. I didn't want that emotion and my wolf's rage to bubble up inside of me. I was simply too tired to deal with it all at the moment.

"My consent. I accepted you and despite the fact I never actually consented to the bonding it was implied." It was the only reason that my wolf wasn't wanting to take a pound of flesh or more from our mate. She knew we had already accepted doing a bonding with him we just didn't do so verbally.

"That doesn't change-"

"It's all that is keeping my wolf from attempting to tear you to pieces for forcing a claiming. My consent was implied and I do not wish to hear more of it." I looked up at him, a frown on my face. The more he questioned it, the more my wolf questioned it, and the more dangerous and angry she became. I didn't want to be the reason Bennett got hurt and I didn't want that bitter feeling in my throat. I truly didn't. I wanted to revel in the closeness we were currently sharing.

There was a small pause as he swallowed before looking down at me. His expression was so forlorn it almost felt like a sharp pain was sent through my chest. "I'm *so* sorry." The words were filled with guilt and shame and I simply buried my face back into his shoulder, holding him tightly.

"I know." It was enough. I knew how he felt. His emotions were swirling around me just as frantically as mine were.

I wasn't sure how long we stayed like that but the moment I shivered Bennett let out a small curse and rubbed at my arms. "We need to get you inside. It's cold out." He pulled away from me before quickly scooping me into his arms. My feet felt almost frozen and I noticed my teeth were chattering. I scowled slightly but wrapped my arms around his neck as he carried me up the stairs and into the house.

"This is what I get for wearing a t-shirt and pyjama pants outside in the middle of April." I muttered it and Bennett chuckled slightly. I frowned when I realized he was heading towards the stairs to go up to my room. "What do you think you are doing?" The words were almost icy as I asked them and he froze, staring down at me in confusion. Irritation, agitation and frustration all hit me at once. Intense and powerful to the point it made my head hurt.

"I'm taking you to your room." He sounded almost wary and I gave a rather short and bitter laugh.

"Oh no, Bennett. You claimed our bond. There is no fucking way in *hell* that you are just going to dump me on my bed and slink away with your tail between your legs." I stared at him, the thought of him just sending me to my room to deal with all the emotional bullshit alone, enraged my wolf. "You are going to carry me down to your room. We are going to spend the night there because I will not tolerate being separated from you right now. I refuse to become a sobbing mess again and I refuse to let you wallow in misery and guilt. Am I understood?" His blue eyes narrowed in almost slightly frightened amusement and I looked at him expectantly.

"Bennett. *Am I understood*?" I said it slowly and a smile spread across his face. If I thought what I felt for him before the claiming was intense, I was horribly wrong. My heart seemed to jump start in my chest. It was highly unpleasant but I enjoyed it at the same time.

"You aren't very frightening with puffy eyes, tangled hair, and a red nose." He had that breath hitching, heart turning smile still on his face and I scowled at him playfully.

"One more word." I held up a finger and stared at him. I knew I wasn't scary. I was well aware of that but the emotions that were wreaking havoc on my body didn't know it and they seemed to be in control at the moment. "Let's go to bed and no more talk about how horrible I look at the moment." He opened his mouth as if to disagree and I levelled him with a look that simply had a small smile cross his mouth as he turned and carried me towards the basement stairs.

I had stopped shivering, the heat from his body and my wolf were enough to warm me up. He carried me down the stairs and into his room. His scent enveloped me and made me sigh in relief or pleasure I wasn't sure. He set me down on the bed and crouched in front of me.

He held my hands as if he were afraid they would break. "Maricella, please under-"

"You are my mate. Our relationship has sped forward faster than I would have liked but there is no reason for you to act like I'm a fragile little doll." I snapped it out before letting out a sigh and pulled one of my hands from his and rubbed at my aching forehead. I didn't feel like myself and I *hated* that. "I'm sorry. My emotions are taking my mouth for a joyride." I felt upset that I couldn't control the raging emotions bombarding me and tears filled my eyes. Bennett made a sound in the back of his throat.

"No crying, sweet one. It's okay." He cupped my face in his hands and brushed my cheeks bones with his thumbs. "Don't cry."

"I'm just a blubbering, emotional mess! I can't help it!" I sniffled and wiped at my eyes before I grabbed his shoulders and pulled him close. "Just stay close to me, alright? It helps." I pressed my cheek to his chest and let out a shuddering breath before he gently wrapped his hands around my waist. Without warning he lifted me up and settled me on my back in the bed. He hovered over me for a moment, my heart started beating frantically in my chest before he kissed my forehead softly.

"I will *never* take another decision from you, Maricella. For the rest of my life I will pay for what I took from you." He moved over me and lay down beside me. I felt my heart slow down and I turned onto my side to look at him. His blue eyes were slightly dark and the darkness of the room made it hard to see his features properly, even with my enhanced senses.

"We can work through this together, Bennett." My words echoed what he had told me in Amber's office and he let out a sigh.

"I'm a really shitty person, Maricella. I'm emotionally cold, I enjoy being a harshly sarcastic, bitter asshole to the people around me and I don't like physical contact." A small silence fell as he let out a sigh. "I don't think that will ever change but you're my *mate*, Maricella. You're what makes every day in this shitty world worth living." His words were soft and I felt a warmth move through my chest as I shifted fully onto my side as I looked at him in the dark.

"And I'm a former omega with a serious amount of issues that would make *anyone* turn around and walk away when they hear them... but you stayed." I reached out and he took my hand in his pressing his lips to the backs of my fingers as heat slowly flooded my system. "I will never be a hundred percent okay with everything that happened to me but I know that just being with you, will help me." I let out a small sigh. "We make quite the dysfunctional pair, don't we?" We did and for some reason I preferred it that way.

"A pack warrior that has troubles with anger management and a sweet, kind female who was broken for a male's pride and has a long road to recovery. That's not dysfunction. I think it's perfect." He was smiling at me and I couldn't help it as I pulled my hand away from his and went up on my arms. I dipped my head down and kissed him softly. He was right, this was perfect. We had our issues and troubles but we were perfect for each other.

He bunched his hand in my hair and I relaxed into him, letting the heat of the kiss roll through me and fill me. I pulled back from the kiss and giggled slightly, touching my lips with my hand. Bennett growled playfully before pulling me down onto his chest. I looked at my hand, the scar had faded to white. Bennett pressed his hand to it, lacing his fingers with mine before kissing my knuckles again.

"No matter what happens, Maricella, I will be by your side and we will deal with it together. You aren't alone anymore." His words made a warmth spread through me faster. I wasn't alone because he would always be by my side. "I love you more than you could possibly know, Maricella." His words brought a flood of love to my chest and tears to my eyes.

"I love you too, Bennett. *So* much." I swallowed thickly, trying to push the tears away. I couldn't and simply buried my face into his chest. I held his hand tightly and wondered how on earth I had gotten a mate as perfect as Bennett. Our words shifted something inside of me and I felt a smile grow on my face. I had a long road to go, a long and *hard* road to travel, but I knew that with Bennett by my side I would make it to whatever waited me on the other side. I didn't have to look back anymore, I had the future in front of me with my mate by my side.

"We're in this together, you know that right?" His voice was soft and I nuzzled his chest.

I could feel that smile on my face as I tugged his hand towards me and I kissed the back of it softly. "Together." Hot tears pricked my eyes and I held him close. "I like the sound of that."

EPILOGUE

Four Months Later

I sat in the summer sun on the porch, a book in my lap as I read the words carefully. It was an adventure romance novel. The heroine, Avaline, was cast aside from her lord lover, Anthony, and as a result she became bitter and ran away. Only to be captured by pirates who she then defeated and stole their ship. It was exciting and I was having a hard time fighting the urge to flip to the back to see if she got together with the pirate captain in the end. He was a true gentleman. True he was a terrible asshole in the beginning but Avaline kicked his ass seven ways to Sunday and stole his ship in return for his dickish behaviour.

I chuckled lightly at the remembrance of how she threw him, beaten and bruised, onto a deserted island with his first mate as she waved at him with the hat she stole from his head during their sword fight.

Any male worth his salt knows better than to treat a lady as such, you cad. Now you are left without a ship and the lady for your boorish behaviour. If you ever get off of this island, Ryder. Be sure to get some lessons from a true gentleman and you might get the ship back.

What about the she-devil who stole it?

That, my dear Ryder, is one lady no man can have.

I smiled and shook my head, turning back to the book. Currently, Anthony was trying to win her back after seeing her at a ball, not knowing that she and Ryder were going to rob the party goers at the stroke of midnight. Her life was filled with adventure and romance and I *almost* envied her. Almost because Ryder was no Bennett. The thought of him filled my chest with happiness and love. Four months we had been together and despite some set-backs and blow ups I was beyond happy with him by my side.

It had taken a month before my emotions had settled enough for me to feel remotely normal and I had been thankful for it. I wasn't sure if I could handle more borderline bipolar moments like I had been experiencing during the first month of our bonding. I was quick to anger, quick to cry, I became oppressively happy at the drop of a hat and the only time I felt remotely stable was when Bennett wrapped me in his arms and rubbed my back. The world faded away and it made me realize that the claiming didn't affect him as it did me. I knew it would have bred a bit of resentment but the guilt he had over it was enough to make me push it away.

I wasn't sure how long he would hold onto his guilt for but even now I could see a flash of it in his brilliantly blue eyes and it always made me wince. He didn't need to be guilty, not about the claiming. I had forgiven Luka, my wolf too. After we had gotten control over our emotions we realized everyone had just tried to help and that the situation was just a consequence to that.

I frowned and tucked my bookmark into the book, knowing I was too distracted to continue reading. Bennett was running patrols and Alpha Linton was coming for a visit. It had been nearly half a year since I had last seen him and the visit had me more than excited. Bennett, on the other hand, not so much. I knew he was jealous of me being around other unmated males he didn't know but I also knew how hard he tried to push his possessive nature away so I could be with my friends.

So when he got tired and snappy with them or became a touch possessive with me, I let him. I would lean towards him, touch him, let him and his wolf know that despite everything surrounding me, that I was his and he was mine. We had made a vow that we would take on this life *together* and I would remind him of that ever single chance I got. I was invested in us just as much as he was, if not more so.

I set the book in my lap and looked towards the trees, enjoying the small breeze that blew across the sweat on the back of my neck. The days were almost oppressively warm and I found myself spending more and more time outside. My pale skin had acquired a slight tan from the constant exposure to the sunlight and my hair had lightened, the rays bleaching it just a fraction. Bennett was very fond of pressing his face into my hair and inhaling before telling me the strands smell of honey and sunshine. I let out a content sigh and relaxed further into the rocking chair Bennett had placed on the porch for me. I didn't ask him why he had done so but I appreciated the gesture. It had quickly become my favourite place to relax.

"Davin says Alpha Linton just pulled onto the road." Bailey's voice was sweet and soft. I tapped my lap with a smile and she giggled before climbing into the chair with me, throwing her legs over mine. I leaned my head against her shoulder, the smile still firmly on my face. Bailey had progressed quicker than anyone had thought she would and I knew it had to do with Davin. Even I had progressed much quicker with Bennett around, much slower than Bailey but it was a start. It seemed having a mate made the process much easier. I thought it had to do with having someone there for you unconditionally that would help you through the moments you felt like you couldn't show anyone else..

After her submission about omegas had been passed to the Hunters, Amber had started writing a medical thesis for the shifter medical community about mental and emotional trauma and how to most effectively treat it. Shifters, much like the mundanes, didn't really have the facilities or programs in place to deal with serious mental or emotional trauma and in most cases, didn't have the knowledge to fix it. We healed so easily physically that we almost tended to forget that our mind was a completely different matter and I was pretty sure nearly all of the shifters that ever existed had some sort of mental issue at one point or another.

Despite that, Amber still needed more people to test her theories on. She needed control groups and variables to figure out a good baseline. She was currently using my first two years as a control baseline because after bonding with Bennett my progress increased, slowly but it was still an increase. However she wasn't sure if the mate bond was helping or if it was just based on a person by person basis.

"You know you're my best friend right?" Bailey spoke softly and I hummed in acknowledgement. "I am serious, Mari." She was glaring at me and I couldn't help the smirk that tugged at my mouth.

"I know, Bailey. You are my best friend too. Now why are you bringing it up?" I opened my eyes to look at her and she gave me a sweet smile before throwing her arm around my shoulder and kissing my cheek.

"No reason. I just wanted to remind you." She giggled as I rolled my eyes. Her hand slipped down and snatched the book from my lap. "Ooooh. *She-Devil,* is it as hot as the cover suggests?" She looked at me innocently and I snatched the book from her before lightly tapping her on the head with it.

"It's just as hot as the cover makes it out to be. Ryder and Avaline are a serious power couple, I'll have you know." I lifted my chin, her attempts to embarrass me failing miserably. There was nothing wrong with reading romance novels.

Bailey tilted her head, giving me a look that was far too innocent. "I know. I've read it and in the end she gets pregnant and they take down the Southern Trading Company before heading to stop slavery in Africa." At her words my mouth dropped open in shock.

She spoiled the ending.

The fucking *brat*!

"Bailey! You-you've *ruined* it!" I stared at her and she simply laughed loudly before bolting off of the chair. I followed her, ready to beat her over the head with the book she just ruined. Never in a *million* years would I have thought she would spoil a book ending for me. That was just *cruel.*

I wasn't fast enough and she was already in the house. That was something else we had learned in the four short months she had been at the house. Bailey was incredibly fast. I sat down on the porch stairs, silently fuming as I clutched the book in my hand. I had really enjoyed it too.

I stared at the cover. It had a handsome dark haired male holding a nearly half naked fiery red haired female on some rocks by the ocean. I stared at it darkly. It was *ruined.*

"Hey, what did that book ever do to you, Mari?" At the booming voice I snapped my head up, my foul mood forgotten as I took in the red haired male I called Uncle Bruce.

"Uncle Bruce!" I jumped to my feet and laughed as I ran towards him. He picked me up and spun me around. His hazel eyes twinkled as he set me down, holding onto my shoulders gently.

"Six months is much too long. Remind me to come back out sooner next time." He gave me a crooked grin that I returned with a smile of my own, even as he ruffled my hair.

"It's okay, uncle. You are an Alpha, you are allowed to be busy." I reached up and smoothed my hair down and tucked it behind my ears.

"Should never be too busy for friends and family. So where is that snake in the grass, Jace?" He winked at me and I gestured to the tree line. Uncle Bruce's gaze zeroed in on my hand before he grabbed my wrist and looked at my palm with bulging eyes. "Who do I have to castrate?" He roared it out playfully but I simply laughed and shook my head at his dramatically playful words.

"I found my mate. It is only natural that we claim the bond." I watched as he pointed from my hand to my face almost in accusation.

"And where was *I* during this? Why was I not given a courtesy call to tell me that my favourite female in the whole world, my honorary *niece*, had found her mate and got claimed?" Despite the angry face he had on, his eyes were twinkling and I couldn't help but smile at him. He chuckled and hugged me tightly. "I'm happy for you, Mari. Who's the lucky guy? Does he have a title? Power? Respect? We all know how much you wanted to be Queen of the Shifters." He winked at me and I laughed loudly at his words. Queen of the Shifters indeed.

"He's a pack warrior. Bennett Aldridge." I looked up at the burly male and he narrowed his eyes in suspicion before looking over his shoulder.

"Lace, I want you to find out all there is to know on this... *Bennett Aldridge*." His face pinched as if he tasted something sour. I lightly slapped his shoulder before looking around him. A small and rather delicate looking female with empty black eyes was the only person he could have been talking to. She was wearing a black tank top and black cargo pants with combat boots. Her entire form showed a still wariness.

"Don't do that. He's just being crazy and over-protective." I smiled at her, despite how her entire aura wanted to make me shiver. She was powerful, I knew she was just from looking at her but nothing hung off of her. She was as normal as me and Bailey and it didn't sit right with me. She was hiding something and it put me and my wolf on edge.

"Lace isn't much of a talker. I found her about five months ago. Had gotten herself in a tight spot with some bad people so I helped her out." He sounded proud and I blinked before nodding. That would explain some of why she was with him.

"I owe him my life." Her voice was soft and even. I looked at her but her eyes were still empty. I felt mine go wide as she suddenly stared at me. It was as if I were looking into death itself. She stared at me intently before she moved so quickly I jumped in alarm. She stood by my side but slightly behind, as if guarding me.

"Lace, don't do this right now." Bruce groaned as if exasperated.

"I must protect your weakest side. That was a part of our agreement." Her tone was still soft but I could clearly hear the hard steel that ran through it. The softness seemed to be just how her voice sounded, the hardness seemed to be more natural to her attitude.

"But *Maricella*?" He gestured to me and I looked over my shoulder at the female who seemed to be a few inches taller than me. My eyes were drawn from her face to the side of her neck where a thick scar slashed down the side of it to her shoulder. I felt my eyes widen as I took it in.

"She is your weakest side." At her voice I yanked my eyes away from the scar only to realize that she was covered in them. There were thick ugly scars on her arms but in between them were swirling patterns of raised skin. A faint glimmer of beauty behind what appeared to be cruelty.

"Really? That little detai-"

"Major detail, Alpha."

"Why are you so irritating, Lace?" He groaned it out and I looked at him, tearing my eyes from Lace's scars. He was pinching his nose in irritation.

"I'm starting the facts, Alpha." The more I listened to her voice the more it made me aware that she was hiding something. It felt like Ezekiel in wolf form after I had seen him in human form, as if her power was muted somehow.

"So?"

"The fact you find the truth irritating is completely irrelevant to the situation at hand." At her words I nearly choked. Uncle Bruce never took disrespect well but he didn't seem angry at her words, just irritated. "While you remain here, I shall be by your weakest side. When we leave I shall return to your previously discussed weakest side. This is how the agreement works." I frowned in confusion and he rubbed his temples.

"I should have left you to the wolves. You give me a headache." He gritted the words out and rubbed at his temples once more before pinching the bridge of his nose, exhaling loudly.

"Perhaps, but you have created this mess and now we must deal with it as it is." Lace's voice never wavered, never rose, never lowered. It was almost eerie how monotone it seemed to be.

"Maricella, this is Lace. Lace, this is Maricella. Ignore her disrespectful tone. I can't get her to stop because if I tried she would annihilate me." He sounded serious and I stared at him in shock. "I've seen her take down bigger males than me, Mari. She's small but don't underestimate her." I looked between her and Uncle Bruce and she tilted her head.

"I've killed people for less, Alpha. You are safe with me, little wolf." With that she went back to staring forwards. I shivered but nodded. As much as she made me wary I was pretty sure she was telling the truth.

"Sorry about that, Mari. Lace does what she wants." He let out a sigh before wrapping me in a hug once more.

"It's okay. I'm sure she will join in on the endless fun we have." I rolled my eyes at the words and Uncle Bruce laughed.

"Such dry humour. I'm going to find Jace." He kissed my temple before striding off, leaving me with the strange female whose name matched her appearance but not her attitude.

"You hide your power, don't you?" I turned around and looked at her. She narrowed her eyes at me as if studying me. I felt cold under her gaze.

"Yes." The word came out clipped and cold and I swallowed before nodding. I felt a bit better knowing what it was that she was hiding. It relaxed my wolf as well, only a fraction though. We weren't exactly comfortable being around a wolf as powerful as her, even as muted as her power was.

"That's a good strategy." I looked at her and her narrowed gaze went slightly amused. At least that is what I believed it was, her mouth twitched slightly but her eyes remained empty.

"It is." It was strange how soft and melodic her voice was but how hard it was at the same time. Like silk over a knife's edge. Soft but underneath it all was cold, sharp metal.

"How many people fall for it?" I shifted on my feet and she crossed her arms over her chest. My eyes were once again drawn to the strange swirling scars on her arms. They were a stark contrast to the thicker scars. I wondered what she had gone through to get them before I shoved the thought away. It did me no good to wish to learn the suffering of others while still trying to deal with my own. I knew I would only compare them and minimize my own. Perhaps I would be able to in time but not now, not yet.

"All of them. Alpha included." She tilted her head again and I was reminded of the wolves. I took a subtle inhale through my nose. There was a faint scent of wild to her but nothing extreme enough to remove her entire scent.

"Okay. I won't say anything." I watched as her eyes widened slightly. I would have thought surprise but the rest of her face didn't move so I couldn't accurately gauge what she was feeling.

"Why, little wolf?" There was a darker undertone to her voice and I shrugged slightly.

"It's not my place to say anything about you, Lace. Your business is yours." I clasped my hands behind my back and rocked back and forth on my bare feet. She made me feel a bit off balance. I didn't entirely know how to act around her.

"You are a smart one. How easier this world would be if everyone lived like you." At her words I simply smiled before moving back to the house.

I picked up my book and sat down again. "I'm sorry you are stuck babysitting me." I set the book on my lap as I watched her.

She moved up the stairs, the boots clunking on the wooden boards. "It is my duty." She jumped onto the porch railing gracefully, leaning against one of the columns and sitting down on the thin wood. I was faintly impressed. I knew if I tried that I would end up with a mouthful of dirt or a face full of porch floor.

"You can do whatever you want. There is food in the kitchen, books in the living room. We have cable and movies as well. Just make yourself at home." I looked out towards Bruce's fancy SUV. I never understood his fascination for newer and bigger vehicles. Older ones worked just fine. Our jeeps were old but they ran perfect on most days.

"I will not let you leave my sight." There was an edge of finality to her voice and I nodded.

"Okay. Fair warning. I am boring." I raised the book, giving it a small shake and she said nothing in return. A thick silence fell and I glanced over at her. "What are the scars? The swirling ones?" I couldn't help myself, wolves were curious creatures by nature and I wasn't an exception.

"Proof that I am still alive." Her tone made it seem like the end of the discussion and I didn't want to pry more. I looked over to the trees and sighed. Bennett still had another hour of patrolling to complete before he could come back. "Little wolf, there is an evil in this world. Humans and shifters that prey on the weak, like you. Do not trust anyone or you will end up like me." Her words were cold and I shivered as I looked at her. Her expression was harsh and I nodded.

"I like pain, little wolf. I do not care for my own life. Do not become like me. Keep that innocent and naive spark in your eyes. Do not let anyone snuff it out." It was like her words were a warning and I swallowed before nodding again. She was a strange shifter, a *very* strange shifter, but I liked that she trusted me enough to tell me what she had.

"Okay, Lace." I pursed my lips at her name. "Did you know the name Lace is an Irish name meaning warrior?" I had been helping Angie pick baby names. She and Seamus found out three months ago that she was pregnant and she was ecstatic. The entire pack was excited at the news. It would be the first birth in our pack's history. It wasn't a very long history but it was still significant for us.

"I did not." She said it curtly and I looked at her carefully.

"It suits you." I looked her over. The delicate nature of the name suited her appearance but the meaning of it suited her attitude. "You are a capable warrior, I'm sure."

"You do not have any idea, little wolf, of what I am capable of." Another warning from the strange shifter Uncle Bruce had saved.

"I don't plan on finding out. I don't do violence or blood." I shrugged and she let out a cold chuckle.

"Good. Stay in your bubble of protection." She sounded pleased and I stared at her, bravely meeting her cold gaze even though I wanted nothing to do but hunch under it.

"I was an omega, Lace. I know what it means to be beaten down and abused. I know how cruel this world can be to people like me. I am not deluded or innocent to the world that surrounds me. I just don't like it or wish to see it." My words must have surprised her slightly because she frowned darkly. "I have had that innocent little spark snuffed out of my eyes as a child. The spark you see now is hope and love but never innocence or naivety."

"It seems I have underestimated *you*, little wolf. I apologize." Lace stared at me, her gaze flashing with something for a brief moment. "We are more alike than I thought. It is strange how two similarities can end so differently." She said it casually, as if remarking on the weather but I understood what she was saying.

"It is strange, Lace, but no two people are the same." I let out a sigh before standing and moving towards her. I held out the book. "Take it. It might amuse you or work for starting a fire." I waved it slightly before she flicked her gaze from it to me before slowly reaching out and taking it in a pale, dainty looking hand but I could see the calluses on her fingertips and the faint scars she had on it. The inside of her arm had the faint outlines of the word *Mori* in almost a block like letters. I shook my head trying to look everywhere but her scars.

"Romance is useless." She said it slowly as she looked at me and I shrugged.

"It is more like an adventure with an undertone of romance. It's not very often a mundane female beats up a pirate captain, steals his ship, and starts a life of crime after a male breaks her heart." I watched as something flashed in her black eyes.

She nodded slowly. "Thank you, little wolf." She set the book in her lap, covering it with her hands. I didn't want anything to do with the book after Bailey spoiled the ending and Lace looked like she could use the offer of friendship or even just the gesture of a gift. I smiled at her with a nod before going and sitting in my rocking chair. I stared at the far tips of the mountains as I pulled my feet onto the chair and let out a happy sigh.

"Do you trust your mate?" Her voice was almost colder than previous and I nodded.

"With my life." I turned my head and her black eyes were nearly piercing through me. I shivered slightly, unable to stop the reaction.

"Foolishness, little wolf." The words were icy and her eyes turned hard and sharp like shards of obsidian.

"Why do you say that?" Her gaze made me uncomfortable and I nearly sighed with relief when she looked the other way.

"Matings only end in betrayal." There was a flare of fiery rage in her voice. It was the first time since she had arrived that her voice showed emotion but just as quickly as it was there, it was gone.

"Some do, others don't because some people find it easy to cast others off and others find they can't." I shrugged slightly, eyeing her warily. "There are good people in this world and there are bad. Sometimes, when the world seems endlessly tainted by the bad, you just need to look for the light of the good because it will always be there." I frowned slightly before looking towards the trees. Jace and Bruce were laughing loudly as they came from the treeline. Despite the previous four months, I hadn't been able to stop my fearful reaction to Uncle Jace. It had lessened but it was still there. Trauma had a strange way of changing how you viewed the world, of how you reacted to it. I missed that relationship I had with Jace but my body and mind still locked up, still froze, and still feared him. I had to work through that.

Almost, as if sensing his presence, Amber was on the porch, moving to stand beside me. Her warm hand reached out, holding my shoulder gently. I leaned my head against her arm, craving the comfort that came from her touch. Our bond had strengthened considerably, falling just under our skins. She knew when I was distressed or scared, an instinct in her driving her to protect my wolf and I. She squeezed my shoulder in reassurance as Uncle Jace and Bruce reached the stairs.

"Lace, I know you're wanting to stay and watch Maricella but could you please, for several minutes, come with Alpha Lawrence and I? We are discussing certain things." The way he said it made Lace slowly get to her feet with a nod. I noticed the book was still firmly held in her hand as she threw me a glance, looking between Amber and I before she headed inside.

"Who was that?" Amber's voice was sharp as if her instincts were kicking into high gear at the unknown threat.

"Lace. She's Uncle Bruce's guard." I left it at that before smiling up at her, her blue eyes softened as she brushed her knuckles down my cheek. I felt the ever familiar tensing in my stomach when she looked at me.

Guilt was eating away at my insides. I felt like I was betraying her. Every little thing I had learned about her I had quietly told my father, trying to give him an edge if he were to ever come for her. I wanted him to be happy and the only thing that seemed to do that was his bond with Amber.

True I made him happy but when he spoke of Amber I could tell how it lifted him up, how it smoothed over everything in his life and he felt right. There was a lightness in him that came with the thought of his mate and as much as I loved helping him the guilt of betraying Amber ate away at me. I just wanted them both to be happy and proud. The feeling was grating and irritating. The bond demanded I make my parents proud of the future they created, despite the fact neither of them helped in creating me, in the biological sense.

I pushed everything away and held my smile on my face. She squeezed my shoulder once more before moving over to the railing and leaning on it, a small, sad smile crossed her face. I could never discern what she was thinking. She was never easy to read when she didn't want to be. It had to do with her past, one she never really opened up to me but one I could sense. The hurt and broken could always sense when they were in similar company.

I looked out towards the mountains again. "The view is always nice." I said it off-handedly and Amber sighed, the smile growing wider.

"It is, isn't it?" She let out another sigh, a peaceful sound that made me relax. I closed my eyes, snuggling into the warm beam of sunshine I found myself in. I liked our small territory, it was never busy and was nearly always quiet. Except for when we had a newcomer cross our borders, then again I was always kept away from them. Bailey and I would be held captive in the study by our mates. Not that we minded, any excuse to spend time with each other and our mates we took but too much of it usually had me crawling up the walls with boredom, much to Bennett and Davin's amusement.

I could hear the sharp groaning of the steps before a familiar and wonderful masculine scent filled the air around me. I found a smile on my face before my eyes opened. A bouquet of flowers was in my vision and I made a surprised sound at the beautiful wildflowers.

I reached out and took them from Bennett, a happy smile on my face as I looked them over. He must have freshly picked them because some of them still had roots with dirt on them. The sweetness of the gesture had me blushing crimson with a warmth spreading through my entire body as Bennett kissed the corner of my mouth. I wanted to melt into a puddle of mushy goo. Bennett's sweet little gestures made me melt from the inside out.

"What the hell, Bennett? Why are you giving her shit naked?" Davin's voice was obnoxiously high pitched and Bennett's low growl of warning made my cousin make a sound of anger. "Well *excuse me* but you are prancing around *naked*!" He hissed the words out and I turned my head to look at them. Bennett was pulling on a pair of shorts and I felt a rush of liquid heat go through my at his muscled form.

"Davin, he gave me a bouquet of flowers, not his penis." At my words both males froze and Amber snorted, trying to hold back laughter.

"I bet you would like that, Mari!" Angie's voice came from the open window above the porch and I glowered up at the roof of the porch, trying to ignore the burning in my face. I glanced over at Bennett and he simply smirked at me and I felt a wave of heat hit me from the mate bond. I gave him a warning look and he simply winked at me, making my heart flutter.

"You guys are disgusting." Davin made a face.

"Oh shut up, Davin! You're just mad cause you ain't gettin' any!" Angie sang the words and I smirked slightly. After she discovered her pregnancy she took great fun in tormenting everyone but Bailey and I. I truly believed she got off on knowing they couldn't really retaliate without Seamus flipping out.

"And your emotional pregnancy hormones are getting on my nerves." He muttered it under his breath and I could hear a sharp inhale from the window.

"Seamus! Davin's being an asshole!" The tone in her voice made me think of a child tattling on their sibling.

Davin gritted his teeth and pinched his nose. "This house is going to shit." He muttered it under his breath and punched Bennett's arm. "I'm going to take over for patrol before Angie convinces Seamus to try and kick my ass. He's like an overprotective dog with a meaty leg bone when it comes to her." Bennett nodded in acknowledgement before moving towards me.

I felt my heart turn over in my chest as he stood in front of me. Heat radiated off of him and I would have found it uncomfortable in the summer sun but it simply made a liquid fire run through my veins and pool in my lower stomach.

We hadn't completed the claiming. He had promised me he wasn't going to take any decision from me and at the moment I was still too messed up to have an intimate form of relationship. I knew Bennett wanted it and on some level I did too but my brain wouldn't let me. There was too much going on and I knew there would be a time when there wasn't and I was glad that Bennett would wait for me to reach that point.

I stared at his chest, my eyes taking in the familiar lines of the tattoo above his heart. His memorial for me. The lines were crisp and the colours brilliant. I had traced every line on the tattoo and the feeling it brought me was one of satisfaction and an intense happiness. There were no words on the tattoo but the fact that I knew it was for me was enough.

Bennett said nothing as he gently picked me up out of the chair and took my spot, settling me back in his lap. I leaned against him as he slowly started to rock us back and forth. I nuzzled his skin and sighed happily before closing my eyes. "How was your day?" He sounded genuinely curious, as he did every time he asked me something. He was attentive and thoughtful. He never pressured or raised his voice to me.

"The same as every other day." I reached up and touched his neck, moving closer to him. I loved feeling his skin sliding along mine. The fire burned hotly in my veins and I enjoyed it, letting it sink deep into me.

"Luka phoned again. He says it's time for me to help him with his pack. He requested you come as well." His words were low and I mulled it over. I would be out of my safety zone and that always brought issues but the thought of going somewhere else, somewhere new, was highly alluring. Besides it was to visit Luka and I knew he would never let anything happen to Bennett or I.

"That sounds nice. How long?" I opened my eyes and watched his pulse dance under his skin as I brushed his slightly sweaty skin with my thumb. I resisted the urge to bury my face into his neck and inhale his heady scent.

"He said a week at most." Bennett had no qualms and his nose brushed the skin of my neck as he inhaled deeply. Shivers moved through me as his arms tightened on me slightly, his large, warm hands gripping me firmly.

"Okay. It will be nice to get away for a little bit." I titled my head allowing him more access to my neck. His lips trailed across my skin, leaving goosebumps as I looked out towards the forest. He hummed an agreement, the sound vibrating my skin, leaving little shock waves of pleasure in its wake. I bit the inside of my bottom lip as I watched the treeline.

I froze as I watched several figures leaving the safety of the trees. Bennett stiffened in response to me, a low growl escaping him as he snapped his head to the people leaving the forest. He tightened his grip on me before he stood up, gently moving me towards Amber.

"Get her to the study and get Jace." His voice was low and Amber nodded quickly before wrapping her arms around me, moving me towards the door.

"Amber June Blanche. I've come for you." At the familiar timbre of the loud voice both Amber and I stiffened. I looked over my shoulder and tears filled my eyes when I saw my father standing tall, his chin lifted and his brown eyes hard. Amber turned around, I could feel her sudden anger, her inability to escape riling up her wolf into a frenzy. "I have come to claim my mate. If I cannot have you, I will take your rejection so I can find another." His words were like hard steel and I moved closer to Bennett, reaching out and touching the bare skin of his back. He pulled me to his side tightly and I looked over the group of people. Their eyes were all downcast, their skin pale, and their frames nearly skeletal. I inhaled sharply at the sight of them.

Omegas.

"I have already told you, Andrew Lawrence. I cannot be with an Alpha." Despite the slight waver to her voice Amber's tone was just as cold and hard as my father's. The bond between me and them twisted slightly. It was uncomfortable and I didn't really want to know what would happen if they broke their mate bond.

"Could you be with the brother of one?" At his words a thick silence fell and I could feel Amber's confusion. I glanced at her pale face before looking at my father who took several steps forward, holding out his hands. "I come to you with no pack, no territory, and no title. I come to you as I stand. Nothing more, nothing less. You said you couldn't be with an Alpha so I'm no longer an Alpha." Amber inhaled sharply and my mouth dropped open. In all of the conversations I had with my father he never mentioned that.

"Why?" The hardness in her voice had faded to vulnerability. She wasn't sure how to process what had happened and my father swallowed.

"Because I would give up *everything* for just a chance to spend the rest of my life with you. You're my mate, my life, my future. You're like a mother to my child and I would do *everything* in my power to be with you." His voice softened the more he spoke and I realized Amber had climbed over the railing to move closer to him.

"You gave it up?" Her voice sounded so fragile that I wanted to wrap my arms around her and my father nodded.

"I gave up everything I had for a chance to be with you. Amber June Blanche, will you have me or will you reject me?" He stared at her, his brown eyes taking her in as if she were his lifeline in a stormy ocean.

"You aren't an Alpha?" Her voice trembled as her body did as she took a few shay steps towards him, her arms wrapped around herself tightly.

"No." He shook his head and she moved closer.

"Will you ever hurt me?" The words twisted at my heart and I made a sound in my throat as I leaned forward, the urge to wrap her in my arms was growing. Bennett held me tight to his side, as if sensing my urge to move to her.

"As long as I live and breathe I will do everything in my power to keep you safe and loved. I would *never* harm you, I couldn't fathom it." He took another step and I watched as Amber's form continued to shake. She looked on the verge of breaking or bolting and I didn't know which it would be.

With a muffled sob she threw herself at him, wrapping her arms around his neck tightly. My father looked stunned for a moment before he wrapped his arms tightly around her, smoothing down her honey blonde hair and whispering in her ear.

I felt tears in my eyes at the rather intimate and private display. A blush coated my cheeks. They were my parents, I didn't want to see them kiss and make up, no matter how sweet the scene was. I pressed my face to Bennett's side and he let out a chuckle.

"I take it this means Alpha Lawrence will be living here with Alpha Lawrence." At his words I couldn't help the smile that tugged at my mouth. It would be confusing but I knew it would settle eventually. I glanced at them and my father had let Amber go, wiping at her tears, a loving smile on his face as he placed kisses all over her face. I glanced at the omegas that stood behind him. I counted six and I swallowed. They were forgotten ones, just like the rest of us.

I stepped closer to the railing and I watched as Uncle Jace came from the backyard, Uncle Bruce following him. Lace glanced at me before her eyes shifted to Bennett. She gave a sharp nod as if satisfied with my mate or the safety he provided before she looked back at her Alpha. Uncle Jace clapped my father on the back before turning to the cowering group of omegas.

He glanced at me before shaking his head. "Need a bigger fucking pack house." He muttered it more to himself than anyone else and I couldn't help the smile that crossed my face. Bennett moved closer, pressing his lips to my shoulder. I shivered at the action, heat spiralling through my veins. "My niece, Maricella, will come help you." He gestured for me and Bennett gently lifted me over the railing, setting me on the ground.

I walked over and looked at the rag tag group of omegas. My father reached out and grasped my shoulder before kissing the top of my head. I leaned into the contact before I focused on the scared shifters in front of me. "Welcome to Oblitus, forgotten ones. You can stay or you can choose to leave but know we are all here to make sure you get better." I could feel Bennett moving behind me and I let out a sigh as they all looked at their feet.

"We should know." Bailey was suddenly by my side and she grabbed my hand, smiling at me before looking at the group. They would become better, we all would. I watched as their eyes snapped up to look at us. Their eyes shining dully with a faint form of hope. "After all, we were omegas too."

PACK GLOSSARY

Packs shown in order of appearance.

Pack Tacita

Current Alpha: N/A

Next-in-line: N/A

Beta: N/A

Delta: N/A

Pack Healer: N/A

Pack Doctor: N/A (Was specified to be female)

Pack Counsellor: N/A

Known pack members:

Lucas Simmons- Was mated to Maricella and rejected her, nearly causing her death.

Emerson McIver- had conflict with Bennett over his sister Linnette.

Linnette McIver- had a sexual relationship with Bennett Alderidge before he mated to Maricella.

Ingrid- was a rather cruel female to the omegas, the status of her is currently unknown.

Notes: Not much is known about the current pack structure or the people within it. However the former beta was killed by Victor after a trial that exposed a lot of the corruption and harm caused by Beta John.

~~~~

Pack Oblitus

Current Alpha: Jace Lawrence

Next-in-line: Davin Lawrence

Beta: Andrew Lawrence

Master-At-Arms: Jay Newport

Delta: Bennett Aldridge

Pack Doctor/Counsellor: Amber Lawrence (Formerly Blanche)

Known pack members:

Seamus Holfstader- Mated to Angela (Angie) Moore. Was rejected by his mate and ended up at Oblitus to be treated for said rejection.

Angela Holfstader- Mated to Seamus Holfstader. Ended up at Oblitus because she was banished after harming the son of an Alpha who rejected her little sister and publicly humiliated her. Currently pregnant.

Jay Newport- Master-At-Arms for the pack, he was a wanderer that found his way to Oblitus. Has been rejected as well.

Collin Ferris- Was banished from his old pack for reasons he has not discussed.

Bailey (last name unknown)- Mated to Davin Lawrence. Former omega of Pack Tacita.

Maricella Alderidge- Mated to Bennett Alderidge, former omega of Pack Tacita. Adopted daughter of Amber Blanche and Andrew Lawrence. Cousin of Davin Lawrence. Niece of Jace Lawrence. Birth daughter to Victor Dohi and Petunia Brooks.

Victor Dohi- A wild on the territory. Is the birth father to Maricella Aldridge. His mate died in an attack orchestrated by John Simmons.

Six currently unnamed shifters- from Pack Veritas where they were held as omegas.
~~~~

Notes: Oblitus only just got its official pack ranking and is still mainly a pack where people go when they have nowhere else to turn to.

~~~~

Pack Fortis

Current Alpha: Luka Sterling

Beta(s): Michael and Ezekiel (Both are wilds, shifters who hide inside their wolves and do not come out. This is remarked to be an odd choice for betas.)

Master-At-Arms: N/A

Delta: N/A

Pack Doctor: N/A

Pack Healer: N/A

Pack Counsellor: N/A

Known pack members:

N/A

~~~~

Pack ????

Current Alpha: Bruce Linton

Beta: N/A

Master-At-Arms: N/A

Delta: N/A

Pack Doctor: N/A

Pack Healer: N/A

Pack Counsellor: N/A

Known pack members:

N/A

Notes: Bruce's pack has a strong alliance with Oblitus due to his affection for Mari. Not much else is known.

~~~~

More packs and members will be added as we meet them.
~~~~

AUTHOR'S NOTE

I know it's such a strange place to end a story but I never intended to write a drama filled tale with villains and evil. This was more of a *snapshot* of the life of a young female gripped with trying to figure out her inner demons and finding out that love can be the best form of combating the demons that try to swallow us whole. This book is just one part of her life. Just one small portion of the life of a character named Maricella Charlotte Lawrence.

I'm sorry if you didn't like how it ended or if you expected something else when you started to read this book. I never intended to disappoint but it is what it is. Maricella's life is far from exhilarating. She is no Avaline and this book is not called *She-Devil.* However I hope you did get some enjoyment out of the story as I got a lot out of writing it.

In fact the world I have written the characters in, is vast and wonderful and I want to spend so much more time writing about it and I believe I may. I want to write more stories that show how the Old Ways can destroy a shifter, how the Mountain Alphas choose their mates, how the bonds Mene so easily forged can be just as easily broken with one of her vessels. I want to write more stories that can give you a glimpse of Oblitus and the familiar members it has. I want to write more about the Alpha Gatherings and the feuds it has, creates, and even ends. I want to write about the other types of creatures that live in this world. Vampires, witches, fae, spirits, and many more.

I hope to write more soon and I hope that each story is as easy to write as *Red Ribbons* was. It took me to write this story. Three short months. It is astounding to me that I managed to write this tale in such a short period of time and I am happy that I managed to actually finish it. This, I hope, is the beginning to a wonderful world filled with wonderful characters but I need some time.

So until then, my dearest readers, keep on reading and I hope to be back soon with maybe a sneak-peek to a relationship that may or may not have our dearest Luka Sterling.

With warmest regards,

Anna M. L Koski

ACKNOWLEDGEMENTS

There are many people I wish to thank for helping me make this book a possibility. First off is the lady I dedicated this book too. Without Jenn Lile, I doubt I would have written this series. She found this book on wattpad and shared it with a facebook group and the rest is, as they say, history. So she holds a special place in this book just for that.

I would like to thank my 'over the pond' friend Mel. She has always been so supportive of me and my books. She voraciously reads everything I write and she is a true friend that I love to bits. (I know you are reading this and you deserve the shout out! You are a great friend, you really really are!)

I would also, once again, love to thank my readership and community for their unfailing support and appreciation in all that I do in my writing. They are always full of encouragement and happiness and never once let me fall. I appreciate all their comments and reviews and just general positivity they have towards, not only me, but everyone in my community. Thank you guys for making my community as amazing as it is.

And of course my last thank you. I need to thank my laptop. This beast has been with me through over twenty manuscripts and has sacrificed a screen, a hard drive, and left mouse button. This laptop has carried me through so many books and I hope many many more.

Thanks my lappy top, you the real MVP!There are many people I wish to thank for helping me make this book a possibility. First off is the lady I dedicated this book *to*. Without Jenn Lile, I doubt I would have written this series. She found this book on wattpad and shared it with a facebook group and the rest is, as they say, history. So she holds a special place in this book just for that.

I would like to thank my ‘over the pond’ friend Mel. She has always been so supportive of me and my books. She voraciously reads everything I write and she is a true friend that I love to bits. (I know you are reading this and you deserve the shout out! You are a great friend, you really really are!)

I would also, once again, love to thank my readership and community for their unfailing support and appreciation in all that I do in my writing. They are always full of encouragement and happiness and never once let me fall. I appreciate all their comments and reviews and just general positivity they have towards, not only me, but everyone in my community. Thank you guys for making my community as amazing as it is.

And of course my last thank you. I need to thank my laptop. This beast has been with me through over twenty manuscripts and has sacrificed a screen, a hard drive, and left mouse button. This laptop has carried me through so many books and I hope many many more.

Thanks my lappy top, you the real MVP!

ABOUT THE AUTHOR

Anna M. L. Koski grew up on the family homestead in the rolling hills of Southern Saskatchewan. She has always been an avid writer and has a boundless love of literature.

Time has not lessened her desire to write but has only seemed to make her passion for it that much stronger as the years have gone by. You will likely find her staring at her laptop writing page after page of her stories even in the wee hours in the morning.

She has a great love of encouraging others to follow their dreams and to pursue their passions. She believes a life is only well lived if it is lived in happiness and contentment. She lives by her mother's motto and encourages others to do the same.

The tallest trees have the strongest roots.
Never forget where you came from.

UP NEXT

FORGOTTEN
BOOK TWO
FORGED IN FIRE

SUMMARY

~~~~~~~~~~~~~~~~~~~~~~~~~

It's not about how hot the fire is.

~~~~~~~~~~~~~~~~~~~~~~~~~

Different metals react differently to heat. Some, like gold and aluminum will melt at a low heat and others like iron and steel require immense heat to melt. However people were different and Shey Lazera wondered how hot the fire would need to get before she burned up and ceased to be.

Shey had been rejected. She was no stranger to it. Her own mother had suffered rejection more than once. The first time had been her grandfather casting her mother out of her rightful place as his heir. He was stuck in the Old Ways, refusing to allow a female to become his successor. Then Shey had been born through fire. A rejection had forced her mother to give birth to her prematurely.

So it came as no surprise to her that she was not destined to have a mate. She had been rejected so many times she almost enjoyed the fire, the burning that covered her body. Each wave of fire separating her and her wolf, each wave chipping away at her wolf's spirit until she was barely noticeable anymore, her power diminished.

She was viewed as weak by the Alphas who had the misfortune of pairing with her. As a result she was rejected by each and every one she came into contact with. That is why she wandered aimlessly through the neutral highways, avoiding the Hunters trying to put her into their system.

So she was rather pissed when she stumbled into a territory, fucked up an escape attempt and was drug soaking wet in front of yet another Alpha. She was surprised to feel his weakness. He was not the firstborn yet he held the position of Alpha. What surprised her was his adamant refusal to reject her like she wanted.

~~~~~~~~~~~~~~~~~~~~~~~~~

It's about what you are made of.
~~~~~~~~~~~~~~~~~~~~~~~~~

~~~~~~~~~~~~~~~~~~~~~~~~~~~~

Luka Sterling had been forced into the Alpha position after an accident killed his two older brothers and his father. He had taken up the mantle to take it off of his fragile mother but he knew it did not belong to him. He was a weak Alpha that had needed constant training just to be ready in case anyone tried to take his claim as Alpha.

He surrounded himself with only those he trusted and very few people fit that description. His two guardians, Ezekiel and Michael, were his only friends and they were wilds. They spent all of their time in wolf form but they protected him fiercely and loyally. He was a weak Alpha with no true Beta or mate. He had been rejected once and that had been enough for him to not try again.

So he was more than surprised and more than irritated when members of his patrol drug a half drowned dark haired beauty with green eyes as cold as ice, into his office. He hadn't wanted a mate and his first thought was to reject her until she opened her rosy lips and demanded he do just that.

Something about the practically human spitfire made him want to dominate her, to force her to submit under his demands but every time she opened her mouth nothing but fire and derision slipped out. She taunted him to give in and let her burn. Something he found himself unwilling to do just to watch her face twist with irritation and rage. His dark haired beauty seemed to crave the burn only his rejection could give her and he found it left a sour taste in his mouth.

~~~~~~~~~~~~~~~~~~~~

What are you made of?

~~~~~~~~~~~~~~~~~~~~

Luka struggles to hold onto his Alpha position while he clings to a female who seemingly wants nothing to do with him but for him to burn her alive with a rejection. He holds her tighter because as she taunts him and pushes him to the very edge of his control, he finds he wants her to burn for him in a completely different way.

Shey tries her hardest to push Luka away but her Alpha mate seems perfectly content with vexing her plans. She can feel them spiralling down into a path she isn't sure she is ready for but he is dragging her down regardless. He is demanding her compliance and her trust as he holds out his hand as he prepares for them to jump over a cliff into the unknown.
~~~~~~~~~~~~~~~~~~~~

Only together can they find a balance and equilibrium. She needs Luka to show her that she is worthy of love and Luka needs her to show him just what kind of Alpha he was meant to be.

ONE

I looked at the various papers scattered on my desk that needed to be dealt with. Just *looking* at them threatened to have my head splitting from pain. I closed my eyes and rubbed at my face. Five years of Alpha bullshit and I was nowhere near the level my father had been. Hell, I was nowhere near the level my second eldest brother, Derek, had been at. The thought of them sent a dull pain through my chest and I sighed.

Five years since I had been shoved into the Alpha position. Five years since my father and two brothers had died. Five years since my mother had lost her mind to grief and five years I had to put up a front to everyone around me. Some days all I wanted to do was put a gun in my mouth and pull the trigger just to be free from everything but I would never do that to my mother or the pack my family had spent so long building.

I took off my glasses and placed them on the desk before I leaned back in the chair and resisted the urge to set the entire office on fire. If the paperwork was burned then there would be no paperwork to do. That thought had a lot of merit but I knew I couldn't.

I let out a heavy groan and pressed the heels of my palms to my eyes. It hurt slightly and caused a kaleidoscope of colours to emerge but it made me feel a bit more in-control. I was putting off the inevitable, I knew I was. I had Hunter forms to fill out, bank statements to process, bills to pay, pack members to file. Too much paperwork to deal with in one go but I had been putting it off and it had only compounded. I knew it would compound into a bigger mess but I had put it off anyway. That was on me.

The door to my office opened and I took a subtle sniff. The smell of forest, wolves, and dirt entered my nose and I relaxed as the sound of bare feet scuffed against the hardwood. Despite what everyone thought, Michael and Ezekiel did come out of wolf form on occasion, just never when anyone else was around. Which is why it was so surprising Kiel had done so with Maricella. True, he viewed her as a pack member but he rarely shifted in front of others. The door closed and there was the sound of cracking bones as one or both of them shifted.

"I should make you guys a doggy door." I muttered it out and was suddenly bombarded with images of what I could do with said doggy door. I chuckled, feeling a bit more relaxed as they showed me their displeasure. I pulled my hands away from my face and blinked at the ceiling, clearing the colours from my eyes. "Okay, okay. I'm sorry. No doggy doors. Besides I think your fatasses would get stuck in it." I chuckled as Michael snarled before putting his front paws onto the arm of my chair. His hot, foul breath brushed my face and I wrinkled my nose in disgust before shoving on his wide chest, without looking at him.

"You need to start brushing your teeth. I think I can still smell last Friday's rabbit on your breath." I smiled at the low huffing sound he made as he did as I requested. I let my eyes wander to Ezekiel who had taken up his usual spot on the couch below the wide window. His bulk took up the entire couch and I was reminded of him holding Maricella's hand. She looked like a child next to him and it made me smile. "Bennett and Maricella will be arriving tomorrow." At my words both wolves perked up. Michael let out an excited bark before bounding around my desk. I laughed at his puppy-like antics as he ran around and around.

Despite what people thought about wilds and how they couldn't be trusted, once you had their loyalty, there was nothing they wouldn't do for you. I trusted the two wilds with everything I had. Our friendship had extended nearly ten years for me and Ezekiel and eight for Michael and I. They never challenged me because to them while we were equals, I held the authority of the pack. They were content with being my second in commands. Not that they really did much. When they were around the pack with me they were silent, watchful, and volatile. When they were alone they did as they were doing, Michael acting like an idiot and Ezekiel sprawled out on the couch looking deceptively lazy.

I winced as there was a loud cracking bang and yelp. I darted my gaze to Michael who had slipped on the hardwood and had crashed into an overstuffed chair by the bookshelf. I rolled my eyes as he whined at the broken chair. Ezekiel let out a huff before turning his head the other way. I found it highly amusing. Michael wasn't a puppy nor was he the size of a dog. He was nearly four feet at the shoulders and should have realized that bouncing around the room like he was a smaller wolf would always end up in an injury.

He walked over to me, holding his front paw up in an almost pathetic manner. He waved it slightly and whined sadly. I put my glasses back on and crossed my arms over my chest as I watched him make an especially pathetic spectacle of himself. He looked at me through sad brown eyes and I shook my head.

"What did you expect? You went bounding around the room like a toddler given a redbull and you broke another one of my chairs." I gestured to the wreckage he had just made before pointing to the chair that was held together with duct tape. I didn't wish to spend any of the pack's money on frivolous items so I never replaced anything in my office if it broke. "What is Gamgam going to say to me, Michael? She's going to be very upset with me." I shook my finger in his face, speaking to him like a child before he snapped at my finger. His sharp teeth just missed my hand, all pretense of injury gone. I smirked at him as I leaned back in my chair once more. I let out a sigh and reached out to scratch his head.

You couldn't really tell he was a dangerous shifter from the way his ears flopped slightly and his tongue hung out. His eyes closed as I hit a particularly itchy spot on his scalp. He looked ridiculous but it made his transformation into a lethal weapon that much more powerful. Ezekiel always looked like he was three seconds away from ripping a person's throat out. Michael, on the other hand, was playful and approachable until he snapped without warning.

He placed his head on the arm of my chair and I absently scratched at it as I sorted through the papers on the desk, feeling relaxed enough to try and figure them out once more. I sorted the bills from the rest, only being interrupted when I stopped scratching Michael and he tugged on my shirt arm with his teeth, wanting me to continue.

Just being around my two guardians was relaxing. I knew they always had my back and I never had to worry about my life when they were around. I hated dealing with the pack when they weren't with me. I wasn't stupid. I could feel the heated glares that spoke of death. Some of my pack members believed I was too weak to lead and I knew I was but I held on in my father's memory and in the memory of my brothers. I did it for them. However, I was always in danger when I dealt with the pack.

I tugged on Michael's ear as I looked through the Hunter requisition forms. They were looking for several rogues that skipped check-ins. There was always the possibility that packs caught sight of them and so they sent requisition forms so they could use the territory to search for the wayward rogues. I could only count three of them and I signed off on them quickly before watching them curl up and disappear in a puff of smoke that smelled like lavender.

The Hunters would be in and out before I started my little weeding project five days from now. I didn't need them questioning my decisions about my pack. Having the Hunters sending Enforcers into my pack would only fuck my plans up. I needed to have a low profile while we banished or killed any and all dissenters in my pack. I rubbed at my forehead, pushing the thought away. I focused on the bills, writing them down in the business account ledger.

The pack owned the rights to two iron mines and owned several businesses in the nearby mundane town. That didn't include the logging company my father had started before I was born. It had slowed down as we waited for the replanted trees to get stronger. We worked in pulses. Every five years we would slow down the logging and work on restoring the areas we logged in and then five years after that we sped up again. All the ventures brought significant money to the pack and I was always careful to save and limit spending.

So far I had managed to be able to save enough to be able to send eighteen out of the twenty two children to college on a full scholarship if they so wished it. I had named the scholarship after my brothers, to let the pack know that despite the fact they were gone they would still take care of what would have been theirs. I wanted to carry their legacy forward, to not let the pack forget them.

There was a knock on the door and I looked up, running my hand through my hair. Michael stiffened before taking his spot beside my desk.

Ezekiel wasn't long in following, low rumbling growls filled the room as they warned the person that they were unwelcome. "Come in." I watched as the door opened and a gruff looking male looked around. The growling coming from Ezekiel grew louder. He didn't much care for Dylan Colter and I agreed with him completely. The male wasn't a wolf, he was a spider crafting a web around me.

"There's an Alpha Thorn here." He spat it out before looking me over. "*Sir*." The derision in his tone was enough to make my wolf's hackles rise but I fought it off, shoving him away. Ezekiel had no such qualms and stalked around the desk, snarling as he did so. I looked Dylan up and down, wondering if I should let Ezekiel take a chunk out of him. It was tempting but I needed to keep everything normal until the pack wide sweep.

"Bad day, Dylan? Even so, you should probably watch the tone. They don't like it when *anyone* gets snarky with me." I stared at him, wishing I had the power to have him submit under my gaze but he held his head high right up until Ezekiel snarled once more and advanced. At the threatening wild that wouldn't hesitate to rip his throat out, Dylan grudgingly bared his neck before glaring at the wooden floor. I held out a hand and Ezekiel's growls stopped immediately but his form remained ready to spring at a moment's notice.

I gave Dylan a smile he did not deserve. One had to keep up appearances. "Thank you for being so understanding. Ezekiel can be a handful sometimes. I will be right down to see to our guest." I stood up and walked around the desk as Dylan left quickly. He had always been the most vehement dissenter of the pack but I had to play nice. For now.

I walked out the door flanked by Michael and Ezekiel. We moved down the hallway and down the wide staircase towards the front door. I had never understood why my grandfather had such an extravagant place built. We had just about a hundred pack members but most of them lived in the small village just five minutes from the pack house. So as a result there were rarely more than ten people in the house during the day and even less during the night.

I pushed open the door and looked at the rather large civilian Humvee that was parked rather rudely across the entire driveway. It was filthy and beat up looking but it matched the pack it drove around. I watched as a large male stepped out of the driver's side. I nodded at him in respect. Ezekiel and Michael sat down beside my legs as he opened the back door to the vehicle. It let out a rather irritating screech of misused hinges before a tall female stepped out. I let out a sigh. She hadn't made it then. She looked almost dejected as Alpha Thorn placed an almost gentle hand on her shoulder before leading her towards me.

"Alpha Thorn, it's nice to see you but not in these circumstances." I looked at the female and she discreetly wiped at her eyes. I felt a pang of sympathy for her but I pushed it away. She had tried her best and not everyone could handle the trials the Mountain Alphas had for their mates. I moved down the stairs and grasped her arms. "No matter how you did, you still brought pride to our pack, Jessie. You were mates with a *Mountain Alpha*, that alone demands pride and respect." I grasped her chin and smiled at her.

She gave me a weak smile in return. "Really, Alpha Sterling?" She sounded defeated but I simply nodded before giving her a hug that she returned tentatively. The rejection had shaken her and I knew she had truly wanted to complete the trials. It was a big thing to be a mate to a Mountain Alpha. It spoke of great strength and resilience.

"You get yourself home. Your parents haven't stopped worrying about you since you left. I am certain they will be more than glad to see you. Tomorrow we can see about arranging a picnic celebrating your arrival back home." I had seen my father arrange similar things when he had been Alpha. He always celebrated the small things with pack members. A shifter returning from college or one going away. New babies and pregnancies, anything he heard about he loved to celebrate and even back then I could see how much it made the pack love him.

I let her go and patted her shoulder before she walked towards the village. *Noah, please escort Jessie back home. She looks like she needs a friend.* I sent the mind-link to him, knowing they were close before Jessie left two months ago. They had been nearly inseparable, the best of friends from what I had seen and heard. Despite how long it had taken I had made it my business to know of my pack members. It made it easier to pick out those who didn't like my leadership.

Yes, sir! His excited relief was nearly overwhelming and I blocked him out and looked at Alpha Thorn. His form was wide and muscles seemed to come to him naturally. I wasn't a short male by any means but he still had six inches on my height. His frame was coated in authority and power. It rolled off of him affecting everyone around him. I was lucky that my position as Alpha didn't make me want to kneel before him but it made my wolf wish to challenge him. I shoved him away unwilling to let him influence me. Azrael's dark blue eyes scanned the area and his mouth was pulled down into a rather cold frown.

"How many did she manage?" I watched as he shook his head, his raggedly cut brown hair moving around his face. His entire form spoke of the wilderness he and his pack resided in. A good amount of scruff covered his jaw and he scratched at it absently.

"Three out of five but only a few of mine." His voice was low and rumbling. It reminded me of an avalanche for some reason, maybe because both an avalanche and his voice were cold and deadly. "She did better than I thought. A sweet and soft female but sweet and soft females don't last long in Algus. It's best she failed, she can stay where it's safer for her." His frown deepened and I nodded. If he said she wouldn't survive then it was best for her to be where she would be safe and that was at home, regardless of how she was feeling at the moment.

"You'll find yourself a strong mate, Alpha Thorn." That much I was certain of. He was actively seeking a mate and I knew he would find one that would pass his trials. It was just a matter of time.

"I know." He let out a sigh before staring at me. "Formalities over, Luka. It's a long drive back home. Could I stay the night?" His face relaxed slightly and I chuckled but nodded.

"Of course, Azrael. As I said before, my house is your house." I gestured to the stairs before starting up them. "Supper should be ready in about an hour. You can stay in the same room as before, shower up if you want. I need to go back and work on my paperwork." I ran a hand through my hair and Michael and Kiel walked into the house after me.

"Fuck the paperwork, Luka. Have a drink with me." Azrael sounded exhausted and I shook my head.

"That's what I have done for the past few weeks, now it's beyond ignoring." The pile of paperwork that I still had left to do was enough to make me want to tear my hair out or blow my brains out. I wasn't sure which. My two guardians headed up the stairs and I turned to look at Azrael.

"You lowlander Alphas are so strange. Need to fill out a form just to take a shit." He said it with disgust and I let out a laugh. He wasn't exactly wrong.

"That's what we get for living close to the Hunters. They don't like going up to the mountains so you guys don't get nearly as much paperwork." I shrugged and he shook his head before tugging on his slight beard. "You should shave. It looks like someone glued pubes to your face." I tilted my head at him and he let out a booming laugh before shaking his head.

"I believe you're right, Luka. I'll see you in the kitchen in forty-five minutes and don't think I'm above dragging you out of your office by your tail." Despite the laughter I knew he was being serious. Mountain Alphas were very family orientated so meals were eaten together in the place they were made. They didn't see the need for dining rooms or other such formalities. Azrael expected me to eat in the kitchen with him and my mother as was proper by his customs. Refusing to eat with your family was seen as a great insult and serious disrespect to your parents and guests if you had any.

"I'll keep my eyes on the time then. I would like my tail to stay attached to my ass." I nodded at him before I moved up the stairs.

Alpha Thorn and I had met at an Alpha Gathering two years ago. He was intimidating but he had seen me floundering and the Southern Alphas gathering like vultures and helped me out. We weren't exactly friends because I didn't truly think Azrael was capable of having friends but we were more than acquaintances and we weren't exactly business partners. I opened my home to him when he was travelling through and we had an understanding that anything either of us said after we finished with formalities wasn't to be taken literally.

I walked into my office and laughed loudly as Michael stood on my desk, pissing all over the paperwork I had yet to complete. He had taken everything I had finished off the desk and placed it on the floor but the rest was now covered in rather potent smelling urine.

I covered my nose and coughed despite the laughter. "Fuck, Michael! That stinks!" I hurried over to the window and threw it open before looking down at Ezekiel. "Where were you when he decided this was a good idea?" I looked down at him and he simply rolled onto his back and gave me an uncharacteristic wolfy grin in response.

I shook my head and glared between the two of them, trying not to smile. "I needed to do that and now I have to get new ones and tell everyone it's because you pissed on my desk." I pinched my nose closed and glared at Michael who looked completely unrepentant as he jumped off my desk. I let out a sigh and rolled my eyes. "I guess we can go see mother." Ezekiel jumped off of the couch and Michael started to follow but I pointed at him.

"You, kind Michael, pisser on office furniture, are going to stay here and clean up your mess." I stared at him and he whined pathetically. "No. I don't want to throw out that desk. It was my grandfather's desk and I want it spotless by the time I come back." I watched as he lowered his fur and tucked his tail between his legs in an attempt to look small but I simply glared at him. "I mean it, Michael. After you are done, clean up and come down for dinner." I gave him one more look and turned around. A wide grin crossed my face as I walked out of the office. When Ezekiel left the room I closed the door behind him. I patted his head and we quickly went down the stairs and towards my mother's room.

I had to move her out of the master bedroom and down to the main floor a few months after the accident. She needed to be close to the front door and her room had to be big enough to accommodate a nurse as well as herself. Currently the nurse, May, no longer needed to stay with her in her room but she had a separate room close by so she could keep an eye on her. I didn't want to have May far away in case something happened with my mother.

I pushed open her door, ignoring the almost antiseptic smell of her room before moving over to where she sat in her wheelchair by the window. "Luka, darling, how are you?" Her voice was thin and wavering and her smile was almost lackluster but I ignored it all and kissed her cheek gently. Her skin seemed almost paper-thin and I smiled down at her.

"I'm fine." I crouched down and took one of her hands in mine before pressing a kiss to the back of it. Her veins were visible and her hand felt so delicate I was constantly afraid I would break it if I held it wrong. "How was your day?" I looked up at her and she gave me another sad smile.

"I missed them today. When are they coming back again? I hate it when my males are gone." She let out a soft sigh and I wanted to wince. I wanted to do a lot of things when it came to my mother but I kept the mask on for her. To give her some semblance of happiness after her entire world crashed down around her. Doc Howard said she had less than two years left depending on how she declined as her illness progressed. It could be more time or it could be less, he wasn't sure. "When they come home, make sure to get them to wash up. I have a special supper planned." She squeezed my hand absently as she glanced at me.

I nodded slowly in response. "I will, mum." I gently placed her hand back in her lap before standing up. Ezekiel nosed passed me and set his head in her lap.

She gave a small chuckle like she always did when she saw him. "Such a silly thing to have a dog for a pet, Luka." She patted his head gently before rubbing at his scar. He let out a groan and she looked up at me with a small smile. I knew what was coming and it hurt me as it always did. "Luka, darling, how are you?" She looked at me and I bit back a sigh and smiled instead.

"I'm okay, mum. Let's go out into the garden. It's a beautiful day out." I pushed open the doors to the garden I had made for her and Ezekiel walked out into the sweet smelling air as I gently wheeled her outside.

"This is beautiful. Your father must have done this to surprise me. I'll have to thank him when he gets home." She gave me such a serene smile that I felt my breath hitch in my chest. I bent over and kissed her temple before heading into the garden, looking for flowers I could pick for her.

She had something similar to the mundane illness Alzheimer's, one of the only known cases of the shifter equivalent of it. After the trauma my mother had suffered when my father and brothers did, it had just happened. The doctor said it was most likely the shock of losing so much of her family and her mate bond that caused the rapid deterioration of her mental state. She was stuck in a time when my father and brothers were alive. She was constantly forgetting conversations or repeating them over and over again. I tried my best to be patient and keep her happy despite how badly it was tearing me up inside to see her as she was.

My mother had always been a strong female. She knew exactly what to say or do to lift your spirits. She was quick to give a reprimand but there was never a time when she wouldn't hug you, kiss your cheek, or tell you how proud of you she was. Not just strong emotionally or mentally but physically. She had always insisted on running patrols and participating in training. She said there was no use in being a delicate wallflower, she wanted to be able to protect the pack just like everyone else did.

Now she was a thin, sick, delicate creature confined to a wheelchair and at the mercy of her deteriorating mind. She was fragile now and oh so delicate. It was against everything I had grown up with and it seemed to make the hurt that much worse. I had known what she had been like before and now I suffered with her, watching in silent agony as the female that had raised me all but disappeared.

I looked at the bouquet of flowers I had picked and headed back to where I had placed her. Ezekiel was sitting by her wheelchair with his head on the arm of it as she scratched at his scars. I appreciated how gentle he and Michael were with her. They never growled where she could hear and allowed her to yank and tug on their fur or ears without retaliation. I trusted them with her more than I trusted any of the pack members other than May.

I stopped in front of her and she smiled up at me. "Luka, darling, how are you?" She moved her hand from Kiel's head and he nudged her arm. She chuckled at the action. "Such a silly thing to have a dog for a pet, Luka." She tsked at me and I crouched in front of her before gently placing the flowers in her free hand. "Oh, these are so beautiful, Luka! Thank you. You were always the sweetest of my boys." She smiled brightly at me and I nodded.

"Benjamin used to bring me frogs. Such an adorably evil little boy. He knew I hated them and Derek would show me handfuls of worms but you always brought me flowers." She looked down at them before her face fell. "Your father was going to pick me some flowers up for our anniversary. Do you know when they will be home?" She looked up at me and I kissed her forehead gently.

"Soon, I think." I watched as her face brightened and guilt ate away at my stomach. Doc Howard told me to not feel guilty about the lies because she never remembered but she was my mother and I had always spoken the truth to her. The white lies I told her weren't hurting her, they were making her happy but the guilt was still there. "Let's sit and watch the garden for a few minutes." I watched as she nodded before I stood up. I carefully sat on the bench beside her wheelchair, she was staring at the garden with a small smile on her face.

I reached over and picked up her hand, she looked at me, a slightly surprised look on her face before she smiled. "Luka, darling, how are you?" Her grey eyes were shining and I patted her hand gently.

"I'm fine, mum. Let's watch the garden for a bit." I watched as she turned her head and stared at the garden in awe.

"Your father must have done this for me. He's such a sweet male. When will he and your brothers be home?" She looked over at me with a small frown on her face and I kissed the back of her hand.

"Soon, mum. They should be home soon." I watched as her face lit up and she gave a happy nod.

"That's good. I have a special supper planned for them. I am going to make all of their favourites. Benjamin loves my lasagne and your father simply adores steak and potatoes. Oh and Derek loves chicken parmesan. That sounds good, right? You think they will like it?" She looked at me with happiness shining in her grey eyes and I nodded and kissed the back of her hand again.

I pushed away the feeling of tears burning my eyes as I squeezed her hand gently. "It sounds wonderful and I'm sure they will love whatever you make for them." I watched as she looked down at her lap and saw the flowers. A bright smile covered her face and I clenched my jaw.

"Oh you are the sweetest of my boys, Luka. Benjamin used to bring me frogs. Such an adorably evil little boy. He knew I hated them and Derek would show me handfuls of worms but you always brought me flowers." Her voice trailed off and another small frown appeared before she looked at me. "Your father said he would bring me flowers for our anniversary. When do you think he will be home?" The look she gave me made my chest tighten and I blinked away tears.

"Soon. I promise you." I leaned over and kissed the side of her head. It was painful going through the motions with her but no matter how many times she asked me the same question I would always answer because she was my mother, despite how fractured and broken her mind was.

"Lily, how did you- Oh Alpha Sterling!" May's voice sounded shocked and I looked over my shoulder towards the door.

"Hello, May." I gave her a small smile before I looked at my mother and kissed her head again. "I'll be right back." I moved around her and headed towards the slightly plump female I had hired as my mother's nurse. I glanced over my shoulder and Ezekiel resumed his position by my mother's side.

I led the nurse back into the room and she looked at me sadly. "She didn't eat today." Her voice was low and I nodded. I had gathered that much for her fixation on making food for my father and brothers when they got home. "I think you might be able to convince her. She was getting agitated when I tried."

"Thank you, May. I think I'll be able to get her to eat." I frowned, if I could convince her that it was a small meal before supper and only for politeness with Alpha Thorn she might eat something. Despite everything she was forgetting she never forgot how to be a polite Alpha Female. "Any other changes?" I watched as May walked over and grabbed her chart.

"Not really but she isn't improving either and looking at her charts from two weeks ago she's still declining. Not rapidly but enough to cause concern." She gave me a sympathetic look and I nodded before rubbing at my forehead. I knew she wasn't getting better. I knew she was slowly declining and her health would get worse but I didn't like hearing about it. She was my mother and I just wanted her to be safe and healthy and despite how safe she was, her health was something I couldn't control.

"I understand, May. I thank you for your diligence in caring for her." I gave her a tight smile and she shook her head.

"She was a good Alpha Female for this pack and I love her, as we all do. You don't have to thank me for something anyone would have done. The pack is a family and she was at the head of this family for many years." She gave me a curt nod before setting the chart down and moving to stand beside me. She wrapped me in a motherly hug. I appreciated the gesture and hugged her back.

May was like an aunt to me. She and my mother had been close before the accident and there wasn't anyone else I would trust my mother's health and care to. "I know it hurts you to see her like this but you're doing so well with her. She never smiles as much for me when I'm around. It brightens her day for you to come and do things with her." She gave me one more squeeze before she let me go, holding me at arm's length. "No matter what they say, you're a great Alpha. You put this pack before your own needs and you take care of your mother just as intensely. They are too blinded by what the meaning of power is to see that you're just what this pack needs." Her hazel eyes crinkled at the corners as she gently patted my face.

I gave her a small, thankful smile. "Alpha Thorn is here. Would you like to bring mother and yourself to the kitchen for dinner?" I watched as she let out a small shudder at the mention of the Alpha. Not everyone was as comfortable with Azrael as I was and even then it was a cautious comfortableness.

"So Jessie didn't make the trials?" Despite the small frown she had on there was relief evident in her voice.

I shook my head slowly at the question. "Azrael says she did better than expected and she has still brought pride to the pack despite not making it." I was positive of that and I knew most of the pack would feel that way as well. Two months the pack had waited with bated breath not sure if we should be proud or scared for Jessie. I knew everyone would be happy to have her back, regardless of her failure.

"Mate to a Mountain Alpha. That certainly is something to be proud of despite not making the trials. She was strong enough to be paired with one." May gave a firm nod and I chuckled slightly.

"She might not see that now but it's something she will grow to understand in time." I was certain she would be okay as time went on. Azrael had let her down gently, as he did with every female he had put through the trials. He had let her down gently and brought her home. Despite what anyone thought of him he wasn't a cruel monster. He did care for the females in his own way. He had told me before that it was better to reject them and bring them home than to let them die on the mountains. I looked at May once more. "So will you join us for dinner?" She gave a small jump and an embarrassed smile crossed her face.

"Yes, yes. Sorry about that, Alpha Sterling. We would be more than happy to join you for dinner." She nodded and I gave a sharp whistle, Ezekiel was by my side within a few seconds and I nodded to May. My mother was in good hands with her.

I led the wild out of the room and looked towards the stairs. "Michael!" My voice echoed through the large room and I was sent images of the now clean office through our mindlink. I chuckled and patted Ezekiel's head. "Okay, you can join us for dinner!" I bit back a smile as I could hear his nails scrambling along the hardwood as he bolted for the stairs. "*Slow down*, Michael!" As usual he ignored my warning and halfway down the stairs he tripped and tumbled the rest of the way, yelping in surprise as he did so. I shook my head and pinched my nose in irritation.

Every single time.

Every. Single. Time.

He would go too fast and fall down the stairs. I didn't understand how he even managed to kill people in moments like the one I had just witnessed. He was a bumbling, overgrown puppy. It was at times like these that I wondered how on earth he managed to kill anything.

This book recognizes the upset this publishing has caused in certain individuals in a certain group but the author of this book does not care about the upset and those individuals can suck it.

Suck it.

www.ingramcontent.com/pod-product-compliance
Lightning Source LLC
Chambersburg PA
CBHW070552310726
48982CB00011B/1556/J

* 9 7 8 1 7 7 5 1 8 5 7 6 5 *